Curse of the Orkney Sea

Joy Jarrett

Literary Wanderlust | Denver, Colorado

Published in the United States by Literary Wanderlust LLC Denver, Colorado.

www.LiteraryWanderlust.com

ISBN Hardcover: 978-1-956615-24-1
ISBN Paperback: 978-1-956615-26-5
ISBN Digital: 978-1-956615-25-8

Printed in the United States of America

Dedication

To Isabelle, Zoe, and Luke, my first and favorite readers of this book. I love you more than all the worlds in the multiverse—imaginary or otherwise—could ever hold.

Chapter 1

Morag stepped outside the terminal, and the ferry slid against the dock with a terrible screech like a wounded animal as if the boat were warning her away. *Run. Turn back.* The black and white ferry was the only thing visible on the water. Fog obscured the view of some of the other islands. Morag was heading toward Tullimentay, the farthest flung isle in Orkney. A couple dozen people clattered up the metal gangway to the ferry, and Morag followed with her family, her hand slipping on the wet railing.

She spared a glance over her shoulder at the town of Kirkwall. The granite shops and houses faded into the surrounding gray of the North Sea. An old woman in a yellow headscarf, the only spot of color in the bleak monochrome, stood on the dock watching them board with a stern look of disapproval. Morag stumbled on the metal ramp, and Hamish plowed into the back of her.

"Go, Morag," he said and shoved her.

She elbowed her big brother in the gut. "What's your hurry?"

"I want inside before I freeze to death." Hamish, wearing shorts and a T-shirt, rubbed his muscled arms. "How the hell is it this cold in *June?*"

"Ever heard of a jacket?" She'd never admit it, but she was shivering even in her hoodie and jeans. The frigid wind biting her cheeks didn't help. The other passengers boarding the ferry looked dressed for an Arctic expedition. People said summer didn't exist in Scotland, but she didn't expect it to be this bad. Back home in Colorado, winters got cold—but here, the mist chilled her in a damp and unfamiliar way that reached her bones.

Seagulls wheeled against the dark clouds, and their cries sent jagged black stars spinning across her vision. She clutched her backpack straps to stop herself from batting them away. The stars weren't real. The doctors said it was only synesthesia. Except Morag's senses mixed colors and sounds and music in a 3-D explosion that sounded way more intense than what others with synesthesia described.

She ignored the spinning stars and the shooting green laser beams caused by the barking seals and focused on a different sense. The smell of salt and fish and the stench of diesel hung heavy in the air.

"If Mom didn't hate the sun, we could be in San Diego right now," Hamish said. "Know what's in San Diego? Girls in bikinis." He got a faraway look on his face for a minute before snapping out of it. "Why does Mom hate the sun? Why? Doesn't she know it's the source of all life?"

"And Grandma's skin cancer," Morag pointed out. Their grandmother passed on her pale complexion and freckles to Morag along with her dark curls, blue-green eyes, and a broad face that made Morag look like a medieval peasant. No matter how much her mom protested otherwise.

Hamish snorted. "No chance of skin cancer in Orkney."

At the word Orkney, little blue ovals floated across her eyes like happy bubbles despite the miserable cold. "Orkney is going to be good. You'll see."

"Yeah. Good for your stupid art portfolio."

"It's not stupid, Hamish."

He huffed out a long-suffering sigh. "Accept your D and move on already."

"Since I want to go to an *art* college, I can't accept a D." Morag's mouth soured— she'd also failed the AP exam. Well, she wouldn't fail this time. She was taking the class again this summer remotely.

And it didn't get much more remote than this.

"Chill," Hamish said. "You don't see me worrying about college."

As a senior, he *should* be worrying. Hamish was great at sports, but not exceptional, and his mediocre grades meant he wouldn't get any scholarships. She and Hamish were only a year apart in school, and it would be expensive for her parents to put two kids through college so close together. Yet her parents dipped into the college savings to rent an honest-to-god castle with two other families for the summer. If it worked out the way she hoped, it would be worth every penny and solve more than one of her worries. But all the more reason to retake that art class. Morag's grades *were* exceptional, and *she* could get some scholarships.

Hamish blew on his hands. "Why do you think your portfolio will be any better this time?"

The question stung, but she could tell Hamish was genuinely asking. "Because Orkney is a romantic setting. It'll be the inspiration for my portfolio."

"Romantic." Hamish rolled his eyes. "I know why you're really excited about this trip."

Morag's stomach dropped. Had Hamish figured out her crush on her best friend's brother? Juliette and Paul were still in the ferry terminal with their parents making some last-minute purchases in the gift shop, but they'd be along any moment.

Hamish jerked his head toward their parents up ahead.

"Orkney's not magically going to fix them."

He was talking about their parents, not Paul. "It'll be better here." She took a deep breath and pushed away her anxiety. There had to be hope for her parents still. Why else would her mom arrange this trip? "They had their honeymoon in Orkney, remember?"

"You think I forgot why Mom gave us Scottish names that sound like a cat vomiting? *Hey-mish. More-rag.*" He said their names like a puking noise, but it was an old joke, and Morag didn't laugh. "Ugh. Mom's ruining my summer to make me live on an island with, like, five people and a million sheep."

"Over eighty people live on Tullimentay."

Hamish laughed without humor. "Wow. Traffic must be a nightmare."

"Couldn't you *try* to have a more positive attitude? Mom and Dad need less stress. They need us to—"

"Be one big happy family? Come on, Morag. It's not our job to solve their marriage problems."

Maybe Morag *couldn't* fix them, but she could make it easier on her parents, right? Hamish never thought about that kind of stuff.

He growled like a bear. "Why did the line stop? This sucks."

"Would you stop whining already? Here." Morag reached into her pocket, pulled out a Cadbury bar, and held it out to him.

"Hey, thanks." He ripped open the purple wrapper with his teeth. "I need the calories to stay warm."

Within moments, the chocolate disappeared, and Hamish's smiling face was smeared with chocolate like a toddler. Riding his candy high, he gave her a friendly nudge. "Line's moving."

Morag started to move when something below the grid of the metal gangway caught her attention. A large shape floated in the water. A shark? A dolphin? She stopped, and Hamish stepped on her heels.

"Morag, seriously, go."

She ignored him and bent over to peer through the squares.

"What's that?"

The dark shape—vaguely human—didn't move or swim. Instead, it started sinking. "Look." A skeletal hand drifted toward the surface. Her heart thudded heavily in her chest. Before she could make out more details, the shape melted into the murky water. "Did you see that?"

Hamish raised his eyebrows. "What?"

"You didn't see it? A skeleton or something. A human one."

"A human skeleton?"

"Don't say it like that. I saw a shape down there. Like a body."

He stared down. After some time, he said, "I don't see anything. Maybe you hallucinated it?"

"Hallucinated? Real nice, Hamish." People at school had called her Hallucino-Girl before she'd learned to control the impulse to reach for shapes moving across her vision. Shapes were one thing, but—"I wouldn't hallucinate a *body*."

"Okay, whatever. See you up top." Hamish knocked into her shoulder as he overtook her on the ramp, and she let him go. For him, knocking into her shoulder passed as an apology.

She stared down and caught only the white flash of a Styrofoam cup bobbing in the dark water. Already she began to doubt herself. It hadn't been her synesthesia, but it could've been an overactive imagination. Seaweed and driftwood and shadows—or even the rotting body of a seal made more sense. Add in jet lag and no wonder she thought she'd seen a dead person. She was so tired, she *felt* like a dead person. She'd gotten maybe six hours' sleep in the past two days of travel. A flight from Denver to London. London to Aberdeen. Aberdeen to Kirkwall—the last on a frighteningly small plane—and a two-hour ferry ride ahead to get to Tullimentay.

Morag yawned as she crested the ramp. On the deck waited a man with a white beard, navy jacket, and a captain's hat who looked like he belonged on a box of frozen fish sticks. His hand rested on his chest in a noble pose. Before she had time to reconsider, she opened her mouth. "Do you get a lot of dead seals around here?"

His hand spasmed on his chest in alarm. "What's this ye're talkin' about now?" His Orkney accent was unlike anything Morag had ever heard. Black and silver chains undulated across her eyes at the sounds.

"I thought I saw a dead seal or something in the water."

"The water can make ye think ye see all sorts of things. Best ye get inside. We'll be leavin' shortly." With impressive speed for a man his age, he darted up the staircase to the wheelhouse, like he was desperate to get away from the weird American girl asking him about dead marine mammals.

Fat raindrops splattered down, and she hurried into the cabin where passengers sat scattered on brightly colored plastic seats. Condensation dripped down the windows, and the stuffy space smelled like Hamish's socks after football practice. Hamish slouched in a seat near the front of the ferry. Their parents sat a few rows farther back on their own, maybe wanting to reminisce about their honeymoon in Orkney.

Or not. Judging by the way Mom's face had gone a delicate jade green, her motion sickness was back. As a maternity nurse practitioner, she delivered a lot of babies. A miracle of life, sure, but also a ton of blood and guts. Didn't bother Mom at all. But put her on any type of craft—air or sea—and she hurled non-stop. How would she cope with filling in for the regular midwife this summer when it meant traveling on boats and little planes to different islands to deliver babies?

The only reason this trip was happening was Mom's old friend, Magnus. Mom loved to tell the story of how she cut her hand on a broken champagne glass during her honeymoon. Magnus had been the new doctor on Tullimentay who gave her stitches. At the time, Mom was halfway through her nurse practitioner program, and she'd grilled him about what it was like to practice medicine somewhere as isolated as Orkney. They'd stayed in touch ever since, which was why Magnus thought Mom would be great for the position, but clearly, Mom hadn't told him about her severe motion sickness.

Constant vomiting was probably not the best way to rekindle her parents' marriage. What if this trip only made things worse? Before Morag's thoughts could spiral further, her best friend burst into the cabin looking all blonde and beautiful as always. How did Juliette and her family do it? After all this traveling, Morag's family could've been extras for *The Walking Dead* while the Gaspars looked like the glossy photo of the fake family that came with picture frames.

Juliette flounced over and dropped into the seat next to Morag, smoothing out the flowered dress she'd sewn herself. Textile art was her obsession, and she'd embroidered iridescent beads on the skirt. She clapped her hands together. "Only two more hours, and we finally get to see Screeverholme Castle. It's so exciting."

"Thrilling," Hamish added in a flat voice.

Juliette pulled out her phone and snapped a selfie of her and Morag. "I want to document this." She showed Morag their photo, and Morag sighed in resignation at her Medusa-like hair. Juliette outshone her in every picture, but her friend was so lovable and unassuming, it was hard to resent her.

Juliette held up her phone again. "Need one of you too, Hamish."

Hamish gave Juliette a toothless smile.

"Excuse me," Paul said.

Morag looked up at him, and her heart jumped. He was only an inch or two taller than Morag and bordered on slight, with a face made for sketching. Perfect proportions with full lips and thick lashes framing eyes as gray as the North Sea and hair the color of sand. In a word, gorgeous.

To reach the last empty seat, Paul had to push past her. Morag accidentally-on-purpose didn't pull her legs in far enough, so his legs brushed against hers. She wished she could slow down time to savor his body heat, but it was over all too quickly as he slipped by.

He gracefully folded himself onto his seat and pulled a paper bag from his dripping raincoat. With a rustle of paper, Paul took out a guidebook. "The cashier at the terminal told me about the etymology of Screeverholme."

"Whoa, wait," Hamish said. "Like there's gonna be bugs at this castle?"

"You're thinking of entomology. The study of insects."

Hamish stared.

Paul cupped his elbow in one hand and rubbed the other down his mouth like a college professor being patient with a particularly slow student. "You have no idea what etymology is, do you?"

Was it possible to find a guy's vocabulary sexy?

Hamish pulled his CU Boulder hat low on his forehead. "Ask me if I care."

"Word origins?" Paul sighed. "*Quel imbécile.*"

Imbécile. Morag snorted. Right then, she couldn't agree with Paul more. Hamish *was* an imbecile who didn't care about anything—college, their parents—while she was left to worry about everything. She waited to see if Paul would continue in French. She loved hearing him speak the language, fluent thanks to his Parisian mother, Françoise. She was a famous artist, and along with Paul, also the object of Morag's infatuation, albeit of a different kind.

"Anyway," Paul said, "'Screever' means a cold wind in some Orkney language."

"A cold wind?" Hamish used the tone of someone saying *rotting fish heads.*

As if on cue, a gust of wind pummeled the salt-encrusted windows of the cabin with rain. The ferry pulled away from the terminal, only discernible by the movement and chugging of the engine.

"Wow," Hamish said. "I can hardly wait to get to Screeverholme now."

In the row behind them, someone cleared their throat, and

the four of them turned to look at a man with a red, craggy face. "Visitin' Screeverholme, are ye?"

"We're going to live there for the summer," Juliette said.

The man's bushy eyebrows lifted. "The last of the Tullochs finally died, and the island is rid of them, and now the castle's to be invaded by Yanks?" Morag's mom said it *tuh-luck,* but this man said it in that Scottish way like he had something stuck in his throat. *Tuh-luchhgh.* He chuckled, though he didn't sound amused.

Morag's family was distantly related to the Tullochs, but perhaps that might be a detail to keep to herself. "You didn't like the Tullochs?"

The man's puckered mouth said it all.

"We're not exactly invading." Juliette sounded affronted. "It's just for summer vacation."

The man barked a laugh. "A summer holiday at Screeverholme? It's on its own wee island off Tullimentay. Tullimentay is the farthest north, the loneliest of Orkney. There's naught to do, and it's always cold. Oh aye, that sounds a grand holiday—if ye love freezin' all the time."

Hamish dropped his head in his hands with a groan. "So, I packed my swimsuit for nothing?"

"Ye packed yer swimming costume? That's the daftest thing I ever heard." He gave another humorless laugh and licked his chapped lips. "Ye'll no' be swimming at Tullimentay. The waters around it are treacherous. Don't go in unless ye've a death wish, lad." His juicy chuckle turned into a coughing fit.

Hamish shared a look with Morag that said, *Dang, this dude is freaky.*

Their mom rushed toward them. At first, Morag thought she was checking if the man was bothering them. Instead, she raced past into the tiny restroom. A few moments later, Morag was mortified to hear retching. She glanced at Paul, whose nose was buried in his guidebook. There was no way he couldn't hear it, too.

"She's no stomach for the sea." The creepy man pulled out his own book.

A couple of minutes later, Morag got up and knocked on the bathroom door. "You all right in there?"

"Eurggh," Mom answered, which sounded bad, but Morag thought was her way of saying she was okay.

She returned to her seat and avoided eye contact with Paul.

"Your poor mother should have considered breaking up the trip like the Bacons," he said.

Paul was right. Mom was worn out from being sick, and Morag had never been so exhausted. The Bacons had the right idea taking their time on the journey. Morag couldn't wait to meet the third family joining them for the summer. When her mom found out about the opportunity to rent Screeverholme Castle, she wanted more families to come along to split the cost. Morag had been best friends with Juliette since kindergarten, so it had been a natural choice to invite the Gaspars. As a programmer, Dad could work anywhere. He'd suggested inviting his coworker, Mr. Bacon, a single dad of three. The Bacon family opted to do a few days sightseeing in Edinburgh first. Smart.

Morag yawned and stared at a stack of orange life vests. Their bright color kicked off a psychedelic pop song in her head.

She yawned again and drifted off to sleep for a while.

Suddenly, Morag lurched out of her seat to sprawl on the cold floor. What the hell was happening? Had she fallen off the seat in her sleep? Her fingers scrabbled for purchase and closed around someone's leg. Paul yelped, and she blinked in confusion to see him lying on the floor as well. She gripped his leg as the ferry tipped to one side with a muted *boom*. Vibrations reverberated through the linoleum, and someone shrieked. The ferry righted itself, and a heavy silence ensued.

Paul cleared his throat and looked at her fingers clutching his leg. "You all right?"

Morag nodded and hastily removed her hand, wondering if it was obvious how much she wished she didn't have to.

"What the hell?" Hamish grabbed Morag's upper arm and hauled her to her feet. "You okay?"

"Yeah, thanks."

Paul climbed from the floor and stood beside a wide-eyed Juliette. He pressed his nose against the window. "We hit something."

"No shit, Sherlock." Hamish hung his hands on his hips.

"But what did we hit?" Morag joined Paul by the window and wiped away a circle on the glass to peer out. Nothing but gray sea and sky and fog. Everyone on the ferry talked at once, and as their excited voices merged into one sound, green lights flashed outside the window.

"Can you see anything?" she asked Paul. It was probably her synesthesia set off by everyone's voices, but she couldn't be sure. The lights looked so real. Something about them made her afraid.

Paul turned his attention from the passengers back to the window. "No. It's too foggy."

The captain, his hat gone, hair disheveled, and a wild look in his eye, slammed open the cabin door and glanced around. "Everyone all right?"

"What happened?" asked Dad.

"We hit a buoy."

"A buoy? That was an awful hard hit."

The captain stared her father down. "If everyone is all right, we'll be on our way again."

The red-faced man spoke behind Morag. "I'll call Ben and let him know."

The captain gave the man a curt nod and left the cabin. In his wake, the only sound was the purr of the idling engine as the ferry bobbed in the water. Poor Mom darted for the bathroom again.

"Did you smell him?" Hamish mimed tipping a glass. "Guy's been drinking. Maybe he hit another boat."

Morag peered through the chilly window again but saw

nothing. No boats and no buoys. The ferry rolled on the waves, heaving up and down and side to side. More retching came from the bathroom.

As Morag fought her rising seasickness, her hopes for the trip sank.

Sank like whatever she'd seen in the water.

A moment later, the ferry's engine rumbled again. An hour later, everyone sighed with relief when the ferry bumped against the pier at their final destination. They shuffled off the boat into the clawing wind, the air extra cold after the fug of the cabin. Morag shivered. At least the rain had stopped. She reached into her backpack and pulled out a scarf—her favorite because the scarlet color always made Vivaldi's *Winter* play more perfectly than anything she could manage on the piano. She wrapped the scarf around her neck before heading down the gangway.

She glanced back at the ferry and saw no sign of damage from their collision. The gangway led to an ugly concrete pier, incongruous against the breathtaking backdrop. A few shafts of sunlight stabbed through the dark clouds to make the low green hills of the island glow emerald in the gloom. A folk rock song played for only Morag to hear.

Juliette clutched Morag's arm. "Isn't this beautiful?"

"Oh yeah," Hamish said. "Nice beach. Great for barbecues, right?"

Sheer rock cliffs wrapped around the island and dropped straight into the roiling sea. Juliette's fingers slipped away, and Morag scratched absentmindedly at her arm.

"Sweet, sweet terra firma." Mom stepped off the gangway and looked tempted to throw herself onto the ground and kiss it.

As people shuffled off the gangway onto the pier, family and friends reunited. They sent a mix of curious and suspicious looks in the direction of Morag's group. Off to the side, a man lifted his hand and waved at Mom, and she waved back. She led them off the ramp over to him.

He had to be in his twenties, though he dressed like an octogenarian in a tweed jacket and flat cap. "Ye must be the Davidsons and Gaspars. I'm Ben, the caretaker of the castle." His sober face was about as friendly as the ominous clouds.

Was this the same Ben the man on the ferry was going to call?

Morag started to speak, then cleared her throat of a scratchy feeling. Hopefully, she wasn't getting sick. "You heard we hit that buoy?"

A muscle twitched along Ben's jaw as he studied Morag, but before he could respond, Morag's father gave introductions. Ben didn't look too pleased to get the roll call of all eight Davidsons and Gaspars, and he kept eyeing their luggage and then his small, blue Fiat. "We'll have to take it in turns. I can't fit ye all at once in my peedie car." He sounded irritated, although nobody *had* suggested he could fit them all in.

Another gust of cold wind swept across them. Morag's scalp tingled, and her neck itched. The respite from the rain would be short-lived. A few drops splashed onto the hood of Ben's car. He proceeded to tie a teetering stack of suitcases on the roof, and the two dads shot each other dubious looks. "Ferry loupers," Ben muttered.

"What's that mean?" Juliette said in her ear, and Morag shrugged.

Goosebumps broke out over her skin, and selfishly, Morag hoped she might go in the first carload to the castle. She rubbed her neck and tugged away her scarf, but the itching intensified and spread to her face. She scratched at her cheeks, stinging like they'd been slapped by an icy hand.

Ben opened the passenger door, and Hamish said, "I call shotgun."

Morag tried to protest, but her tongue felt thick and clumsy. She drew a breath, and it was like breathing mud through a straw. An invisible hand gripped her lungs. Air, she needed air. She sucked in and only managed to wheeze. Clutching at her closing throat, she struggled to push out the words before she ran out of breath completely. "I—I can't breathe."

"Morag?" Juliette's worried face swam across her vision.

Morag slipped into blackness.

Chapter 2

"**O**uch!" Morag's eyes flew open, and she stared up at her family circled around. Her thigh stung, and her heart pounded in her ribcage like a trapped bird. She clawed at something covering her mouth and nose.

"Leave it." A man crouched by her head. "It's oxygen." He held a metal tube in his hand and lifted it so she could see. "Epipen. It might make ye feel a wee bit strange for a few minutes."

Morag tried to orient herself. Her fingers scrabbled at rough concrete. Someone's jacket served as a pillow under her head. She craned her neck and saw she lay under an overhang near the ferry terminal.

Mom kneeled nearby, crying, and Dad squatted with his arm around her. It was the first time Morag had seen her parents touch in a long time. Hamish stood by her feet, his face pale and drawn.

What happened? She tried to sit up, but the man put his hand on her shoulder, and she stilled, remembering. The crushing sensation in her lungs, the panic of not being able to breathe.

Why? To reassure herself, she drew in a long breath through the oxygen mask. It tasted sweet. Was oxygen sweet? Oh god, had she almost died? Her body trembled, and she laced her fingers together on her stomach as if it would hold her together.

"This will hurt a bit." A needle slid into her arm, and she winced. The man handed a bag of fluids to Dad, who took it without question and held it high. Her heart still pounded, from the epi-pen or her close brush with death, or both.

Liquid moved down the IV tubing and into her arm. Her mom touched the tube and gave the man a heavy look. "How hypotensive is she?" The undercurrent of fear rippling through her mother's words shot a jolt through Morag.

A stethoscope hung from the man's neck, and he put the earpieces in and began pumping the blood pressure cuff Morag hadn't noticed on her other arm. He recited out some numbers to her mother, who sagged in relief and bent to pull Morag into a tight embrace. When she finally let go, her dad handed Mom the fluids bag so he could hug Morag, too.

"You scared the shit out of me," Dad whispered.

Morag decided in that instant she never wanted to see that look on her parents' faces again. What the hell had happened to her? She wanted to ask, but for now, she enjoyed the sensation of oxygen moving into her lungs again. Something she'd taken for granted before today.

"All right, give her some air," Mom said.

Hamish rolled his eyes at Morag and shook his head at their mother's typical overbearing behavior, and Morag smiled, her cheeks pressing against the plastic of the mask. She never wanted to see her brother that scared again, either.

Juliette and Paul huddled with their parents about ten feet away. A new feeling beyond confusion and fear began to creep in. Embarrassment. It provided the motivation she needed to try to speak.

"What's going on?" The mask muffled Morag's voice.

"Anaphylactic shock," the man said. "A bad allergic reaction."

An allergic reaction? "To what?"

"We're goin' to figure that out." The man's Orkney accent caused undulating silver chains to dance across Morag's vision. "I'm Magnus, the doctor here, but ye've probably heard of me."

"Nice to meet you." Morag croaked like a geriatric frog as she tried to raise her voice to be heard through the mask.

He smiled. "Same."

"Can I sit now?"

Magnus helped her into a seated position. "Nice and easy. Ye gave everyone quite a scare. If ye don't mind, I'll take ye to my clinic."

"Yes," Mom said. "Please."

Morag sat against the wall of the building. She must've looked a little dazed because Hamish gave her a questioning double-thumbs-up. "You good?"

She nodded. Morag's skin still itched, but her throat no longer felt like a closing fist. Now she was awake again and talking, the Gaspars moved in closer. For the first time, she noticed some strangers lingering near the terminal, sending glances and outright nosy stares in her direction. Morag made brief eye contact with Paul before turning her head away. She couldn't think of a time she'd been more embarrassed. Even when she fell off the stage at her piano guild recital.

"Is she going to be okay?" Juliette darted in to squeeze Morag's hand.

"She'll be fine. Right as rain, soon enough," Magnus said.

"Why don't we have Ben take us up to the castle?" Mike, Juliette's dad, gave his wife a meaningful look, and Françoise nodded. "I'm sure Morag and her family will join us soon."

Juliette squeezed her hand once more and allowed her parents to lead her back toward Ben who waited by his vehicle.

"We need to get Morag into my car." Magnus wore an olive-green sweater that matched his eyes and made Morag hear a stripped down version of a song by a Denver band. The doctor eyed her hulk of a brother. "Could ye carry her?"

Hamish bent and hooked one arm under Morag's legs and the other under her shoulders. She wasn't sure she trusted her brother not to drop her. Her father lifted a silver oxygen tank while her mom carried the IV bag.

Hamish hefted her up with all the care and delicacy of someone hulking a big bag of dog food, and her shoulder knocked painfully into his collar bone.

She clutched his neck. "Hey, careful."

He readjusted her in his arms. "Geez, Morag. Good thing I've been working out so much. You weigh a ton."

Hamish grunted theatrically as he carried her toward a waiting Land Rover. She smacked his arm, but he only gave her a quick reassuring squeeze against him and chuckled, sounding giddy with relief. In a rush of affection, it hit Morag again that her brother had been terrified about his little sister.

Terrified because she'd almost died.

Magnus opened the rear door so Hamish could place her in the back seat. They situated her IV bag and oxygen, and everyone else piled in the vehicle, her dad in the front beside Magnus, and Hamish and Mom propping her up on either side in the back. Mom reached over and took Morag's hand in hers and blinked rapidly, keeping her eyes toward the front of the vehicle.

It wasn't exactly an ambulance, but there wasn't exactly a hospital to go to—only the small clinic where her mom would be working. In fact, Morag didn't see many buildings at all on their drive across the island. It was smaller than she'd expected, a landscape of vivid green crisscrossed by stone walls and punctuated by a village of scattered houses, one church, a teeny school, and a few shops. Tullimentay lay in solitude, a fixed lifeboat for its inhabitants living on the gray sea, held back only by the strength of the rocky cliffs.

Morag imagined that gray sea roiling up over the island drowning them all. The sensation from before, the struggle to breathe, overwhelmed her, and she took a deep breath to make sure it was only a memory. Her mom released her hand

and stroked her hair before leaning her head to Morag's for a moment as if she too needed to reassure herself Morag was okay.

Sheep kept moving across the road, forcing Magnus to stop while they passed. The slender animals pulled themselves from the rocky beach, munching on seaweed of all things.

"What are they doin' out?" Magnus muttered. "They should be in their punds. The sheep court will have a fit if the sheep dyke's broken again."

"What's a sheep dyke?" Hamish whispered in her ear.

"Probably a wall," she whispered back.

"And a sheep court?"

"No idea." Morag's mask hid her laugh as she imagined lordly lambs at a fancy ball.

Magnus stopped outside a single-story stone building. A plaque read *Tullimentay Clinic.* Hamish climbed out and reached for Morag, but she waved him away.

Mom's eyebrows drew down. "Let him carry you."

"No, I'm fine." Morag stepped from the Land Rover, pleased to find her legs, though shaky, held her up. Her mom held her firmly by the elbow as if Morag might blow away in the stiff wind and led her inside behind Magnus. In the clinic's tiny waiting room sat a girl with long red hair and more freckles than Morag. Somehow, her freckles made her prettier by highlighting her huge green eyes. Hamish stirred and stood taller.

"Dad!" the girl said. "I got yer call. Everything's on, just like ye told me."

"Thanks, Ingrid. A cup of tea wouldn't go amiss, either."

Mom tucked Morag into one of the two beds in the ward with antihistamines feeding into her IV and stood guard by her bed, Dad at her side.

Magnus handed her some pills and a glass of water. "Steroids."

"Watch out. Morag's gonna get cut like me!" Hamish flexed his biceps.

Ingrid, coming in with a tea tray, laughed at his dumb joke, and he looked pleased with himself.

"Ye seem to be doin' grand enough, now," Magnus said, after checking her vitals. "We'll monitor ye a few hours, but seein' as yer mum's a medical professional, I feel comfortable sendin' ye home tonight."

Hamish turned on a television and found *Scooby Doo* dubbed into another language. "What are they speaking?" He lifted his head at the TV in question.

"Gaelic," Ingrid said. "No one speaks that in Orkney, but they do in other parts of Scotland."

"Oh, yeah. Of course." Hamish nodded, as if he'd known all along, and was soon laughing at Shaggy's antics making a huge sandwich.

"Ye don't have any allergies ye know of?" The doctor brought Morag's attention back to the unpleasant matter at hand. "Or asthma?"

Morag looked at Mom, waiting for her to answer as usual, but her mother only gave her an encouraging nod. "Uh, no. No allergies. Or asthma." She bunched the blanket under her hand.

"Can ye tell me what happened?"

Morag glanced at Hamish and Ingrid. They stood by the TV chatting in low voices not listening to this conversation. Good, she hated all this attention. "So, yeah. Uh, I was standing on the pier, thinking it was cold." Just talking about it made her feel cold again. "My scalp felt tingly, and my neck and face itched. Then I couldn't breathe." She swallowed hard before continuing. "That's all I remember." Though she wished she could forget it completely. What was happening to her?

"Hmm. So ye were feeling cold? I'd like to try an experiment."

Magnus disappeared and returned with an ice cube, which he placed on her forearm. "This might get a bit uncomfortable."

Three long minutes later, he pulled the ice cube away and gave a triumphant, "Ha! Cold urticaria."

Mom stepped forward to look at the angry welt on Morag's arm. "An allergy—to the *cold?*"

Dad's eyebrows shot up.

"Aye. It's rare. A person can get hives. Swelling. Or in a severe case like Morag's, anaphylaxis. Damp cold is the worst and going in cold water would be dangerous."

"Whatever made you think of it?" Mom said.

"Probably never would've, but we had a resident on Tullimentay with it."

"We're from Colorado," Dad said. "It gets cold there. Morag's never had a reaction before."

An image popped into her mind. Morag walking to the school bus in January in single-digit temperatures, her shoes squeaking on the powdery snow, and her mother shouting at the door that her hoodie wasn't warm enough and to come get her winter coat. Morag had laughed her off in embarrassment. Didn't her mom see all the dumb boys wearing *shorts* at the bus stop? She'd be fine.

And she had been. "Why is this happening now?"

Magnus tossed the ice cube in a nearby sink with a *clank* that made a silver bubble float up in Morag's head and pop. "It can come on quite suddenly."

Morag latched onto it. "It happened like the second I got here. Is it something to do with the island?"

The doctor looked startled. "The island? No, I don't think so. Why would ye say that? Perhaps it's to do with the damp." He rushed on. "Fortunately, it can stop as suddenly as it starts. It's quite treatable."

"How?" Dad said.

"Don't get cold." He smiled. "Have an epi-pen at all times. Take antihistamines every day."

"Antihistamines sound easy." Relief warmed Morag as much as the blanket tucked around her.

"Aye, every day. More if the weather's goin' to be cold and damp and windy."

"So, a regular day in Orkney?" Mom wrapped her arms around her middle, wearing a horrified look.

"Aye." The doctor chuckled, but Mom clearly didn't share his amusement.

"We've just learned Morag has an allergy to the cold," Mom said. "An allergy that's particularly bad with the damp, and we've brought her to a cold and damp island. She went into anaphylaxis and nearly died, and I'm supposed to be okay with giving her some Benadryl every day and calling it good?"

"But I didn't die." Morag's face warmed even as a cold chill slithered through her gut at the truth in her mother's words.

Mom shook her head. "No. No way. I don't think Morag should be here."

Morag sent her father a pleading look.

Dad blew out a long, slow breath and ran his hand over his stubbled face. "Now, Lisa. We're already here. We'll follow doctor's orders and—"

Mom shook her head harder. "No. We can't stay here with Morag."

Now it was the doctor's turn to look horrified. "Lisa, ye're no' thinkin' of leavin', are ye? We've a bumper crop of babies comin' this summer. At least, by Orkney standards. I'm countin' on ye to help me."

"Oh, *I'm* not leaving." Mom's lips set in a thin line. "But Morag is. I'll call Aunt Helen. Morag can stay with her for the summer."

Hamish winced. "Oof."

"Mom, no." No way she'd stay with Aunt Helen. Recently divorced, she dressed three decades too young and took dance classes. Not ballroom or salsa. *Pole dancing.* "I want to stay." She didn't want to die, of course, she didn't, but Magnus said the treatment was easy. A couple antihistamines every day. Morag remembered the squeezing feeling in her throat, the panic when she couldn't breathe. But she thought of Paul's serious, gray eyes. Her art portfolio and the beauty of the island begging to be drawn. "I want to stay," she said again.

"Bill?" Mom looked to Morag's dad for support. He shrugged,

and her mom huffed out a sigh. "Typical. Well, Morag. This isn't your decision to make. Tomorrow, we're getting you off this island and on the next flight home."

Magnus held up his finger. "About that. The next ferry won't be runnin' for three more days."

"It still only runs twice a week? Fine. The next ferry it is. Morag doesn't go outside until then."

"Orrrr," her father stretched out the *r's*. "We see how Morag does over the next few days on antihistamines. See if she might be able to stay."

Go, Dad. Good plan.

"Aye, that's a grand idea if ye ask me."

Her mom sent Magnus a look that said no one had and turned to Dad. "She almost died."

"I'm aware." He crossed his arms. "She's my daughter, too, you know? But Morag is sixteen. I say we let her decide for herself."

"*You* say?" She tucked in her chin, then seemed to remember herself and clamped her mouth shut.

An awkward tension settled over the room. Ingrid loudly cleared away the cups of tea, and Magnus checked Morag's IV tubing even though she was sure it was fine.

Morag's face flushed so hot she couldn't imagine being cold again. "Hey, guys. Let's see how I do, okay? Now we know what we're dealing with, I'll take the antihistamines, I'll bundle up warm, and it won't happen again." She spoke the words to reassure herself as much as her mother.

"Everybody is exhausted," Dad said. "Things will look better when we get some rest." He put an arm around Mom's shoulder, but she eased away.

Their summer was off to a great start.

Chapter 3

It wasn't until after ten p.m. that Mom finally agreed Morag could leave the clinic. She couldn't wait to see Screeverholme Castle. It was late, but being so far north on the globe, the sun was only starting to set, leaving the landscape in a dimness just shy of full dark that Magnus called the *simmer dim*. He also had a funny name for the fog clinging to the ground—the *haar*.

They'd been driving a few minutes when Magnus slammed on the brakes.

"What's that?" Dad asked.

Morag sat in the back seat sandwiched between Mom and Hamish. Hamish knocked his head into Morag's trying to peer out the windshield. "Ow." Morag shoved him away.

Magnus stopped and climbed out of the vehicle. In the misty glow of the headlights, something lay in the road. Magnus lifted an animal in his arms, and everyone in the car gasped as the headlights caught the startling red of a bloody sheep. Its belly was a mess of exposed guts.

"It's a dead sheep," Dad said helpfully.

Hamish covered his mouth. "Oh, man. That's so gross."

Morag's stomach, full of the delicious shepherd's pie sent over by Magnus's wife and subsequently scarfed down by her family an hour ago, agreed with a sickening twist. It didn't help the shepherd's pie had been made with lamb.

Magnus carried the sheep to the roadside and climbed back into the running Land Rover. He held up his hands, and in the interior light of the car, revealed the sticky red on his palms. He asked Dad to open the glove box and pass him the bottle inside. A moment later, the scent of hand sanitizer filled the air.

"Hit by a car," Magnus said.

"The driver didn't stop to deal with it?" Dad said.

"Even our tiny island has its share of bad apples." Magnus put the Land Rover in gear. "Fortunately, the good people here far outnumber the bad."

What was that expression about one bad apple spoiling the bunch? Morag snuck a quick glance at the poor torn-up sheep as they passed it. She only hoped it hadn't suffered.

Screeverholme Castle came into view, and she instantly vowed to stay no matter what Mom said. The gray sandstone castle stood on its little island connected to Tullimentay by an arching stone bridge about a hundred feet long. The castle appeared to grow out of the rock like a living entity. Only the narrowest perimeter of the island separated the castle from the sea, with the exception of the strip of land to the left sloping to a tiny beach. Higher up from the beach near the castle, some dark shapes rose from the misty ground. Gravestones? Morag hugged herself against the chill.

Moss and lichen dotted the castle walls, and yellow light glowed in some of the windows. A four-story, rectangular tower stood on the right opposite a long, two-story wing on the left. A squat building connected the two halves of the castle into a U shape. Nearest the bridge lay a small hexagonal tower on its own, a gatehouse perhaps, and the blue Orkney flag whipped in the wind above its steep roof.

The sight made Morag hear bagpipes. For once her brain decided to use a natural association.

"It's magical." She climbed out of the Land Rover, unfettered from the IV and oxygen mask she'd endured all day. She started across the bridge and stared up at the castle. A hush enveloped the place, and the only sound was a soft lapping of waves against the rocks below, prompting Mozart's Piano Sonata Seven to play.

"Let's get you inside where it's warm." Mom waved for Morag to hurry. Ben appeared in the doorway of the smaller hexagon tower, and Morag realized he lived there.

Ben crossed the bridge to meet them halfway and eyed Morag like she was contagious. He jerked his head in her direction and sent Magnus a questioning look. "She all right?"

"Oh, aye. An allergic reaction to the cold is all, but she's fine now."

The caretaker's posture went rigid. "The lass is like Catherine's dad?"

Magnus held up his palms. "I don't want to hear any of that. No' a word."

"What's this about?" Dad asked.

"Nothin' to worry about, Bill," said Magnus. "Local nonsense."

"Ye know that isn't true, Doc."

A strained silence fell between the doctor and the caretaker.

Dad shrugged at Morag, and Mom hooked her arm over Morag's shoulders and swept her along like a swelling tide. "Inside." Mom led their family toward the castle.

"People saw her collapse at the pier." Ben's words followed Morag. "There'll be talk. What would ye propose . . ."

Morag was too far away to make out the rest. Great. The entire island was talking about her, and it sounded like something weird. "What's Ben talking about?"

"Who knows," Mom said. "I remember the islanders here were ridiculously superstitious. Let's just focus on getting you warm." She had the tenacity of a terrier and wouldn't be distracted from her mission to keep Morag safe.

They'd almost reached the imposing castle door when Morag cast one last look over her shoulder at Ben and Magnus. Movement in the water caught her attention. She dug in her heels and managed to jerk free of her mom's grip. "Wait."

Twenty feet below, an otter swam on his back in the dying shadows of the evening. He gazed up at Morag, brown button eyes gleaming in a whiskery face, paws tucked on his chest like he was praying.

"Come on," Mom said. "It's windy."

Ben caught up to Morag and her mom. "What're ye lookin' at?"

Morag gestured at the water, but only rings fanned the surface. "There was an otter."

"An otter?" Ben's fingers dug into the side of the stone bridge as he studied the water like someone scrying for the future and not liking what he saw. "Ye sure? The water can fool a person. Make them think they see things that aren't there." He almost looked frightened, and for an unsettling moment, it reminded Morag of the ferry captain's words.

"Morag, it's cold." Mom tugged on her arm. "Come on."

Ben turned abruptly from the water. "Ye best listen to yer mum and get inside." He pointed at the arched wooden door. Morag noticed a line of silver coins stretched across its threshold, but before she could ask about it, the door creaked open on giant hinges to reveal a curved foyer and stone floor and an excited Juliette.

"Morag." Juliette stood in the wash of yellow light. "Oh my god, you're okay." She pulled Morag inside and into a hug. "Your mom texted. You're seriously allergic to *the cold?*" Morag slid her eyes toward her mother and patted the air with her hands. Fortunately, Juliette, being her best friend, got the hint. "Oh, so, yeah. Let me give you a tour of the castle and show you your room."

"Don't unpack much, Sweetie," Mom said. "Just what you need until the next ferry. I'm sorry, Juliette, Morag needs to rest. She's—"

"Lisa." Dad stepped into the foyer with Hamish and ran a hand through his wild, dark curls. "*You* need to give it a rest."

Mom smiled tightly at Juliette and turned to Dad to speak through gritted teeth. "Bill. I need you to back me up."

"And I think we need a moment to settle in here." His jaw clenched. "You know? In the place you wanted us all to be, whether we liked it or not."

Morag sent her friend a desperate look.

"Let's start that tour." Juliette dragged her deeper into the castle and down a hallway. "What did your mom mean about the next ferry," she whispered.

"She wants to send me home." The words left a bitter taste in her mouth. Her mom couldn't even let her enjoy seeing the castle without ruining it. "But I'm not going without a fight. I just have to convince my mom." Something brushed her leg. A pewter cat with golden eyes did figure-eights around her calves. "Who's this?"

"Malcolm. The owner left all these instructions. Apparently, Malcolm belongs to Ben, but spends most of his time in the castle." Juliette stopped in front of a large wooden table and picked up some papers. "Here's the owner's letter. It's some guy who inherited the castle last year from a distant cousin. Can you imagine?"

Morag scanned directions on everything from how to feed Malcolm to using the boathouse.

"Look at this." Juliette pointed at a paragraph on the third page. "'We ask you please stay out of the graveyard to preserve Screeverholme's history. Some of the graves and stones are very old and in poor condition.' Spooky, right? Here. You'll need this." She gave Morag a laminated map.

Morag studied it for a minute. The castle consisted of two parts: the large tower on the right and the lower wing on the left.

She and Juliette stood in the foyer, and this short wing served as no more than a connecting passage on each floor between the two sides. On the first floor, the map showed the kitchen, library, and study located in the left wing, while the large tower held a grand banqueting hall to the right. The second floor contained a series of bedrooms over the kitchen on one side, and in the big tower was a lounge and billiards room. The third and fourth floors of the tower housed the bedrooms.

Morag waved the map at Juliette. "This sounds like a game of Clue. Professor Plum is in the billiards room with a pool stick. Where are the secret passages though?"

"Duh. You wouldn't put those on the map. They're secret." Juliette pointed at the map to the fourth floor of the large tower. "Our rooms are up top. Our parents are below on the third floor." She pointed to the bedrooms over the kitchen in the smaller wing. "Some of the Bacon family will be on that side, but there's plenty of room on our floor if anyone wants to join us. Should we start in the kitchen? The heart of any home."

Morag smothered a smile at Juliette's tendency to sound like an old lady and followed her down a stone hallway. They entered a jarringly modern room compared to the cave-like corridor. The dark wood cupboards stood out against the sparkling white granite of the countertops, and the high-end appliances could have come from a professional kitchen. Tall stools lined a breakfast bar. A long kitchen table sat perpendicular to a bank of windows, and a back door led outside to that strip of land she'd spotted before. It was too dim to see much.

"The graveyard is out there." Juliette hiked her thumb toward the back door and waggled her eyebrows. "Creepy."

Morag stepped to the back door and peered out the window. In the murky darkness, the water surrounding their small island glittered malevolently. A humped hill squatted to the right at the far side of the graveyard. In the dim fog, the gravestones looked like the blurry outlines of huddled figures. The idea sent a thrill coursing down her spine as if a skeletal finger traced each knob of her backbone.

"Come on," Juliette said. "Don't you want to see the library?"

Morag felt simultaneously annoyed and relieved to be pulled from the gothic scene before her. As she turned away, she caught a glimpse of movement near the graves. No more than a shadow moving in the dark mist by a headstone. Wind blew the mist, and a skeletal figure appeared. She blinked, and it was gone.

Juliette, sensing Morag's tension, froze. "What is it?"

"I thought I saw something."

"Like what?"

Morag squinted. "I don't know. A shape moving."

Juliette looked out the window beside her. "I don't see anything."

Morag didn't see anything either. She cleared her throat, a little embarrassed. "Yeah, must've been my imagination." Two imaginations in a row. Nothing more than a trick of the light and fog, her brain fueled by what she'd seen in the water earlier. She let Juliette lead her out of the kitchen.

When they entered the library, Morag breathed a sigh of contentment. It wasn't huge, but the ceilings rose so high, the walls seemed to stretch as her eyes followed up the expanse of bookcases. Everything from classics to modern fiction lined the shelves, complete with a rolling ladder for accessing the higher volumes. Thick rugs muted her footsteps, and golden light spilled from the only source in the room, a small lamp atop a baby grand piano. Its polished surface—rosewood if Morag wasn't mistaken—gleamed in the light, beckoning.

She weaved her way through the end tables and chairs to sit at the piano bench and traced her finger over the smooth cover. She imagined the short black keys tucked up for the night in their beds of white.

"I knew you'd like the piano." Juliette clapped her hands together. "Play for me?"

"Maybe the owner doesn't want us touching it." She half-hoped so. Any excuse not to play for an audience.

"The letter didn't mention it. Go on."

"It's probably out of tune." Morag slid back the cover and gently pressed the fingers of her right hand onto the smooth keys to play a C chord. At the sound, pitch-perfect, a green spiral floated over her vision. She shifted her hand up to the more melancholy E minor chord and the green spiral morphed into blue. Someone had kept this piano in good condition. She worked her way through a progression of chords, while Juliette plopped onto a red velvet couch to listen.

Warmed up, she played a piece of Bach she'd memorized last year. The music sent blue and green and yellow notes floating through Morag's mind. Circles and ovals bounced harmlessly off sharp diamonds and trapezoids, bringing the song alive. It made music both enormously easy for Morag to learn and enormously difficult to master.

When she finished the song, Juliette's mouth hung open, her chin propped in her hand as if she'd just heard some great prodigy play. Morag shook her head in affection. Juliette was as enthralled with Morag's music as Morag was with Juliette's sewing, except Juliette truly was a maestro with her needles and thread.

Juliette's large, expressive eyes shone in the low light. "Play one more?"

Morag shut the cover with a decisive, firm thud. "Don't we have a castle to explore?"

A chance to resume tour guide duties proved irresistible to Juliette. As she whisked Morag through the castle on a whirlwind tour, Juliette chattered away about the history of castle fortifications. Morag was too tired to take in most of the architecture lesson. The rooms passed in a blur of dim lighting, heavy wood furniture, and portraits of stern Scots scowling out of oil paintings. The large banquet hall felt positively medieval with a disturbing collection of weaponry covering its walls and a fireplace big enough to roast an ox. Morag already loved the place.

On the second floor, they entered a room labeled *lounge* on the map. Dark beams crossed the ceiling of the long, rectangular space. An inviting collection of squishy sofas and chairs was arranged in front of a flat-screen TV and more dusty books packed the built-in shelves.

"What's that smell?" Morag pointed at the fireplace, curious at the smoky, sour scent wafting from the smoldering fire.

"That would be peat." Morag jumped at the voice, having not noticed Paul sitting on the other side of the room in a wingback chair reading his guidebook. How he could read in this low lighting, Morag had no idea. "Peat's terrible for the environment, of course, but seems the Orcadians are big on tradition, and the place is full of peat bogs." He peered at her now, a touching look of concern drawing his eyebrows together under that mop of silky blond hair. "Morag. You look better. I heard it was cold urticaria?"

Juliette tugged Morag toward the doorway past Paul. "Would love to talk but got a tour to finish. Bye." As soon as they made it into the adjoining room, Juliette rolled her eyes. "Sorry, but you don't want to get my brother started on the topic of peat bogs."

Except Morag did. She'd listen to Paul's confident voice reading from the dictionary, but she wasn't about to tell Juliette that. Juliette flicked on a light to reveal the biggest pool table Morag had ever seen. A wave of exhaustion overtook her, and Morag failed to stifle a yawn.

"Oh, my goodness, Morag. I'm sorry. You must be so tired. Let me show you the bedrooms."

They got lost once turning left in a hall instead of right and ended up on the second floor over the kitchen and had to consult the map. The cat shadowed their steps, meowing from time to time as if in encouragement.

"Maybe Malcolm is lonely." Juliette bent to pet him.

"It's cute he's following us everywhere," Morag said.

At last, she and Juliette climbed a winding staircase to the fourth floor at the top of the biggest tower. Silence pressed heavy, like a physical presence, as they looked down the long hallway. Another spiral staircase was visible at the far end where Juliette headed.

"Our parents all wanted the rooms one floor below with ensuite bathrooms but being on the top floor is worth us sharing a bathroom," Juliette said. "And wait until you see your room. It's the best one. Paul wanted it, but I told him to let you have it after your rough start."

She smiled knowing Paul let her have this room. Morag was so shattered, she'd happily have slept in a broom closet, but when Juliette opened the door, gratitude toward Paul filled her. The cat streaked down the two steps inside. Being in the tower's corner, the bedroom had two walls of windows, flanked by interior wood shutters. A giant bed faced those windows overlooking the sea to the north. Dark beams crisscrossed a plaster ceiling painted robin-egg blue.

Morag grinned. "This is awesome."

Malcolm meowed his agreement.

"Be right back," Juliette said. "I'm going next door to change into my PJ's."

Morag's suitcase lay haphazardly by the door, like someone chucked it in. Hamish, no doubt. She fished her pajamas out of her case. Getting into them was heaven. With another yawn, she headed to one of the windows set deep in a stone niche. The cold from the rock seeped into the space. The stone floor bore a slight indentation, as though it had slowly yielded to the feet of generations of people standing at this window, gazing at the sea.

Her bare feet settled into the indentations, and she looked at the scene of endless water unchanged since the castle's construction. Only the type of boats that sailed the waters of Orkney would've changed. She'd read about the Viking longships in the 800s, bringing invaders and then settlers to Orkney. Oral history claimed the flagship of the Spanish Armada sailed to the Shetlands in disgrace, maybe passing this very island. During WWII, a British naval fleet prowled the Scapa Flow around

Orkney. The North Sea had seen it all, she was sure, and in its long history, sunk many secrets in its vast, empty waters.

The island, sitting on the edge of nothing but endless sea and sky, filled her with melancholy loneliness. Which was silly because family and friends surrounded her.

A strange moan came from the hallway. Juliette? Morag opened the door and tripped on the steps. She cursed her clumsiness and looked down the hall. Some faint, echoing sound like footsteps moved away from her down the corridor. "Hello?"

The hallway, like the walls of the library, seemed to stretch and elongate. She counted the bedroom doors, eight in total, including her own. She'd gone with friends to a haunted house in Denver two years ago for Halloween with a long hallway like this, each door providing jump scare after jump scare. Morag hated every second of it. Fed by that experience, her imagination ran unchecked wondering what waited in those bedrooms. Suddenly, those heavy wooden doors could be concealing any manner of horrors—ghosts, starving vampires, crazed axe-murderers.

Malcolm abandoned her, fleeing down the nearest set of steps. Typical cat.

"Juliette?" Her quavering voice bounced off the cracked plaster walls. For the first time, she noticed the light fixtures lining the hallway. Brass mermaids, more like grinning demons than Ariel, each held a single bulb aloft at regular intervals. The one nearest her room winked out, leaving the stretch of floor before her in a puddle of darkness. She swallowed and tried again, louder. "Juliette?"

A long few seconds later, Juliette popped out her bedroom next to Morag's. "What's up?"

"Have the boys gone to bed?"

"I haven't heard anyone come up yet. Why?"

Morag put her hand on the bedroom door across from Juliette's and hesitated. Drawing a deep breath, she pushed it open. The scant light from the hall showed Hamish's suitcase stood near the door. No sign of Hamish, though. "Hello? Anyone here?"

"Stop," Juliette said. "You're creeping me out."

"I heard a noise earlier."

"Maybe it was a ghost." Juliette's gaze darted around the hall. "If anywhere was gonna have a ghost, it's Screeverholme, right?"

Morag swallowed, her mouth dry. Ghosts were fun in theory. Like when reading a gothic book or telling Juliette scary stories during sleepovers when they were younger. The possibility of living with real ghosts in an ancient castle on a tiny island? Not so much.

Juliette grabbed her arm. "Did you hear that?" She cocked her head toward the staircase. "It sounds like someone breathing." She dropped her voice lower. "Like someone's standing on those stairs waiting."

The spiral stairs were creepy as hell. There was no way to see what was coming up them. She heard the noise too, a soft sighing. "Maybe it's the wind?" Fear made her words come out strangled.

Arms suddenly grabbed Morag around the middle. She screamed, and Juliette joined in.

Familiar laughter rolled out from behind her. Morag broke away from Hamish and turned around to punch him in the stomach. Which only made him laugh harder. Her brother must have snuck up the set of stairs at the end of the hallway behind them while Paul had been climbing the nearest staircase, because he crested the top of them now, out of breath and lugging a suitcase.

"That wasn't nice," Paul said. "You really scared them."

"Uh, yeah. Kind of the point." Hamish let out a spooky moan. "Couldn't resist. You should've heard yourselves."

"Super mean, Hamish." Juliette pushed him. "This place is freaky enough."

"Yeah, freaking awesome." Hamish grinned. "I'll admit it,

Morag. Maybe this summer won't be so bad after all."

"And does that revelation have anything to do with Ingrid?" Morag asked.

"Maybe," he said.

"Who's Ingrid?" Juliette's brow furrowed as she looked between Hamish and Morag.

"The doctor's daughter," Morag said. "When I was lying in a hospital bed, Hamish was trying to put the moves on her."

Hamish casually stretched his arms overhead. "Not trying. Succeeding. Ingrid and I are going out tomorrow night."

"Going out where?" Paul leaned against the wall as if too bored by this topic to stand up straight. "There's literally nothing here."

"Guess we'll make our own entertainment." Hamish winked.

"Eww." Morag glanced to Juliette for support, but her friend looked oddly stricken.

Wait. Did Morag and Juliette share a mutual crush of the other's big brother, because *that* would be weird. She could imagine how she'd feel if Paul had just gotten a date with a girl on the island. But did Juliette—her beautiful, sensitive, romantic friend—really have a crush on her oaf of a brother? She shot Juliette a questioning look, but before she could get an answer, Mom appeared at the top of the stairs.

Morag groaned inwardly.

"Hey, Sweetie." Mom came down the hallway, an unstoppable force of maternal worry. "I wanted to check on you and say goodnight." She put her hand on Morag's cheek. "How are you feeling?"

Morag ducked away. "Mom. I'm fine." She wished Paul would go into his bedroom, but he and Hamish stood staring at her.

Mom rubbed her hands over her upper arms. "It's chilly up here, don't you think? I brought you this." She handed Morag a hot water bottle. "Maybe you should come downstairs and sleep in my room. There's a couch you could have."

"Yeah, Morag," Hamish said. "You could sleep with Mommy."

She rounded on her brother. "Would you shut up."

"Goodnight, Hamish," Mom said pointedly, and kissed him on the cheek. "Love you."

Paul lifted his hand in farewell. "Goodnight." He and Hamish both slipped into their rooms.

"It's too cold for you up here," Mom said.

Morag tried to reign in her temper because it wouldn't be worth losing it with Mom. "It's fine. I'll be warm under a bunch of blankets."

"I can sleep with her," Juliette said. "She'd be warmer sharing her bed with someone. If that would make you feel better?"

"Seriously, I'm fine." Morag grit her teeth. "I have my phone. I'll call if I need help." After all the attention, Morag wanted to be alone.

Mom stood debating then hugged Morag. "All right. But if you get cold, come down to my room immediately or call. We just have to get you through these next few days. Sweet dreams. I'll be downstairs if you need me."

Next few days? Not if Morag had anything to say about it.

Morag lay in the huge bed, propped on two pillows, and gazed out the windows. She'd left the shutters open to enjoy the view. The place already had a hold on her. For all its desolation, Morag felt a connection to Screeverholme.

Faint meowing came at her door. She opened it to find Malcolm sitting in the hall, his golden eyes gleaming. He streaked in and leaped onto the bed as if he owned it. Morag settled back in, and the cat was gracious enough to share the covers with a comforting purr, curling up next to the hot water bottle. She'd left the window cracked open to let in the sounds of sighing wind, lapping waves, and the faraway barking of seals.

Morag snuggled under the thick duvet and sank into sleep like a hot bath.

Sometime later, she awoke. It still wasn't completely dark even though the clock read two a.m. The wind no longer sighed, it howled and rattled the windows like something trying to claw its way inside. In the cold room, Morag regretted leaving the window cracked.

Cold was something more than a discomfort now. It was dangerous. She couldn't wrap her head around the strangeness of that. Morag pushed back the duvet with a sigh and got up, toes curling on the cold floor. Tomorrow she'd wear socks to bed. She started toward the window and tripped over Malcolm weaving between her legs.

She stopped at the window, and the stone floor chilled her feet. Morag looked back at the nightstand by her bed, grateful for the epi-pen in the drawer, though she hoped she'd never need it. Once again, the thought she'd almost died today slammed into her with a painful shock. Just as quickly, she shoved the thought away. Only paralyzing fear lay down that path. She'd stay warm, and she'd be fine.

Malcolm was already seeing to that. He sat on top of her feet radiating warmth, a living pair of furry slippers. Standing in the dark, out of bed and exposed, she couldn't help but think of dark things—the skeletal shape in the water and that awful dead sheep in the road. The shadow in the graveyard. How she herself almost ended up in a grave today. So much for not thinking about that. A ripple of fear slithered along her spine.

Outside, sky and sea fused into a never-ending expanse, and the sun lurked coyly at the edge of the horizon, leaving everything washed in gray twilight. She started to pull the shutters closed when a green flash of light caught her attention. Sometimes, her synesthesia reared up without any provocation, her mixed-up senses creating their own show at unexpected times. She squinted, wondering if that's all this was. But no, it wasn't something overlayed on her vision. These lights flickered out at sea, moving underwater. It reminded her of what she'd seen outside the ferry windows.

Malcolm growled low in his throat like a miniature mountain lion. Goosebumps broke out on her arms.

"Bioluminescence," she told Malcolm. "I saw it in a documentary, okay? Just little glow-in-the-dark sea creatures. Stop freaking me out, cat."

She slammed the shutters and scurried back to bed to burrow under the covers. No need to be scared, she told herself. Juliette was next door and Paul and Hamish across the hall.

Paul. She pushed away her fear and pictured Paul in his bed, those long lashes of his lying on his cheeks as he slept. She imagined slipping into his room and telling him she was frightened. Not frightened. That sounded pathetic. She'd tell him she was cold, and he'd throw back the covers and invite her to—

From the hallway came a low moan. Not Hamish this time, she was sure. The wind. That was all. Some kind of acoustic effect. Malcolm curled up beside her again, reassuring her it was nothing to worry about.

Tomorrow night, she'd ask Juliette if she wanted to sleep in her room. Just for fun.

Not because Morag was afraid.

Chapter 4

The next day, Morag awoke late and staggered like a jet-lagged zombie down the spiral stairs toward the siren call of caffeine. She stopped in the kitchen doorway. Paul sat on a bench at the kitchen table drinking his tea in silence. Juliette yawned on the opposite bench, while Hamish and Mom moved around each other in the kitchen looking for food.

Food, though, was in short supply.

Hamish pawed through the cupboards like a starving orphan in a Dickens novel. "Oh, sure," he said to Malcolm, sitting on the floor by his bowl licking a silver-gray paw. "*You've* got food. What about us?" Malcolm regarded him with a golden eye and made no response.

Mom was spooning instant coffee into a cracked mug, but at the sight of Morag, she rushed over and ran her hand over Morag's hair. "You look back to normal."

"Good as new." Morag's throat tightened on the words, an echo of the sensation yesterday. Her throat closing, no air getting in, her vision blackening. She stopped herself. *Enough.*

She *was* good as new this morning.

"Here." Mom handed Morag a glass of water and some pills, and Morag obediently took them.

"See, Mom? I'm taking my pills. All good."

"Aunt Helen said she'd love to have you this summer. Angus and Aileen will be excited."

Morag's empty stomach clenched. She didn't doubt her fifteen-year-old twin cousins would be happy to have a distraction from their mother's midlife crisis. A summer with Aunt Helen was worse than anaphylactic shock. "Mom. Look at me. You said yourself I'm back to normal."

"And I want to keep you that way."

"Morag will never be normal," Hamish said. Morag opened her mouth with a retort, but he continued. "Seriously, Mom. You worry too much. Ingrid showed me the pharmacy at the clinic. Magnus has like fifty boxes of antihistamines. Morag will be fine. Let her stay." Hamish flashed her a conspiratorial smile, and she felt the unexpected sting of grateful tears. "I mean, obviously a Morag-free summer would be cool and all, but Dad really wants her here."

Morag knew Hamish was only teasing about not wanting her around, but she wished he hadn't brought up their dad. Sure enough—

Mom let out an annoyed sigh. "Your father likes to argue with everything I say. He isn't thinking what's best for Morag. I'm going to wake him before he sleeps the day away." Mom disappeared from the kitchen, carrying the coffee mug.

Morag dropped onto the bench next to Juliette, and her friend grimaced in sympathy. "It'll be all right. You sleep okay?"

"Mostly. My bedroom was chilly."

"Mine too," Juliette said.

"Do you want to trade back, Morag?" Paul asked, "Maybe it's too cold with all those windows."

"No way."

"Suit yourself." He smiled over the rim of his cup. "I think I might've got the best room anyway."

"Why's that?" Morag asked.

His smile turned smug. "It's got a secret."

"What secret?"

Paul mimed zipping his mouth shut, locking it, and throwing away the key.

"Whatever." Her curiosity ate away at her, but she wouldn't give him the satisfaction. "Besides, you can't beat the view from my room."

"Speaking of views, how do you like that one?" Juliette pointed at the windows.

"Oh, wow." Morag got up to peer out the window in the back door. In the daylight, stone crosses and headstones clearly marked the raised mounds of burial sites. She thought of the shadow slipping through them last night. At least the gravestones no longer looked like creepy figures. The graves themselves, though, were creepy enough. "Those mounds are weird." She bent to scratch Malcolm as he rubbed against her legs.

"Right?" Juliette said. "You can see exactly where the bodies must lay."

Even creepier was the larger mound beyond the graves, about fifty feet away. Two stone pillars supported a stone beam embedded in the sod to form a doorway onto a tunnel leading into the mound. A boulder rested beside the entrance, like it could be rolled across to seal it. Morag shuddered at the claustrophobic thought, and her throat closed reflexively.

Paul joined her at the window, and his elbow brushed against hers. Her heart sped up at his touch, however brief. "That's an ancient barrow. I'd love to get a closer look."

Morag bit her lip. "That letter from the owner said—"

"I won't traipse over the graves. I just want to see the barrow. I was reading about it in here. Found it in the library." He held up a slim, leather-bound volume entitled *Screeverholme*. "At first I thought it was a cenotaph."

Hamish whirled around from his fruitless search of the cupboards. "Ceno-what now, NerdTurd?"

"Cenotaph. From the Greek. It means *empty tomb*. But I found out from this book it's not empty after all."

"Let me guess?" Hamish said. "Some boring old dude that lived forever ago is buried in there?"

Paul ignored Hamish and opened the back door. The cat shot out, a silver streak like a comet. "Come on, Morag. Let's go look."

The wind from the open door ruffled Paul's light hair. Under normal circumstances, Morag would jump at his invitation, but after yesterday, she hesitated. "I don't think we should."

He cocked an eyebrow. "Are you scared?"

Yes, she wanted to say, but not of tombs and dead guys. She was scared of the cold. Her hand drifted to her throat as she considered. "Fine. I'll get my jacket." She wanted to add, *You know, so I don't go into anaphylaxis and die.*

"Score!" Hamish whooped. "Found some cornflakes."

Juliette made a big deal of going over and exclaiming about his find. How long had she liked Hamish? Was this new, or was Morag that oblivious?

Morag returned a couple minutes later with her jacket and scarf. Surely she was so full of antihistamines and steroids the cold wouldn't bother her. She pulled the scarf over her chin to be safe.

"You coming?" she asked, but Juliette shook her head. Apparently watching Hamish scoop dry cornflakes into his mouth was too fascinating to pull her away. Gross.

Morag followed Paul outside. The castle stood at their backs, and to their left, the ground sloped gently to the tiny, rocky beach. Small waves lapped the shore. To their right, sheltered in the shadow of the castle wall, lay the graveyard on a higher promontory rising thirty feet above the water, the mounded hump of the barrow at its peak.

"Barrows," Paul said, "are long hills of earth entombing the ancient peoples of Britain."

Morag fought back equal parts annoyance at Paul's lecture-mode and a need to impress him. "I know what barrows are."

At Morag's tone, Paul glanced sharply at her. "Of course." He nodded as if remembering Morag wasn't so different from himself. Smart. Curious. Or so she hoped he was thinking.

She considered telling him about that shadow last night but didn't want to ruin the moment. He would only tell her it was her imagination, and he was probably right.

"Anyway," he said. "I read this book about Orkney before our trip. For research. I like to know about a place before I visit." Red spots stained his cheeks. Was he embarrassed in front of Morag? If so, what did that mean? Did he care what she thought? Or was his face flushed only with cold? He hurried on. "I found out there are barrows across the islands. Most are ancient Pictish ones, but this is a burial mound for an old Viking earl. Those were sort of like chieftains in Orkney. He was killed in battle over a thousand years ago."

"A battle between who? The islanders and the Vikings?"

"No, the Vikings *were* the islanders at that point. They'd settled Orkney and lived here. The book was unclear who they battled. Perhaps the settlers fought a new wave of Viking invaders?" The wind tore away his voice, giving Morag a legitimate reason to lean in closer. "Anyway, the earl's long ship was buried in there with him."

Morag barely avoided stepping on a mounded grave. "Doesn't this feel kind of—disrespectful?"

"I have nothing *but* respect for this." Paul waved his hand to encompass the graveyard. "I just want to see if that boulder is engraved."

Morag walked carefully among the fragile gravestones, crumbling from the constant onslaught of time, wind, and rain. How was it the strange mounds hadn't washed away? She pointed at a gravestone. "Wish I could read those. See who the people were, when they lived."

"That's easy. They span from hundreds of years ago to the last century. The book said there are quite a few unmarked Viking graves mixed in, but the ones with gravestones? They're mostly Tullochs."

Her relatives, if she went back far enough.

Near the boulder, a high-pitched snarl cut through the damp air. Malcolm rolled on the ground with a black cat, the two felines locked in an angry ball of fur. "Hey, stop." Morag lunged toward them, and the black cat broke free from the fight and ran behind the mound.

Malcolm's tail was puffed up four times its normal size. She reached down to stroke him, and he hissed before seeming to recognize her. His back relaxed, and his tail deflated. "Poor Malcolm." She scooped him up, enjoying his warmth against her face, itching slightly in the cold. She was okay. The antihistamines would kick in. "You all right, kitty?"

"He's fine. Defending his territory is all. Look. There *is* an engraving." Paul stepped to the boulder and ran his hand over deep etchings in the stone. The sharp letters branched and forked like trees. "Viking runes from a millennia ago."

The growing wind and threatening clouds dimmed Morag's appreciation of the runes, and she lagged behind Paul. She shouldn't stay out much longer. She was like that short story she read in middle school about a family made of sugar that melted in the rain. Why was she suddenly cursed with this stupid allergy? Wasn't her synesthesia weird enough without adding this to the mix?

And now she was getting caught up in self-pity. Perfect.

She stepped beside Paul as he drew closer to the barrow entrance. Under the stone lintel, the short tunnel gaped into blackness. She shivered, though not from cold. Malcolm was having none of it. He leaped from her arms, and the sting of his claws penetrated her thick coat. The cat raced to the kitchen door. Which Morag should do as well. Instead, she took another step into the tunnel. At least it sheltered her from the worst of the wind.

"Do you smell that?" A scent of musty decay wafted from the dark space. "The Viking earl stinks."

Paul huffed. "The body wouldn't smell anymore."

"It was a joke." Not a funny one, apparently. "Look at this." A dead blackbird lay on the ground at the mouth of the tunnel, its delicate yellow feet curled into stiff fists. "Poor thing."

Paul didn't comment and ducked under the lintel. "In here." A short passage led to a wall of earth.

"Don't." Morag grabbed the back of his coat. "I don't think the owner would approve."

Paul tugged away from her. "I'm not going far. I just want a look." He took Morag's hand and pulled her in after him. She might have enjoyed the feel of his skin against hers were it not for the growing scent of rot that turned her stomach. Of course a thousand-year-old body wouldn't smell anymore, so what was it?

"Look." Paul pointed to the ground at an open pair of scissors, the long blades rusty with age. He bent over and closed the scissors with a creaky squeak. In front of the scissors rested a drinking horn wrapped in two metal bands. "Someone left this out here?"

"Does it belong in a museum, Indiana?"

Paul didn't laugh. He reached down, and Morag gripped his hand as dread seized her. "Don't. Please. It's wrong." It *felt* wrong.

"I'm not stealing it. I only want to see it in the light."

Every instinct in her body told her nothing good could come of this. "It's a bad idea to disturb a grave."

"You *are* scared. Really, Morag, I wouldn't think you'd be superstitious."

"It's not superstition." She pressed her lips together, fear winning out over her feelings for Paul. "It's respect. Leave it alone."

Not listening, he wrapped his hand around the drinking

horn and lifted it. "It's heavy."

Morag ducked under the lintel, anxious to be out of the barrow. Paul or not, she wanted no part of this.

"Morag, don't run away." Paul hurried after her.

"Aaaaaahhhhhh!" The shout startled Morag as much as the large shape that jumped into their path, blocking the entrance to the tomb.

Both Morag and Paul shrieked and grabbed for each other, and the horn tumbled from Paul's hands to the damp earth.

Hamish laughed. "Oh my god, you guys were pissing yourselves. That was hilar—what's this?" He bent over and picked up the horn. "Whoa. Did you actually find treasure?"

"Were you spying on us?" Morag punched Hamish in the arm, which he barely registered as he studied the horn.

"Give that back." Paul's voice came low and cold, punctuated by a growl of thunder rolling in the distance.

Hamish ignored him and carried the object farther away from the barrow and examined it. "Wow, pretty cool. This looks valuable, don't you think?"

The marbled horn, maybe from a bull, was wrapped in engraved bands of gold that retained their sheen. Golden dragon feet served as a stand for the horn. "Yes. Now can you put it back?" Morag said.

"Let me see it." Paul grabbed for the horn, and the two boys engaged in a wrestling match when an angry yell caused them both to freeze.

"Hey! What do ye think ye're doin'?" Ben's voice boomed across the graveyard as he left a rowboat on the shore and strode toward them. He wore a red rain slicker, and his face was stormy as the sky.

Hamish shoved the drinking horn at Paul and pasted on a look of innocence.

"What have ye done?" Ben said. His disapproval made him seem older than twenty-something. Morag felt as guilty as if she'd been the one fighting for the historic artefact. Ben snatched the horn from Paul's hands. "Did ye no' read the letter? Mr. Sutherland allowed ye into his castle, and this is how ye repay him? Get back inside."

"I only wanted to look at it." Paul's face set in a mutinous glare, but Hamish had the good grace to look embarrassed. Morag, for her part, said nothing, and the three of them headed back toward the castle as the rain started. Morag looked over her shoulder where Ben was coming out of the burial mound, now empty-handed. He turned to stare into the tunnel, muttering to himself.

They slipped into the kitchen to find their parents at the table with Juliette.

"What were you doing out in this weather?" Mom said.

As if in answer, Ben slammed open the back door. "Yer children were in the graveyard." His dark eyes blazed in his pale face as he fixed each adult with a warning look. "I don't ever want to see any of ye in there again. Mr. Sutherland—and the Tullochs before him—made their wishes clear." Water droplets spilled off his slicker onto the floor.

"I—I'm sorry." Morag slid onto the bench next to Juliette and ducked her head.

Hamish mumbled an apology and pushed in beside her, shoving her against her friend.

Juliette leaned forward to whisper across Morag. "I told you not to follow them, Hamish. That was mean. Now you got them caught."

"What? That's not what—"

"It won't happen again, I assure you," Dad said to Ben, and glared from Hamish to Morag.

Morag gulped. She couldn't afford to lose her father as an ally.

"Paul." Françoise's French accent was obvious in that single syllable. Even scowling, she was lovely, her blonde hair pulled into an artful chignon. A spot of blue oil paint smudged her cheek. "That is no way to start our visit here. Trespassing?"

Paul stayed quiet, still not apologizing himself.

"I'm sorry," Mom said. "Our kids know better. And Morag had no business being out in this cold." She jumped to her feet. "Can I make you some coffee?"

"Aye, please." Ben's gaze finally dropped, as if remembering his manners. He yanked back his hood to send more water droplets flying.

No one spoke as the man sank onto a bench and wrapped his trembling hands around the coffee mug Mom handed him. He seemed to be collecting himself, and Morag wondered if he wasn't so much angry as afraid. Her apprehension at Paul disturbing anything in the barrow flooded back. Was Ben afraid of that, too? It was an unpleasant idea.

"I hate to ask," Mom said, "but is there any way you could take me into town for groceries?"

Ben stared into his mug, as if unable to meet her eye after his outburst. "Aye. I apologize. I should've got more supplies fer ye, but I was busy before yer arrival. I forgot to tell ye I left kippers for yer breakfast. Caught and smoked the herring myself."

Hamish curled his lip at Morag and whispered, "Eww. I thought that fish was for the cat."

"I'll take ye to Sinclair's. It's a peedie shop. Peedie means small," he added, perhaps guessing he was confusing the Americans. "But it's well-stocked, and Catherine—the owner— gets regular shipments of food from the mainland." Ben's eyes narrowed on Morag, and she remembered Ben mentioning the woman last night on the bridge. He'd asked Magnus if Morag were like Catherine's father. How did he mean?

"It's goin' to be a *fissowy* day," Ben continued. "Bring yer waterproofs."

A few minutes later, Mom left with Ben. Since it rained harder than ever, Juliette suggested the billiards room. Paul grabbed his laptop from the table and caught Morag in the hall.

"Sorry I got you into trouble," he said stiffly.

Morag's face flushed. "It's all right." She'd made the choice to follow him, after all. "But maybe don't poke around in tombs anymore, okay?"

"Mm." The noise was noncommittal. As they entered the room, Paul pointed at the giant table in the center like he wanted to distract her, and she let him. "Shall we play pool?"

"Not pool, snooker," Hamish said. "Don't look so surprised, Paul. You're not the only one who knows some shit." He took down a pool cue and chalked the end. "What do you say? Davidsons against Gaspars?"

"Or should we split up?" Juliette sounded a little breathless. "I'll be on your team since I don't know what I'm doing, and you sound like you do."

Morag joined Paul, and it soon became obvious neither one of them could play pool—or snooker. Malcolm jumped onto the table and sat on the edge. He watched the balls clack and swished his tail whenever they got too close.

"Did Ben seem kind of weird to you earlier?" Morag asked, as Paul blew yet another shot and slapped his palm on the edge of the table in frustration.

"It's weird he got so mad when we weren't hurting anything." That mulish look from before crossed his face. "He was furious."

"No." Morag pulled at her bottom lip. "He seemed almost—"

"Scared?" Juliette said.

"Yeah. Like he was scared Paul went into the burial mound."

"You went in there, too," Paul said.

"Because you dragged me in. I told you not to touch that stuff."

"What stuff?" Juliette asked.

Morag told her about the objects at the barrow entrance.

"Dude, we're probably all cursed now." Hamish sank a red ball into the middle pocket.

"Hey, don't say that. *I* didn't touch anything." Morag bit her bottom lip. She supposed she *had* gone into the barrow. "I don't want to be cursed."

"There's no such thing as curses, Morag." Paul pulled a cover off something about the size of a pinball machine but covered in felt like a pool table with several holes in the top.

"There are definitely curses," Hamish said. "Some girl cursed Tyler Jennings, our receiver, after he dumped her at homecoming. He didn't catch another pass the whole season." Hamish sank yet another red ball.

"There you go, Morag. Incontrovertible proof." Paul sniffed. "I think this is a bar billiards table. Want to try it?"

Paul and Morag weren't any better at bar billiards than snooker. Eventually, the cold room drove them back into the lounge where the parents were hanging out. Mike was doing his best to get a peat fire going, but he'd only managed to send thick, white smoke belching into the room with the scent Morag now associated with the castle.

"Dad, the carbon emissions from burning peat are worse than coal," Paul said.

Mike looked to the ceiling, as if seeking patience there. "It's what's here, and it's freezing."

"Well, the U.K. is supposed to be banning it soon, so enjoy your repugnant practice while you can." Paul arched a brow at his father.

"I'll tell you what's repugnant." Hamish looked at Mike and Juliette and shut his mouth.

Paul glared back at Hamish and sat in a wingback chair. Juliette settled on the floor by her father while Hamish threw himself onto the couch with a mournful sigh.

"Aren't you and Ingrid going out this afternoon?" Paul sounded like he hoped to get rid of Hamish.

"Yeah. We're supposed to go for a walk." Hamish punched a pillow. "This rain sucks. Maybe it'll stop soon."

Dad glanced at the window and shared a look with Morag that said *fat chance*. He dug around in a cupboard next to the fireplace and discovered a stack of board games.

Paul opened his laptop. "Better get started on my coding. Earn that money you're paying me, right, Bill?"

Juliette rolled her eyes at Hamish, who shook his head in disgust. Dad was paying Paul for a side project this summer, something to do with the user interface on the company's website, and Morag found it impressive, but even she could admit he'd been bragging a lot.

Hamish groaned. "Man, this rain sucks."

Françoise sketched near the window. The sight reminded Morag of her entire goal for the summer. Morag walked over and lifted her eyebrows in question. Françoise nodded, and Morag came around the easel to look at a drawing of a man walking on a bridge. If she ever wanted to be able to create art anything close to this spectacular, she needed to practice every day. She ran upstairs and retrieved her own notepad and pencils.

Morag plopped onto the sofa by Hamish. Her portfolio would be entirely centered on Orkney. She selected orange and yellow pencils to sketch out the lines of flame and fire Mike was coaxing to life in the fireplace. The deep shade of tangerine ignited a Rolling Stones song her dad loved. *Sympathy for the Devil*. She worked for a while until she noticed her source of inspiration had fizzled out once again, and fresh belches of smoke poured into the room.

Paul coughed, waving his hand in the air. "Hey, Dad, face facts. You're not a pyromancer."

"Pyromancer?" Hamish said. "Dude. Why do you talk like that?"

"Because I have a superlative vocabulary."

"You can shove your vocabulary up your—"

"How about poker?" Dad pulled out a pack of cards with a desperate flourish.

"Sure." Hamish slid onto the floor.

Morag's sketch looked like a kindergartener drew it, and it was going about as well as the real fire, so she joined in. To her surprise, Paul did, too. They started off playing with pennies until Hamish had the genius idea of switching to IOU chores for cleaning duties. Paul proceeded to win every hand. Hamish muttered under his breath, and even Dad and Mike made huffing noises.

Hamish growled after yet another Paul victory. "How are you doing this?"

"By being smart," Morag said and blushed.

Hamish lifted an eyebrow in her direction, and she quickly looked away. If he knew how much she liked Paul, he'd tease her remorselessly. But Hamish only slammed his cards down. "I quit."

Paul shrugged. "Suit yourself. I won't have to do dishes for the rest of the summer."

Ben stuck his head in the lounge as Hamish got to his feet and said, "This blows. Rain or not, I'm walking to Ingrid's."

"If ye come downstairs and help me carry in the shopping," Ben said, "I'll show ye where there's a bike ye can use."

"Yeah, thanks, man." Hamish left.

Paul returned to his computer work, and when it became obvious Morag couldn't engage him in conversation, she headed downstairs to help put away groceries. She passed the open castle door and noticed again the string of silver coins dotting the threshold. Ben marched inside with the last bags, head down against the downpour. Behind him, Hamish wobbled across the bridge on an old bike. Ben slammed the giant door with a resounding *slam*.

"What are those coins for across the doorway?"

"Leave them be," Ben said.

Morag pulled her arms in across her stomach, defensive and guilty at the same time for her earlier escapades. "I am. I just wondered why they're there."

"Protection."

"From what?"

"Irritating questions."

Ben slipped away, but Morag gathered her courage and followed him down the hallway. She dropped the subject of the coins, though. "Still fissolee?"

"It's *fissowy*," Ben said.

"Is that a Scottish word?"

"Orcadian."

"Orcadian." She tested the word, which created jagged towers of blue and black before her eyes. "Sounds like something out of *Lord of the Rings*."

Ben grunted and headed into the kitchen, Morag at his heels.

"I really am sorry about going into the graveyard. I promise it won't happen again."

"Let's hope no damage has been done." Anger radiated off his hunched shoulders. "This isn't yer home. There are things ye do and don't do here, aye? Ye don't go traipsin' about in graveyards. Or messin' about with those coins or—"

"I didn't touch them, I sw—"

"There are things here ye don't understand."

Morag's pulse beat in the hollow of her throat. "Like what?" Ben shook his head, as if annoyed with himself for saying too much. She couldn't help but think of the shadowy shape in the graveyard, the lights at sea. A long awkward pause stretched out, and Ben set the grocery bags on the long bar-top counter with a *clack* of canned goods. Morag cleared her throat and forced herself to go on before she lost her nerve. "You're right. There *are* things here I don't understand. Last night I saw some weird lights outside my window."

Ben turned toward her with a glower. "What did ye say?"

"Lights. Out in the ocean. Sort of greenish. Do you know what they—"

"No." The word came out before she could finish the question, and he buried his head in a cupboard sorting and stacking cans.

"Are you sure? Have you ever seen—"

"No." Again, he wouldn't even let her finish her question. He was lying, she knew it. But why?

"Is it bioluminescence? Glow-in-the-dark squid or jellyfish or something? I saw this nature show once—"

"Probably that."

"It's not the Loch Ness Monster, right?"

Ben turned around and finally faced her with a grim expression on his face. "Monsters aren't real." His gaze flicked to the window and the graveyard or perhaps the sea beyond. "They're for fairy tales." As if that settled the matter, he turned on his heel and left the kitchen.

The thing was, this castle looked straight from a fairy tale, too, and it was real.

So why *not* monsters?

Chapter 5

The tantalizing scent of cooking bacon wafted into the banquet hall, and Morag was ready for some serious banqueting. Françoise was whipping up one of her signature quiches with the same artistry as her paintings, insisting the others enjoy themselves.

The adults sipped pre-dinner drinks at one end of the table while Morag hung out with Juliette and Paul at the other. Juliette wore a billowing blue gown while embroidering the bodice of a green one. Paul buried his nose in a book of Burns poetry he'd found in the library.

It would be impossible to engage Paul when he was deep in a book, so Morag searched on her phone for bioluminescence. She learned there were indeed bioluminescent organisms in the waters off Orkney. Copepods, tiny crustaceans, would emit light if disturbed.

"Blue-green?" she said, reading the description of the creature's light. She'd seen yellowish green. Another article stated the copepod activity occurred in late summer and early autumn. It was only the start of June.

Climate change was screwing up everything in the ocean, so why not her poor little copepod friends?

Mom raised an eyebrow. Morag guessed being in a castle didn't change their strict no-devices-at-the-table rule. She shoved her phone into her pocket with a heavy sigh.

"Should we start a fire in here?" Mike asked, and Dad hastily told him it was warm enough.

Several shields painted with crests hung above the fireplace. Mounted on the walls among the weapons, the heads of deer and boar stared down with sad, judging eyes. An antler chandelier hung over the long table.

"Nobody's cold?" Mike gave the fireplace a longing look. "Morag?"

"Um, I'm okay."

"You sure, honey?" Mom said. "There's a definite draft in here."

"Lisa," Dad warned. "Look at Morag. She's wearing a sweater and a jacket."

"As she needs to do until she's on the next ferry." Mom fixed Dad with a saccharine-sweet smile.

"I'm not getting on it." Morag had no intention of leaving this amazing place. Or the inspiration for her art portfolio. Even if she hadn't managed a decent sketch today. "I don't want to miss out on the fun this summer."

"Morag, be sensible," Mom said. "How fun is this summer going to be with you stuck inside?"

"She doesn't have to stay inside, Lisa." Dad tapped his fork on the table. "That's why she's taking the pills, remember?"

Uh-oh. Thanks to her father's tone, the discussion escalated to an argument that no longer involved Morag and made Mike decide building a fire was actually very necessary.

"Oh, but you know everything." Mom's voice came tight and strained, as if keeping herself from shouting.

Morag shifted in her seat. No danger of hives when she could feel the heat pulsing off her face. Juliette sewed industriously, keeping her gaze on her needle and thread. Morag glanced at Paul, but he was either too absorbed in his poems, or too polite to look up.

"Hey guys," Hamish bounded into the room. Morag wanted to jump up and hug him.

"You're soaking wet," Mom said. "You should go change clothes."

"Leave him alone, Lisa," Dad said. "He's fine."

"I'm really fine." Hamish lowered himself into the chair next to Mom with uncharacteristic clumsiness, a sloppy grin on his face. "Ingrid is really fine, too. She's invited us all to the island ceilidh this weekend. Some sort of Scottish dance." He draped an arm around Mom's shoulders. "You'll love it, Mom. It'll be all cultural and Scottish and shtuff."

Mom wrinkled her nose. "Hamish! Are you drunk?"

Hamish waved his hand in dismissal. "'S only a couple beers at the pub."

Morag shared a look with Juliette, who mouthed *He's totally drunk*. Morag fought the urge to giggle at her friend. Juliette's expression was every bit as disapproving as Mom's. Probably because Hamish had been with Ingrid. At least this turn of events would distract her parents from their argument about her.

"When you say a couple beers, son," Dad said, "how many exactly?"

"Four or five? Who cares? Drinking age is eighteen here."

"You rode your bike like this?" Mom folded her arms over her chest. "Intoxicated?"

"Yep. Major BUI risk. Get it? *B* for bike?" Hamish chuckled. "Besides, what am I gonna hit? Who's gonna arrest me? There're no cops here. No freaking anything here." He sighed. "'Cept Ingrid. I love Ingrid."

"Forget hitting something. *You* could've been hit. Like that sheep, Hamish." Mom, her face splotchy, stood and threw her napkin on the table. "It could've been *your* guts strewn on the road."

"I think you should go upstairs and sleep it off, Sport." Dad stood, too. "I'll help you find your way."

Morag cringed. Did her father really just call Hamish *Sport?*

"I'll come help." Mom hugged her arms tighter and sent Mike a tense smile. He stopped staring and ducked his head back into the fireplace, as if he could escape the tension in the room. Morag might join him in there.

"I think I can manage Hamish on my own," Dad said, but Mom followed him and Hamish into the hall, where they continued arguing loud enough for everyone at the table to hear.

"Let it go." Dad's voice echoed from the stone hallway. "He's eighteen. Having a little fun." They were moving away, and Morag started to relax, only to hear Mom's volume shoot up.

"A little fun? He's completely plastered."

"It's not that bad," Dad said.

"Guys, I think I'm gonna barf." A retching sound came, followed by the splat of vomit on a stone floor, and Hamish handed his mother the win.

Juliette's face twisted in disgust as Françoise swept into the room carrying two trays. "Ready for dinner?"

Paul picked up his fork and knife and snorted. "*Bon appétit.*"

After dinner, Morag headed to her bedroom, too embarrassed to face the Gaspars. Her parents retreated into the lounge to continue their fight—a thoughtless venue since that's where everyone liked to hang out. Stupid Hamish only gave her parents another reason to argue. Why couldn't he make things easier for them like Morag tried to do? At least he'd distracted their mom from the idea of sending Morag home. Unless, of course, she decided to send them *both* home for a fun summer at Aunt Helen's Camp for Sobriety and Warm Weather.

Morag stepped into her dark bedroom and reached for the light switch. Her hand froze. Outside the windows lights flickered in the water. Not only yellow-green, but whorls of blue and purple swirled through the water. The colors touched off a moody alternative song. She snapped a photo on her phone, but all it showed was a few blurry dots.

She crept downstairs, avoiding the lounge where her parents' raised voices carried through the door, and entered the kitchen. Juliette was drying dishes with her mother, and Mike was wiping the counters to pay off one of his IOU's to Paul, who was absorbed in his poetry at the kitchen table. His brows furrowed, and Morag wanted to reach out and smooth his forehead.

Morag swallowed her embarrassment over her parents. "Hey guys, can I show you something?"

"Is anything the matter?" Françoise asked.

Besides her parents having another battle from WWIII? Nope. "I saw something strange outside my window. In the water. Some sort of bioluminescence."

That caught Paul's attention, and he set aside his book. "Let's go look." He got to his feet and pointed at his father. "You're doing a great job with those counters, Dad."

Mike mock-glared at him and shook his head with a smile.

"I think we'll be able to see it from the study." Morag led Françoise, Juliette, and Paul into the dark room, moving past the massive desk and over to the windows lining the north wall. The four of them peered out to sea. Paul stood near enough that when Morag shifted her weight, her shoulder brushed his. He glanced at her, his gray eyes pools of shadow in his Gallic face. Her heart hammered.

"I don't see anything." Paul's gaze shifted to the window again.

"What did it look like?" Françoise asked.

Morag stopped staring at Paul and cleared her throat. "Swirling colors in the water. I tried to ask Ben about them, but he got really weird about it. Same when I asked about those coins outside the doorway. Said they were for protection."

Paul gave a dismissive *pffft*. "These Scots are all superstitious. Have you seen some of the books in the library? Tales of fairies and ghosts and all sorts of nonsense."

Françoise stirred in the dark. "My mother adopted an Italian superstition to put coins on our windowsill at New Year's for good luck. Maybe it is something like that?"

"Mémé lets me keep them on New Year's Day," Juliette added.

"Ben said the coins were for protection, not good luck," Morag said. "Protection from what? He didn't like me asking about the coins, and he didn't like me asking about the lights. What if it's all related?"

"I think," Paul said, "these lights you described are some sort of natural phenomenon, but maybe the locals invented a supernatural explanation, and the coins keep away any danger from them. Of course, the lights are harmless. There are many dinoflagellates in the genus *Gonyaulux* that are bioluminescent. Dinoflagellates are tiny protists—"

"Copepods," Morag said. "I think they're copepods."

"Small crustaceans." Paul nodded in approval. How many people their age would know what a copepod was?

She tried to breathe in the clean scent of Paul without being obvious. It would be easy to reach out and take his hand in her own. Would he mind? "I'm frustrated the lights are gone. I wish you could've seen them."

"Me too," Juliette said.

Françoise walked toward the door. "*C'est dommage*, Morag. Perhaps another time."

Paul followed his mother out, and Morag turned to Juliette. "Want to sleep in my room tonight? In case you can see the lights?"

Her teeth shone in the darkness when she smiled. "To see the lights, right? Not because you're scared."

"Exactly."

Morag and Juliette stared out her bedroom windows at nothing but a slice of moon and its reflection in the shimmering water. No lights. Finally, Morag closed the shutters and climbed into bed next to her friend. They talked for a long time about colleges before falling asleep. It felt like only a few minutes later when a pounding noise awakened them. Morag glanced at the clock—almost two a.m. The doorknob twisted back and forth as the racket continued.

"Morag," Hamish shouted. "Open up."

Juliette flew off the bed and opened the door. Light spilled in from the hallway as Hamish staggered into the room. Malcom raced in behind him. The cat jumped on the bed as Hamish slammed the door and locked it. Morag switched on the bedside lamp and stared bleary-eyed at her brother. He wore plaid pajama bottoms and a scruffy old T-shirt from his basketball team. His dark hair stood on end, and his face was as pale as she'd ever seen it.

Morag swung her legs over the side of the bed. "What's wrong?"

"I—I saw something." Hamish ran his hands through his hair. "It was . . . like a man. Standing at the end of my bed. I couldn't see his face. Just the dark shape of a man." He swallowed hard, his Adam's apple bobbing up and down, and sank onto the desk chair. "On top, it had"—he mimed something coming out of his head—"horns. Curved horns. Like a—like a demon. Like the balfrog in that *Lord of the Rings* movie."

"Balrog?"

"Whatever. The fiery demon guy with horns. And it stank."

Morag's throat convulsed. "Stank how?"

"Dude, like death. Like, you know, a rotting corpse or something."

Corpse. Her thoughts flew to the barrow, the scent of decay Paul swore wasn't the dead Viking earl. Maybe they should get

Paul now, see what he thought of all this.

"What did you do?" Juliette said.

"I asked what the hell it wanted. It opened its mouth." He cradled his hand under his chin and dropped it down to his chest. "Like this far. The cat jumped off my bed yowling and spitting and crap. And the thing walked *through* my door—not the doorway—the actual door—and disappeared."

Morag frowned. "A demon showed up in your room, the cat scared him off, and it disappeared into thin air?"

"That's literally what I just told you."

Morag crossed her arms. "Let me guess. This demon craved the flesh of your sister?"

Hamish's face screwed up in confusion. "What?"

She cocked her head at him. "How stupid do you think I am? You're just trying to scare me again." At least she hadn't run across the hallway all scared to wake up Paul and embarrassed herself. "Stop with the dumb jokes."

Hamish exploded out of the chair toward her, his face contorted. "You think this is a joke?"

"That's literally what I just told you," she shot back.

"Why are you being so mean?" Juliette moved to Hamish and put her hand on his shoulder. "He's terrified."

"Okay, terrified's a strong word," Hamish said.

"How am *I* mean when Hamish is the one trying to scare us?" Morag said.

"I'm not freaking kidding, Morag." Hamish glared at her. "I'm telling you, we shouldn't have gone in that barron thing."

"Barrow." Morag chewed on her thumbnail, not liking the direction of Hamish's thoughts.

Hamish scowled. "Whatever. What if we *did* curse ourselves or something by going in there?" His hand was shaking as he ran it through his curls again. "That's why Ben was so pissed."

Juliette sat on the side of the bed, looking wide-eyed between Morag and Hamish.

The idea hit her with a jolt of fear—Hamish wasn't that good an actor. Maybe he *wasn't* pulling a prank. She got to her feet and met her brother's eyes. "You swear this is true?"

"I'll pinky-swear on Caramel's grave." Hamish held out his little finger and gave her a steady look.

A cold chill settled in her bones. Caramel, their beloved spaniel who died when she was twelve, provided the gold standard in promises between her and Hamish. Any swear made on her grave meant serious business. Suddenly, taking the next ferry off the island didn't sound like such a bad idea.

"Okay," Morag said at last. "I believe you think you saw something."

"I didn't *think* it. I saw it, okay? I saw a demon-man."

If Hamish wasn't lying what was the explanation?

Her brain scrabbled for any ideas that didn't involve believing demon-men were real and then—"Wait. You were totally drunk earlier." Relief flooded in at the obvious cause of all this.

Hamish scrubbed his hands over his face. "Fine. I was drunk earlier, but this was crazy real. Sobered me right up."

"So, you admit you were still drunk when you woke up? Maybe that's why you were *hallucinating*." A spiteful part of her enjoyed throwing that word back at Hamish. See how he liked it.

"I don't know, Mor," Juliette said.

"You saw how wasted he was." Morag enjoyed her own outrage, but another part of her remembered how frustrating it had been when Hamish hadn't believed her yesterday about the skeletal body floating in the water.

Hamish sighed. "Look, this is kind of embarrassing, but can I sleep in here?"

Morag held her hand toward the door. "Why not sleep with Paul? A boys' sleepover."

"Are you kidding? Paul would never believe me."

"But maybe we should keep him safe, too."

"He's on his own." Hamish put his hands together in a

pleading gesture. "Please, Morrie. Just let me sleep on that thing." He pointed at the chaise lounge in the corner.

Juliette touched Hamish's arm. "I'd feel better if you did." Her little smile irritated Morag. But why? Because her friend could do better than her Cro-Magnon brother, or because her brother could do better than her flaky, romantic friend? And what was the matter with her for thinking such unkind things about people she loved?

"Fine," she said. "You can sleep on the floor."

Truth be told, drunken hallucination or not, Hamish's story scared the hell out of her, and she'd just as soon have her older brother around to protect her. They pulled some extra blankets out of the wardrobe and made Hamish a nest on the chaise lounge in the corner. It didn't look too comfortable, but he didn't complain.

Morag crawled back into bed, Malcolm stretched along her side. Time passed. By the uneven sound of Juliette's and Hamish's breathing, they seemed to be having as hard a time getting to sleep as Morag. For the longest time, she kept picking up her head and craning to look at the bedroom door.

But like the ocean with its vanishing lights, Hamish's so-called demon never reappeared.

Chapter 6

Morag awoke to Malcolm meowing at the bedroom door. She got up to let him out and passed Hamish's rumpled blankets he'd left on the floor. He probably went back to his room to sleep off the rest of his drunkenness. It seemed silly in the light of day, like a weird dream. Juliette was gone too, and Morag savored a few moments alone. She grabbed a granola bar from her backpack for breakfast, and her gaze landed on her nearby sketchbook. Her online class began tomorrow, and she needed to get a jumpstart on her portfolio.

Her phone wasn't able to capture the bioluminescent lights, but maybe she could draw them. Morag crunched through the honey and oat bar, considering. She often liked to draw on her tablet, but the art school application stipulated no more than two of the required ten to twenty pieces should be created with digital media. Today, she'd try replicating the lights with colored pencils or oil pastels. She opened the shutters onto a bright day, grabbed the sketchbook, and popped in earbuds. The shimmering colors of music washed over her.

Without thinking, she sang along, but as usual, her synesthesia intensified to the point she couldn't see anything else in front of her but swirls of colorful patterns. That was why Morag normally only hummed or sang wordlessly to music. She stopped singing and concentrated on drawing.

It proved impossible to copy the expanse of dark sea and strangely colored lights on paper. Maybe the lights should be one of her digital media creations. Instead, Morag sketched the rough outline of the otter she'd seen, adding more details, and finally color. The exact shade of his whiskers escaped her. Creamy white or buff? It paralyzed her. She flipped through her sketchbook. So many unfinished drawings. So often shading or perspective eluded her, and she gave up. What was her problem?

She needed to stop the spinning colors if she wanted to remember the otter's face. She turned off the music, and the black and purple of the singer's voice slowly faded. Her hand hovered over the silver box of colored pencils as she tried to conjure up the otter. Sure, she could see imaginary shapes and colors clear as day, but visualizing the subject of her art—that would be too useful for her brain. She slammed the pencil box and stared out the window.

Golden sunlight beckoned her outside. She pulled on jeans, a T-shirt, and a hoodie with a Monet print and tucked her sketchpad and pencils under her arm. She remembered the epi-pen from the nightstand and shoved it in her back pocket.

Downstairs, her father worked on his laptop at the kitchen table. When she told him she was going for a quick walk, he grunted, "Take your pills?"

"Yep." Morag rushed out, eager to escape before encountering her mother, though the weather was nice enough, even Mom couldn't object. Morag didn't like to think about leaving Orkney, but if her mom won, at least she'd get this walk around the main island.

A gentle breeze greeted her outside, wafting the scent of salt on cool air. Under a blazing blue sky, the water glittered azure, shot through near the island's rocky shores with hues of turquoise and aquamarine, as vivid as any of Chopin's Nocturnes.

Over the bridge, the gentle hills of the main island of Tullimentay rolled like a thick carpet of jewel green—the color of an Australian indie pop song she liked. With the magic of sunlight, the island had transformed into a sparkling gem.

The castle shed its creepiness in the light of day. It made it even harder to believe Hamish and his wild story about a demon-man in his room. Morag stepped onto the bridge where sunlight glinted off something. A single silver coin. Where were the rest? Hopefully, Paul wasn't adding coin collector to his amateur archaeologist hobby. Sometimes Paul thought rules only applied to other people—people he deemed not as smart as him.

The unkind thought shocked her. She'd had a crush on Paul since first grade. Those feelings had become such a part of her, she didn't always trust her opinions on Paul—good or bad. Her thoughts got so mixed up at times. No one was perfect, though. You didn't have to like *every*thing about a person to like them, right?

Morag leaned over the bridge, mulling this over as she gazed out at the horizon. A soft splash drew her attention directly below, and she gasped in delight. The otter was back, swimming in languid circles. "Hey, there." To her surprise, the otter moved his head in her direction. Intelligent eyes, large and liquid, gazed back. He appeared to be studying her as much as she studied him.

"Definitely buff-colored, buddy." She set her pencil box on the bridge wall and flipped it open to select several shades of cream.

The otter swam nearer and rubbed his furry face with his paws. He dove under the water, then his sleek head popped back up. Morag sketched in quick strokes, trying to catch the way the water rippled around his chest. The otter rolled over several times and executed a somersault.

She laughed. "Okay, now you're showing off."

"Who're ye talkin' to?"

She jumped at Ben's voice and pointed. "Him."

He stilled at her side. "Oh, no. No' today." Ben pulled a rock out of his pocket and chucked it at the otter. "Get out of here, ye wee mangy sea beast!"

"Stop! What are you doing?" In her shock, Morag reached toward Ben and knocked her pencil box over the side of the bridge, where it landed with a disheartening *plop*. "No!" She leaned over and watched the pencils sink through the water. A final ray of light winked off the metallic silver as it disappeared. She rounded on Ben. "Those were my art pencils."

"I'm sorry." Ben peered over the bridge, but he wasn't looking where the pencils had gone. His eyes narrowed on the otter a short distance away. He plunged his hand into his pocket and withdrew another rock as if he carried them around for this express purpose.

"Don't throw that at him." Morag fisted her hands on her hips. "I'll tell my parents."

Ben seemed unbothered by this threat and let the rock fly. It landed a foot from the otter, who dipped underwater and vanished.

Morag's chest heaved. "What's your problem with otters?"

"They're pests, Miss Davidson."

"How exactly is an otter a pest? What could it possibly do?"

"Take my breakfast, that's what. Steal fish from my nets." Ben drew a slow breath through his nose as if gathering patience and in his customary style, turned on his heel and marched down the slope to the stretch of shoreline beneath the bridge. Morag watched him untie the little rowboat from its mooring and begin rowing around Screeverholme as if searching for more otters.

The guy was insane. Living on a tiny island in the middle of nowhere probably did that to people, making them care too much about catching fish for making smelly old kippers.

Morag sent a longing look to where her expensive pencils had gone to their watery grave. No point taking her sketchbook now. At any rate, the cold breeze made her arms itch, and a faint welt was rising near her collarbone. She should put away the book and fetch her scarf.

She raced to her room, grabbed her scarf off the chair, and turned to leave. Muddy footprints led to her doorway. She must've tracked mud through the castle, but how? She picked up her foot and examined the bottom of her Converse sneaker. Clean and dry, as expected, considering she'd only walked over a stone bridge. Where did the mud come from? Puzzled by the footprints, she crouched down for a closer look. The large prints were too messy to make out much detail, but they grew wider near the long toes, almost like someone with webbed feet. Or flippers. The idea chilled her blood as effectively as the Orkney wind.

She thought of the lights in the water, the demon-man in Hamish's room, and imagined sea monsters with flippers. Wait. *Flippers*. Hamish had a snorkel and flippers, and the idiot probably packed them for this trip along with his unnecessary swimsuit. He must've walked around in them up here to trick her as revenge for not believing him last night. Unless that was all part of the trick too, an act to scare her and Juliette. It was a convincing performance, but she wasn't going to fall for it.

Hamish was *not* going to frighten her any more, and she wasn't going to let her mom make her leave. She loved this place already. A little spooky stuff and a cold allergy weren't enough to keep her away. The sea, the island, the castle—it called to something inside her, filled an emptiness she hadn't even known existed.

She stepped around the wet prints, walked downstairs, and went to find Hamish. She found him sitting cross-legged on the library floor surrounded by a pile of books as high as his shoulders.

"You must've run back here," she said from the doorway.

He looked from his book and winced. "Do you have to talk so loud?"

"You must've run," she repeated.

"What?"

"To get back here in time." Morag came into the library, stopped in front of Hamish, and crossed her arms.

"Do I look capable of running without puking? Remind me never to drink again."

"I know you're trying to scare me."

"What are you talking about?"

"The webbed footprints in the . . ." Her voice trailed off as she realized Hamish was sitting with a *book* in his hand. "What are you doing?"

"Trying to figure out what kind of creature I saw last night."

Forget him swearing on their dog's grave. Seeing Hamish reading presented the most terrifying evidence possible he wasn't joking around. Although reading wasn't the right word. More like staring suspiciously at the pages.

"You can look all day," she said, "but there's no on-switch for those. They're called books. People read them for information."

Hamish glowered. "Ha, ha."

"Seriously, what are you doing? It's freaking me out, seeing you voluntarily reading."

"Of course. You're the only smart kid in the family."

"If not, you're sure hiding it well." She instantly regretted the words, but he barely noticed. Something in the book had caught his attention. Morag studied him. "You really didn't track muddy footprints upstairs?"

"Nope." Hamish, eyes glued to the pages of his book, shifted his foot on the floor to show her his clean Nikes.

If it wasn't Hamish, who? What could make footprints like that? Fingers of dread crawled over her scalp. To distract herself, she picked up the top book only to send the entire stack crashing onto the floor.

"Graceful as always." Hamish squinted at a page.

Morag let the comment slide. It was true, anyway. She might have got the brains, but it came with a generous helping of being a klutz, especially compared to Hamish. She rummaged through the pile of fallen books. *Scottish folklore. Myths of Orkney. The Fairy Realm. Scottish Hauntings.*

"There's gotta be an explanation here for last night." Hamish set aside the book in his hand. "Let me see *Scottish Hauntings* again."

She handed it to him. "There *is* an explanation for last night. It's called too much alcohol."

"I know what I saw."

She decided to change the subject. "Mom and Dad up yet?"

"Went for a walk."

Her parents always went on walks after a big fight. They must have seen a big uptick in their cardiovascular fitness lately.

"You gonna tell them about last night?"

"If you're anything to go by, there's no point. They won't believe me." He sighed. "Mom's still on the warpath about sending you home and maybe me, too. 'Cause, you know, it's not like Aunt Helen doesn't have a pretty deep liquor cabinet herself or anything."

"Yeah, about that. Can you *try* to stay out of trouble? You know Mom and Dad don't need anything else to fight about."

Hamish slammed down the book. "Don't you get it? If they hadn't fought about me being drunk last night, it would've been something else. The way Dad used his fork and knife, or Mom sniffing too much."

"You don't need to add fuel to the fire." She gathered her courage and made herself ask. "Are you drinking a lot at home? Is Mom right? Do I need to be worried about you, too?"

"What? No." He sighed and said it again, more firmly. "No. No more than the average teenager. You need to lighten up and have some fun yourself once in a while. Stop worrying about everything, okay? Or you'll end up like Mom."

Morag flinched like he'd struck her, and Hamish clambered to his feet.

"Hey, I didn't mean it like that. I just—I don't like seeing you get so worked up. You're not responsible for me. *Or* Mom and Dad."

Morag ran her toe over a scuff on the floor. "Excuse me for caring about our family."

Hamish put his arm around her shoulders and pulled her roughly against him. "Hey, I care about our family, too." He tilted his head to the side and knocked it against hers, clicking her teeth together. "You and me. We'll always be there for each other, all right?" He shoved her away. "Now get outta here and leave me alone so I can get through these books."

She couldn't help but smile a little. "Fine. I'm going into town to buy some more pencils." She told him how Ben made her knock her case over the bridge.

"That guy is weird," Hamish said. "Have you seen him rowing around Screeverholme island?"

"Yeah. Almost like he's looking for something."

"Totally creepy."

Morag headed toward the door. "Good luck with your research. See you later."

"Don't forget to take a jacket."

Morag smiled again as she left the room.

Chapter 7

Every step of her walk, Morag mourned her lost pencils. One scene after another presented themselves as possibilities for her portfolio. The stone dyke walled off the beach from the nearby fields, trapping the sheep near the water. She couldn't get used to seeing sheep munching on seaweed, which dangled comically from their mouths. At her approach, the animals scurried around bleating out warnings like the chittering prairie dogs back home.

The breeze wafted through the blond manes of Shetland ponies standing in lush fields dotted with heather. Smoke billowed from the chimney of a stone cottage. The jarring anachronism of a small plane landing at the tiny island airport interrupted the mood. Mom had checked about flights for Morag, but thank god only exorbitantly expensive private flights went in and out.

Farther inland, the scent of damp earth and manure overlaid that of the sea. A squat tower, shaped like a beehive and built of stacked stone, rose in the distance. She'd read about this broch, a tower from the Iron Age built by the Picts. Mind-boggling something so old still stood. Some historians believed the hollow, round towers served as defensive structures. But defense against what, exactly?

The village, no more than a sparse collection of buildings, perched on a slight rise of land in the island's center. One low stone building displayed a sign that read, "Tullimentay School." A wall enclosed the small school and playground, where a dozen children of varying ages swarmed the plastic play structure and swings. They wore navy shorts and light blue shirts with red neckties.

Morag hugged her hoodie tighter against the chill. Those kids were way tougher than her. Cold wind nipped her cheeks, and the warning tingle of hives danced along her skin.

A short line of granite buildings lay ahead—a post office, bank, pub, and her destination, the shop Ben mentioned, Sinclair's. An electronic bell beeped as the door opened into a space the size of a classroom. It smelled of a not-unpleasant combination of the bread sitting on a wire rack near the entrance, and rubber, coming from a nearby pile of rain boots. There was little rhyme or reason to the arrangement of goods on the overstuffed shelves. Dog food sat next to light bulbs. Packets of seeds lay next to lipsticks and ballpoint pens. String bags of garlic, bags of candy, and kites hung from the ceiling. So much drawing inspiration packed into one shop.

"Hallo," said a chirpy voice from the front. "Who's there?"

The warm, stuffy air made her hives feel, if anything, itchier. She tried not to scratch and weaved her way toward the sound. A friendly-looking woman stood behind the counter; an elderly lab lay in front of it. Both of them had black hair sprinkled with gray. At the sight of Morag, the dog heaved himself up and tottered over to lick her hand before collapsing back onto a plaid bed.

"Och, I see ye made friends with Duncan already." The woman lifted her head toward the dog. "Ye must be one of the

Yanks staying at Screeverholme?"

"Yes. I'm Morag Davidson."

"Morag, is it? Well, you'll no' get a more Scottish name than that, aye? Is yer family Scottish?" People here sang more than spoke, and Morag's head danced with colorful patterns as the woman's voice rose and fell.

"We've got a little Scottish in there."

"I'm Catherine." She smiled with her warm, dark eyes.

Ben had asked Magnus if Morag were like Catherine's dad. Morag tried to think of a graceful way to broach the subject.

"Biscuit?" Catherine pushed forward a plate of homemade shortbread.

Morag took one and bit into it, and the buttery cookie melted in her mouth. "Mmm. These are amazing."

"Thank ye." The woman leaned forward. "Are those welts ye have there?"

"It's an allergy."

"So I heard. Word traveled fast about yer wee bit of anaphylaxis."

Morag grimaced. "One way to put it."

"If ye don't mind me askin', what is it ye're allergic to?"

"The cold."

Catherine's head jerked a little. "Really? That's odd. My dad was allergic to the cold as well. All the people in his family going back to his great-great-grandmother, Mary."

"Mine only started when I got here. It's weird, right?"

Catherine nodded slowly. "Do ye know any—"

"Hello?" The bell chimed on the door.

Catherine pressed her lips together as a woman stalked up to the counter. Duncan didn't get up to lick her hand. The woman was in her fifties with dyed auburn hair and blue eyes magnified by large glasses dominating her face. "Did my order come in?"

"Aye, yesterday."

The woman sniffed. "Ye might've called to let me know." She glanced at Morag. "And who's this?"

"Morag. Morag, this is our schoolteacher, Mrs. Heddle."

"Hi there." Morag blushed under the woman's scrutiny. "I—I passed by your school earlier. It looked nice."

"The students are on their lunch break under my assistant's supervision." She said it like Morag had accused her of negligence. "Are ye stayin' all summer at Screeverholme?"

"Yes."

"Then I'd like to extend an invitation to our summer solstice fête at the school. All the island comes. We have games and activities, and the children sleep over in the school. In fact, I'm here to pick up supplies for it." She raised her eyebrows at Catherine.

The shopkeeper pushed off the counter, and with a rolling gait from a bad limp, went into a small room.

"No child ever misses the solstice celebration sleepover," Mrs. Heddle said. "And this year, what with the Tullochs gone, it will be a true celebration, won't it?" She gave a satisfied smile. "Ye will make sure to come, won't ye? And ye'll bring any other children stayin' at the castle."

Why was it cause for celebration to have the Tullochs gone? It's not like she'd known her distant relations, but Morag felt a stab of indignation on their behalf. "Uh, I'll ask my parents."

"Good. See that ye do."

Catherine returned and handed over a large box. "There ye are, Mrs. Heddle."

"Thank ye kindly, Miss Tulloch," the teacher replied, and Morag startled at the woman's icy tone as much as the name. "Nice meeting you, Morag," she added in a kinder voice.

"You, too. Thanks for the invitation, Mrs. Heddle."

"Ye *will* make sure to come on the solstice." It wasn't a question. She hefted up the heavy box and marched out of the shop.

The interaction was weird enough to make Morag want to ask Catherine several questions, but she focused on the most interesting one. "You're a Tulloch? My great-great-grandfather was Douglas Tulloch. Moved from here to Boston a long time ago. My mom told me he was only in America for a few months and died of a heart attack at thirty. Left my great-great-grandmother alone and pregnant. I'm part Tulloch, too."

Catherine blinked a few times as if processing this information. "Can I make a wee suggestion? I wouldna mention ye're related to Tullochs to anyone—no matter how far back it was. Tullochs never were popular here."

To be judged because of a distant name in Morag's family tree was unfair. "But why?"

"Och, ye know, the Tullochs were the lairds of the castle lookin' down on the islanders. Everyone here was glad to be rid of them when old Robbie Tulloch finally died last year."

The guy on the ferry had said the same thing, and Mrs. Heddle said the Tullochs being gone was cause to celebrate. "But you're a Tulloch, right?"

"Aye." Her mouth twisted. "But I was adopted, ye see. Doesn't count to them since I wasn't born on the island. Came here when I was already ten years old." Catherine clicked her tongue. "They don't think of me as a Tulloch—or a local."

Morag didn't know what to say. An awkward silence followed until she said, "Did you grow up in the castle?"

"No, my grandfather's older brother inherited Screeverholme, so my grandad moved into his own cottage when he got married."

"But you must've spent time at Screeverholme?"

"The islanders avoid the castle as much as possible. My family was no exception. Old Robbie Tulloch—he was a second cousin of my father's—never welcomed us there except for the one Christmas he hosted. He'd have made Scrooge look like Mother Teresa. Robbie was a right old bastard." She winced. "Beggin' yer pardon."

Morag might've laughed if her thoughts hadn't snagged on the first thing Catherine said. "Why do people avoid the castle?"

"Och, just bad blood, I suppose." Catherine busied herself

tidying a display of chocolate bars. "A distant relation of Robbie's got the castle after he died. A Mr. Sutherland. From what I hear, he's turned it into a grand holiday rental. More shortbread?" The woman shoved the plate across the counter with such force, one of the biscuits fell onto the floor and into Duncan's bed.

The dog grabbed it with a snap of his teeth.

Catherine's evasive answer sent a current of unease through Morag. Was something wrong with the castle? She pet Duncan's broad head and decided to change the subject. "How did your dad deal with his allergy in such a cold place?"

"He stayed inside as much as possible. Stayed out of the rain. And he never went in the sea, of course." Catherine shifted her weight. "Are ye only takin' a wee peek around my shop, or is there somethin' I can help ye with?"

Morag took the hint and glanced around. "Um." She blushed again. Why had she thought this tiny shop would have what she needed? "I was looking for some colored pencils."

"I'm certain I've some of those." She walked down an aisle, and Morag trailed after, trying not to stare at Catherine moving like someone on a heaving ship. Duncan, with a long-suffering sigh, got to his feet and followed.

"Here they are." Catherine passed her a box of colored pencils a child might use.

Morag pressed her hand to the sinking sensation in her stomach. Class started tomorrow, and she wouldn't have any decent art pencils. She felt doomed already, set up to fail again. They returned to the register, and since Morag didn't have the heart to tell Catherine these weren't what she wanted, she let the woman ring her up.

Catherine placed the pencils in a paper bag along with several shortbread cookies. "Is there anythin' else ye're needin'?"

"You—you don't have any more art supplies?"

"Paint, ye mean?"

"Or, well, watercolor pencils, or um, you know. More professional supplies?"

Catherine's eyebrows shot up. "Are ye an artist? Wonderful. Why didn't ye say so? I've let ye buy stuff for the *sprogs*."

"*Sprogs?*"

"Children. I'm afraid I don't have any real art supplies. What is it ye do?"

"I draw mostly. Digital art. Some painting." Her face burned like a heat lamp.

"Maybe ye can show me sometime? I'm an artist, too. Jewelry." She tipped her head toward a display tree of silver earrings, necklaces, and bracelets.

"They're beautiful." Morag wasn't being polite. It was true.

"Thank ye. Which one do ye like best?"

"Oh, um, I'm not sure." Morag studied the display. "That one." She pointed to a pendant covered in a series of intricate knots.

Catherine plucked the necklace off its hook and held it out.

Morag looked at the price tag and shook her head. "I love it, but I don't have the money."

Catherine continued to hold it out, giving it a shake for emphasis. "It's a gift."

Morag shook her head harder. "Oh, I couldn't. I mean, it's beautiful, but that's too generous."

The woman grabbed her wrist, placed the necklace in Morag's hands, and closed her fingers over it. Morag uncurled them. The silver caught the dusty light and shone brightly. She swallowed. "Thank you. It's really nice of you."

Catherine beamed a smile. "Go on. Let's see how it looks on ye."

"Oh. Sure." She struggled with the delicate clasp. Once on, she was pleased to see the pendant hung in the hollow of her neck.

Catherine clapped her hands. "Aye, that's lovely. I knew it was perfect for ye. Do ye ken there's a ceilidh Saturday night? Yer family should come."

"My brother told me about the kay-lee." Her tongue tripped

over the strange word. "Ingrid invited him. I think we're going."

"Did she now?" Catherine's face turned thoughtful. "Maybe ye won' stay outsiders all summer if she likes you lot."

"The caretaker at the castle sure doesn't like us," Morag blurted out. "And he was mean to an otter."

"An otter, ye say?"

She explained Ben's behavior this morning.

"Aye, I'm no' surprised. Ben's a wee bit barmy, ye ken?" Catherine twirled her finger by her temple. "His family's always been the caretakers of Screeverholme as far back as anyone remembers. The legend goes it's only his family that stands between us and a sea full of monsters."

Morag's heart thudded as she thought of Ben patrolling in his little rowboat. "What kind of monsters?"

"Oh, my mum used to love tellin' my sisters and me tales about frightenin' creatures—shapeshifters and fairies and angry spirits and trolls—but I probably shouldn't be fillin' yer head with nonsense."

Morag's pulse quickened with a thrum of fear. Ben's anger about the otter, the shadow in the graveyard, the lights at sea, and the coins for protection. Oh god. Hamish's demon-man. What if it wasn't nonsense at all?

The bell on the door chimed, and a mud-covered man walked in. "Catherine, please tell me those valves came in."

"If ye'll excuse me, I should get to work." Catherine gave an apologetic smile and limped over to the man.

Was it her imagination, or was that smile tinged with relief, as if the woman had been saved from saying too much? Morag headed for the door, though she would've liked to hear more Orkney stories. In fact, with her childish pencils clutched to her chest, an idea began to take root.

Her pace quickened as she imagined an art portfolio based on the mythology of Orkney. With imaginary creatures, she wouldn't be constrained by drawing realistic subjects. She could sketch ideas with ordinary pencils for now. Her walk across the island had helped her art project, but not quite how she'd expected.

She couldn't wait to dive into those books in the library and do some research—for academic purposes—into the local myths. Finally feeling some real excitement for her portfolio, Morag pushed open the door and stepped into a cold drizzle.

Morag, her skin itching unbearably, ran back to the castle. She rushed into the kitchen, intent on a hot cup of tea, only to discover her mother, medical bag slung over her shoulder. Morag tried to duck out before she was spotted, but the Mom Radar was on full power.

"Whoa. Hold up. Let me see your face." Morag turned around, and Mom gasped. "You're covered in hives."

"Gee, thanks. Hadn't noticed."

Mom gave her The Look, and Morag cringed.

"Were you out in this rain?"

"Yes, but the hives are better already." Morag resisted the urge to scratch. "And it wasn't raining when I left earlier."

"The rain here can catch anyone off guard. You can't go out whenever you please until we get a handle on this allergy. Morag, you could have—" Her phone rang inside her bag, and she sighed, digging around until she found it and whipped the phone to her ear. "Yes, on my way." She hung up and frowned at Morag. "You're lucky I've got a baby to deliver. But this discussion isn't over."

"I'm shocked," Morag said. Mom gave her another look. "I'm sorry. That was rude."

Mom cupped her cheek. "I love you, Morrie. I want to keep you safe. That's all. Please don't go out if it's raining."

"Around here, that's always."

She smiled sadly and tucked a curl behind Morag's ear. "I know. That's why I think you should go to Aunt Helen's."

After that ominous declaration, Morag headed into the library to start her research. Predictably, Hamish left the books scattered on the floor. She dove into the pile, soaking up everything she could about Orkney mythology. Her head swam with brownies, witches, selkies, ghosts, and fairies. By late afternoon, she managed two halfway decent sketches of a sea trow—an ugly, stupid creature known to play tricks on humans—and a giant wandering along the beach among the sheep.

Afterward, she found Françoise in the corner of the banquet hall where the bank of windows gave the best light in the castle for her makeshift studio. Morag watched in fascination as Françoise opened cases of oil paints and arranged a canvas on her easel.

The canvas was half-finished, an oil painting of a woman curled in the fetal position among colorful tubes of paint. The woman's hands were fisted against her chest, and the muscles of her arms and legs corded in quiet desperation. In the face of this brilliance, Morag's sketches of monsters seemed juvenile and crude. Her chest tightened.

The scent of linseed oil formed a cloud around Françoise. "How's your portfolio coming along, Morag?"

In stammered sentences, Morag told her about using Orcadian mythology as the basis for her project. She waited for Françoise's opinion, her fingers laced tightly together.

"That is a wonderful idea." The tendons stood out on her hand as she swept her brush across the canvas with a soft *shoosh,* leaving magic in the wake of the bristles. "Let me know if you want me to take a look."

But the painting had pulled Françoise in. She didn't even notice when Morag drifted away to leave her in peace. It didn't matter. She wasn't brave enough to show Françoise her artwork.

Mom, her hair damp from the rainy journey, sank onto the

bench at the table beside Morag. Dad set a plate of reheated dinner before Mom. It was only the three of them in the kitchen.

"Thank you," Mom said. "I didn't get a chance to eat all day." She shook her head. "It was a difficult breech delivery, and the mother refused to fly to Kirkwall. I don't understand it. The women here seem determined to give birth on Tullimentay at any cost." She took a bite, and with her mouth full, said, "The ferry will be back in a couple days to take you to Kirkwall, Morag. I booked your flights for next Tuesday."

Before Morag could protest, Dad spoke. "Without consulting me? We discussed this, Lisa. We agreed Morag is old enough to decide for herself."

"Bill, she came home with hives. After going to the shop today. She could die going on a *walk* here. Magnus said damp cold is the worst."

"Oh, well, if the illustrious Dr. Magnus said it, we'd better listen." Her father turned to Morag. "Did you take your epi-pen with you today?"

She dug into her back pocket. "Yes."

"You took your pills this morning?" Dad didn't look at Morag though—he stared at Mom—his jaw tight.

"Of course."

"What about a jacket? You remembered one?"

"Yeah." She pulled on the drawstrings of her hood. "I'm wearing it."

"Why did you go out today?"

"It was sunny. I wanted to get some inspiration for my art."

"Why did you come home?"

Mom glared at Dad. "Bill, I get it."

"Morag? Why?" Dad repeated.

"Because it was raining."

"Let me get this straight. You took your pills, had an epi-pen with you, brought a jacket, and you did not stand outside waiting to die like a complete idiot in the cold rain, but came home."

Mom's fork clattered onto her plate. "This isn't a joke."

"I know, Lisa. I'm not joking. Give our daughter a little credit. She can take care of herself. Just like she's going to have to do back home when winter comes."

Triumph and a sick feeling at getting dragged into her parents' fight churned together in Morag's gut.

Dad turned to her. "Morag, what would you like to do about this summer?"

She didn't hesitate. "I want to stay. I have a good idea for my art portfolio. I need to be here to work on it."

"Then it's settled."

Mom shook her head. "No. I don't—"

"Lisa." Dad's voice turned gentle. "Please. Trust Morag, okay? Our kids are going to be off to college before we know it. We need to start letting them make decisions for themselves."

"Oh, like getting drunk and—"

"Lisa. They're good kids."

A beat of silence followed. For once, Dad said something Mom didn't want to argue with. She buried her head in her hands. "Okay. You two win. It's not what I'd choose—"

"I spoke to the owner of the shop." Morag rushed to cut off any further protests. "Her dad had a cold allergy like me, and he managed to live here—so did all the people in his family. We're even distantly related—she's a Tulloch."

"Really?" Mom sounded skeptical. "I thought the last Tulloch here died."

"Catherine was adopted. Her dad was a Tulloch. I can't leave, Mom. I'm getting to know our family history here."

"I don't like this. How can I keep you safe if even a little rain gives you hives?

"They're annoying, but the medications are working. Just some itchiness."

"She's made her decision, Lisa." Dad put his hand on Mom's, and Morag's heart lifted as she saw the moment of capitulation cross her mother's face.

Mom sighed. "I'll cancel the flights."

Morag won—but she didn't miss the way Mom pulled her hand out from Dad's, and in an instant, the victory felt hollow.

Chapter 8

F*issowy* weather trapped everyone inside for two days to
pursue their own activities. Morag attended her first online
art class, causing her to panic about her art portfolio. After
several frustrating attempts at drawing mythological creatures,
Morag found herself drifting more often to the piano.

One of those times, Ben popped his head in the library and
said gruffly, "Ye play well, Morag. It's a pleasure to hear music
like this in Screeverholme." He'd promptly disappeared again.

Morag had looked at Juliette, who wore a bemused smile
at this unexpected compliment, and they'd burst out laughing.
Whenever Morag played, Juliette kept her company sewing the
beading on the beautiful, green gown, which she finished and
presented to Morag.

Morag felt bad she had no drawing worthy to give in
exchange, but her friend said Morag's piano playing was gift
enough.

Paul continued working on the website for her dad, muttering
over his computer all day. Hamish was constantly video chatting

with friends, using his phone to show them outside, and saying things like, "I know. Shocking. It's raining in Scotland. Again."

Little by little, the weather wore down their nerves as surely as the rain wore down the gravestones outside. They were sick of each other's company. Thank god the Bacons were due to arrive any minute tonight. Morag couldn't wait to meet them and see some new faces.

She perched on a barstool at a high-top table against the wall in the billiards room. Her belly was full of the tasty spaghetti they'd had for dinner. Rain lashed the windows, and the only light in the room shone over the pool table where Hamish and Juliette played. The sight started a song Morag loved, with intricately layered guitars and raw vocals.

Paul sat next to her, his laptop untouched, and watched Juliette. Her friend flipped her hair over her shoulder and smiled at Hamish, who was instructing her on how to bank a shot into the corner pocket. From the twisted moue of Paul's mouth, he looked about as thrilled as Morag over Juliette's obvious crush on Hamish.

Juliette took the shot. Her pool stick struck too low and launched the cue ball over the table and onto the floor with a *crack*.

"I think you're getting worse," Paul said. "Maybe you should quit before you tear the felt."

"Maybe *you* should shut up," Juliette snapped in uncharacteristic grumpiness. She flounced across the room to retrieve the errant ball.

Paul opened his mouth to retort, only to yawn loudly. "I'm sure I'd think of some witty insult if I weren't so exhausted. Thanks, Hamish."

"Hey, man, next time I see a demon outside your room, I'll just do nothing. Or better yet, I'll open your door and show him the way in."

Paul slapped his hand on the table. "Yes. Please do. Because I have a few questions for this demon thing. Mainly, why is it only ever *you* that sees it?"

The spaghetti in Morag's stomach congealed to a cold lump at the reminder of last night. At three a.m., Hamish had pounded on everyone's doors to say he'd caught a glimpse of a dark form standing outside Paul's room on his way back from the bathroom. Of course, the hallway had been empty. And of course, Paul scoffed. And of course, Hamish got angry.

Hamish ended up sleeping in Morag's room again. Not that Morag had minded. Last night, Hamish had been stone-cold sober, leaving her with no explanation for her brother's claim. Except, by the time the sun came up, she convinced herself Hamish had only imagined the whole thing because his drunk experience the other night put ideas in his head. Funny how it was easier to believe things in the dark.

Her gaze slid to the gloom of night pressing in at the windows, and a chill spread over her shoulders.

"—your dumb idea to go in that tomb anyway," Hamish was saying, his voice loud enough to pull Morag's attention back from the windows. "It's your fault we're all cursed now."

Paul slammed his laptop shut and stood. "You know you sound like a complete child—"

"The Bacons are here." Dad popped his head around the corner from the lounge. "Françoise let them in downstairs."

Finally. The four of them hurried for the lounge, bouncing off each other and the door jamb in their rush. Mom and Mike got to their feet to join Dad in greeting the new family. Already, Mr. Bacon and a little boy stood in the center of the room.

"Hey, guys." Mr. Bacon dropped some luggage at his feet, and Françoise appeared behind him with a carry-on. "That was some ferry ride, wasn't it, Pete?"

Pete, who looked about five or six, hid behind his father's legs.

"Hi, Gary." Dad stepped forward. "Need a hand?"

"Yes, please." Gary looked like he'd showered in his clothes. Water puddled around him. With his tattoos, beard, and earring, all he needed was a parrot on his shoulder to be the perfect pirate.

A tall, lanky boy with black hair and dark eyes pushed his way in to stand beside Mr. Bacon and Pete. He might have wanted his hair to be spiky, but whatever his intended style, it hadn't survived the barrage of Orkney weather. A drowned porcupine came to Morag's mind. His black hoodie was sopping wet. Firelight glinted off the rings in his eyebrow and lip, and a barbell piercing spanned the entire top of his ear. The piercings drew attention to his sharp features, and to the sparkle in his black eyes. Morag could see how other girls might find him attractive, but he wasn't her type. At all.

She wouldn't have guessed he was Juliette's type either. That didn't stop her best friend from straightening beside her and staring.

"What's up?" The boy lifted two fingers in salute. At the graceful movement of his hand, Morag heard a song by her favorite band.

Interesting choice. Maybe she wasn't immune to his good looks after all. Confusion fluttered in her chest, and she looked at Paul, who gripped his laptop in front of him like a shield.

"I'm James." That deep, rumbling voice sent a pleasant shockwave through her brain.

Hamish, possibly sensing another troublemaker, saluted back. "Hey. Hamish."

A girl about Morag's age staggered in through the circle with an army-green duffel bag. Her head of purple and red hair triggered her own song for Morag by an LA indie pop band full of fun energy and chaos.

"James, you think you might want to help?" She stuck out her tongue, flashing a silver piercing.

"What? Oh, sorry, Ivy. I was just excited to see the castle."

Hamish leaped up and everyone scurried out to help the Bacons. Morag's allergy prevented her from going outside, but she could at least carry things upstairs. She went down to the entry, grabbed a guitar case, and headed back up.

"Careful with my baby." James followed her up the stairs with some bags.

Great, she'd spend the summer being regaled with bad renditions of *Stairway to Heaven* or puce-colored covers of Greenday. A boy back home played mediocre guitar at lunch in the hall and refused to let any of the starry-eyed girls gathered around him touch his "precious dreadnought." She knew how these guys were and held the case toward James. "You want to carry it?"

He gave her a crooked smile paired with a disarming nose crinkle. "Nah. I trust you."

James and Ivy took rooms on the same floor as Morag and the others. Gary, along with Pete, chose two connecting bedrooms in the opposite tower on the floor above the kitchen. After the Bacons settled in, everyone gathered in the banquet hall. The adults sat at one end of the long table, the kids at the other. Morag's mom made a casserole Morag thought paled in comparison to Françoise's cooking, but no one complained.

Mike was getting better at building fires. Hardly any smoke billowed into the room.

Morag caught Paul in her peripheral vision, staring at the Bacons like they were aliens. James had stripped to a T-shirt, and his left forearm was covered in intricate, locking tattoos of sunbursts and rings. It reminded Morag of the patterns she saw when she played Rachmaninoff. Ivy opted for a flying hummingbird on the inside of each wrist, and a delicate dragonfly flitted across her collarbone. As far as Morag could see, Pete, who was indeed six, didn't have any tattoos—yet.

The Bacons gushed about their trip to Edinburgh, which included a visit to the castle, some dungeons, and a walking ghost tour of graveyards.

"There's a graveyard here," Juliette said. "We're not supposed to go in it, but that didn't stop my brother."

Paul stiffened. "I was merely examining the old Viking burial mound."

"What's that?" Pete pushed around the casserole on his plate, his dark eyes darting about the room.

"A hill where they buried people and their things a long time ago." Paul lowered his voice so only those sitting nearest could hear. "I found gold in there."

"Really?" Pete said.

Paul nodded.

"There's seriously a graveyard?" Ivy grinned. "Do you think this place is haunted?"

"Here we go." James laughed and seeing their questioning looks, added, "Ivy loves the supernatural, the occult, horror movies, ghost hunting shows. She's really hoping this place is haunted."

"Is it?" Pete got up and leaned against his dad. "Are there ghosts here?"

"Maybe," Gary said at the same time Dad said, "Of course not."

Pete pulled on his dad's sleeve. "I wanna sleep with you."

"Maybe if you ask nicely, you can join him," Morag said under her breath to Hamish.

"You wait, Mor. When the reaper comes calling at your door, don't say I didn't warn you—or Paul." Hamish glared at them both, in a bad mood since his parents refused him a beer while James, the same age, sat with a pint.

Still, his words chilled her, and Morag scooted closer to the crackling fire. The flames danced yellow and orange, swirling in a way that reminded her of the lights at sea.

Copepods. That was all.

One of the books Morag found in the library last night gave her an idea for the perfect outing to inspire her portfolio. The morning, if not exactly warm, was at least sunny. Even better,

Mom was at the clinic seeing patients with Magnus. They were all in the kitchen settling down to plates of scrambled eggs, sausages, fat loaves of bread, fried potatoes, and a mountain of paper-thin crepes with Nutella.

"Would anyone like to check out a cave?" Morag asked after breakfast.

James, clad in a hoodie, black skinny jeans, and Doc Martens with blue and green plaid laces, turned from stacking bowls in a cupboard. "Sounds cool."

She smiled, pleased. But why did she care so much what this boy thought?

"Can I come? Can I come?" Pete jumped up and down, waving a dishtowel. In the Bacon family, even six-year-olds helped with chores. Pete dried while Gary washed up and James put away.

"Can *you* come?" James screwed up his face, and Morag waited for the crushing blow when he'd tell his baby brother no way. Instead, James said, "Would it be an adventure without you, buddy?" He ruffled his little brother's hair.

"Yeah!" Pete jumped higher.

Against her will, Morag swooned a little to see a guy be that nice to his younger sibling. She wished Hamish had been that nice to *her* when they were little. To be fair, she and Hamish were less than two years apart, while Pete was twelve years younger than James.

"Keep an eye on him." Gary scooped fresh coffee into the maker.

"Have I lost him yet?"

Gary laughed. "A couple of times."

"Well, I found him again, didn't I?" James slapped his hands together. "Okay. Who's coming?"

Hamish set his mug on the counter. "Count me in, man."

At this, Juliette looked as excited as Pete and agreed to come along, too.

"What about you, Paul?" Françoise asked.

He slumped over a geology book at the table. "What?"

Morag held her breath. It seemed to slowly sink in everyone awaited Paul's response, and he looked up from the pages, startled. "Oh, the walk? No, thanks."

"Come on, it'll be fun," Morag said.

"Stop reading and go see some real geology." Françoise pointed toward the doorway. "Go. Get some fresh air." She wrestled the book off her son, twisting his fingers until he yelped in pain and let go.

"Fresh air. Wonderful." Paul shuffled out of the kitchen with a bored expression painted on his face.

Trust Paul the bibliophile to think reading about a cave was more exciting than seeing a real one—or spending time with Morag. The idea stung.

They grabbed bags of chips and bottles of water. Morag wore stretch pants under her jeans, two pairs of socks, a hoodie, and her waterproof coat. She stuck a navy-blue beret over her curls. She wasn't taking chances.

Morag paused in the entryway in front of the map of Tullimentay hanging on the wall. She pointed out the cave to the others. "It's on the west side. We'll need to walk across the whole island."

They set off across the stone bridge, all of them in high spirits except for Paul.

Ivy stopped in the middle of the bridge and stomped her foot along with what was meant to be an imaginary staff. "You shall not pass," she roared like Gandalf, followed by a belting laugh.

Paul chuckled, and jealousy twinged in Morag's chest. Not jealousy of Ivy, who'd mentioned her girlfriend back home no less than ten times last night—but for not thinking of the reference herself. She knew *The Lord of the Rings* was one of Paul's favorites. Why couldn't she ever figure out a way to get his attention—other than almost dying from a weird allergy, of course. She glanced down for her otter friend, but he wasn't around. Thankfully, neither were any balrogs.

Few trees stood on the island, and the wind blew unobstructed to ruffle the tufted hillocks of grass. The stone walls enclosed swaths of green fields as well as stretches of road, leaving cattle free to roam over it. Pete slipped from James to run toward a nearby cow. A farmer waved his arms and shouted.

"Sorry." James lifted his hand in apology and rushed to catch Pete.

The farmer approached, a black and white border collie trotting at his side. It was the muddy man in Sinclair's who'd asked for valves. Morag braced for a lecture, but he only smiled at Pete.

"Young man, if ye keep chasin' the cows, ye'll put poor Kate out of a job." He said it *coos*.

"I'm sorry." Pete looked ready to cry.

The farmer pulled off his flat cap and gave Pete a playful smack with it, underscored by a wink. "Och, don't cry, son. It's only my cattle are half-wild, and they don't take well to people. Grumpy sods, the lot of them." His smile faded, and his tone turned serious. "Mind ye leave the animals alone on the island, ye hear me?" He leveled them with a stern gaze. "That goes for every one of yous. Respect the animals, leave them alone, and they won't be botherin' ye, aye?"

This odd warning created a strained silence until Morag broke it. "What animals would bother us, sir? The only wild animals I've seen around here are birds and an otter."

The man's eyes narrowed, and he rubbed his gnarled hand over his wool sweater with a scratching noise. "Otters belong in the sea. Stay away from it. The water's rough, and there's all manner of dangers in it." Abruptly, the man's tone turned congenial again. "Right, then. I'm off. Kate and I need to finish our work in time for the ceilidh tonight. I hear I'll be seein' ye there." He marched off toward his tractor, a man bent on escape.

James ran his fingers through his spiky hair, sharp and shiny black in the sunlight. "Did anyone else find that a little bizarre?"

"Uh, more than a little," Ivy said. "What was that all about?" She held up her finger in warning and did a passable impression of the old man. "'Stay away from the sea.' Like what kind of dangers is he talking about? The Kraken?"

Morag gave a weak laugh. "Well, when I was at the shop, the owner told me Ben and his family apparently think they're the only ones keeping the islanders safe from a bunch of sea monsters."

"Yes." Ivy jumped up and down with excitement, much like Pete might. "There are seriously monsters here?"

Paul made a guttural sound deep in his throat. "There's no such thing as monsters."

"Except I saw one." Hamish casually ripped open a bag of chips and crunched into one.

"You joking?" James's eyebrow ring lifted.

Hamish shook his head. "Not in the slightest. I saw some scary shit in my room one night."

"That's a cuss word." Pete shot Hamish a scandalized expression.

"Tell me everything." Ivy punched Hamish on the arm for no apparent reason other than to emphasize her need to know.

Paul rolled his eyes and started walking again, but when no one joined him, he stopped and turned around. "Here we go again. I'll summarize. Hamish got drunk and thought he saw a 'demon-man'"—here, Paul curled his fingers in air quotes—"and we're all supposed to believe we brought a curse on ourselves by going into a tomb."

Juliette glared at Paul. "Hamish isn't a liar." Which Morag had to agree was true most of the time.

"Thanks, Juliette." Hamish flashed her a thumbs-up and shoved another chip in his mouth.

"Whoa, whoa, whoa," Ivy said. "Wait up. Demons? Tombs? Curses? That's a lot of terrifying stuff to unpack."

"That *is* pretty scary." James cocked his head at Pete clinging to his arm. "Maybe tone it down, okay?"

"Okay, *Dad*." It was Ivy's turn to roll her eyes. "Pete, you can handle this, right, buddy? Or do you want us to treat you like a baby?"

Pete's wide eyes took up half his face. "I can handle it."

"Hell yeah, you can." Ivy held out her hand for a fist bump, which Pete returned before hastily grabbing onto his big brother's arm again. Ivy turned to Hamish. "Spill it."

Everyone resumed walking, passing pebble-dashed houses and stone cottages, while Hamish told the Bacons about how he, Paul, and Morag went into the barrow before Hamish saw the horned figure that night.

James's mouth turned down, and he nodded several times as if considering how he felt, and then finding what he felt was impressed.

"That's crazy," Ivy said, in the same tone she might say *I won the lottery*. "You cursed yourselves with demon visitations? Wow." She tapped her mouth. "But what does that have to do with Ben and the sea monsters and that farmer being all weird about animals?"

"No idea, but there's been other weird sh—stuff." Hamish glanced at Pete. "Our ferry ran into something on the way over here—"

"It was a buoy," Paul said.

"Right." Hamish sprayed a mouthful of chips in Paul's face as he spoke. "The captain was so freaked out because we hit a *buoy*."

Paul wiped the crumbs off his face in disgust and moved to walk beside Morag and Juliette.

"What do *you* think it was?" James asked.

Hamish shrugged. "I don't know, but something scared our captain. Plus, Morag thought she saw a body in the water that day."

"No way." Ivy rounded on Morag. "Really?"

"I don't know." Morag slid her gaze to Paul, feeling a little ashamed of how much she craved his approval. "It looked like a human skeleton, but it was probably a sea animal."

"More like a sea *monster*," Hamish said.

"Oh, my god." Paul rolled his eyes so hard, Morag swore she heard them rattle back in his skull.

Juliette looked at Hamish with a quiet desperation Morag recognized in herself a moment ago trying to impress Paul. "Maybe Hamish is right, Paul. Something's in the water. Morag keeps seeing those lights in the ocean at night, too."

Paul groaned. "Cephalopods."

"Copepods," Morag snapped, surprised at a sudden burst of anger.

Paul reddened. "That's what I meant."

"Copepods—little plankton things?" James encouragingly smiled at her, and Morag blinked in confusion. Another teenager knew what a copepod was? And here she thought Paul was the genius. In a flash, she realized she was angry not at Paul, but at herself, for her pitiful need to impress him all the time.

"Probably the lights I'm seeing in the water are copepods. They glow in the dark like fireflies." Morag drew a deep breath and glanced at Paul. "But I also saw a shadow moving through the graveyard our first night here. And I saw a muddy footprint outside my room that looked like it had webbed toes, and I don't know who made it." There. Those were the facts. The Bacons could make what they wanted of it, and Paul too, for that matter.

"A ghost in the graveyard. And a sea monster came into the castle?" Ivy clenched her hands into fists. "This is so exciting."

Pete pressed himself against James who said, "Probably enough monster talk."

For a bit, no one said anything. No doubt everyone's thoughts swirled like Morag's. They neared the schoolhouse, and being a Saturday, the playground stood forlorn. One of the swings creaked in the breeze, and the sound made a bronze-colored starburst explode across Morag's vision.

"Can you imagine going to such a tiny school?" Ivy said. "I'd love to see inside."

"Maybe you can," Morag said. "I ran into the teacher, and she invited us to a summer solstice celebration at the school."

"A solstice celebration sounds cool." James plucked up the flagging Pete and swung him onto his shoulders.

"Yeah. But she was pushy about making sure we came." Morag thought again of the woman's order. *You* will *make sure to come on the solstice.* "Almost like she was anxious about it."

"It's quite common for cultures to develop anxieties and strange customs around solstices," Paul said. "There's a particular superstition around the estival solstice when pagans believe evil spirits come out."

"'Particular superstition around the estival solstice'." Hamish used a mocking singsong. "What the hell even is an estival solstice?"

"The summer solstice," Paul said.

"Dude, then just say that. Why can't you talk like a normal person?

"Shut up, Hamish," Morag said, without thinking. Paul's head snapped in her direction. "You don't have to be mean," she added, "just because big words scare you." She hoped to make it sound like a sibling spat rather than the reflex to defend the boy she liked. Judging by the way both Paul *and* Hamish were studying her, she'd failed. "Hey. Look at that church." She pointed at the weathered building standing alone on a hill. "Bet it has a graveyard." The words came out louder than she'd meant, but the distraction worked as everyone turned to look.

"Let's check it out," Ivy said. "I love cemeteries." She charged up the hill, and the others followed behind with a mixture of laughter and groans.

They walked around all four sides of the stone building, but there wasn't a graveyard. Ivy sagged in disappointment.

"It makes sense a small island like this would need to conserve space," Paul said. "Perhaps they cremate people."

"Or give them burials at sea." Ivy's eyes lit up as she gazed out at the water. "The beaches around here are probably crawling with ghosts."

"Hey, Einstein," Hamish said. "Why does Screeverholme have a graveyard?"

Paul opened his mouth, shut it, then opened it again. "Different rules apply to lords of castles?"

They approached a cluster of houses, and Hamish pointed out a two-story stone house with smoke billowing out the chimney. "That's Ingrid's place." The old green Land Rover sat in the front yard along with several cars in various states of disrepair. Hamish stuck his hands in his pockets. "So, uh, I was thinking we could ask Ingrid along."

Morag glanced at Juliette, who wore a look of devastation. Morag was struck with pity for her best friend. How could Juliette not see Hamish was a terrible match for her? They had nothing in common. Hamish was loud and simple and into sports—he was rough edges, while Juliette was sensitive and romantic and soft like the fabrics she worked with.

Now Morag and Paul, on the other hand had lots in common. They both got good grades and liked reading and . . . her brain floundered to find something better than that, but fortunately a couple of shaggy dogs raced around the side of Ingrid's house to greet them, and she shoved her thoughts aside.

A pleasant smell of woodsmoke and burning leaves hung in the air. Hamish knocked on Ingrid's front door. A woman who must have been Ingrid's mother answered and leaned out to get a better look at their group. James waved.

The woman didn't wave back. She shouted for Ingrid, who bounded out a minute later.

Hamish normally went for cheerleaders or girls who found nothing more riveting than Hamish's exploits on the football field or basketball court. It was fascinating seeing him with Ingrid, in dirty jeans, a red rain slicker, and dark green rainboots that sparked a 90's song by Garbage, *Only Happy When it Rains*.

Hamish made the introductions with uncustomary shyness. Interesting. He took Ingrid's hand with a fierce expression as if daring anyone to say a word.

They continued along the road. Morag asked Ingrid what to expect at the ceilidh, and she regaled them with descriptions of the different Scottish dances.

"I don't have to dance, do I?" Hamish said in horror.

"No, but ye'll be the only one who isn't." Ingrid nudged him with her elbow. "It's all right if ye're scared, Hamish."

"Do I have to wear a skirt?"

"If ye mean a kilt, then no. Orcadians don't have tartans. That's for Highlanders, but some still wear kilts for fun."

A bank of gray clouds gathered out to sea. The wind picked up, sending strands of dark hair across Morag's face and sticking them to her lips. She plucked them off and tucked her hands deeper into her pockets, pushing her fear of the cold down in there as well.

Ingrid nodded toward the western tip of the island where a tall white lighthouse speared the air like a monolith. "Are we goin' to visit the lighthouse? Or the broch?" She pointed to the ancient stone tower in the direction of Screeverholme.

"We're going to a cave," Paul said.

Ingrid stopped so fast, she jerked Hamish into a stumble. "Ye're goin' to Hellyaskaill?"

Morag snapped. "So that's how you say it."

The blood in Ingrid's face drained away to leave her freckles in stark relief on her pale skin. "I'm no goin' with ye." She tried to drag Hamish in the opposite direction, but he stood his ground.

"Whoa. What's up? Why don't you want to go?"

Unable to get Hamish to budge, Ingrid yanked her hand out of his. "It's forbidden."

"Forbidden?" Ivy said. "I like this cave even more."

Their group formed a curious ring around Ingrid and Hamish.

Morag looked at Juliette, who gave a helpless shrug, but perhaps looked a little pleased at the idea of Ingrid leaving.

"Why is it forbidden?" Morag said.

Ingrid sighed. "Ye wouldn't understand. Ye're no' from here. It's dangerous. It's where they take people."

"Where *who* takes people?"

Ingrid glanced around, her mouth and eyes perfect circles of fear. "I can't say. Just—ye can't go in there, all right?"

"Come on, Ingrid," Hamish said. "What's there? Have you been inside the cave?"

"No, but I've heard stories of bad things in Hellyaskaill, aye? People get lost in there."

Morag didn't like the idea of getting lost in a cave—or encountering bad things. Ingrid's fear proved to be contagious, and she was about to suggest abandoning the plan when Paul snorted.

"I, for one, am curious to see this cave," he said. "Let's not get silly about some local legend."

Ingrid's bright green eyes sparked with defiance. "It's no' a silly legend, okay? You shouldna go in there."

Hamish put his arm around the girl. "Maybe we should listen to Ingrid. I don't want to upset her."

"You mean you're too scared." Paul crossed his arms over his chest and cocked his head in challenge.

"I'm not scared, okay?"

"Ye would be if ye had half a brain in yer skull." Ingrid pulled his sleeve. "Stay with me, aye?"

"Yeah, Hamish, stay here, you big chicken."

"Dude, shut up."

Paul began clucking.

"Shut. Up."

To Morag's surprise, Ivy joined in with the clucking and upped it to elbow-flapping.

Hamish turned to Ingrid, his eyes pleading. "Explain why we shouldn't go in the cave. What is it?"

"I can't say."

"Why? Tell me, and I won't go in there."

She jutted her chin up. "Ye'll have to trust me."

Paul and Ivy danced around them both, crowing and clucking and flapping. Morag fought back a giggle at their childishness and her own giddy fear.

Hamish held up his hand and shouted. "Stop. Seriously, both of you, stop." He turned to Ingrid and in a quieter voice said, "I saw something. In the castle."

Paul slapped both hands to his forehead and slid them down his cheeks. "*Mon Dieu.* Not the demon-man again."

But Paul stayed quiet during Hamish's recounting of the barrow and the horned figure as if he too was curious how Ingrid would respond.

"Is that what's in the cave?" Hamish asked.

Ingrid's shoulder lifted. "I don't know. I just know ye shouldna go in there."

"If you can't tell me what it is, then I'm going in." Hamish glared at Paul, and Morag shrank as he included her in that scowl. "Maybe we'll see something, and I can prove it wasn't me being drunk or imagining things."

"Ye'll curse yerself going in," Ingrid whispered.

"I think I'm already cursed now." Hamish kissed her forehead, and Morag sensed Juliette stiffen beside her. "I'll be careful, I promise. I won't stay long. I'll look out for the others. If you guys want to go?" He glanced around their group.

Everyone nodded with varying degrees of enthusiasm, but nobody said no.

Ingrid let out a long sigh. "Fine. If I canna talk ye out of it, I'll wait here." She shifted her gaze to each of them in turn. "To make sure ye get out alive."

Chapter 9

Despite Ingrid's warnings, once someone used a word like *forbidden* to keep people from doing something, it always had the opposite effect. Human nature, plain and simple. Morag discovered she wasn't immune either. Her curiosity was piqued, and she was determined to go to Hellyaskaill. Everyone huddled on the top of the headland, waiting for someone to make the first move.

Since it was Morag's idea in the first place, she said, "Let's go."

Pete tugged on James's ear. "I don't wanna go in the cave, Jamie."

"Maybe you can stay outside with Ingrid?" James sent the girl a questioning look.

Ingrid nodded grimly. "Better he doesn't go in there." Pete slithered off his brother's back and crossed to Ingrid's side. She took his hand. "We'll stay here, Pete."

Paul swung his backpack from his shoulder and unzipped it to take out some flashlights. "Found these in the castle." He passed them around.

"Ye'd better hurry. Rain is comin'," Ingrid said as she clutched Pete's hand. She made a dramatic picture with the wind swirling her red hair around her face.

Hamish stepped over to Ingrid and kissed her cheek while Ivy said, "Ooooo.".

He always had an easy way with the opposite sex which Morag envied since she was awkward with boys. Girls loved Hamish for that confidence, Juliette included, it turned out. Her friend was gnawing her lip, staring at the water. White caps dotted the choppy surface, in as much turmoil as she appeared to be.

"Come on." Ivy started toward the cliff's edge, and Juliette hurried after with Hamish and James following.

"Don't go in far," Ingrid called. "Ye'll get lost."

Morag turned toward the rocky outcrop by the lighthouse where the sound of the sea grew louder with every step. The vivid, lush green turned into a tumble of dark rock dropping steeply into the water. Here and there, natural plateaus broke up the rock face. A natural staircase of stones led to a narrow cave mouth, halfway down the bluffs. Waves churned up a yellowy-gray froth, and the scent of dead fish wafted on the building wind, blowing the dark clouds closer. Exploring the cave appealed less now they started down toward it.

Morag fell into step beside Paul and shivered.

"Make sure you keep warm, Morag." His concern was enough to warm her all on its own.

"Do you think this is safe?"

"I might not believe in local superstitions, but Ingrid is right to warn us to be careful given people have gotten lost inside. We'll take a brief look around. I don't want to worry her too much or disrespect the locals."

"Like when we went in the barrow?"

Paul cleared his throat. "I didn't mean to upset Ben that day. Or get you in trouble."

Morag might have responded, but it took all her concentration to pick her way over the rocks. Mist curled against the cliff, shrouding the cave's entrance. A chill stole over her cheeks, and she yanked her scarf over her mouth and nose. Her foot slipped on a wet boulder, and Paul grabbed her arm. Her heart pounded, as much from the feel of his grip as almost falling.

He helped her from the boulder, and her skin tingled where it touched his. He guided Morag over the rocks, and she pretended to have trouble negotiating them, even though that offended her feminist sensibilities. The rocks turned to rough gravel at the cave's entrance, where plants clung to the cliffside. The mist drifted into long fingers and collected at the opening of the cave like a hand over a screaming mouth. The sight filled Morag with dread, and her hand convulsed in Paul's.

Perhaps misreading it as a hint, he dropped it. "You can manage?"

She nodded, hoping she didn't look as disappointed as she felt.

The mouth of the cave ran in a diagonal slash in the rock face. The sight played a haunting song. The rhythm of it throbbed like the beat of a broken heart in Morag's mind.

Ivy approached the cave entrance, and her nose wrinkled up. "What's that smell?"

"Probably Hamish," Morag said.

"Not funny." Hamish punched her in the arm, making Morag yelp in surprise. "Now *that's* funny."

"Yes," Paul said. "Hitting girls is always the height of comedic genius."

Hamish pushed past Paul. "Step back and let the real men go first."

"Suit yourself," Paul said. "They do say 'fools rush in where angels fear to tread.'"

Hamish pushed his arms out at his sides. "You calling me a fool?"

"Ok, while you two are bickering, I'm just gonna . . ." Ivy

pushed between the two boys and into the cave.

Hamish rushed after her, followed by Juliette.

Paul pointed his flashlight in front of Morag. "After you."

She stepped in and smelled something, too. Wet dog mixed with salt water, smoke, and fish. A layer of slick, green algae slimed the walls. The cave entrance narrowed to a tunnel just wide enough to accommodate two people walking side-by-side. Ahead, brave Ivy walked first, followed by Hamish and Juliette shoulder-to-shoulder, then Morag and Paul, and James bringing up the rear. Morag's shoes crunched on something. She directed her flashlight down, afraid she'd see bones, but it was only gravel and bits of broken seashell.

After a couple of minutes, the tunnel twisted away, blocking out the sunlight, but out of the wind, it wasn't as cold. The algae gave way to dry walls of dull rock where their flashlights cast bobbing shadows. Ahead, the twisting tunnel bounced back the others' voices in odd ways.

As the tunnel slanted downward, James kept stepping on Morag's heels and apologizing. She slipped on the gravel, and James caught her before she fell. A jolt like electricity zipped through her body when he grabbed her.

"Careful." He gave her a lopsided grin that left her unsteady again.

"Thanks." Morag shook her head to clear the muddled feeling and stepped more carefully over the increasingly steep ground. How deep did this cave go? The tunnel narrowed, and Paul and Morag slid past each other when the width forced them to walk single file at times. She might have enjoyed it if not for her confusion over her body's reaction to James and her growing anxiety about going farther into the cave. For now, though, there was no danger of getting lost as there was only this tunnel to retrace.

"Anyone else getting hot?" Ivy called back.

The air was growing heavy and warm, like a greenhouse.

"Wait," said James. "Come look at this." Morag and Paul

stopped and turned. James used his phone light to illuminate some deeply cut symbols in the rock wall. "Kind of looks like hieroglyphics."

"They aren't." Paul's response was instant. "Not runes, either."

"Any idea what it is?" James said.

For once, Paul didn't know and shook his head.

"Paul." Morag tugged on his arm and pointed higher up the wall. "Look."

It was crude but still clear. A simple curled wave represented the sea, and a figure, hardly more than a stick person, walked out of it. The figure had long hands and flippered feet, reminding her of the strange footprints. Beyond the figure was the outline of a huge man with horns sprouting from his head. Morag swallowed hard. "The demon-man," she whispered.

James ran his fingers over the etched figures. "Creepy. I wonder how old they are. Ancient? Or some kids last week?"

"They look old." Paul took out his phone and snapped a few photos. "Fascinating."

James glanced down the tunnel where the others had disappeared, his face drawn, and met Morag's gaze. "We shouldn't get separated in here."

Ivy, Hamish, and Juliette must not have noticed the rest of them had stopped.

"Hey, Hamish," Morag shouted. Her voice bounced back through the tunnel. "Wait up."

"Come on," Hamish shouted back. "I can hear running water up here."

James started after the others. "You coming?"

"Yeah, one second," Morag said.

James strode off into the dark, his flashlight dancing on the walls, and left her and Paul alone to study the carvings. She found Paul's hand and squeezed it. "Paul. What if Hamish really saw one of those?"

"What if horned demon-men are real, and one visited your

brother's room? Morag, be serious."

"I am. We went in that barrow, and *that* night Hamish said he saw this man with horns. Now we find an etching of one inside the cave Ingrid warned us not to go in."

"Yes, she warned us because people have gotten lost in here before. The islanders made up scary stories to keep kids out." By the light of the flashlight, his expression brightened. "Bet you anything this man with horns is part of the island mythology, and Hamish saw or heard about it somewhere. Had the idea planted in his subconscious so when he was drunk, his brain thought he saw *that* guy." He released Morag's hand and pushed his index finger into the carving of the horned man.

Slow relief trickled in at the idea. "You think so?" Morag pressed herself against Paul.

"I do. It makes sense, doesn't it?"

"I guess so. More sense than believing in monsters."

His expression softened. "I think you and I might be the only logical people in this group."

"We should stick together then."

"Hey, Morag," Juliette called from ahead. "Where are you? We don't want to get separated."

She silently cursed Juliette for ruining the moment, though she didn't mind leaving the carvings behind. They hurried and caught up with the others.

"How far are we going?" she asked Hamish in an irritated voice, even though he wasn't the one to shout for her.

"I think the cave opens out up ahead. I can hear running water echoing. Do you guys hear it?" Hamish slowed. "I feel like a giant pit is going to open under our feet."

"Don't say that." Juliette smacked him on the arm.

"We saw some carvings on the wall back there," Morag said. "A figure with flippers and a guy with horns."

Hamish recoiled. "What?"

She described the etchings, and Hamish and the others painted their light along the walls, but there was nothing along this stretch. "Hamish? Do you think you saw or heard about the horned man before? Had it planted in your subconscious?" Morag turned her flashlight to see his response.

"No. Stop blinding me." He snatched her flashlight. "I swear. Never saw or heard anything about it before that night. Why won't you believe me, Morag?"

She slid her eyes toward Paul and back to Hamish, her annoying brother, but also one of her best friends when he wasn't driving her crazy. She couldn't ignore her gut anymore. Not with that carving as proof on top of it. "Fine. I believe you now, okay?"

Paul groaned, but she did her best to ignore it.

"Finally," Hamish said huffily. He knocked his shoulder into hers with a small smile.

The tunnel took another steep downward turn around a corner, and Morag's feet splashed through an inch of water on the floor. All at once, the tunnel opened into a large cavern, about the size of her school cafeteria with a ceiling so high, the blackness swallowed their flashlight beams. Now she'd given in to believing Hamish, to believing herself and the weird things she'd seen, being in the cave was suddenly terrifying. As if to underline this, hissing noises echoed off the rock walls of the space.

"What's that?" Juliette gripped Hamish's arm, the gesture no longer flirtatious. Morag grabbed his other arm, grateful for his solid presence.

Like a whale surfacing to breathe, a jet of water sprayed high into the air from the middle of the cavern and sprinkled them with frigid salt water. Hamish shoved Morag behind him, taking the brunt of it.

"Stay back, Morrie." Hamish leaned forward a little. "Guess there *was* a giant pit."

Paul frowned and stepped beside Hamish. Morag ignored Hamish's warning and inched toward the hole, perfectly smooth and circular, about ten feet across and twice as deep.

Water swirled around and around with a roar, then slid away on a sucking sound. Then only a soft *shush* remained as they stared down in a long silence.

"That was insane." Ivy's voice reverberated off the cavern walls.

"Is the tide coming or going?" Paul stepped back, picking up his foot and letting it fall with a splash. "This is as far as I'd like to explore. It's not safe for Morag."

"Yeah. I don't want to worry Ingrid." Hamish backed away as well.

James and Ivy had already moved toward the perimeter of the room, talking to each other in excited, hushed tones.

Morag couldn't seem to move. The swirling water hypnotized her, and she heard the distant strains of Camille Saint-Saëns' *Danse Macabre* with a cold sort of dread as she stared into the writhing darkness. It was horrifying to think where she'd get sucked to if she slipped and fell in, yet she couldn't tear her eyes away.

"Back up, Morag," Paul said. "We don't know how often the water erupts like that."

A flash of spinning green light shot past below and disappeared. Morag whipped around feeling triumphant. "Did you guys see that?"

"What?" Hamish grabbed her jacket. "Come on, you're making me nervous standing so close."

"Yeah, Morag," Juliette said. "Let's go."

Annoyed, Morag yanked free of her brother. "I saw those lights again. Come look for yourself."

Paul shook his head. "I'm not risking getting knocked down that thing for some dinoflagellates."

"Copepods," Morag said impatiently.

Hamish took another step back and spun in a circle, shining his light around. "Hey, look at all these tunnels."

Paul took another step back. "I have zero interest in exploring those."

"Yeah, I'm good," said Juliette.

Morag continued to stare into the black hole waiting for the lights to reappear until suddenly, she didn't *want* to see them again. She didn't want to be in the cave anymore, and it struck her as imperative they leave. "Guys, I don't think we should be here."

When no one responded, Morag finally turned around to look at what the others had noticed. Tunnels, eight of them, twisted off the main cavern like the tentacles of a giant octopus. In the shadows of the cavern, all the tunnels looked the same. Morag hurried to Paul, panic swirling in her like the dark water in the hole. "Which tunnel is ours?"

Ivy pointed her light. "That one."

"Are you sure?" Ingrid warned them people got lost. Morag's phone light wasn't cutting it. "Give me my flashlight." She clawed at Hamish. "Give it to me."

"Okay, okay. Chill." Hamish slapped the flashlight in her hand.

"It's okay, Morag." Ivy smiled and pointed at one of the tunnels. "Those are our footprints." Morag was too relieved to be embarrassed at her panic. "I just want to peek in each tunnel."

"No. We need to go," Morag said.

"I'll be quick," she said.

Juliette hooked her arm through Morag's. "Stay with me, okay?" Morag nodded and squeezed her friend's arm.

"Careful." James's voice echoed from the other side of the cavern. "This tunnel drops straight down."

James and Ivy were the only ones enthusiastic about investigating, peering in each tunnel going counterclockwise while Hamish and Paul attempted to look brave, but mostly hung near the exit tunnel.

The hole in the cavern hissed like a nest of angry cobras, and Juliette's fingers dug into Morag's arm. "Time to leave."

They headed toward the way out. Morag didn't look down any of the tunnels they passed.

"Do you hear that?" Juliette clutched Morag. The sound of running water was replaced by a low growling like a dog—a really big dog—from the tunnel to their left, the last before the exit tunnel.

Morag hunched her shoulders as if she could hide in her jacket. She caught the strong scent of fish and wet dog and something musky. Before she could think better of it, she turned her flashlight toward the sound. The beam didn't quite reach a dark shape looming in the shadows. Momentarily paralyzed, she and Juliette exchanged terrified looks. Despite her fear, the same morbid curiosity that compelled her to go into the cave in the first place took hold of Morag. "What is it?"

The shape heaved forward a step, and Morag was very sorry for her curiosity.

A giant, shaggy brown bear, so huge its head was level with her shoulders, glowered back with glowing blue eyes filled with rage. Morag's insides shriveled to make room for her thundering heart.

An angry roar filled the air. Juliette shrieked.

"Run!" Morag's scream prompted the others to react. Ivy and James had completed their circuit of the cavern and returned to the exit tunnel by Hamish and Paul. The four of them all ran, and Morag and Juliette followed.

Cold water splashed over Morag's feet. Behind, another roar echoed through the cavern. She glanced back to make sure the bear didn't follow. So far, it hadn't moved.

Their beams bounced along the tunnel, lighting the others in front who slowed to wait for them. They jostled against each other through every agonizing twist and turn.

"Morag!" Hamish bellowed. "What the hell was that?"

"A bear." Her mind jumped to the tales of shapeshifters she'd read in the library.

"There aren't bears in Orkney," Paul panted. "Maybe centuries ago, I suppose they could have migrated—"

"Bro. Shut up and go." Hamish shoved Paul, accidentally

knocking him into Ivy.

No one cared the tunnel was too narrow for them all to squeeze through as they pinballed along. Morag's shoulder hit the rock wall with a burst of pain, but she didn't slow. The others stumbled out the entrance ahead, and Morag and Juliette plowed through them into sheets of water. It drove against the rock face like fake movie rain. In an instant, Morag's clothes hung wet and heavy on her body.

"Did you really see a bear?" Hamish shouted over the rain and glanced back at the entrance.

Juliette nodded, her face white.

"I swear, Hamish," Morag said.

"That's crazy," James said. "Are you sure?"

Ivy rounded on her brother. "They said so, didn't they? You heard that growling, too."

Already, Morag's neck was beginning to itch. "I'm cold."

"It's freezing." Juliette clambered over the slippery boulders toward the path leading up the cliff face.

Morag followed. "No, Jules, *I'm* cold."

"Oh. Oh!" Juliette did a double-take. "Oh, no."

"What?"

"Your face is blotchy. Hamish, look at her face."

Standing in the icy rain, shivering and breaking out in hives, she'd rushed headlong from the bear into a different sort of doom. Was her throat closing from fear or the allergy? Everyone gathered around.

"Why are we stopping?" James asked.

"She's allergic to cold," Juliette said. "Do you have the epi-pen with you?"

Morag nodded. "I'll take another antihistamine." Her swelling hands struggled to pull the pills from her pocket. "Help me with the blister packs."

Hamish stripped off his jacket and held it over her like a tarp while Juliette popped out two pills.

Morag gulped them down.

"You can be allergic to cold?" James said.

"Shut up," Hamish snapped.

James held up his hands, water cascading off them like a fountain. "No offense. Just never heard that before. Can I help?"

"We need to get her somewhere warm," Juliette said. "Fast."

"This was a terrible idea," Paul said. "We never should have come."

"Then why did you?" Hamish snarled. "Oh, wait. I remember. Your mommy made you."

"Can we concentrate on helping Morag?" Juliette guided Morag over the rocks and onto the cliff path.

Hamish put his arm around her, sharing his body heat. "Hang on, Mor. I'll text Ingrid to get the car. Here, keep her warm." He handed her off to James, who pressed Morag to his side.

Even through her fear and cold, Morag's body responded with a *zing* like hot lightning at James's touch. She stumbled and clawed her way up the path, the task made harder by the driving rain. Below, the sea pummeled the rocks with punishing blows.

"No signal." Hamish shoved his phone into his pocket.

When they finally reached the top of the cliff, Ingrid and Pete were nowhere to be seen.

Chapter 10

James whirled to face Hamish. "Where's my little brother?"

"Ingrid probably took him back to her house to get out of the rain. We gotta get Morag there, okay?" Hamish pulled Morag into a jog.

The stretching feeling in Morag's face and arms distracted her from the memory of the giant bear with the gleaming blue eyes. Panic clawed at her throat. Or else it was the beginning of anaphylactic shock. Inside her pocket, her fingers curled around the epi-pen. The smooth tube anchored her and presented hope, but she didn't relish the idea of administering it. Getting shot up with what was basically adrenaline wasn't a sensation she was eager to experience again. How long to wait for the antihistamines to kick in?

Juliette, Paul, and Hamish ran beside her. Juliette's colorless face didn't do much for Morag's panic. Itchy snakes writhed along her back where her cold, wet shirt clung to her skin. She ran faster.

"Should we give you the epi?" Paul said.

"I don't know." Morag rubbed her neck, triggering a fresh crop of welts. "Maybe." She needed to keep moving, to reach shelter, and she wasn't sure she could after using the epi-pen. At least not for a little while.

Hamish exchanged a grim glance with Paul, so out of character for her brother. Morag's heart sped up. The Bacons followed close behind, exchanging nervous looks Morag didn't miss.

"Maybe you should do the epi-pen," Paul said. "Once it affects your breathing—"

"Ingrid's here." Hamish let out a deep breath as the Land Rover Defender crested the hill.

The vehicle pulled up, and Ingrid rolled down the window. "Need a ride?"

Hamish opened the front door, and Morag climbed into the passenger seat. Ingrid took one look at her and cranked up the heat. Warm, delicious blasts of air washed over her. The radio played unexpected country music, and orange and brown rectangles ran in lines like train cars through Morag's mind. The sensation proved too much, and she switched off the radio.

The others jumped into the backseat, and the Bacons piled onto the extra bench in the cargo area.

James slammed the door. "Where's my brother?"

"He's back at my house, warm and dry, which is where we'll get Morag in a minute." Ingrid wrestled the steering wheel. The road was fast becoming a quagmire, and the Land Rover spun, spraying an arc of mud high into the air, before shooting forward. Ingrid glanced at Morag, and her mouth tightened. "I told ye the cave was cursed."

"It's not the cave. I'm already cursed with this stupid allergy." The warm air enveloped Morag like a blanket. Already, the tightness in her chest was easing.

"Still, I told ye no' to go in there, didn't I?"

Juliette sat behind Ingrid and spoke straight into the girl's ear. "You were right. There was a bear in there."

The result was electric. Ingrid's hands jerked on the wheel, and the freckles on her face stood out livid on her white skin. "A bear, ye say?"

"It was huge. With weird blue eyes."

"Tell them," Paul said. "Orkney doesn't have bears."

"Orkney doesn't have bears," Ingrid repeated robotically.

Two minutes later, the Land Rover skidded in front of Ingrid's house.

"Listen, everyone," Ingrid said. "No' a word about any of this. Ye can't tell my mum ye went in the cave. Don't even tell her ye went near it. Ye didn't listen about goin' in the cave, listen to me about this, aye?"

Everyone murmured in agreement.

The front door whipped open to reveal Pete and Ingrid's mother, her face drawn and angry.

"Hey, I feel better already," Morag said. "Maybe you could drop us off at the castle. I don't want to bother your mom."

"I'm no' allowed near the castle."

"Uh, it's a small island," Paul said. "Where exactly *are* you allowed to go around here?"

Hamish gave Paul a disgusted look.

Ingrid remained silent, lines of worry creasing her forehead. She eased the vehicle close to the door. Morag climbed out and walked the two feet to the front step. Something shiny glistened around the doorstep. More silver coins. Was Magnus, a doctor, not immune to island superstitions either?

As Morag came into the entryway, Pete hopped up and down. "What's wrong with your face?"

"Hush, child." Ingrid's mother began stripping off Morag's jacket.

The house, cluttered but clean, smelled of cooked sausage, fabric softener, and woodsmoke. Morag stepped into a lounge where a fire glowed. Magnus sat on the couch, dressed in a kilt and white blouse. He raised his cup of tea in greeting before a startled look crossed his features, and he leaped to his feet.

"Joyce. Epi-pen." He winced and shook spilled tea from his hand.

"No, I have an epi-pen with me, but I'm feeling much better. No wheezing, just hives. Uh, where's my mom?" Morag looked around as if her mother might be lurking behind one of the curtains.

"Screeverholme. Only had one patient on account of the ceilidh."

Relief poured over Morag, as warm as the heat pouring from the fireplace. Her mom would hear about the reaction. There was no avoiding that. But hopefully, she wouldn't see Morag in this state, which must be bad considering the way Joyce stared.

Water dripped from the ropes of Morag's hair onto the carpet. She pressed her curls against her jacket in an attempt to stop it.

"Ye're the lass allergic to cold, aye?" Joyce said. "Like Catherine's father." A look of revulsion crossed her face, but as Ingrid entered the room, she seemed to recover herself.

"Ingrid, go run Morag a hot bath. I'll make tea." As the others piled into the small room, Ingrid's mother did a quick headcount, and to her credit, didn't bat an eyelash at the cups of tea she'd need to make.

Ingrid led Morag up a narrow set of stairs. She opened a cupboard at the top and took out a fluffy turquoise towel before entering a bathroom with a cork floor and deep tub. She twisted on its tap with a squeak, and steam immediately wafted into the air.

"Go ahead and get in. I'll find ye some clothes." Ingrid studied Morag's obvious curves. "I think I've something that'll fit."

After stripping, Morag sank into the tub and watched the hot water wash away the hives. The aching itch dissolved, and the tightness in her throat eased. She put her warm hands on her cheeks and touched her eyes, where the swelling had disappeared. Good to know hot water was an instant cure. A few minutes later, Ingrid entered the bathroom carrying a pile of clothes and a cup of tea. Morag shrank down and tried to disappear into the water. Ingrid averted her eyes and set the cup of tea on the edge of the tub. She stopped at the door, her back to Morag.

"My dad will drive yer friends to the castle when they finish their tea and then take ye when ye're ready. Remember. Say nothin' about where ye've been today, aye?"

"I won't," Morag promised, humbled by Ingrid's hospitality.

Later, dressed in sweatpants and a long-sleeved T-shirt, she opened the bathroom door. A girl of seven or eight, with the same red hair as Ingrid, sat cross-legged in the hall, her back against the wall.

"Pete told me ye went to the cave," the little girl whispered. Ingrid either forgot to tell him to keep quiet, or he couldn't control himself. "Did ye see the Fin Folk?"

Whoa. The Fin Folk?

Morag slid down the wall to sit beside the girl, both of them considering the other. "Who are the Fin Folk?" The girl looked wary, but on a stroke of inspiration, Morag said, "Never mind. You're just a little kid. How much could *you* know?"

The girl crossed her arms and stuck out her bottom lip. "I know loads of things. I listen when my parents think I'm asleep."

The musical Orcadian accent coming out of a child delighted Morag, but she suppressed a smile and made herself sound doubtful. "Do you even know what they look like? Where they come from?"

"Of course, I do." She glanced to the stairs, where the voices of her mother and Ingrid drifted up.

Morag waited, not wanting to spook the girl out of talking. She did, however, fix her with a skeptical look.

"They come from the sea." The words darted out, hushed and lightning-fast, like silver fish through water. "They have long hands and feet, webbed like a duck, seaweed for hair, and sharp, sharp teeth."

Webbed feet, like the footprints. The girl's hands jerked in her lap, and she guiltily gnawed her lip. That didn't stop Morag from asking her more. "Do you know what they can do?"

Without warning, the girl leaped to her feet, dashed into her room, and a minute later, returned with a worn, old book. She stopped at the top of the stairs, peered down as if to check the coast was clear and placed the book carefully in Morag's lap. The girl flipped it open to a page with a drawing of a man with flippers for hands and feet, seaweed for hair, and glowing eyes. The opposite page showed a small rowboat, glowing eyes peering from the bow.

"They change shapes into anything. Boats, driftwood, fish." Or maybe a *bear?* The little girl's voice dropped to nothing more than a breath of sound. "And they can take ye into the sea. Forever."

The words undid much of the good of Morag's hot bath as a chill slipped over her scalp. Her fingers convulsed on the edge of the book, and she flipped to a page, quickly scanning the text describing Finfolkaheem, the underwater city of the Fin Folk. She wanted to read all of it cover to cover, but the girl shut the book and held out her hands.

"Give it back. Please. I'm no' supposed to show it to anyone, aye?"

Reluctantly, Morag handed it back. "That's a pretty scary story."

"It's no' just a story. And Ingrid says there's somethin' much scarier than the Fin Folk out there."

"Does it have horns?" Morag whispered.

The girl paled. "I can't say their name. Not ever."

"Tell me," Morag pleaded. "I saw a shadow in the castle graveyard. Are we in danger?"

"Bridget," Ingrid called upstairs. "Mum says ye have to go help set up for the ceilidh."

They both jumped. Bridget sprang up and put her finger to her lips. She disappeared into her room and returned without the book. With a flash of swinging red hair, she pounded downstairs.

In all the drama, Morag forgot about the ceilidh tonight. Fat chance Mom would let her go after this, but she'd do her best to convince her she felt fine. More than anything, she wanted to be around the people of Tullimentay, to see if she could glean more information about these Fin Folk. She didn't remember seeing this particular Orkney legend mentioned in any of the books in Screeverholme's library.

She remembered the ferry captain's expression when they supposedly hit the buoy. She'd seen the flipper-like prints in the hallway, seen Ben's reaction to the otter, and remembered the warnings from the islanders to stay away from the water. Ingrid had been terrified of the cave. The cave with its carvings of the flippered figure and the horned man.

What if the Fin Folk, insane as it sounded, might actually be real? Bridget's words haunted Morag.

And they can take ye into the sea. Forever.

Chapter 11

Morag's mom surprised her by putting up no resistance about the ceilidh since they'd be inside, only insisting Morag wear warm clothes. So while everyone else dressed up for the ceilidh, Morag looked ready for a polar expedition. Or maybe lunar exploration.

Juliette wore an empire-waist dress in vermilion that perfectly complemented her blonde hair. Ivy wore a button-down shirt and pants, as did the boys. Paul, in the spirit of the event, wore a red plaid tie that made him look grown-up and handsome. Morag, on the other hand, could hardly move under a coat, sweater, shirt, thermal underwear, two pairs of socks, and thick gloves. Her only concession to dressing up was the silver necklace Catherine had given her, hidden under the layers.

"There." Mom pulled a hat over Morag's ears and wrapped her face with the red scarf until only her eyes peeked out.

"You know I need to breathe," Morag said, but it came out, "Bbm fmm eee mmmfm."

The entryway filled with the rustle of people sliding into

waterproof jackets. James wore a green kilt with a leather jacket and carried his guitar case. Was he playing tonight?

Ben, in his kilt, stood by the door, and to Morag's surprise, also carried an instrument case—what looked to be a violin. Without even needing to hear it, Morag saw the copper violin notes shimmering in her mind. He'd agreed to drive her, Juliette, and Mom to the ceilidh.

Ben's eyes narrowed on James and his guitar case, and he turned to face Morag. "Ready?" he growled.

Morag waved goodbye to the group who'd be walking since *they* wouldn't die in a little rain. She held an umbrella aloft in the drizzle and raced across the bridge with Juliette and Mom. Ben strode along, craning to look over the bridge.

Watching for shapeshifting Fin Folk? Morag couldn't stop thinking about the bear in the cave. Bridget said they could change into anything.

Morag wanted to talk to Juliette about Bridget, but she couldn't with Ben and Mom around. Once they got in the car, Morag yanked her scarf down and gasped for air.

She caught Ben giving her a calculating look in the rearview mirror. "We don't have a piano player for our band. I've heard ye play," he said. "Interested?"

"I—I don't think so." The idea terrified her, especially since she had a propensity for falling off stages. "What kind of music do you play?"

"Ceilidh music, of course. Folk music. Mostly easy chords. I'm sure ye could handle it fine."

Mom turned around in the front passenger seat. "You should play, Morag."

"You totally should," Juliette said.

"Mm." Morag hoped the sound was noncommittal.

"Have ye ever been to a ceilidh?" Ben asked.

They all answered no.

"Then ye're in for a treat." Ben broke into the first real grin Morag had seen from him.

That had to be a good sign, right?

A group of men hunkered against the wind and rain outside the village hall, cupping cigarettes protectively like they held baby chicks in their hands. As Morag passed, she caught a snippet of conversation.

"—time of year. They're killing the sheep again."

"Aye," said another. "Got two of my flock day 'afore yesterday."

Morag remembered the dead sheep on the road that first night. Magnus said it had been hit by a car, but these men said *they were killing the sheep*. Who were *they?*

"Did you hear that?" Morag whispered to Juliette.

"What?" her friend said.

Ben held the door for them.

"Thanks for the ride, Ben," Mom said. "If you'll excuse me, I need to help Joyce with the food." She hurried in through the open door.

"Ben?" Morag said. "Did those men say something was killing their sheep?"

Something unreadable crossed Ben's face so quickly, Morag might have imagined it. "Sometimes a rogue dog kills a lamb or two. Now can we stop with the conspiracies for once, Miss Davidson, and enjoy a nice evening? In ye go."

Could it be a dog killing sheep? Morag had seen that bear herself. She tried to shake off the chill skittering down her spine and stepped inside where recorded music played.

Most of the island had come, though it still wasn't enough to fill the large hall. At the far end, the band was setting up next to a piano on the dark stage. A bald man hefted an accordion strap over his shoulder. Another man with a thick beard settled himself at a drum set, and one picked up a mandolin. The woman next to them blew a few notes on a flute-like instrument causing Morag to see pewter cylinders dropping from the air like rain. The flute player waved at Ben. He headed over, stopping to kiss an attractive young woman with more passion than Morag would've expected, and joined the band.

People, many dressed in tartan, congregated at one end of the hall. Joyce burst through a swinging kitchen door with plates and brought them to a nearby table, raising cheers. Her mom grabbed a platter of small pies off a pass-through counter to the kitchen. One table held kegs of beer and an army of pint glasses.

Folding chairs lined the room. A little boy and girl sat backward on them, hanging their heads upside down until their hair touched the floor. The girl's skirt flipped over her face to reveal pink underwear, and the boy laughed until his mother noticed.

"Thorfinn, stop that."

The kitchen door swung open again on a yell. Catherine's lab, Duncan, slunk out, wolfing something down and shaking his head in the way of foolish dogs eating too-hot food.

In one corner, Ingrid talked with a couple of teenagers. She waved at Morag and Juliette but looked deep in conversation.

"Should we go over there?" Morag said, but Juliette's shy shrug said no.

Catherine stopped scolding Duncan to come greet them, the dog trundling along beside her.

"Hallo, Morag." Catherine took Morag's hand and squeezed it. "Who's this lovely lassie ye've brought?"

Morag introduced Juliette, which Duncan took with great formality, licking her hand.

"Ye're wearin' yer necklace?" Catherine asked.

The urgency in the question disturbed Morag. "Yeah." She pulled the necklace out from her layers to show her. "Thank you again."

"Och, it's nothing." Catherine leaned in closer. "As long as ye promise to always wear it."

Juliette shared a puzzled look with Morag, and Catherine hastily added, "Free advertising for my jewelry, ye see." She dashed back to the kitchen as fast as her limp allowed.

"That was weird," Juliette said.

"This necklace is silver. Like the coins." Excitement washed through Morag. "I think Catherine gave me this for protection."

"From what, exactly? And why only you?"

Morag shrugged. "Maybe because we're sort of related?" In whispered tones, Morag told Juliette everything Bridget said that afternoon about the Fin Folk and the other, scarier thing she couldn't name.

Juliette traced the beading on the bodice of her dress in a nervous gesture. "Probably just a bunch of stories to scare kids." She sounded like she was trying to reassure herself rather than believed it was true.

They stood around awkwardly and watched the schoolteacher show a young girl some steps on the dance floor. As the teacher spun around and spotted Morag, she stepped in front of the girl as if to shield her. Oblivious, the girl tugged at Mrs. Heddle's hand, but the woman slipped away and headed straight for Morag and Juliette.

Everyone in the room watched the teacher stop directly in front of Morag. "How old are ye, lass?"

Morag gulped. "Sixteen."

"I hadn't realized ye were as old as all that. Ye're a wee bit old for the solstice fête, so ye needn't worry about coming, aye?"

"Uh, okay. I was going—"

The woman pivoted on her heel and marched back onto the dance floor. All around the room, people snuck glances in their direction.

"Did you just get *un*invited to the solstice celebration?" Juliette's mouth pursed with indignation. "Rude."

Morag sensed the thread of tension in the room. Some people whispered behind their hands at one another, while sending looks their way. "There's a *lot* of rude and strange behavior going on around here."

"Catherine's nice." Juliette flashed a bright smile, trying, as always, to stay positive, and Morag bit back any further comments.

The band was warming up when the rest of the Gaspars and Bacons arrived. Paul joined Morag, and her pulse tripped. Mom came out of the kitchen to say hello.

"Hey." Hamish spread out his arms. "Where's the beer?" Mom smacked him as people continued regarding them, the obvious outsiders.

"Hello, everyone." James stepped forward and lifted his hand in greeting. The appearance of a leather-clad American teenager in a kilt with facial piercings ratcheted up the staring to murmuring. He started toward the band, hefting up his guitar, and addressed the man with the accordion. "Still okay for me to join in?"

"If ye think ye can play ceilidh music," boomed the man. "And we'll soon see about that." He waved James over with a welcoming grin and blasted a few merry notes on his accordion, overwhelming Morag with concentric purple circles. The band resumed its warm-up, and the tension in the room broke.

A group of people swept Morag along the tables where something called an Orkney pattie was shoved in her hand. Pints got passed around, and Morag ended up holding a beer until Mom plucked it away. More people gathered on the floor to try dance steps, bursting into laughter. Morag bit into the patty. Delicious, deep-fried meat and potato filled her mouth. After a suitable time for eating, the accordion player stepped in front of a microphone. The small crowd stampeded from the table to bunch near the stage.

The big man cleared his throat. "Name's Crusher. I'd like to welcome our visitors from the States." He raised a glass and took a drink. "Ah. Music is thirsty work."

"Ye havena played anythin' yet," pointed out one helpful person.

"*Thinkin'* about playin' is thirsty work. That was only a *peedie* sip. Let's toast our guests. To new friends." He gulped his beer in several swallows and wiped his mouth with the back of his hand.

"To new friends," they echoed, some laughing while others exchanged uncomfortable glances.

"We've a young lad here," Crusher continued, "who says he's listened to some 'Scottish folk music.'" His giant fingers did air quotes. "So's he's thinkin' he can join right in. What d'ye think? Should we let him?"

James wriggled into his guitar strap and saluted the crowd.

Paul groaned. "He's going to suck, isn't he?"

"Aye, or no?" Crusher asked.

"No," Paul muttered under his breath.

Ingrid's friend, a willowy brunette girl, watched James with hungry eyes and shouted "Aye!" louder than any of them.

"Right, then. The lad plays. Do try to keep up." Crusher shared a conspiratorial wink with the crowd and launched into a lively polka. A pleasant rainbow of dots, like confetti, bounced around in Morag's head.

Attempting to cross the room, she landed in the middle of a jostling country dance. She and Paul squeezed through until they reached the safety of the chairs and sat.

Ben's bow flew over his violin at a feverish pitch. The woman with the flute bobbed her head, filling the hall with piercing notes. Everyone clapped. James strummed along. He'd peeled off his jacket to a black T-shirt, revealing his tattoos. Standing in a pool of golden light, he worked his fingers on the fretboard, and the muscles of his left forearm jumped as he fought to keep up with the band.

Ingrid's friend was still watching him with that hungry look, and Morag experienced an inexplicable stab of jealousy.

Paul studied the scene, no doubt analyzing every detail. "Can you imagine being part of such a rich cultural heritage? What do we have back home? Football?"

Crusher stopped playing. The flute dropped out, then the drums and mandolin. With the blaring accordion gone, only Ben's violin and James's guitar remained, a delightful combination of copper and gold. Crusher slid a microphone down on its stand and placed it in front of the guitar for James.

Morag couldn't imagine having attention focused on her like that.

Ben's violin sang, the guitar thrummed, and the crowd danced with the frantic energy created by this musical battle. At last, Ben tipped his head in a bow and stopped so James played alone.

"Show-off," Paul said quietly, while Juliette sent Morag an impressed look.

James clearly felt music like Morag did. He bent the notes to his will, keeping the tune distinctly Scottish and building to a crescendo. With three final strums, the song ended.

The crowd exploded into applause and cheers.

"That's my boy!" Gary shouted.

While Morag might've been embarrassed by that kind of parental outburst, James grinned at his dad.

Ben grabbed the microphone, and his eyes found Morag sitting at the edge of the room. "I'd like to invite another new friend up here to play." He pointed. "Aye, Morag. We need a piano for our next song, and ye've the talent for it."

Paul raised his eyebrows at her in question.

"Go on, Mor. Get up there." Juliette shoved her.

James held out his arm toward the piano and gave her an encouraging smile while the entire hall waited in silence, all eyes on her. Catherine nodded at Morag, her parents gave her a cheesy thumbs-up, but for some reason, it was the sight of the squinty-eyed Mrs. Heddle that propelled her onto the stage.

Ben gave her a few minutes to glance over the music while people took a quick break for more food. Her pulse slowed as she recognized the color themes of the songs. She could do this. Hidden among the notes of the sheet music was a stunning jumble of browns, reds, and golds, like toasted marshmallows, Irish setters, and aspen leaves in autumn.

Without preamble, Crusher counted them in. "One, two— one, two, three."

She struggled with the first few measures until she stopped fighting the music and let the colors wash over her. The accordion's purple and the violin's copper meshed with the gorgeous golden guitar and the red and brown of the song itself until a tapestry wove through her ears, her eyes, between her fingers on the keys. The threads of color kept perfect time, and the sound of people's feet stomping on the floor took on its own sand-colored vibration underneath.

Morag was compelled to join in wordless song. Her voice created another layer of harmony. The colors stood out more vividly, the shapes more sharply defined than any synesthetic sensations she'd ever had. As with James, the others dropped out until it was only the piano and Morag's strong voice. Lost in the music, in the synergy of the musicians around her, she forgot to be nervous. The shapes and patterns morphed into actual images of Orkney, of the island, of the crashing waves, and Screeverholme, as clear as a film in her mind.

When she brought the song to a close, the crowd stood silent and transfixed for a few long moments until erupting into another round of loud applause and whistles.

Unexpected laughter spilled from Morag, and she blinked back tears at the pure undiluted joy of being one with the music, one with her synesthesia, one with the people in the room.

"Isn't she great?" Crusher said. "Take a bow, Morag."

She ducked her head and bobbed a curtsy, wiping away a tear.

Hamish shouted, "That's my sister!" and everyone laughed.

The next song was a lively sea shanty that had everyone singing. Morag played another half-hour until the first break. She didn't understand it, but the music flowed from her of its own accord, so she didn't even have to think.

During the break, Crusher pulled her aside. "As far as I'm concerned, ye're welcome to join us anytime. Now, go. Dance." He shoved Morag in the back with his ham-hock hand and sent her flying.

The crowd welcomed her with cheers and outstretched hands. Crusher called the steps of Strip the Willow and the Dashing White Sergeant. Sweating and smiling, everyone around her in the same state, Morag couldn't remember what it felt like to be cold. Paul threw himself into the dancing with unexpected enthusiasm. His face flushed as he whipped Morag around by the arm. She threaded her way down the line of dancers and barely recognized her mom when she passed. Her whole face was glowing with something Morag didn't see often anymore.

Happiness.

Morag ducked under the lifted arms of Hamish and Ingrid. Belting out a laugh, Ivy hooked her arm through Morag's, Paul grabbed the other, and they spun in a circle with several others. Crusher shouted out the steps until he was hoarse.

At the next break, the crowd staggered like drunken sailors to the kegs. Morag gulped water by the pint and enjoyed watching one of the girls in Ingrid's group try and fail to flirt with Ivy, who was probably texting her girlfriend. The sun finally set, and while gloom pressed in at the windows, it couldn't get in. Laughter rang out. Arms were thrown around shoulders. Gary practiced a funny jig with an elderly man. Françoise joined Joyce in serving cups of tea to those not drinking beer—or those who'd drunk too much. Mom collapsed in a chair and fanned herself, and Dad gave her a goofy grin.

James caught Morag's eye and sent her his crooked smile, their gazes locked with the secret look of two people who'd shared something magical. Heat, thick and sweet as sun-warmed honey, filled her.

Crusher got the crowd back under control with a sad, slow song, and the crowd joined in. The heavy Orcadian dialect, sprinkled with Norse words, made the lyrics incomprehensible, but Morag couldn't miss the longing in the music. The Americans understood the song in their own way, humming and swaying in the press of people. Camaraderie overtook Morag, a feeling of goodwill for everyone united in this single, exquisite moment.

As the evening drew to a close, parents carried sleeping children and murmured farewells. A few people came over to shake hands with Morag and the rest of their group. Françoise and Joyce kissed on the cheeks, James high-fived a white-haired man, and everyone couldn't stop smiling.

It hit Morag. Music was the cultural language of Orkney, the way to their hearts. She was fluent in it. She and James spoke it to the islanders tonight. Though the people of Tullimentay might have been suspicious of the newcomers, they hadn't been able to resist the music James and Morag played, and they'd won over more than a few with it.

She pulled on her scarf, trapping the warmth of the hall against her skin, and stepped out into the chilly night unscathed.

Morag hastily got into pajamas before the cold seeped in. Malcolm dashed to the window and meowed, drawing her over to the open shutters. Once more, her feet settled into the indentations in the stone.

What compelled people to stand here staring out the windows for centuries? The sea? Or something *in* the sea? Apprehension coiled in her gut like a waiting snake as she thought of the Fin Folk again, of Bridget's words, of the impossible giant bear she and Juliette had seen.

Moonlight glimmered off the water in wavering silver paths. She propped her foot on her knee and pulled on a thick sock, unable to tear her gaze from the unending gray sea and twinkling starlight, weak in the incomplete darkness.

Green light exploded in the water. Streaks of green and

yellow raced outward from the center of the explosion, as fast as shooting stars, and filled Morag with an inexplicable terror. The moonlight shimmered on the black sea once more as if nothing had happened. Her fingers curled around the shutter. Copepods no longer made sense as an explanation for these lights. Morag waited to see them again until the cold wind snuck around the edges of the window. She slammed the shutters closed and climbed into bed. Malcolm leaped up to curl in a ball by her feet.

With an effort of will, she shoved away the lights, the bear in the cave, horned men, dead sheep, and Fin Folk. Instead, she let her mind replay the music of the evening, an experience she never would have had without the urging of Ben or the encouragement of James. She couldn't believe she'd played the piano in front of a group of people. Played songs she'd never seen, no less, and sang her wordless music.

This place was getting to her. Orkney was changing her. The loneliness, the eternal expanse of sky and sea, the isolation. The haunting landscape, beautiful as it was, inspired a longing for connection with people.

And she'd never connected with anyone like she had playing music with others tonight. She hadn't known how much she'd craved that connection, but now that the hunger was awakened, she'd have to feed it somehow.

She turned on her side to face the nightstand where her sketchbook lay, an accusing blank rectangle of white in the darkness. She waited for the guilt to flood in over those empty pages, but it didn't arrive.

Which was almost as strange as everything else happening here.

Chapter 12

Morag opened her shutters to a clear sky. The sparkling blue sea made it hard to remember how it was last night— black, menacing, and exploding with strange lights. Harder still to imagine she'd seen a huge bear in the cave. The more time passed, the more it took on a surreal, dream-like quality.

Morag was the last to arrive in the kitchen. She inserted herself into the mealtime chaos to butter an English muffin.

"Turns out you were wrong, Hamish," Mom said. "There *is* a beach here. With real sand and everything. South side of the island if you're interested."

"Looks like a great day for it." Gary stood at the back door sipping coffee and watching Pete play with his toy cars on the kitchen floor.

A plan was made, and an hour later, their group headed across the island on foot. The weather was kind enough to let Morag get away with wearing only a long-sleeved shirt and jeans. Not a whisper of wind touched them. Beyond the village, the sea lay like a mirror, its surface reflecting a few clouds in the blue sky. Seagulls screamed, sending stars spinning across Morag's vision. She closed her eyes and inhaled the salty air, warm and soft. When she opened them, Mom was smiling at her, and for once, her smile didn't hide any other strain or concern.

"There's the seal skerry, Pete." James pointed out a large, humped rock in the water, covered in seals.

Low bluffs sloped gently to the beach. Where the bluffs smoothed out flat to meet the sea, the dyke continued, providing the barrier for the sheep. People were doing something to the wall in the distance. Along the bluffs, the village hosted a craft fair, busy with people taking advantage of the weather. Morag had never seen so many people on Tullimentay as she and the others walked the narrow street lined with booths of food and crafts.

"Hey, ferry loupers." Crusher raised his hand in greeting. His accordion hung off his broad chest by a strap, and he wore a black fedora. The rest of the musicians from last night, including Ben, were setting up chairs under a canopy. "Come and join us."

Morag and James made their way to Crusher while the others trailed behind to peruse the wares being sold.

"What are ferry loupers?" Morag remembered Ben using the term before.

"Och, don't be mindin' him," the flute player said. "He means it affectionately. It means people who aren't local. Plenty of those here today visiting from all over Scotland and maybe even"—she gave a fake shudder—"England." She laughed, and Morag joined her.

Crusher slapped James on the back and tipped his hat at Morag. "Would ye like to play with us again? Tomorrow afternoon in the hall at two?"

She lifted her eyebrows at James.

He smiled at her. "I'm in. Morag?"

"Yeah." She flashed a shy smile at the musicians.

Crusher shoved a CD in her hand. "Orkney music. On the house." A table beside him was covered in CDs selling for ten pounds. "Bring those songs back to the States, won' ye, Morag? We need to keep our music alive."

She wasn't sure how she'd play the CD. Crusher must have read the uncertainty on her face and handed her a flyer as well, which gave her a website and their YouTube music channel. "Listen to that tonight. Tomorrow, we'll teach ye more." Behind him the musicians readied themselves.

Crusher plopped down on his chair, and he and the others began a rousing reel. Morag's head filled with rowdy tessellations of yellow and red squares. She breathed in the music like a scent until she realized James watched her.

"They really liked us," he said as they walked on. "It was easy to play music with them." He turned his hand sideways and slid it through the air. "Like we just slotted into the band."

"I know." Morag stopped at a stall where a woman spun wool on a wooden spinning wheel. Thick sweaters hung near a sign that said *Made with local wool*. Morag bought one. It was expensive but looked so warm, it would be worth every penny.

When Morag returned with the sweater, Mom stood in the middle of their group, her brow furrowed. "The weirdest thing happened. This woman told me we should all leave before the solstice—before it's too late for us."

"What?" Morag thought of how Mrs. Heddle uninvited her to the solstice fête.

"She must be crazy."

Pete yelled, "The beach! The beach!" He raced past the last stall and sprinted to the staircase leading to the bay. Everyone followed, the sight distracting Morag from Mom's disturbing story.

The turquoise water lapped at the soft sand. It was as though Morag had been transported to a different island. They finished laying out blankets when a shout rose from the other beachgoers. Morag followed their points and gasped. The menacing black dorsal fins of a pod of killer whales sliced through the glassy water close enough to hear the sibilant *fwoosh* from their blowholes as they surfaced. Their gleaming black and white bodies caused the quivering notes of panpipes to play in her mind.

"Incredible." Ivy grabbed Juliette and danced them across the sand, throwing back her head with a laugh to reveal her tongue ring, sparkling in the sunlight.

Morag's chest expanded on a deep breath of fresh sea air, filling her lungs and heart with a wild exhilaration. Everyone on the beach watched the whales' passage, and they surfaced a few more times before veering toward the open sea. The apex predators of the ocean slid through the water and disappeared.

She thought again of what the farmer had said on their walk to the cave, and it took the luster off her joy.

There's all manner of dangerous things in the water.

The adults spread out their blankets a good distance away. James and Ivy were making a sandcastle with Pete near the water. Morag took the opportunity to share with the others her conversation with Bridget yesterday. When she finished, she shot a look at Paul, readying herself for his dismissal.

Paul let a handful of sand run through his fingers and said just what she'd expected. "Island superstition."

Morag didn't agree with Paul, but she couldn't stop herself from downplaying the conversation. "Bridget was helpful with all that info because I'm making my art portfolio about Orkney mythology. Like that cave drawing of the horned man."

"Morag." Hamish sat up on his towel. "This isn't mythology. Something real is going on."

Paul harumphed and tossed a handful of sand in his direction. "Where's your proof?"

Morag wouldn't mind some solid proof herself. If only she'd thought to take a photo of the footprints or the bear.

"Dude, my proof is we poked around in a graveyard, and

then a demon-man showed up in my room."

"Fine. I'll go poke around in there again and see if the demon-man makes another appearance." Paul crossed his arms over his chest. "I'll even stay up all night waiting for it."

"Sure, if you're the world's biggest dumb ass," Hamish said.

Juliette's eyebrows drew together. "You said you wouldn't go in the graveyard again."

Paul dusted the sand from his hands. "I'd love to do a rubbing of those engravings in the stone."

Hamish made a rude comment about rubbings, which Paul ignored.

"I'd love a photo of the runes to send to a university for translation," Paul said. He gave Hamish a pointed look. "And going in the burial mound is a good way to prove there's nothing to fear."

Morag touched Paul's arm. "I don't think you should go in there."

Paul groaned. "Not you, too."

Morag knew he wouldn't listen to her fears and tried a different approach. "It's like Juliette said. We promised Ben not to go in the graveyard again."

"I don't remember making that promise."

No, Morag had. She argued some more with Paul, but he was stubborn, and she gave up. Despite Hamish getting the nice beach he wanted, complete with one brave woman in a bikini, he got bored and suggested a walk farther along to see what was happening at the sheep dyke. The Bacons abandoned their sandcastle to join them. James and Ivy held Pete's hands and lifted him high into the air. Paul picked up a piece of thick, white shell and examined it. Yesterday, Morag might have found this behavior endearing, but today it irritated her.

"Isn't that your girlfriend?" Paul said to Hamish as they approached.

Sure enough, Ingrid, Bridget, and their parents were busy working on the wall, along with several other families. It had suffered some damage like a giant carelessly bashed its way through. Flat stones spilled everywhere, blending in with rocks on the beach. A few nearby sheep let out plaintive bleats, as though disappointed their chance at freedom was blocked.

"Hamish, isn't that your *girlfriend?*" Paul repeated the question loudly enough Ingrid's dad whipped his head in their direction and started over.

"Paul, come on. Stop." Juliette played with the ribbons on her tunic shirt and eyed the two boys.

"You're dead." Hamish used his scary-calm voice.

"Ooo, I'm so scared." Paul shook with mock fear.

Hamish rushed toward Paul, but Magnus stepped in front of him and put his hand on Hamish's chest.

"Ye look like a strong lad with youthful energy. Why don't ye lend us a hand?" Magnus sounded stern but had a twinkle in his eye.

James bent at once and picked up a flat rock. "Whoa. Heavier than I expected."

Paul snorted and picked up a rock, disguising his stagger with a big step.

"What happened here?" Morag asked.

"Collapsed," Magnus said unhelpfully.

Thorfinn, the little boy who'd hung off the chair at the ceilidh, popped up from a rock like a jack-in-the-box. "It was a wolf."

Pete dropped James's hand and ran over to his new friend.

Thorfinn turned to Pete. "The wolf got that sheepie." He pointed at a humped shape under a nearby tarp. Pete squatted down with Thorfinn, and they both studied the blood-stained fabric with twin looks of morbid fascination.

Morag's throat tightened at the sight, recalling the men's conversation outside the hall at the ceilidh and that dead sheep in the road.

"Thorfinn," said his mother. "Ye ken well enough that poor animal got hit by a car."

"It *was* a wolf."

"That's enough."

"It was. I saw it last night." Thorfinn threw his arm in the direction of the stone houses by the street fair. "From my window. It was huge. Smashed right through the rocks and killed that sheepie and scared all the others."

"There are no wolves in Orkney," his mother said. "This old wall gets battered all the time by storms. Now mind me and leave it be."

The boy crossed his arms and stuck out his lower lip.

"Wanna play?" Pete pulled on Thorfinn's arm.

The two boys ran off and the adults, rather than looking amused at Thorfinn's overactive imagination, exchanged concerned looks that set off Morag's weirdness radar. She and Juliette also exchanged a look. They'd seen a bear themselves, so why couldn't this boy have seen a wolf? Was she supposed to believe the islanders were such terrible drivers they hit sheep at this rate? That poorly behaved dogs were snatching them left and right?

A tiring half-hour of stacking stones crawled by. Hamish wiped the back of his arm over his sweaty forehead and bent to examine the dirt at their feet.

"What are you doing? Morag asked.

"Looking for wolf prints. You saw that bear"—Hamish sent her a meaningful look, and she nodded in acknowledgment that he believed her—"and Thorfinn saw that wolf. We all know something strange is going on, and we need proof. And not by going back in that barron." Hamish pointed at Paul in warning. "I mean it."

"You mean barrow," Paul said, his expression bored.

"Man, whatever. You're such a—"

Before they could find out what exactly Paul was, an ungodly racket from the bluffs interrupted them. It was hard to tell at this distance whether it was shrieks of laughter or people being tortured.

"What in holy hell is that?" Hamish shrank back from

Joyce's disapproving squint.

Suddenly, Joyce's face melted into a wide smile. "Magnus, it's Iain and Freyja's blackening."

Magnus grinned and set his stone on the wall. "I forgot, what with this wall business. Let's go and see."

"Blackening?" Hamish asked Ingrid. "You don't burn people alive here or anything?"

Ingrid shoved him. "It's a tradition here before people get married."

They trotted up the bluffs where an old farm truck stopped. Sitting on the tailgate were two people in overalls covered in something sticky and black with a fair amount of what looked to be flour, cornflakes, and possibly cooked spaghetti stuck all over them. The bride and groom-to-be wore smiles that glowed white on their mucky faces. Behind them, people stood in the back of the truck. They were shouting, whistling, and banging on drums. Most everyone from the beach and people in the houses had come to witness the spectacle.

"Gross." Ivy shot Morag a look of delight. "What's on them?" Ivy had to shout over the banging drums and ruckus of drunken people.

"Treacle," Ingrid said. "Like molasses."

Mom made gingerbread cookies with molasses every Christmas. Morag found it nearly impossible to clean the sticky substance off the measuring cups. She couldn't imagine being covered in anything worse.

"And a goodly amount of cow shite," Magnus added.

Okay, that was worse. Morag snorted, and Ivy burst out laughing.

"Wow," Hamish said. "You guys need some new traditions. What's wrong with taking a guy to a casino or something?"

"When you can tar and feather people?" James said.

Joyce sniffed. "This teaches the couple humility. That they can face any trouble together."

"And it's good fun for everyone else," Magnus said.

In demonstration, a man burst from a house and pelted the couple with eggs. The groom jumped off the back of the slow-moving truck, ran over to the egg-bearer, and hugged him, covering him in treacle mess as well. Everyone howled with laughter.

"I hope they aren't getting married any time soon," Juliette said. "That must take days to clean up."

"Oh, they won't be getting married until well after the *simmer dim,* of course," Joyce said.

Morag's ears perked at this strange declaration. "Why's that?"

Joyce froze. "Oh. Erm, well, no solstice weddings. Unlucky." She hurried over to the truck to heckle the couple.

Bears. Wolves. Fin Folk. Superstitions about the solstice.

Someone on the truck dumped another bucket of treacle over the groom's head. Every time Morag turned around, things got a wee bit stranger. Only she suspected not all of them were as harmless as this messy tradition.

The weather held until the next evening when the wind picked up again. Morag's new sweater kept her toasty as she walked back to the castle with James, swinging his guitar case. They were both riding the high of an afternoon playing music with the islanders. Morag's wordless singing had been a hit again with the other musicians, who were curious about her style of vocalizations. Ben offered surprisingly warm encouragement for her to pursue her odd singing. Morag was still so excited about the music that she hadn't thought of the Fin Folk or the horned man or the bear in the cave once the entire afternoon.

"I love the music here." James's black eyes sparkled with happiness.

"Me too. The colors in the music are amazing. I get pictures in my head I've never seen before—" She stopped herself. Her face warmed. "I'm sorry. I sound like a lunatic."

James slowed. "No. I'd love to hear what you mean."

She told him about her synesthesia, the way her brain mixed everything. "When I was younger, I wasn't as good at hiding it. Sometimes I'd grab at the air to try to catch the shapes floating by. Kids made fun of me."

"It's that real?"

"I think I have extra vivid synesthesia. Makes me look like a space cadet."

"I never noticed. Could be you're hyper-conscious of it."

She watched her feet instead of James. "This guy back home calls me Moron the Hallucino-Girl."

James laughed. "Wow, he's so jealous."

Morag met his gaze, and now the tips of her ears burned. "Jealous?"

"Yeah. *I'm* jealous." He offered a crooked grin, and at the flash of dimples, Morag's heart did a funny somersault. "To experience music on a whole new level like that, and you don't even need drugs?" He raised his finger. "Don't do drugs, by the way. They're bad for you."

"And you know this from experience?"

"Are you kidding? This body is a temple." James gestured at his facial piercings and ran his hand down his tattooed arm.

Morag laughed, but her brain caught on the image of *her* hand running down his arm. With a guilty pang, she thought of Paul and forced herself to concentrate on the conversation.

"Anyway, I think your synesthesia is cool as hell," James said. Another flash of that dimple and another flip-flop in her chest.

Morag let his opinion soak in, surprised at how much it mattered. "Yeah, well. It makes music easy for me, but also super hard since it scrambles the music sometimes."

"You did fine this afternoon. Crusher and Fiona loved you. Even Ben was smiling."

"It's the Orkney music. It all comes together perfectly in my mind here."

"Yeah, this place is amazing." He nodded at Screeverholme rising ahead.

She drank in the sight of the castle, perched on the island. Movement then drew her attention to the smaller tower where Ben lived. A black canine shape slunk along the wall and disappeared around the corner. "James. Did you see that?"

"What?"

"Okay, this sounds crazy, but I saw a huge wolf walking along that tower."

"That kid got to you yesterday." James nudged her with his elbow and laughed.

"I'm serious."

His eyebrows drew together. "Okay. Could it have been a dog?"

"No, it was massive." She squinted at the shadows of the castle walls but saw nothing. "I—I must have imagined it."

"Yeah? You sure?" James ducked his head to look at her face.

"Yeah." She *must* have imagined it. There and gone again, a play of the light. She hesitated to step onto the bridge and swept her gaze over the castle and surrounding sea. She spotted Ben in his rowboat rounding the far side of the castle. What was he doing?

She hated herself for it, but Morag cowered behind James as they stepped onto the bridge. It seemed to take an eternity to reach the castle, and once they did, she found something as disturbing as the wolf. A note nailed to the castle door, flapping in the wind.

Leave this island before it's too late. Tullochs are a curse to us all. You're not wanted here.

James read over her shoulder. "Whoa. Not cool."

Only one person on the island knew Morag's family was related to the Tullochs, and she didn't think Catherine would betray her. She ripped the paper from the nail and turned to James. "Why would someone do this?"

"A bad joke?"

Which turned out to be exactly what the adults said. All except Morag's mom who remembered the lady from the day before.

"Someone wants us gone," she muttered.

It wasn't a comforting thought.

Chapter 13

Over the next few days, Morag and the others enjoyed some walks, a trip to Catherine's shop, Ivy's horror movie marathon, Snooker championships, and a whole-castle game of hide and seek when they couldn't find Paul for a full hour when he seemed to vanish. She knuckled down on her portfolio, fighting back panic that none of her drawings were very good. Her best one was James playing guitar, but since it had nothing to do with her portfolio's theme, she kept it hidden.

She and James fit in a couple more music sessions with Crusher and his band, and Crusher hoped to do a recording together soon.

A cold front moved in, and the clouds hung around the horizon like bored teenagers looking for trouble. At breakfast, all three families squeezed onto the long benches at the kitchen table, James on one side of Morag and Juliette on the other.

The Bacons announced that Mr. Murray, a white-haired man at the ceilidh, invited them onto his fishing boat for a trip around the island. He'd sighted the killer whales again, and if they hurried, they could see them before the storm moved in.

"See?" James bumped his shoulder against Morag. "Our music got us all kinds of invites and connections."

Our music. Something confusing fluttered in Morag's chest.

Paul's face appeared outside the window before he quickly ducked down. Not fast enough. Françoise slammed her coffee cup on the counter and ripped open the door. "Paul. What are you doing out here?"

Paul stepped in, blond head held high, and fixed Morag with a meaningful look. "I only did a rubbing of the engravings on the stone by the burial mound."

Oh, Paul, you idiot. Thank God Hamish wasn't down yet.

Françoise put her hands on her slim hips. "You're not to go in there again. Ben would be so angry."

Paul didn't take his gaze from Morag. "It won't hurt anything. You'll see. *Nothing* will happen. I got what I wanted so I won't go back again."

Françoise might've said more, but it got lost in the commotion of scraping benches as people left to prepare for the outing. Morag tried to tamp down her annoyance with Paul for inviting trouble.

She dressed in warm clothes and black jeans she hoped James would appreciate. Why was she even thinking that? When she returned downstairs, her parents stood in the entry with their arms crossed.

Uh-oh. A united front.

"Your mother and I discussed it," Dad said. "We don't think it's a good idea for you to go. The wind will be—"

"You disagree with everything Mom says, but *now* you side with her?"

She regretted the words the second they left her mouth. Her dad's face crumpled before rearranging itself to neutral. Worse, James stumbled onto the scene. His darting eyes revealed he sensed the tension.

"Do you want to have an attack out on the water?" Mom

asked.

"I'll be fine. I've got my epi-pen and pills." Morag considered her mom's question though and imagined herself on a boat with her throat closing and—no, she wouldn't go there again. "I haven't had even a hint of hives in days."

"Morag, no. If you keep arguing, I'll—I'll—"

"What? Ground me? You've basically already done that. Sorry, Mom. You got no leverage."

"Watch your tone, young lady."

"Mom." She snuck a look at James, who busied himself tying his Doc Martens.

Mom put her hand on Morag's arm. "I know it's disappointing, but we want to keep you safe, Sweetie."

She hid her face in her hands and wished James weren't here for this. She was only snapping at her parents because she knew they were right. It wasn't her best moment.

"We'll stay here with you," Dad said. "So you don't have to be alone."

"No. I'll use the time to work on my portfolio. Besides, isn't Ben always around?"

"Not today." Her mother raised her eyebrows. "He's at his girlfriend's in the village."

Ben was gone. She thought of that large lupine shape skulking around the tower, and she suddenly didn't like the idea of being alone in Screeverholme.

"I can see you don't want us to leave." Dad's reasonable, patient voice provoked Morag into contrary stubbornness.

"Seriously. Go. No one else should miss out on life because of *my* problem." The self-pity sounded pathetic, so she forced a smile for their sake.

"Well, if you're sure."

"I am." She wasn't, but she'd never let on in front of James.

Her parents gave her strict instructions to stay inside and fussed over her as Françoise joined them in the entry. As humiliating as it was, Morag enjoyed her parents agreeing about something.

Mom wrung her hands. "If you have any trouble, it's going to be hard to get back here quickly."

"The island is not that big." Françoise slipped on a pair of gloves. "I have Joyce's number. If Morag has any trouble, she can call." She handed Morag a slip of paper.

Mom sighed. "All right."

Morag smiled when Dad linked his fingers through Mom's, and Mom didn't pull away.

Everyone crowded the entryway, and chaos briefly ensued until the door slammed shut. A booming silence followed in their wake.

Morag wandered toward the library with the good intention of doing a Fin Folk sketch. Her footsteps echoed in the empty castle, and she pushed open the library door with a creak to find the dim room filled with shadows.

Her sketchbook lay on the end table, but the piano beckoned instead. She needed noise to distract her from the oppressive silence. She'd practice some of the songs for Crusher's recording. Lively ceilidh music would drive away any fear. For a while, it worked, as the colors in her mind guided her hands over the keys, but all at once, it scared Morag when she couldn't hear anything except the piano. She stopped playing and strained her ears.

Only the grandfather clock ticked in the corner.

What was she thinking letting everyone leave her alone for the day to knock about in a centuries-old castle on an isolated island?

She shut the piano hard enough the hammers jangled on the piano strings. "Sorry." She smoothed her hand over the closed keyboard. Whistling for bravado, she went into the kitchen to make tea and toast. Something scratched at the back door, and her chest tightened, but the noise was followed by a loud meow. She opened the door, and Malcolm streaked in like a silver bullet with a poofy tail. Morag leaned out and glanced around the graveyard but didn't see anything out of the ordinary. Her gaze traveled to the barrow.

Where Paul had been poking around just this morning.

She hastily shut the door when something thumped. Morag whipped her head around, and Malcolm hissed. It sounded like it came from the floor above. Maybe something fell in a wardrobe upstairs.

Morag swallowed hard and cocked her head to listen. The sky darkened as a cloud moved in front of the sun. Another soft thump. Then another. Footsteps. Malcolm arched his back, his golden eyes fixed on the ceiling. She gripped her cup of tea, taking comfort from the warm ceramic.

"Ben?" Maybe he'd returned to Screeverholme. "Is that you?"

The footsteps stopped directly overhead. She stared at the spiral stone staircase leading upstairs.

Or down to her.

Morag snatched the poker from the kitchen hearth. She felt simultaneously safer holding it and more frightened. She could go upstairs and investigate. If she were *insane*. She stood in the kitchen, tea in one hand, iron poker in the other, and waited. The digital clock on the microwave flashed. 10:03. 10:04. Malcolm's Halloween cat pose relaxed, and her heart rate slowed, only to race again at a soft scrape. Like a foot dragging across the floor. Her breathing sounded loud in her ears.

The soft thudding continued across the floor. Back and forth, the length of the kitchen. Deep in his throat, Malcolm growled.

She could call Ingrid's mother, but what would she say? *The castle is haunted, can you please come get me?* She could lie. Tell Joyce she was having an allergic reaction and needed help.

10:05. The footsteps stopped. She looked again at the spiral staircase, the way the wall curved into shadow. How easy to imagine the feet of a ghostly figure appearing, then the legs, a hand curled around the stone, the leering face of a specter— maybe one with horns.

She had to get out of the castle.

Still holding the poker, she ran to the entry, grabbed her jacket, scarf, and hat from the coat stand, and ripped open the castle door onto the windy morning. Malcolm shot out and dashed to the hexagonal tower where Ben lived, slipping through a cat door.

Rather than experiencing relief at escaping the castle, the empty landscape of Tullimentay on the other side of the bridge only ratcheted up her fear at how truly alone she was. Only sky and sea and wind-whipped grass before her, and behind, the stern façade of Screeverholme. The wind whistled and tossed her hair.

She pulled gloves from her coat pocket and pulled them on. It was chilly, but not raining. She could walk to town, kill some time at Sinclair's with Catherine or visit the little cafe. Hey, she'd hang out in the post office at this point. All she knew was she couldn't go back in that castle. She'd make her parents understand why she had to leave.

She wrapped the Vivaldi-inducing scarf around her neck and over her mouth, cinched the hat tight over her ears, and started across the bridge. No silver coins remained. Who—or what— took them? The weight of unseen eyes pressed heavily on her back. She looked back over her shoulder where the second floor drew her gaze like a magnet to the window above the kitchen.

Behind the lace curtains lurked the silhouette of a man, horns curving up from his head. She breathed like she'd been running hard. She blinked, and the shape vanished. Her heart thudded as she tried to convince herself it hadn't happened, but she couldn't. Paul had gone into the barrow, and now the demon-man was back.

A surge of anger overcame her fear for a moment. Stupid Paul. Who was the *imbécile* now?

Although—this could be the proof they needed. She took her phone from her pocket and willed the shape to return to the window. She stared for a long time wondering if she were brave enough to go inside to investigate when a soft splash from the water drew her attention.

Another noise rose from the water, like a chirping bird. The sound escalated to the piercing screams of an animal in horrible pain. Had Malcolm fallen into the water?

She gripped the poker and leaned over the bridge. Whatever was making the noise was right below. She dug her fingers into the mossy stone and heaved herself onto the bridge wall to look down.

Below, an otter shrieked, caught in a net. He thrashed and whipped about. The screams were unbearable. She ran to the end of the bridge where it connected to Tullimentay. The land fell away to the water, pooling around dark rocks. The otter wasn't too far from them.

If she could get down to the water's edge and climb across the rocks, she could reach the otter without getting wet. She briefly considered finding the boat in the yet unexplored boathouse but doubted it would fit between the rocks. There was only one way to reach the otter—going across on foot. Poker in hand, she started down the hill, so steep she had to scoot on her backside.

It could be a trap. Bridget's words. *They change shape.*

The screams continued unabated. She couldn't stand to see an animal suffering. She reached the water's edge. From there, she could see the otter's mouth falling open with heartbreaking cries. Sharp white teeth flashed. He twisted and spun, the net tangled around his flailing paws.

She'd thought she could clamber across to the otter, but now she was down here looking at the dark slippery rocks, it seemed a much more precarious journey. The water wasn't so much lapping the rocks as slapping them. That water was dangerous. The man on the ferry, the farmer, Catherine—they'd all told her so.

She tried to think, but the animal's cries bored into her head, creating jagged black and red spikes across her mindscape. She sighed, knowing what she had to do.

"I'm coming." Morag peeled off her shoes and socks and ignored the cold. She imagined slipping under the water, slipping into unconsciousness like the day she arrived. But if that happened now, she wouldn't wake with her family peering down. She'd be dead. Was an otter worth it? If something happened to her, how would her family ever forgive her for being so reckless?

The otter's screams grew quieter. She needed a plan. Nothing brilliant presented itself. Get to the otter and back to land as quickly as possible, get inside, and warm up.

Inside. She'd momentarily forgotten the footsteps, the monstrous figure in the window. She stared at the castle, a great pile of stone rearing out of the sea. Already, her feet were swelling. She could walk into town and try to get help.

The phone weighed her coat pocket down. She fished it out and called Ingrid's mother. No answer.

The otter's struggles grew weak, and its cries came less often. If no one freed it from the net, it would drown. How ironic for an otter to drown. Morag rolled her jeans to her knees. She tossed her jacket, phone, hat, and gloves onto the bank, took a deep breath, and stepped into the sea. The water bit with icy teeth at her ankles, then calves, then knees. The first rock rose up, and she placed her hands and feet on it, trapping the poker between her palm and the rock. She counted eight rocks to the otter.

She crouched on the slippery rock. Arms out, she stepped onto the next one, using the poker for balance like a tightrope walker uses a pole. A jagged point dug into the arch of her foot, but she kept her balance. Seven more rocks. Hives, like angry red flowers, bloomed on her feet.

On the fourth rock, she lost her footing. Her right leg plunged into the water, slamming her other knee into the rock. She gasped as white-hot pain knifed through her. Somehow, she managed to hang on. Her heart hammered against her ribs like a drum, the desperate soundtrack to her efforts.

An itching ache crept up her calves. *Keep moving.* She used the poker like a cane and propped herself on the rock to step onto the next, ignoring the throbbing in her knee. On the next to the last rock, a wave smashed down and sprayed icy water as high as her waist. She started to fall backward but arched her back and windmilled her arms to catch herself. After that, she didn't hesitate and stepped onto the final, small rock.

About three feet away, the otter lay on his back, alternating between violent flutters and complete stillness like a moth caught in a spider's web. Morag perched on the balls of her feet while her knee protested. Blood seeped through her jeans. After all that, she still couldn't reach the otter. Up close, he was cute, even with the smell of fish wafting off him. Whenever he stopped moving, his body collapsed into despair, his whiskers drooping. His paws were entangled in the net.

The net. She might not be able to reach the otter, but with the poker, she might be able to reach the net stretching along the bridge. Squinting, she saw additional nets spanned its length. A rage as cold as the water welled up within her as any goodwill she felt toward Ben over their music vanished like peat smoke up a chimney.

She gripped the poker with her swelling hand and managed to snag the barbed end on the netting and drag it close enough to grab. As soon as she pulled, the otter went limp. With a mighty yank that almost sent her flying off the rock, she freed the net from the bridge. Hand over hand, she hauled it through the water, tugging the otter along like a child's toy. He was heavier than she'd expected.

Then he was beside the rock, and her courage failed. What if the otter *was* a shapeshifter, intent on pulling her into the sea to marry him? Or—a teensy bit more realistic—what if he bit her? Or thrashed and knocked her into the water? If she fell in, the frigid water would be over her head. She looked back at the return journey and wanted to cry.

Instead, she focused on the task at hand and attempted to lift the net from the otter. It was no use; the otter was too tangled.

"I'm gonna have to touch you, okay?" Morag wheezed. "Please don't hurt me."

The otter gazed up with eyes the color of rich earth. An uncanny understanding passed between them. The first touch seemed to shock them both as Morag and the otter trembled. His fur was sleek, the smoothest thing she'd ever felt. She could only imagine how soft he'd be when dry. Creamy spots speckled his brown chest. A thick, rough pad covered the bottom of his webbed paw and caught on the net.

"Easy, okay?" She kept a wary eye on his mouth while working his paw from the net. What she needed were scissors. Sure, a poker, she had that. Who didn't go for a stroll without a trusty iron poker? But some sort of cutting implement? No dice.

The otter didn't struggle, only watched her with the same wariness she did him. Her efforts caused her to knock the poker into the water. The dark shape sank through the water, revealing the bottom was deeper than Morag had realized. Her heart tripped. Desperate to get back to dry land, she hurried to continue her work.

As she bent over, her silver pendant swung forward, and she'd swear the otter's gaze latched onto it. After what felt like an eternity, she freed the first paw. At the increase in freedom, the otter slithered back and forth on his back.

"Hang on. We have to get the other paw."

The otter stilled again. Thanks to the released tension, the second paw came free faster. She gently lifted the net from the animal. He looked at her unblinking for several seconds before flipping over and dipping below the water. He resurfaced about fifteen feet away and turned to look at her again. The next time he came up, he was a dark spot in the distance.

Morag wanted to drag all the nets in, but she couldn't with her swollen fingers. She headed back for shore, knee throbbing, hands and feet like itchy blimps. The cold had worked its way to her core, but she managed to keep her footing all the way back.

By that time, her fingers didn't work well enough to roll

down her jeans or pull on her socks. She snatched on her jacket, rammed her swollen feet into her shoes, and wrapped the scarf around her neck.

Her phone rang. It was Ingrid's mother. "Hello, who's called me?"

"Morag."

"Is everythin' all right?" She sounded worried.

"I'm fine." If you didn't count the impending anaphylaxis. Could Joyce hear her wheezing? Morag quickly thought up a reason for calling. "I'm alone at the castle and got bored. Thought I'd call Ingrid."

"Ingrid's out. They left ye alone in *that* castle?"

Morag didn't like the way Joyce said it, like it would be acceptable to be left alone in other castles, but not Screeverholme. "Everyone went out on Mr. Murray's boat and with, you know, my cold allergy, I couldn't go."

"I worry about ye with that allergy, Morag. I don't think ye should be here. Ye should be somewhere sunny and hot and far from Orkney. The sooner the better."

Joyce's words, like a warning, chilled Morag further. Could Joyce have left that note on the castle door? They said goodbye and hung up. Morag had more pressing concerns than Ingrid's mother. She needed to warm up right away.

Which meant returning inside the castle with whatever might be lurking there. After seeing that wolf by Ben's tower, she knew danger prowled outside, too.

Her knee pulsed in pain with each step that brought her closer to the castle—to shelter—and to the impossible possibility of the figure with horns. She slowed, and her pulse jumped in her throat. How could she go back inside? But hadn't she just managed a brave and dangerous thing saving that otter? She would *not* let fear dictate her actions. She squared her shoulders and continued across the bridge.

Chapter 14

The castle door creaked open like something from one of Ivy's horror films. Morag stood in the entryway and listened. Utter silence hung in the castle, but she couldn't shake the feeling something waited within its walls.

She yelped when Malcolm brushed past her to go inside, but the fact he wanted in gave her the courage to step over the threshold.

Maybe the footsteps were only knocking pipes or the castle's heating system, and she'd worked herself up over nothing. Hamish's drunken story, the cave drawing, stories of mythology, and Paul going into the barrow this morning—it had all acted like a spark on dry tinder, fanning the flames of her imagination into a roaring fire.

Except she knew that wasn't true. No matter how insane it seemed, she believed Hamish. She'd seen that horned man in the window herself and the bear in that cave.

Her teeth chattered hard enough that she worried she'd chip one. An invisible hand gripped her throat, threatening to close off her airway. After the experience at Ingrid's house, she knew hot water would stop the reaction but going for a bath upstairs where the footsteps had been, where she'd seen the dark figure, was more than she could handle. The lounge and its low-burning fire were also on the second floor. The main floor felt safer, closer to the front door and potential escape over the bridge.

She'd go into the kitchen and find a large bowl to soak her feet. Drink a piping hot cup of tea. And sit in the room directly below the footsteps, next to the shadowy spiral staircase at the table with the view of the graveyard.

Whistling as loud as she could, she marched into the kitchen, wishing she still had that poker. "If anyone is here, do *not* mess with me." She'd intended to shout, but it came out faint.

The day grew darker, and the silence shredded Morag's nerves. She could no longer tell whether her shutting throat and pounding heart were from her allergy or being afraid. She needed a distraction before her fear morphed into outright panic. She switched on the flat-screen TV mounted on the wall and also turned on the overhead light and the electric kettle. Immediately, with the brightness and everyday sounds of commercials, she felt braver. Her breathing came easier. It was harder to be scared during an ad for toilet cleaner, and the kettle burbled comforting noises.

Malcolm, curled up on a chair at the end of the table, watched her with one eye as she dug into the cupboards and found a deep, stainless-steel bowl. Wonderful hot water splashed into it from the tap. She let the water run over her numb hands, bone-white except for the red welts, which faded away like her receding fear. Triumph rose like a rising bubble in her chest. She was learning how to deal with this cold urticaria business.

She set the bowl on the floor, sat on the bench nearest the cat, and slipped her feet into the water. Sharp needles of chilblains stabbed her feet as they warmed. Once it eased, she noticed how much her knee hurt. Like really hurt.

She winced as she pulled back her pant leg—the denim sticking with blood—and took advantage of the empty castle to curse loudly. A deep gash ran around the outside of her kneecap. Her mom could stitch it up, no problem, but Morag needed to think of a good story. Like she slipped on one of the stone steps. That was believable.

She cupped her hand and rinsed the cut with hot water from the bowl. Mom's medical bag was upstairs, exactly where she didn't want to go. She blew out a breath and rolled her jeans back down. She'd live.

After pouring a cup of tea and shoving bread in the toaster, she waited at the back door to stare out the window. Wind moaned at its edges. She avoided looking at the graveyard and watched the gray clouds roiling over the horizon. Her thumb smoothed over the pendant at the hollow of her neck. Surely with the worsening weather, Mr. Murray and his fishing boat would head back with her family soon.

Her gaze landed on the graves, the built-up mounds like miniature barrows. Her imagination worked double-time as she envisioned the rotted bodies lying inside—a skeletal hand shooting up through the earth. A soft thump had her whirling around on a yelp.

Her toast had popped up.

It was going to be a long day.

Fortunately, Mr. Murray *had* chosen to head back early. Morag only waited one excruciating hour before everyone returned, transforming the castle from a spooky, haunted pile of rock to a fun place filled with laughter.

"What did you get up to?" Dad pulled a bag of popcorn from the microwave and hissed as he burned his fingers. Which he did every time.

"Nothing much." Morag sat at the kitchen table and enjoyed

the commotion. "Did you guys have fun?"

"Mom and Juliette both puked." Hamish took the bag from Dad and ripped it open, spilling popcorn on the floor.

Juliette hid her face in her hands. Mom, however, seemed unbothered, used to the indignity of a weak stomach. Morag hoped she'd recovered enough to stitch up her knee.

With unnerving maternal instincts, her mom came over and kissed the top of her head. "You survived the castle by yourself?"

"Mostly."

Despite the tumult of a kitchen crowded with five adults and seven kids trying to get snacks, everyone stopped at her words.

"What do you mean 'mostly'?"

Morag knew the adults—and Paul—wouldn't believe her. She didn't know how to begin explaining everything, but she needed them to be aware, to be on their guard for danger in whatever inexplicable form it might take. "I thought I heard footsteps above the kitchen. And I saw this dark shape of a person upstairs." She caught herself before saying the figure was in the window, or she'd reveal she'd been outside.

Hamish slopped hot chocolate over his hand. "Ouch. Say what?"

"Yeah." Dad pointed at Hamish. "What he said."

Morag locked eyes with Hamish, who lifted his eyebrows in question and subtly mimed horns coming from his head. She nodded, and Hamish came and put his arm around her. She leaned her head on his shoulder for a moment in thanks he was on her side.

Paul's brow furrowed. "Could there have been an intruder? There are a lot of valuable items here. Maybe someone thought everyone left, and this was their chance."

"All I know was the footsteps were upstairs."

"Ben?" Françoise asked.

Mom shook her head, her mouth drawn in concern. "His car is gone. What about that note on the castle? Is someone trying to scare us away?"

"Let's go investigate," Dad said to Mike and Gary.

"Sure," Gary said. "Pete, maybe you can tell Morag about the killer whales."

Pete's scared expression transformed as he told Morag about their trip. A little while later, the dads returned looking relieved.

"All clear," Gary said. "You're sure you heard footsteps, Morag?"

Everyone stared at her, but Paul's gaze weighed the heaviest. "I definitely heard sounds upstairs," Morag said slowly. "And Malcolm was freaking out."

"All right, that's it." Dad slapped his hands on the kitchen counter. "We need to report this to the police."

"I don't think that's a good idea," Mom said.

"Of course not," Dad muttered. "Because I said it."

"No. I don't want to make things even worse with the islanders."

"So we're supposed to stand by and do nothing when one of them breaks in and scares our daughter?" Dad pulled his cell from his pocket.

"We have no proof," Mom said. "Isn't it possible Morag's imagination got the better of her alone in a spooky castle?"

"Sounds likely." Paul actually smiled at Morag. She wanted to slap him.

"Morag is sixteen, not six. No offense, Pete." Dad turned to the little boy, who slurped his hot chocolate and watched the conversation like a tennis match. "She said someone was walking around upstairs. I'm not going to just let this go."

Mom put her hands on her hips. "Oh, but you're happy to ignore a life-threatening allergy?"

"Lisa." Dad's voice took on that warning tone he used with his kids.

"Bill." She bounced the tone back.

"Oh, the bread is good here." Françoise took a big bite of toast.

Gary held up his slice. "I love the bread in Europe. Best bread

I ever had was in Belgium." He winced. "I mean, it probably tied the bread in France."

"No, no," Françoise said. "The bread in Belgium is quite tasty, too."

Morag cringed at their clumsy attempt to defuse the tension. Her parents never cared how uncomfortable they made everyone else. Why couldn't they be like Françoise and Mike, who never fought?

Embarrassment radiated off Hamish as well. She'd thought their parents were making progress. They'd looked so happy at the ceilidh. She wouldn't add to this argument.

"Hey, you know what? Mom's probably right. It was pretty spooky being alone here. The cat was hissing and growling and scared me. Probably the plumbing making a knocking noise or something." Hamish tipped his head at her in an *Are you serious?* kind of way, and she rushed on. "Anyway, I tripped on the stairs and hit my knee on a step." She whipped back her pant leg, and those closest to her gasped.

Ivy grinned. "Disgusting," she said at the same time James winced and said, "Ouch."

"Why are your pants wet?" Paul said.

Trust him to notice. "I, uh, spilled some water."

Paul gave her a funny look, which she ignored.

Hamish leaned over for a closer look. "Oh, man. I'm gonna barf."

The gash wasn't bleeding, and in some ways, that was worse, making the grisly wound more visible.

"That needs to be stitched," Mom said unnecessarily. As Morag had hoped, her mother switched to medical mode.

Morag sat on the toilet seat lid in her parents' bathroom. Dad's shaver rested by the sink, surrounded by a circle of dark whiskers. Mom's loofah hung from the showerhead. It was strange being in their intimate space, an intrusion of sorts.

Mom opened her medical bag and pulled out supplies with swift and efficient movements. "That's a nasty cut. Why didn't you clean it? You know better."

Facing the prospect of a shot and stitches, Morag didn't feel as calm as she'd hoped. "I was scared to come upstairs, okay? After what I heard."

Mom snapped on gloves. Plastic rustled as she opened the syringe and suture packets. "Something obviously spooked Hamish, too. I saw the books he was reading in the library. Sweetie, don't you think it was your imagination?"

"Whatever you say. I don't want to add to you and Dad fighting." Her voice dropped. "You do that enough on your own."

Mom sighed. "Here we go again."

"Well, you do. All you do is fight. Only now you get to do it in front of everybody. It's embarrassing."

"All couples fight."

"Juliette's parents don't."

Mom snorted.

"What?"

"You're still young. Sometimes everything isn't what it seems."

"Of course. I'm a little kid, right? I couldn't possibly understand." Morag actually *didn't* know what her mom meant, but as usual, she was being discounted as a child. The anxiety, building over the past year, clawed its way from her chest with an awful question. "Are you and Dad getting a divorce?"

Is our family going to be ripped apart? Will nothing be the same again?

Morag waited for the instant denial, the reassurances everything would be fine. Even though she wouldn't believe the words, she wanted them. She *expected* them. Instead, Mom went into the bedroom, retrieved the chair from the desk, and dragged it in front of the toilet.

"Mom?" Her voice caught. She wouldn't cry and make it

worse. Morag pressed her trembling hands to the tops of her thighs and held her breath.

"I'm just thinking about what to say." Mom let out a slow sigh. "You don't want to be treated like a little kid. I'm trying to give you an adult answer."

"So you *are* going to get . . . one?" She couldn't bring herself to say the word again.

"I wasn't planning on running to the courthouse the day we get back if that's what you mean."

That made her feel worse. Like Mom thought about doing it, just not immediately.

Mom sighed again. "I'd be lying if I said Dad and I never considered divorce. We're very different people." To Morag's surprise, Mom smiled. "That's what first attracted me to him. He was different from me—or anyone I knew. So much more easy-going than me, and he always saw things in a new way."

"So what's going to happen?"

She lifted her brows. "I don't know. But you're right, Morag. You're not a little kid. You're sixteen. Whatever happens, you'll be all right."

Outrage filled Morag. How could her mother think she'd be all right because she was sixteen? She wouldn't be all right if her parents divorced when she was thirty. Parents were supposed to stay married. *Her* parents were, at least. Divorce was something that happened to other families.

Mom touched Morag's good knee. "You know your dad and I love you. And I'll always love your dad."

"Then how can you even think of divorce?"

"Because life's complicated, Morag."

Morag swallowed past the golf ball-sized lump in her throat. "Can we just drop it and get me stitched up, please?"

"You asked, Morag."

"Because I was stupid. I thought you'd make me feel better, but you made me feel worse."

"Then maybe I should have lied." Her mom's matter-offactness stung because Morag knew she *could* have easily lied, and part of her wished she had. Mom picked up the syringe. "Ready?"

Unable to speak, Morag nodded. When the slow burn of anesthetic spread around her knee, she let the unshed tears slip down her cheeks under the cover of physical pain. Once Mom finished the injections, she hooked her finger under Morag's chin and tipped up her face.

The same blue-green eyes as Morag's looked back, large and gentle. "Hey. I'm not saying we won't get divorced, but we haven't given up yet, either. All hope isn't lost, okay?"

Morag didn't respond. Her mother worked in silence, cleaning the wound, and stitching the ragged edges together until a neat crescent of black sutures snaked around her kneecap.

If only it were as easy to stitch up the wounds in her parents' marriage.

Chapter 15

Morag limped downstairs and followed the sound of voices to the billiards room. The adults were nowhere to be seen. Neither was Juliette. More than anything, she wanted to talk to her best friend. She couldn't face talking to Hamish about what Mom said. Not yet. Hamish and James were playing snooker, Ivy was watching something on her phone, and Paul was in the corner on his laptop.

"Where's Juliette?"

James was bent over the snooker table. He paused before taking a shot, eyes on the cue ball. "Taking a nap. She wasn't feeling well after feeding the fishies." The balls clacked softly, and a blue solid one thunked into a middle pocket.

"Nice," Paul said. Morag wasn't sure whether he meant the shot or the disgusting description of Juliette's seasickness. He'd draped himself over a chair by the fireplace in a pool of light from a nearby Tiffany lamp.

"You all right?" Hamish leaned on his pool stick and watched Morag with narrowed eyes.

Great. *Now* he was observant? She forced a smile when she wanted to scream at Hamish their parents were probably getting divorced. "All stitched up."

Hamish frowned as James banked a shot off the side and sank another solid into a corner pocket. "Tell me what you saw today. The horned guy."

She hesitated. "You have to promise not to tell Mom or Dad. I don't want them fighting again."

"Uh, that's a given."

She sensed Paul and Ivy still themselves to listen, and Hamish and James both leaned on their pool cues. Morag took a deep breath and told them everything—the footsteps, the figure in the window, rescuing the otter.

"Not a wise choice given your cold allergy," Paul said from his corner. "Hardly worth risking your life for an otter."

Hamish rolled his eyes. "Back to the evil dude in the window. He had horns? Like a demon, right?"

Paul said, "Seen a lot of demons, have you?"

Hamish ignored him. "Could you see its face?"

Morag shook her head.

"What do you think it is?" Ivy asked. Her phone lay forgotten on a side table. Likewise, Hamish and James set their pool sticks down.

"It's like a demon. I'm telling you," Hamish said.

"Could it be a ghost?" Ivy had looked more and more pleased as Morag told her story.

"No idea." Morag licked her lips and twisted the pendant on its chain. "But I've been doing some research on the Fin Folk."

"The what?" James asked. Of course. He'd been building a sandcastle with Pete when Morag had told the others about it at the beach.

"Mythical creatures." Paul shut his laptop. "Sort of an amalgam of Norse and Scottish legends."

"What's an amalgam?" Hamish whispered to James.

"A mix," James said, surprising Morag with his vocabulary

prowess.

"Good to know."

Paul continued. "The point is, they're the stuff of fiction. You know? *Made-up* stuff?"

"They're shape-shifters who live under the sea," Morag said, "but they come onto land sometimes."

"What for?" James asked.

"They kidnap humans for spouses. If a Fin Folk woman doesn't find a human husband, she becomes an old sea hag."

"Oh yeah, I think one teaches English Lit at my school." Ivy laughed hard at her own joke but sobered as Morag shared everything she'd learned so far. It felt right for them to be taking it seriously. Morag avoided looking at Paul. "I'm wondering if the horned figure showed up again because Paul went in the barrow this morning."

"You *what?*" Hamish pushed himself off the pool table toward Paul. "Why the hell would you do that?"

"You can't possibly think me going in the burial mound makes a demon-man appear," Paul said.

"Yeah, I do."

"Wow. That lowers my already low opinion of your intellect considering I think you're an idiot."

Hamish took another step toward Paul's corner. "Why don't you come over here and tell me that to my face? See what happens."

"Hamish." Morag glared at her brother, but his back was to her.

He'd gone into an aggressive gorilla stance—shoulders back, chest out, and hands balled loosely at his sides, ready for action. "*You're* an idiot for going in that graveyard again."

Paul stood from his chair and swiveled his head, looking for something. Spotting his laptop sleeve, he slid the computer inside before striding toward the lounge.

"That's what I thought." Hamish pushed his chest forward in a fake-out lunge.

Paul, to his credit, gazed back with a bored expression. "You're only making a fool of yourself. I've studied tae kwon do for ten years. Do you think I'm scared of *you?*"

"You should be. And if I catch you in that graveyard again, I'll kick your ass."

Paul shook his head with a little laugh. "I'll leave everyone to their fear-mongering." He wiggled his fingers in the air. "Ooo. Watch out for the Fin Folk."

Paul might have been annoying Morag lately, but she didn't like her brother threatening him. She threw Hamish a dirty look and followed Paul into the lounge. He was nowhere to be seen. Morag walked into the hall but didn't see him there, either. How did he get away so fast? Sometimes he seemed to disappear into thin air.

She returned to the billiards room and marched up to Hamish. "What's the matter with you?"

"What? The guy's so annoying. And weird."

James picked up his pool stick again. "To be fair to Hamish, Paul's pretty conceited."

"He only seems weird and conceited because he's so smart."

James held out his hands. "Hey, I got nothing against weird." He waved his hand over his tattooed and pierced body. "You think I don't know I look like I'm in a nineties punk band? I've got an eyebrow ring, okay? Weird's cool with me. Smart, too. Having a big ego is another matter. Paul's having a major lovefest with himself."

"He's confident."

"He's arrogant," Hamish snapped.

Morag's instincts to defend Paul softened her recent doubt of him. Paul wasn't as arrogant as he seemed. He only came off that way because he was awkward. He was intelligent and interesting, and he could be nice when he wasn't acting like a know-it-all. And he was hot, in an intellectual way.

"One of these days," Hamish said, "he's gonna get a beating acting like that."

"He really is good at tae kwan do."

Hamish sneered. "Morag, would you stop defending your little boyfriend?" Morag spluttered, but Hamish cut her off. "Oh, yeah. I've seen the way you look at him. You've liked him for years."

She had—for almost her whole life—and she didn't know how not to. Stomach churning, she glanced up and accidentally met James's eyes. A flicker of something that might have been disappointment crossed his features.

"Hamish, stop," she said through gritted teeth, sliding her gaze toward James.

"Oh, don't worry. They already know." Hamish pointed at James and Ivy, and Morag's face pulsed with heat. "You know Morag has a crush on that dumb ass, right?"

James ran his hand over the snooker table, his attention captured by a rip in the felt. Morag sensed the sympathy embarrassment radiating from him and felt a surge of gratitude toward the guy for sharing her pain.

Ivy had no such qualms about joining in the discussion. "I figured out Morag likes him, but I can see the attraction."

"Are you kidding me?" Hamish said.

Ivy twirled a lock of purple hair around her finger. "Paul's all blond and brooding and smart and speaks French. *Ooh, la la.*"

"Oh, yuck." Hamish made a gagging noise. "Maybe you can start a fan club with Morag." He put his hands on his cheeks and batted his eyelashes. "She's in wuv with wittle Monsieur Paulie."

A seething fury roiled inside Morag, but for the life of her, no clever retort came to mind. "I—I hate you, Hamish."

As she left the room, she heard him say, "Ouch." Like it hurt. "Too far?"

"Definitely," James answered. "Not cool."

"I know. I wasn't even mad at her. It's that asshole Paul who pisses me off. Do you know—"

Morag couldn't catch the rest of his words on her way out of the lounge. She already regretted saying she hated Hamish. If her parents divorced, she and Hamish would need each other more than ever.

Unbidden, she recalled a memory from when they were kids. Their parents had taken them bowling, and the loud music and crashing pins overwhelmed Morag with pulsing shapes until she'd crouched on the floor with her eyes squeezed shut and hands clamped over her ears.

Another little girl from the next lane giggled, and when she'd opened her eyes, the girl and her friend were pointing at Morag. "Why is she being such a weirdo?"

"You shut up, Ugly," Hamish shouted. "My sister's a weirdo because she's special."

Tormentor and champion in equal parts. That summed up her brother. She didn't hate Hamish. She never had.

She climbed the stairs with a heavy heart. The lidocaine hadn't worn off yet, and the skin around her knee felt tight and numb with each step. She was glad Juliette was sleeping up here. Being alone upstairs frightened her. She paused outside her friend's room.

"Juliette?"

No response. Thank god Juliette hadn't witnessed Hamish's outburst. If she knew about Morag's feelings for Paul, it would be so uncomfortable. Then again, Morag knew Juliette liked Hamish. Juliette wasn't stupid. If even *Hamish* had seen her crush, Morag hadn't played it as cool as she'd thought. Juliette must have noticed, too.

A worse realization hit her like a face full of cold water. *Paul* must know she liked him.

She groaned, planning to hide in her room and never come out until it was time to go home. That sounded doable. She opened her bedroom door and wrinkled her nose at the smell.

Like fish and salt water and a murky, musty scent. Sort of like the bear, but not quite.

"What *is* that?" She looked around the room but saw nothing to explain the smell. She sank onto the bed and glanced at the clock on the bedside table. Her heart somersaulted in her chest.

Lying on her nightstand was her silver case of colored pencils. The pencils that had tumbled off the bridge and into the water.

Chapter 16

Morag reached for the pencil case. Maybe someone had surprised her with a new set of pencils. She flipped the latches with a metallic click and opened the box. The pencils' outer coverings were bubbled and wrinkled from being waterlogged. She held up the case and saw the crooked *M.A.D.* of her initials etched into the bottom. Morag Abigail Davidson. Her parents hadn't thought through those initials.

How could her pencils be back?

She set the case down and noticed a paper lying underneath. She licked her lips and turned the sheet over. Only her drawing of the otter. She blew out a long, shaky breath.

Did Ben fish the pencils out of the water for her? She sniffed the box. A hint of seawater and that odd wet-dog scent hanging in her room.

She stared at the drawing, trying to think, and absentmindedly ran her thumb along the edge of the paper. Another sheet was stuck to her drawing. Gently, she eased apart the two papers.

It was a drawing. A good one. Better than Morag's work.

And *this* artist captured the otter's colors perfectly. They'd also captured the rich, sable black of Morag's curly hair blowing in the wind as she'd climbed over the rocks to the trapped animal, the deep red of her scarf flowing over her shoulder.

Something was written in letters too faint to read. Morag switched on the bedside lamp and thrust the paper underneath. They weren't letters, but some kind of weird symbols. Familiar ones. The same symbols were carved in the cave next to the figure with the flipper hands and feet.

She clapped her hand to her mouth.

For some time, she studied the paper, memorizing every detail. She finally set it aside and looked up. The poker from the kitchen—the poker that had fallen in the water today—rested against the wall behind her door. A trembling started in her belly.

Who'd seen her rescuing the otter? Morag's brain tried and failed to come up with anything that made sense. Even if she could convince herself Ben had retrieved her pencils somehow, he wasn't on the island today. If someone had seen her help the otter, how could they possibly have found her pencil case *and* the poker in the water? It would be like finding two proverbial needles in a haystack.

Unless it was something very at home in the water.

Her mind drummed out the words in a tattoo. *The Fin Folk, The Fin Folk, The Fin Folk.*

Stop it. She whipped open her bedroom door, eager not to be alone anymore.

Morag sat on Juliette's bed, pillow hugged to her chest, and told her friend everything that happened today, minus the part about Hamish announcing her crush on Paul. Sleep creases crisscrossed Juliette's cheek after her nap. She wore a long, white nightgown, and even rumpled from sleep, she looked like a woman in a Pino Daeni painting or the Lady of Shalott herself.

"Juliette? What are you thinking?"

"Sorry. This is crazy. We have my imbecile brother going in that barrow again and now Hamish *and* you have seen a man with horns. You and I saw a bear in the cave, and you saw a wolf. That kid Thorfinn talked about a wolf knocking down the sheep wall."

Morag reminded her about the farmers at the ceilidh discussing the dead sheep and the one on the road her first night on the island.

"You saw footprints in the hall. Your pencils and the poker got returned to you. And this." Juliette sat with the drawing in her hand, her blonde hair forming a curtain around her face as she stared down at it. "Not even my mom could draw something this good." She looked up at Morag. "How do we explain all this?"

Morag bit her thumbnail. "I'm starting to think the Fin Folk is the only thing that makes sense."

"Okay, let's consider our evidence. Why would we think that?" She sounded like Paul for a second, and Morag smiled in spite of herself. Juliette picked her phone off the bed and scooted close to Morag. She bumped Morag's knee, making her wince. The lidocaine was wearing off, and her knee throbbed deep inside.

Morag tipped her head toward Juliette as she typed in *Fin Folk* on her phone.

"I couldn't find much on them when I tried searching before," Morag said. "The same stuff Bridget told me about Fin Folk. Shapeshifting, living under the sea, kidnapping humans." Morag blinked as Juliette added a few words like *Orkney* and *mythology.*

"Whoa," Morag said. "You found way more sites than me."

"Boolean search operators, my good woman."

Morag laughed. Juliette *would* know how to search like a librarian.

Her friend scrolled quickly and straightened with excitement. "Listen to this. 'Some people believe they can keep the Fin Folk from taking them by leaving out silver or wearing it. Explains your necklace.'"

"And the silver coins on the bridge and outside Ingrid's house." Morag fisted her hands at her mouth, torn between excitement and fear. "Whatever's happening here, one thing's for sure. The islanders believe in the Fin Folk."

"Agreed." Juliette shivered and rubbed her hands down her arms. "You know what else is weird? Mr. Murray suggested we might like to go to this other island, Sanday, over the summer solstice."

"There's that solstice thing again."

"Yeah. And he got really pushy about it. When your parents wouldn't promise to go, he got angry. That's when we started back."

Morag ran her thumbnail over her phone case. "Remember Mrs. Heddle wanted us to come to the solstice celebration, and then uninvited us. Why?"

"I don't know, but it's in two days. Mr. Murray made it seem like staying here would be dangerous. Why doesn't everyone leave then?"

"Beats me. Maybe we're the only ones in danger?" An unpleasant possibility, like a bad smell, drifted up through her thoughts, and she wrinkled her nose. "Or maybe *we're* causing the danger? Going into the barrow. Me rescuing the otter." Morag curled her fingers into Juliette's duvet and resisted the impulse to dive underneath it while Juliette returned to her scrolling.

"Ugh. Look at that drawing."

Careful of her knee, Morag pressed closer to peer at the image on Juliette's phone. A creature, gangly and round-shouldered, with large, bulbous eyes, two slits for nostrils, and flippered hands and feet, crept out of the sea, a menacing snarl on its face. Something struck Morag about the picture. "Juliette.

It doesn't have any horns."

"An artist's impression?"

"Can I?" Morag gestured for Juliette's phone, and she handed it over. Morag scanned the lines of text for new information. "Check this out. 'The Fin Folk have the power to transform into any creature they wish. They often prefer to take the form of—'" Morag swallowed, her mouth instantly dry.

"What?"

"'They often prefer to take the form of seals and otters, though they have sometimes been known to transform into a fearsome bear.'"

"A bear?" Juliette blanched, and she and Morag looked at one another with twin open-mouthed stares.

"This is all real. It has to be. The Fin Folk are real and on this island. So many myths are rooted in truth. Only this thing is more than rooted in truth. It *is* the truth."

Juliette nodded, wearing the expression of someone working on a difficult calculus problem. She kept nodding for a while and gasped. "I bet that otter you saved was trying to trick you. Take you for a wife." She shoved her slender finger at the drawing of the Fin Folk. "And *that's* no selkie turning into a hot guy."

"Okay, hang on." Morag scrubbed her face. "This is insane. Why didn't the otter turn back into a fin—folk—fin person—and grab me? Why return my pencils?"

"Maybe the otter *was* trapped, and you saved him. Think how many fairy tales have mythological creatures who grant you a wish or pay a debt when you save their life. Maybe he returned the pencils as a thank you." She gave a proud smile.

Morag had already realized it was a thank-you of sorts. That was obvious. "So, they're *not* dangerous?"

"I don't want to find out. Do you? Plus, you said Ben hates otters. Maybe because they're Fin Folk shapeshifters. If they were benevolent, why would he be afraid?"

"True," Morag said slowly. "And that bear chased us. They're killing the sheep." She shuddered, recalling the eviscerated animal.

"Maybe the Fin Folk guy had to repay you for saving him, and now it's back to Fin Folk kidnappings and forced marriages." Juliette snapped her fingers. "Or the only reason it didn't attack was your necklace."

"The otter did seem to stare at it." Morag touched her necklace and decided Catherine believed more of the Orkney myths than she let on.

Juliette unfolded her legs and climbed off the bed to pace. "Whether we brought the danger or not, it sounds like the islanders believe something dangerous *is* going to happen on the solstice. Which means we're not safe. We have to tell our parents."

"Like they're going to listen." Morag pulled her bottom lip. "We need some sort of concrete proof. We need to show them exactly what the danger is if we want to be taken seriously." She plucked the paper from the bed and traced the symbols with her finger. "I think I'll ask your brother about these." She avoided eye contact with Juliette because even the mention of Paul made her face flush. "He knew something about the runic symbols on the barrow. He might know what these are."

Juliette rolled her eyes. "If he doesn't, he'll make something up. I'm getting something to eat. My appetite is back big-time."

Morag tucked the drawings under her arm and followed Juliette downstairs. Juliette headed toward the kitchen while Morag stuck her head in the lounge. Françoise, beautiful in a blue sweater, sat in a chair sketching while Mike sprawled on the couch near the fireplace, a book in his lap. As always, the Gaspars were the picture of civilized marriage.

She approached Françoise, working on a drawing of a woman gazing out a window. The longing and despair showed clearly on her features. Morag's work would never be that brilliant. "You guys know where Paul is?" Ugh. Why did she have to blush in front of his parents, too?

Françoise flashed a tight smile. "I believe he is in the library."

"Thanks." She found him there, sitting so still on the sofa, she didn't see him at first.

"Hey," she said. He jumped and dropped his book in his lap. "Sorry. Didn't mean to scare you. And sorry about my embarrassing brother threatening you earlier."

"What do you want, Morag?" The impatience in his voice stung. "I suppose you're here to tell me I shouldn't have gone in the burial mound?"

"Well, yeah. I wish you hadn't." She dropped onto the couch beside him. "Because I *did* see a man with horns in the window after you went in there."

He pinched the bridge of his nose. "It had to be your imagination."

She let that slide for now. "I wanted to ask you about some symbols I found. Since you were interested in those runes."

"Funny you should say that. I've already heard from a runic expert at the University of Oslo. He didn't know what those symbols in the cave were from my photo, but he translated the runes on the stone from my rubbing." For some reason, he looked apprehensive.

"Wow. That was fast. What does it say?"

Paul hesitated. "You're probably going to work yourself into a dither over this."

"A dither?" Morag narrowed her eyes at him. "Can you just tell me what it says? Please?"

He reached for his laptop on a side table and flipped it open. "Fine. It turns out those runes are a curse."

"A *curse?* What's it say?"

Paul huffed out a sigh and read from his laptop screen. "'Here lies Earl Sigurd Rognvaldsson and his men. Any who awaken them shall die. Until Rognvaldsson falls the final time, he and his men shall live forevermore.'"

"You went into the barrow and *tried* to wake them up?"

"To be fair to me, I didn't know the runes were a curse at that point. But it doesn't matter because curses aren't real."

It was her turn to sigh. "Then I want an explanation for everything happening. You know? Horned men in the castle. The Fin Folk craziness. How the Fin Folk are related to the burial mound." That was one thing she couldn't figure out.

"They're not. Because none. Of. It. Is. Real." Paul set the laptop aside and gave her a disappointed look. "You strike me as far too sensible to get caught up in this hysteria."

"I'm not. I mean, I am. I'm not getting caught up, and I am too sensible." She rubbed her forehead. "But I know what I saw. I wanted to talk to you because you're logical and scientific."

Paul relaxed some, looking mollified.

"I want your explanation for something strange that happened."

"Here we go." He sent a pained look to the ceiling.

"No, listen. You're going to help me think of an explanation for what happened to me."

By the time she finished telling him what she'd found in her room, they sat so close on the velvet sofa that his leg was only inches from hers. He seemed too lost in thought to notice their proximity as he stroked his hand over his hair and stared into the middle distance. Morag shifted on the couch, accidentally bringing their legs even closer. She scooted away a little, confused. Shouldn't she want to touch him? She liked him, right?

"The pencils and the poker," Paul said at last. "Those had to be Ben. Your hypothesis he retrieved them is sound. You said he felt bad when he caused you to knock the case into the water. If the items fell into one of his nets, he could have easily pulled them from the water."

"My mom said Ben's been gone to his girlfriend's in the village."

"He must have come back at some point. The symbols on the drawing are trickier to explain." His hand traveled to the top of his head again, smoothing over his blond hair she'd admired for so many years. "Can I see it?" He gestured toward the papers.

Morag handed him the drawing.

Paul studied it. "I'm not familiar with these symbols, but I concur they look like those in the cave. More like hieroglyphs than runes." Their eyes met. Flustered, Morag looked at the floor and back up. He ran his finger over the figure of her in the drawing. "It was foolish of you to go in the water. You could have died."

She brought her gaze back to his face. "Would that upset you?" She cringed, knowing she sounded like a simpering girl in a vampire romance.

"Would it upset me if you died?" He snorted. "Morag, we've known each other a long time and I—I care about you."

Was that true? Embarrassment flooded her body like warm liquid. Paul *had* to have known she liked him all this time, and yet he'd never done a thing about it. Maybe what he really liked wasn't Morag, but Morag's adoration of him. "You care about me?" Her tone came out as skeptical as Paul discussing the Fin Folk.

He nodded, and his gaze dropped to her mouth. After an awkward moment, Paul cleared his throat and looked back to the paper. "What's this?" He pulled out her drawing, which she hadn't realized was still stuck to the other paper.

"That's mine." She tried to grab it, but he held it out of reach. "Can you please give it to me?" She wasn't ready to share her artwork with Paul. He squinted, bringing her drawing close to his nose, then pulling it back. "It's not one of those Magic Eye pictures." Paul easily foiled another of her attempts to snatch it away with his upraised elbow, like some sort of tae kwon do move, which it probably was. She sighed and gave up. He'd already seen it. Finally, she couldn't stand it any longer. "So? What do you think?" She might as well have stripped off all her clothes for how naked she felt.

Paul took a sharp breath through his nose. "It's—it's not bad."

"Not bad?" Her heart dive-bombed into her stomach.

"I like the way you did the otter's whiskers."

"The *whiskers?*" She ripped the drawing from him. The corner tore off and remained in Paul's hand. "Can you give me the other paper, please?" She stood and held out her hand, relieved it wasn't trembling.

"Morag." His tone was chastising.

A noise drew her attention to the doorway. James strolled into the room with his guitar case and stopped in front of the bookcases. Just perfect.

"Morag?" Paul repeated, and she slid her gaze back to him.

"What?" She dropped her voice. "This is why I didn't want you looking at my drawing."

"But I did. And you asked me what I thought." He sounded so reasonable, she wanted to scream.

"And you made it clear."

"Did I?"

"Not bad means not good either." To her mortification, tears stung her eyes.

Paul sighed. "It *is* good, Morag."

"But not great."

"Do *you* think it's great?" he shot back, getting to his feet. "Look. Maybe I'm not the best judge of art when I have Françoise for a mother."

She swiped at a tear. "You mean my ridiculous, childish artwork could never compare to hers?"

"My mom is an artistic genius. You think you're going to be in her league when you're fifteen?"

"I turned sixteen four months ago." How did he not know that?

"Regardless of your exact age, my mom has worked at her art for decades. You, on the other hand, hardly ever seem to be working on yours so I don't know why—"

James coughed. "You might want to stop there, man."

"Fine." Paul threw up his hands. "In the future, if a girl asks my opinion about something, I won't share it."

"Ding, ding, ding." James put his finger on his nose and pointed at Paul. "Now you're catching on."

Paul shoved the other drawing at Morag and stomped out. With Paul gone, the tears spilled over. One good thing, she thought bitterly. Paul had distracted her from the Fin Folk. She sank onto the couch, set the other paper aside, and stared at her drawing through blurry eyes.

"Hey." James sat beside her, setting the guitar at his feet. "You okay?"

"For someone who has zero artistic ability, I guess so."

"I didn't mean to intrude." James rubbed the back of his neck. "So, uh? Do you mind if I take a peek?" He held out his hand. "I can lie if you want." His expressive mouth curved into a lopsided smile.

"What the hell." She handed the paper over. "And no lying."

He looked at the drawing while twisting the ring through his eyebrow. "*I* like it," he said, in a way implying others understandably might not. Or maybe she was reading way too much into his tone.

"Do you—do you think it's good?"

James tipped his head side to side. "It's decent. Don't feel bad though. Because this one"—he picked the other drawing off the sofa—"is amazing."

"That one's not mine." Her voice was cold enough to give her hives.

"Oh." A loaded silence stretched on. The clock ticked in the corner. "Um. I actually came in here to find you and see if you wanted to jam."

"Jam?" Conflicting emotions of indignation and flattered amusement battled within her.

"Yeah." He nudged her shoulder with his. "Because you know what's *really* amazing? Your music. Your piano playing. I've been wanting to play with you all day."

The flattery won out for a brief, pink moment of pleasure. "Thanks. I'd love to. Maybe later, though?"

"Sure. After dinner?" He gave her a hopeful, cheesy grin.

"Okay." She gathered the papers and walked out. She held her head higher than she might've otherwise.

The good feeling lasted as far as the kitchen as one question in her conversation with Paul kept nagging her.

Do you think *it's great?*

The little voice, the one that more often than not spoke harsh truths, gave an immediate answer.

No. No, she *didn't* think her artwork was great. No matter how hard she tried to capture the shapes and colors in her mind, she never could. Only crude approximations fizzled from her pencils or paintbrushes. And she planned to study art in college? She was an idiot.

Or maybe this was just a crisis of confidence.

If she wanted the truth from someone she trusted, there was only one person to ask. Question was, did she want the answer?

Chapter 17

Rain battered the windows in the banquet hall as evening settled in, and the lights flickered ominously. Light reflected off swords and knives on the walls, although streaks of rust dulled some of the older blades. Even with the fire, the hall remained chilly. Morag tugged the collar of her turtleneck over her mouth and breathed slowly, enjoying her warm breath with each exhalation.

The Bacons had cooked a vegetarian casserole, and Morag's stomach growled in anticipation at the heavenly scent. Everyone sat at the long table with an ear-shattering scraping of chairs on stone. The chair next to Mike, however, remained empty. Morag glanced at the easel in the corner where the painting faced the window. She knew it was the one of the desperate woman lying curled among her paints.

"Where's Françoise?" she asked.

Mike whipped his cloth napkin from under his silverware like a magician doing a tablecloth trick and put it in his lap. "Not feeling well, I'm afraid. Would you please pass the garlic bread?"

Her shoulders sagged with both relief and disappointment. Sooner or later, she'd have to speak with Françoise. And Ben so she could ask about her pencils.

"When's Ben coming back?" Morag asked.

Mom stirred from her place a few seats down. "He decided to spend a few days with his girlfriend. Something about making sure they were together on the solstice, whatever that's about."

Morag waited to see if the adults would mention Mr. Murray's forceful suggestion they all leave for the solstice, but no one did. Nor did they discuss the woman at the craft fair or the note on the castle door. It made her want to scream with frustration.

James switched on the stereo on the sideboard. The dulcet tones of Ella Fitzgerald swept out, the round, deep purple notes large enough to fill even the big hall. She hadn't listened to jazz in forever, and she closed her eyes for a minute and let the notes dance across her eyelids. The purples and yellows clashed and coalesced, bobbed, and dipped into melting pools of color.

When she opened her eyes, she caught James watching her with a curious tilt of his head. She ducked over her plate and shoved in a bite of barley and bulgur casserole.

"This doesn't have meat in it,"—Hamish said with a full mouth—"and yet, it's delicious."

"Imagine that." Any sarcasm Ivy might have intended was softened when she crossed her eyes and stuck out her pierced tongue at Hamish.

Hamish raised his fork in salute. "Way to go, granola munchers."

"Well, we are from Boulder," Gary said.

"Kind of ironic," Hamish said through another mouthful. "You're vegetarian, and your last name is Bacon."

Paul snorted into his plate. "Tarzan knows the meaning of irony?"

"So," Dad cut in, heading off any argument. "I've been talking with Mike and heard you kids are getting whipped into a frenzy about some kind of monsters or something?"

Morag frowned at Juliette, who gave a sheepish shrug and whispered, "It was worth a shot."

"Something called the Fin Folk?" Dad said.

"All part of the fun of a big, creepy castle, right?" Paul chuckled like he was another adult indulging the children. "Like an episode of *Scooby Doo.*"

Green, turquoise, and orange flowers shimmied across Morag's vision as she heard the theme song in her head.

Juliette glared at Paul and sent Morag a desperate look. "My parents won't listen. I told them when one of us disappears into the sea to marry some flipper-freak, don't say I didn't warn them."

"What are you guys talking about?" Pete stared at them with round eyes.

Gary tapped Pete on the nose. "They're just making up some silly, spooky stuff."

Juliette straightened. "We're not making—"

"No." Mike pointed his knife at Juliette. "You're scaring people. This needs to stop. Now."

Juliette hunched into her chair and sent murderous eye daggers in her father's direction. Never, in the whole time Morag had known Juliette's family, had she seen Mike get the slightest bit angry.

"So, Billie Holiday?" James said. "Greatest or latest? Personally, I don't think she comes close to Fitzgerald. What?" he said, obviously taking note of Paul's incredulous face. "A guy has a few tattoos, and suddenly he can't know jazz? Or blues, soul, hip-hop." James counted on his fingers. "Bluegrass, for sure. Latin, reggaeton, pop, classical, alternative, and hard rock. Quick, everybody tell the person next to you your favorite genre."

James had a knack for sensing someone's discomfort and easing tension. Morag watched him throughout dinner, saw him tell Pete a knock-knock joke while cleaning up his spilled juice, and heard James laugh at a story his dad told. She liked the sharp angles of his jaw when he laughed like that, appreciated the masculine slope of his brow, and the way the tendons in his hands moved. Before, when she'd looked at Paul, she'd wanted to sketch him. Something she might not be very good at, it turned out.

Looking at James made her want to make music with him—and she was starting to suspect she might be quite good at *that*.

Mom was talking to Hamish. "Why don't you invite Ingrid here sometime? She seems nice."

Hamish's hand twitched. It probably pained him to hear a girl he liked described as *nice* by their mom. "I did invite her. Several times. Said she's not allowed at the castle."

"Not allowed?" Dad said. "What's that about?"

Hamish shrugged. "Something about her parents never getting along with the Tullochs. They don't want her at Screeverholme."

"Huh." Mom chewed slowly. "Like an old clan feud or something?" Her eyes lit up, as she no doubt imagined a drama fit for one of her beloved historical romances.

Hamish raised his eyebrows meaningfully at Morag, which told her there was more to it, but he wasn't about to say it in front of Dad and Mike.

Mom launched into an old family story about Grandma's ongoing fight with a neighbor over her begonias. Dad smiled and nodded at Mom, whispering something in her ear. Could people sit side-by-side, talk in each other's ears, smile and nod—and plot their divorce?

She couldn't stand to hope it would be all right, and she couldn't stand not to hope. Between her fears about the castle and creatures in the surrounding sea, her crisis of self-doubt as an artist, and her worry over her parents' marriage, it was a wonder there was room for Ella and her purple notes in Morag's head, but she squeezed it in nonetheless.

Morag came out of the bathroom and found Paul standing in the hallway, hands clasping and unclasping in front of him. Had he been listening to her use the toilet?

"I'm sorry, Morag. For earlier."

She blinked, at a loss for what to say. "It's okay." But it wasn't. Even if he'd only been being honest about her drawing, she couldn't forgive him so quickly. Her desire to be an artist felt integral to her. For him to painfully shred that dream into confetti with a few careless sentences—that was hard to forgive. At least for a little while.

"I meant what I said earlier." He held up his hand. "Not the thoughtless art critique. I mean when I said I care about you." He shuffled his feet.

"Like a little sister?" She picked imaginary lint off her shirt.

Paul stepped closer. "No."

She met his eyes, shimmering in the dim light.

"There you are." James walked into the hallway. "I found some sheet music in the library . . ." His voice trailed off. "I'm interrupting again, aren't I? I have terrible timing." He backed away. "Sorry. Pretend I was never here."

Just days ago, Morag would've done anything to have Paul standing in front of her, about to profess his feelings. But rather than stay to listen to the boy she'd been infatuated with since first grade, she found herself saying, "Wait, James. I'm coming."

He smiled uncertainly. "Great."

"Morag?"

She looked back at Paul. "We're gonna play some music. Want to come?"

Paul tucked his hands in his pockets and rocked back on his heels. "Maybe later."

If Paul liked her, why didn't he come along or ask her to stay and talk?

And if she really liked art, shouldn't she be hurrying off to work on that instead of following James? But her guilt didn't stand a chance compared to her anticipation of playing music with him.

Morag floated upstairs at the end of the night. For three glorious hours, she and James made colorful music that made her forget her troubles. Creating music with other people was the equivalent of slipping on 3-D glasses for the first time at a movie. The colored shapes popped out. Rather than distract her from the music, as synesthesia sometimes did when she played alone, the 3-D shapes *guided* her through the music.

The euphoria wiped away her earlier sadness and made her forget her throbbing knee as she climbed the stairs with the others, laughing and joking. With their music, she and James had caused everyone's good mood—except Paul, who'd finally joined them in the library only to work on his laptop in a corner.

Once they'd crested the spiraling stairs, however, the mood changed. A deep silence hung in the hallway, stretching into darkness. The events of the day washed over her like the icy water of the North Sea. The otter, the drawing, Paul going into the barrow—the horned figure in the window. She turned to Juliette.

"Don't worry," her friend said. "I'm sleeping in your room tonight."

Hamish spread his arms wide and smiled at Morag. "Little sis. Wanna be roomies?"

James laughed. "There's a sofa in my room. You're welcome to crash on it."

"Thanks, man." Hamish slapped him on the back.

"Are you scared, too, James?" Ivy was grinning, clearly enjoying the excitement.

"A little creeped out," he admitted.

"Wow," Paul said. "You all really believe this Fin Folk

nonsense?"

Hamish's jaw tightened, and he fisted his hands. "You think you're so smart, Paulie, but there's a lot you don't know."

Paul looked at Morag, his gaze lingering. "Maybe about some things," he said softly. He gave his head a little shake. "But there's no such thing as supernatural shapeshifters from the sea." Paul pushed between them. "Sorry to interrupt your fear-fest slumber party, but some of us would actually like to get some sleep." He disappeared into his room with an abrupt, "Good night," and slammed his door.

Hamish put on a baby voice. "'Some of us would actually like to get some sleep.' Loser."

Juliette winced, and James patted her arm. "I'm with Paul. Let's get some shut-eye."

Morag shivered as she pulled on pajamas. "Don't you think it's extra cold tonight?" Familiar itching danced over her skin. Angry at being cursed with this allergy, she pulled on her socks with a vicious tug.

"It is." Juliette frowned at her.

Morag went to the radiator on the wall and put out her hands. Heat rose from the metal, but it didn't make a dent in the chill.

"I can see hives on your neck, Mor." Juliette's concerned look was both touching and irritating. "You should get under the covers."

Malcolm meowed from the foot of the bed as if encouraging her, too. Morag climbed into the chilly sheets and heard the faint sound of barking seals in the distance. The shutters were open. "Hang on." She jumped up and crossed the room, her knee protesting, and gasped at the sight. "Juliette." She waved her over. "The lights are back."

Juliette joined her at the windows. The lights pulsed and

shimmered and circled under the water in bright yellows and greens.

"This is the closest I've ever seen them." Another shiver crawled over Morag's skin. The lights filled her with sharp fear.

"I wish my stupid brother hadn't gone in that Viking grave today," Juliette said.

Something stirred in Morag. "I only saw the silhouette in the window today, but the horns—now I think about it, they're like horns on a Viking helmet."

"Maybe it's a ghost. And my brother woke it up."

"Ghosts *and* Fin Folk?"

Juliette shrugged. "This place seems full of the supernatural."

The lights outside moved in patterns like a secret message Morag couldn't quite understand. "I'm getting everyone."

She strode into the hallway and pounded on Paul's door. Not waiting for an answer, she knocked on Ivy's and James's rooms as well.

Hamish yanked the door open an instant later. "You feel it too, don't you?"

"Feel what?"

"Evil," Hamish breathed.

Ice water flowed down Morag's spine, and she slapped his arm. "Don't be so dramatic."

"I'm not kidding."

She stared at her older brother, assessing his levels of seriousness. Which, if she had to rate, she'd put somewhere between "extremely" and "deadly." She tugged on his arm. "Come here. I want to show you something."

James joined Hamish at the doorway, and Ivy slipped out of her room.

Paul stuck his head into the hall, looking like a grumpy old man whose lawn was being overrun with children in cleats. "What's going on?"

Morag headed toward her room, passing Paul on the way. "Come see the lights."

She was afraid they would've disappeared, but if anything, they flashed closer than before.

"Whoa," James said.

"Yes. Bioluminescence." Paul made a show of yawning. "Very pretty show by Mother Nature. Can I go back to bed?"

"Dude, this isn't Mother Nature," Hamish said.

"No," Morag said. "I think it's the Fin Folk."

"You really think so?" Ivy was dancing around.

Slowly at first, then going so fast her tongue could barely keep up with her words, Morag summarized everything she and Juliette had discussed this afternoon. It all led to the Fin Folk.

Ivy, Hamish, and James all talked at once. Ivy asked something about the solstice, while James spoke about the possible meaning of the lights. Hamish's words came out loudest.

"Guys. If Ingrid's not allowed at Screeverholme"—he circled his index finger in the air to encompass them all—"maybe *we* shouldn't be here either."

Juliette, pale and drawn, stopped gnawing on her lip and said, "Let's get our parents."

"Good idea," Hamish said. "If my dad sees this—"

"He'll say what I said," Paul interrupted. "You'll look ridiculous for being *eighteen* and crying to Mommy and Daddy in the middle of the night over light-up plankton."

Morag started to speak, but Paul cut her off. "Yes, Morag, the islanders buy into this Fin Folk legend. Who can blame them? It's a spooky place on the edge of beyond. The weather's bad. There've been so many shipwrecks here. People made up stories about loved ones being stolen by the Fin Folk because it was easier than believing they drowned. And that legend carried over into silly superstition today. I can give you natural explanations for everything you listed. *We* believe in science and logic." He looked directly at Morag, his eyes pleading. "Right?"

He seemed desperate for her to agree. Whether it was because he felt alienated, or because he was scared, she wasn't sure. "Paul," she said gently. "Every scientist knows you can't deny what the data is telling you just because you don't like it. It's telling us there *isn't* a natural explanation for this."

Paul buried his face in his hands and groaned. "Morag, please, I need—"

She shivered. "I'm sorry, but *I* need to get warm." She reached past Hamish, who watched the lights with a stupefied expression, and grabbed the shutters.

Something moved at the edge of the water.

"What's that?" She pointed at the dark figure crouched on the rocks. Weak light glinted off the curving horns on his head. "It's the man with horns."

"Ha ha," Paul said. "Very amusing."

Everyone ignored him.

"Horns?" Hamish shoved her out of the way. "Where?"

"Down by the rocks." Morag shoved him back so she could point it out. In the dim light, she struggled to find the shape, but then caught movement again. The dark figure toppled forward and slipped under the water as if something dragged it away.

"I don't see it," Hamish said.

Morag blinked. "It—it's gone." She shook her head. "It was crouching by the rocks, then disappeared in the water. I swear."

"I believe you," Hamish said.

Malcolm growled low in his chest. "It's all right, kitty." Juliette stroked him, and his tail puffed up.

"See, Paulie?" Hamish said. "Even the cat knows something is wrong."

"This is wild," Ivy said. "Don't you love this?"

"No." Morag slammed the shutters, barely missing her brother's nose. "I don't. And I don't know how I'm going to sleep wondering what might be creeping into the castle, but I'm exhausted." Her knee throbbed, and despite her fear, she gave a jaw-cracking yawn.

"None of us should sleep alone." Juliette eyed her brother.

Ivy held out her hand. "Paul, want to sleep in my room?"

Paul rolled his eyes and strolled from the room, but Morag caught more than a whiff of bravado in his actions.

"Why don't you sleep with us, Ivy?" Juliette said, and the girl hastily agreed. From fear or excitement, Morag couldn't say.

"You guys will be all right?" Hamish said.

Morag yawned again and nodded. "Everybody lock your doors and windows."

James took Morag's hand and gave it a quick squeeze. "We're right down the hall if you need us."

"Yeah, yeah." Ivy arranged some blankets on the chaise. "Gender-stereotyped roles of masculine protection, yada, yada. We'll be fine."

They said their goodnights and Morag expected to spend the whole night terrified the demon-man would reappear. But the exhaustion of the long day hit her like a stampeding bull. She fell into bed beside Juliette with Malcolm on her feet and dropped into a troubled sleep filled with dreams of hungry wolves.

Chapter 18

Morag slipped downstairs in the early morning, carrying her drawing tucked inside an art book. Her stiff knee ached as she crept around the castle. Both the lounge and billiards room were empty. She continued to the first floor, half-hoping and half-dreading Françoise would be painting in the banquet hall.

Empty. She didn't like being alone in the castle. She headed toward the kitchen and was relieved to hear someone clattering dishes around.

"Coffee?" Gary held up a pot. "Tea's nice, I guess, but I'm not British, you know? Enough's enough."

Morag smiled and took the coffee to be polite. "Have you seen Françoise? I was hoping to talk to her."

Gary shook his head. "Think we're the only ones up. You having trouble sleeping?"

"Sort of." She considered telling him about the lights at sea. He might not be as quick as Dad or Mike to discount her. Before she could find out, Gary whipped open the back door of the kitchen onto a morning thick with the Orkney *haar*.

"What're you doing, Pete?" He sounded alarmed.

Morag followed Gary outside. Heavy fog shrouded the graveyard, reducing the headstones to shadowy shapes. Pete was visible only as the vaguest form until she got nearer. The dark-haired boy squatted in the graveyard in front of a headstone, digging with a plastic shovel and bucket, a canvas sack of sand toys beside him. Several mounds of dirt surrounded him, an echo of the towers of Screeverholme.

Gary and Morag approached Pete, who grinned. "Hi, Dad. I'm making a sandcastle."

"He keeps coming out here," Gary said quietly. "A few days ago, I found him playing in the burial mound if you can believe it."

Morag's stomach curled in on itself. Had Pete seen Paul in there and followed suit? She glanced at the shadowed entrance to the burial mound and shuddered at the image of the little boy inside that dark tunnel while the horned man loomed over the child. Gary crouched down and spoke in low tones to Pete, busy adding to his sandcastle and blissfully unaware he used grave dirt as his building material. While Gary was distracted, Morag crossed the graveyard toward the barrow. About ten yards from the entrance, she spotted the rusty, old pair of scissors stabbed into the earth. She drew on her courage and peered inside. Thankfully, the dead crow was gone, but a cold fist of dread squeezed her chest as she saw what else was missing.

The drinking horn.

As she crossed back through the graveyard, both Gary and Pete watched her with curious eyes. She bent down in front of the little boy. "Pete? Did you take anything from there?" She pointed at the burial mound.

He shook his head hard.

"Are you sure?"

Pete nodded. Gary shot her an odd look, but Morag didn't want to press the matter and get anyone in trouble. Because if it wasn't Pete, there was only one other logical conclusion. She straightened and spoke to Gary. "Does Ben know Pete's been in the barrow?"

Gary pressed his lips together. "No. Let's keep it that way, okay?" he said under his breath. He turned to Pete, whose face was smudged with dirt. "Pete, buddy, I told you not to come out here. I should explain why."

A few sentences from his father sent Pete into tearful wailing. "I didn't know, Dad. I didn't know."

Morag scanned the graveyard and shivered in revulsion at the hole Pete had made in the damp earth. She wanted to join the boy in crying. What fresh horror would visit them in the castle after this?

"We'll help you fix it," Gary said. Together, he and Morag helped Pete return the dirt to its rightful place.

Morag patted the soil in a brave attempt at affection for the grave's inhabitant. Who knew? Maybe it might mollify the horned man. "See, Pete. All better. I bet the person buried here liked some company for a while."

That was possibly the worst thing she could've said to a six-year-old. Pete's lower lip trembled, and he slipped his hand into his father's, dragging the sack of toys behind him. "I wanna go back inside."

The three of them were all too happy to leave the graveyard and return to the kitchen, with its smells of coffee and oatmeal to banish the lingering discomfort over Pete's gruesome sandcastle.

"Here you go." Gary set a bowl in front of his son at the table. Morag leaned against the breakfast bar counter and watched.

"Dad, I don't want oatmeal!" The graveyard experience had left him churlish, and he shoved the bowl away.

Gary made a show of looking furtively around. "All right, Pete. Don't tell the others, but I've found something magical for oatmeal." He whipped a green can from behind his back. "It's called golden syrup. You're supposed to be seven or older to eat it, but I'll let you try it if you promise to eat all your breakfast."

"Da-ad," the little boy said. "Is it healthy? It has to be healthy."

"Oh, totally healthy. Because it gives you energy."

"Okay." Pete grinned and wiggled his bottom tooth while his dad drizzled syrup off a spoon. Gary pushed the bowl back. Pete took a small, thoughtful bite, followed by a much bigger one.

"I'm telling you," Gary said in a conspiratorial tone to Morag. "It's getting harder and harder to fool kids into eating their necessary sugar these days." He dumped out Morag's now cold coffee and poured her a fresh cup.

She took a sip. It was strong enough to fly out of the mug and punch her in the face. She lifted her chin toward the golden syrup can. "Is that stuff good in coffee?"

"Don't think so. Guess that coffee's a little potent." Gary set a sugar bowl on the breakfast bar and plopped on the bench next to Pete at the table. "So. You and James sure play some great music. Maybe you should start a band. As long as it wouldn't distract him from his studies."

"His studies?" James told her he'd dropped out of school in March, not even bothering to finish his junior year, and got his GED.

"Yeah, he's doing some online college courses. Advanced Calculus and Linear Algebra."

"Really?"

"Try not to sound so shocked. James loves math. Believe it or not, he's pretty sharp."

"I'm not shocked. He seems sharp." She realized it was true.

"Yeah. School's always bored him to tears. He fell in with an iffy crowd for a while which got him in trouble. We got him tested, and the kid's off-the-charts smart. He's applying to colleges for next year."

Morag mulled that over. She'd always thought of Paul as the smartest person she knew, like he had the market cornered on intelligence. It was most of the reason for her big crush. Of course, there were lots of smart people in the world, and it occurred to her that even though she valued intelligence, there were other important aspects to attraction. Kindness. Humor. Chemistry. Could two people playing music together be—

"Can I have more oatmeal?" Pete asked.

"More oatmeal?"

"Please."

Gary got up and carried Pete's bowl to the stove.

Morag pushed off the counter. "If you see James, can you tell him I'll be in the library?"

"Gonna play some more music?" Gary smiled knowingly, and she blushed.

Great. Now she was giving him the wrong idea about her and James.

Or was she?

Morag settled at the piano with a selection of music. After a while, she leaned back on the bench, resisting the urge to pound the keys. She squinted at the first measure. It was an intriguing, haunting melody from one of the songbooks James had pulled out. It looked well within her abilities, but every time she hit the fifth measure, a jarring orange triangle appeared and scattered the other notes.

She played the note over and over, hoping to grow immune to the orange of the B-flat, but the stupid orange triangle smashed into her vision every time. She could still play the song, but when she hit that B-flat, it took time to recover and continue. Usually, B-flat was a pleasant enough amber oval, but in this particular song, her synesthetic brain decided to torture her.

She snatched the book from the piano and thumbed through it until she found another song with B-flat. Amber and oval—it caused no problems when she played *that* one. Sometimes she hated her weird brain. After her conversation with Paul, she'd tried convincing herself music was her thing, but that was crazy to think when some music created explosions in her mind that made it impossible to play.

Maybe she should stick to art after all.

As if summoned by the idea, Françoise entered the library. "Good morning, Morag. Gary said you wanted to speak to me?"

Morag's throat thickened like she'd swallowed mud. She glanced at the art book on the coffee table, her drawing tucked inside. The otter wasn't her best work, but she'd thought it was good before Paul's assessment. She could show Françoise the drawing of James, but Morag wanted to show her the same thing Paul had seen.

Perhaps sensing Morag's hesitation, Françoise asked, "Are you okay?"

"Yeah. Well, no. I—I wanted to ask your opinion about something."

"Of course." Françoise gracefully turned her hands palms up. Everything she did was graceful.

Morag left the shelter of the piano and crossed to the coffee table. Moment of truth. Was she strong enough to hear it? Yet what was the point of pursuing a dream if she had no talent? Why study art and waste her time? Better to know now than thrash around for years before swallowing the bitter pill of reality. She grabbed the art book and sat on the couch.

"Will you look at my drawing?" she said before she could take it back. "And tell me the truth?"

Françoise's mouth curved into a gentle smile as she sat beside her. "I would love that, Morag. I will tell you the truth."

Morag opened the book and handed over the drawing.

"Ah, this is nice." Françoise ran her finger over the page. "I like the way you've captured the playfulness of the otter. It is good."

Relief trickled in. "It's good?"

Françoise nodded, her eyes earnest. "Yes."

Morag took a deep, bracing breath. "But not great?"

"Morag, what is this about?"

"I showed that to Paul. He said it wasn't bad, and I got kind of angry at him."

"Ah."

"Basically, he implied I wasn't that great. An amateur."

Françoise folded her hands over the drawing and tilted her head. "Do you get paid for your work?"

Morag stared at her lap. "No."

"Then, you're an amateur, no?" She let out a tinkling laugh.

Impatience overcame Morag's fear of the truth. "Do I have any real talent, or is Paul right?"

Françoise placed her cool hand on Morag's arm. "Morag, I love my son. But sometimes he is—how do you say it?—quite full of himself. I can only imagine what he said to make you feel bad."

"So he's wrong?"

"Well, no."

There was that bitter pill, stuck in Morag's throat.

"Wait," Françoise said. "I'll explain. Art is subjective, no? What one person loves, another hates. It doesn't make it bad. It makes it art for one and not for the other."

"I just want a straight answer."

Françoise threw up her hands. "I cannot give you that. You can draw. You are smart, so you can learn new techniques if you study hard. All that matters is if you love art."

Morag read between the lines and didn't like the message. "You're saying I don't have natural talent?"

"Perhaps not, but that doesn't happen very often. It doesn't mean you can't create art that pleases you. That pleases other people, too. And that makes it art. If it makes you feel passion, you should always follow that." She paused, pulling on her ear. "If I might say something, it seems to me you have a natural talent for the piano."

Morag picked at the arm of the sofa, unable to meet Françoise's gaze. "The piano drives me crazy. And performing in front of other people is terrifying." And wonderful, but she didn't say that.

Françoise laughed. Morag looked up, and for the first time, noticed the woman's eyes were bloodshot like she'd been crying.

"If the piano drives you crazy," Françoise said, "if it makes you uncomfortable, causes you pain, then it is most definitely your gift. Of that, I am certain."

"Shouldn't you love it though?"

"You do love music. I see it shine on your face."

"Then why's it so hard?"

"Morag, do you know how hard art is for me? How hard I must work at it? It drives me crazy all the time. It's called being an artist, and you are one, too." Françoise handed her back the drawing. "If you love doing this, don't stop. But don't ignore your true gift either. Better to be yourself than try to be like someone else." She softened the pointed remark by patting Morag's hand, but it didn't stop the wash of embarrassment. Had her hero worship—like her crush on Paul—been so obvious?

Morag stared at the drawing, letting the words sink in, no matter how much they hurt. "Thank you for being honest."

"Any time." She sounded tired.

"Are *you* okay?"

She smiled brightly, but it was fluorescent light compared to the sun of her real smile. "*Bien sûr.*" Of course.

Morag knew a lie when she heard one. As for the rest of what Françoise said, it held the unmistakable ring of truth.

Orange notes and all.

Chapter 19

Everyone was eating lunch the next day when Gary plopped down at the kitchen table with a cheese sandwich. "That was some storm last night."

"Yeah," Dad said. "Poor Lisa got called in the middle of the night, and she's still not back. Another tricky birth with a woman who refused to leave the island. Lisa said it was lucky it turned out okay because it would've been impossible to transport the mother to Kirkwall in that storm."

"It was crazy. Never heard so much knocking and creaking," Gary said. "Pete was terrified."

"Knocking?" Juliette frowned at Morag.

They'd heard the wind and rain and seen the lights at sea during the storm last night but hadn't heard any knocking.

"Yeah." Gary rapped his fist on the table. "Like this. All around our windows. I don't blame Pete for being scared. I felt a little scared myself. Sounded like some monster trying to get in. I mean, it really did." He glanced toward the kitchen doorway, presumably checking to see if Pete was still in the lounge watching cartoons before he continued. "And we kept hearing creaking noises in the walls."

Morag and Juliette exchanged nervous glances.

Dad forked up a mouthful of runny eggs. "Didn't hear any knocking on our side of the castle. Must be the way your wing faces into the wind."

Or into the graveyard. Goosebumps broke out on Morag's arms. Maybe someone hadn't appreciated Pete digging around in their grave.

"Probably ghosts," Ivy said.

"Or angry Fin Folk," Juliette said. Mike gave her a warning scowl. She sent Morag a *They just won't listen* look and whispered, "One more day until the solstice."

"No more spooky talk." Dad clapped his hands together. "What's everyone's plans for the afternoon?" It was a clumsy change of subject, but it cemented an idea for Morag.

Dad and Mike could say what they liked about what Gary had heard. Morag had her own theories, but she needed more information. Taking advantage of Mom's absence and the break in the rain, she didn't hesitate. As soon as people heard she was going to Sinclair's, they wanted to join her, but she knew it would be better to do this alone. So instead, she got stuck with a long shopping list from everyone.

When Paul requested some licorice, Morag dropped her voice to a whisper and though she'd already asked him several times before, she still said, "You swear you didn't take that drinking horn?"

"No, and stop asking." He was loud enough that everyone in the room glanced their way. "Did it ever occur to you that Ben might have removed the horn for safekeeping? I'm not a thief."

"Okay, okay." Morag supposed Ben might have put it somewhere, but unfortunately, he wasn't here to ask. "I'll see you later."

Morag set off over the island, thinking how when she'd arrived here, it was as though she'd returned home to a place she'd never been, like migrating birds following in the flights of their parents or sea turtles returning to their birthplace to lay their eggs. Were people so different? Perhaps something called them to a place. A deep-seated connection borne out in the genes.

Morag moved past a herd of shaggy cows standing against the backdrop of the ancient broch, a view that should have inspired her. Françoise said there was nothing wrong with pursuing art if it brought her pleasure, but how could it when Morag knew there was no future there? With no chance of becoming great, art—and her art class—didn't appeal much anymore. She had no desire to draw the scene.

Instead, she let the rich jewel tones of the island create notes in her mind. The green of the fields played a G chord, the gray sea sounded a melancholy A minor. She took advantage of her solitude and sang a wordless melody that expressed her feelings far better than any lyrics could.

Before long, she arrived at Sinclair's, and the beginning of a song had taken shape, a song of the island. She'd never taken songwriting seriously before, but maybe it was time she did. It wasn't too late to drop her AP art class and enroll in a music one.

The bell chimed when she pushed inside the shop. A pungent smell of burned coffee hung in the air. Morag moved down a crowded aisle to the counter, and Duncan pushed to his feet with a big sigh to greet her. Muttering came from the back room, and Catherine appeared a moment later carrying a coffee maker with a brown scorch mark up its side. Her entire face shifted from frustration to a beaming smile.

"Oh, hallo, Morag. Coffee maker's packed up as ye can see, and I'm none too happy about it, but ye've cheered me right up." She clapped her hands together. "I've ordered something for ye, but don't feel ye have to buy it."

Morag's heart sank as Catherine pulled out a box of watercolor paints from under the counter.

Catching her expression, Catherine said, "Wrong sort of thing? Don't worry. I'll try to flog it off on some other islander." She chuckled, but it didn't hide her disappointment.

Morag ran her hand down the paint box, the colors sparking a song from an Icelandic band. "No, they're great. It's me that's not."

"What do ye mean?" She lowered herself onto the stool behind the counter and massaged her hip.

"Turns out my artwork isn't very good."

"Och, well. If ye could play piano like that, be as gorgeous as ye are, *and* a great artist too, I'd have to hate ye."

Gorgeous? She'd never use that word to describe herself and couldn't suppress a smile.

"Ye know, my father was a musical man himself. Most of the Tullochs were, but most especially Mary Tulloch. She'll be one of yer ancestors, too. Famous around here." Morag bit back a sigh of frustration. As much as it was interesting to hear of her family history on the Tulloch side, she needed to somehow steer the conversation to the Fin Folk.

"They say Mary came from the Fin Folk," Catherine said.

Morag's mouth fell open, never expecting to get to the topic so easily—or in such a bizarre way. Her distant relation came from the Fin Folk.

"I take it ye've heard of them? Even though we're no' supposed to speak of them."

"I've heard them mentioned." Morag wouldn't implicate Ingrid's little sister. "I read some books in Screeverholme about the legend."

"Mary Tulloch was a legend herself. Here, let me show ye something." Catherine reached under the counter and hefted out a huge, leather-bound bible, which she set down with a thud. She opened the cover to reveal an intricate family tree scrawled with different handwriting to fill the entire page. "Remind me again of yer great-great-grandfather's name? The one who went to Boston?"

Morag swallowed hard. "Douglas."

"That's what I thought." Catherine ran her finger over the script. "Here we are. Douglas Tulloch. His mother was Mary, making her your three-times-great-grandmother."

The dramatic moment conjured a bit of Beethoven's *Symphony No. 5.* for her. Mary wasn't just a distant relation— she was a direct ancestor.

Catherine turned the bible toward Morag and pointed at another name. *Alexander.* "That's Mary's father. Went missin' as a teenager. Taken by the Fin Folk." She clucked her tongue. "More likely he buggered off to the mainland, back when the islanders could leave. Since Mary's time, leaving never goes well. Or so they say."

"What do you mean?"

"If anyone born here leaves the island and doesn't return every solstice, they're cursed with nothin' but bad luck, and then they die."

"My ancestor left for Boston, and he died young."

Catherine tucked her chin in a skeptical look. "Trouble is, people die, don't they?"

"But just a few months after leaving?" Morag couldn't stop the buzz of excitement coursing through her. She sensed she was getting close to understanding what the Fin Folk meant to the islanders. *For* the islanders.

Catherine waved her hand. "Ye get a few coincidences and suddenly, everyone's frightened to leave. Girls grow up thinkin' if they try to have their babies elsewhere, they might die in labor—and their babies, too. Can you believe it?"

"Whoa." Morag's mind raced. Guess that explained why her mom had been dealing with women who wouldn't go to a hospital to give birth. "What's that have to do with Mary though?"

"A few years after Mary's father went missin', a little girl of two was found wanderin' near Hellyaskaill wearing the queerest clothes made of seaweed. Everyone knew at once it was Alexander's daughter. She was the spittin' image of him. Save for her skin, which they said would light up."

"Light up?" A bioluminescent *human?* She thought of the lights at sea. "How?"

Catherine shrugged. "This was all ages before I was born. She died in the 1940s at over a hundred years old. They say being half Fin Folk helped her live so long. There were other rumors. More believable ones."

"Like?"

"Like Alexander got a girl pregnant on another island and scarpered off. And the mum got tired of takin' care of a crippled girl with a bad allergy to the cold. Her mum must've dumped her on Tullimentay. Very clever, if ye ask me."

"Why's that?" Morag's brain struggled to make sense of the seemingly disconnected information.

"Alexander's parents took in Mary." Her mouth twisted. "They guessed the Fin Folk brought her back because they didn't want a crippled child. All the islanders looked out for the poor girl, afraid the Fin Folk would be angry if they didn't—and they claim from that time on leaving the island led to disaster." Her voice took on a bitter note, a scorched brown like the coffee. "That's why I say it must've been her mother. She made sure her bastard daughter with a bad limp was well-cared for."

Morag glanced at Catherine's cane resting against the counter, and Catherine noticed. "Oh, aye. I've a bad hip too, but where Mary's came from an injury, mine's thanks to untreated hip dysplasia as a child and a botched surgery. But ye can bet the islanders noticed and found me even more suspicious with my Tulloch name." She rolled her eyes. "Even though I'm no' related by blood."

Duncan groaned as if their conversation disturbed his sleep.

This was crazy. Morag *was* related by blood to someone who supposedly came from the Fin Folk. "That sucks people treated you that way. I can sympathize with people being suspicious. I thought people were weird at first at the ceilidh because we're outsiders, but maybe it's because of my cold allergy making them guess I'm a Tulloch."

Catherine blew out a breath. "That's my fault. The mornin' of the ceilidh, I was on the phone with a friend and mentioned ye're related to the Tullochs. I didn't know Mrs. Heddle was in my shop, and she overheard. She's been in a panic ever since, frightenin' some of the other islanders about it."

"She *un*invited me to the solstice. Guess I know why, but what is she so afraid of?"

"That ye'll draw the Fin Folk here." She made a scoffing noise deep in her throat.

"You don't believe any of it?"

Catherine didn't answer. She only folded her arms over her chest. Perched on the stool with her eyebrows drawn down in disapproval, she reminded Morag of her mom. Suddenly, she felt childish.

"Everyone else around here seems to believe it." Petulance crept into Morag's words.

"Aye, I know. Better than anyone. Has me feelin' an unwanted outsider even after bein' here since I was a young lass. Everyone skulkin' about me like my presence will summon an army of Fin Folk. I'm fed up with talk of solstices and curses."

Chastened, Morag bought a moment by crouching to pet Duncan, gazing at her with sweet eyes. Her necklace swung forward as she bent down. She took a deep breath and straightened. "I read how silver is supposed to distract the Fin Folk. Or you can use it to bribe them into leaving you alone."

Catherine's gaze slipped to the side. "Ye think I gave ye the necklace to help fend off the Fin Folk? Morag, really."

"Why *did* you give it to me?" She softened it by adding, "It was really kind."

"Why? Because I thought it suited ye. That's all." Catherine spun her silver ring around her finger and wouldn't meet

Morag's eyes.

Morag couldn't help but think what an expensive necklace it was to give away just because it suited her. "But why did you tell me to wear them all the time?"

She sighed. "The islanders believe in the Fin Folk. I thought if they saw ye wearin' the silver, it would help ye fit in. Make them trust ye more, aye, since they'd be suspicious of yer cold allergy? And it does suit ye."

"You really don't believe any of it?"

"Ye're makin' me regret I ever gave it to ye."

Morag didn't like to push Catherine, but she knew it might be her only chance. Time was running out. "What's the deal with the solstice?"

Catherine slipped off the stool. "I'm done with this conversation. Now if ye'll excuse me, I'm goin' upstairs to my apartment and gettin' my electric kettle."

Morag remembered the shopping list in her pocket. Which was worse? Returning to Screeverholme empty-handed, or shopping in Sinclair's right now?

"I'm sorry, Catherine. I was only curious." She *was* sorry, too, to have upset someone who'd only ever been kind to her—and sorry for herself as well. She'd wanted to tell Catherine everything and thought she'd found one adult who might take her seriously and even have some advice.

Catherine blew her hair off her forehead. "No, I'm sorry. Ye hit a nerve is all. I shouldna lashed out. See what happens without coffee?" A tentative smile tugged at her lips. "Forgive me?"

"Definitely." She smiled back and pulled out her list. "I've got a lot of shopping to do."

"Let me know if ye need any help. Keep an eye on my shop while I'm upstairs?" Catherine started toward the outside staircase to her apartment, then stopped. "Morag, all these stories—they do contain some good advice. Ye'll stay away from the sea, won' ye? Don't get it into yer head to go explorin' the water what with all these stories flyin' about. The tides are dangerous. There's been many a drownin' over the years. With yer cold allergy—promise ye'll stay away?"

Morag's breath caught in her throat as she forced a nod. Because just like that, Catherine's warning made her reconsider the woman's beliefs all over again.

Chapter 20

When she left the shop, heavy clouds darkened the sky, making it feel like dusk instead of mid-afternoon. Morag broke into a run across the island, determined to beat the rain and eager to share what she'd learned. She clutched the shopping bags to her chest over her pounding heart. By the time she crossed the bridge to Screeverholme and pushed open the castle door, fat raindrops fell from the sky. Panting, she climbed the spiral stairs toward the lounge and plowed straight into James.

"Morag." He caught her in his arms and took the bags, a tricky feat in the tight confines of the spiraling stairwell. "Are you all right?"

She braced her hand on the cool stone and tried to catch her breath. "Sort of?"

It was dim in the scant light leaking through the arrow-slit window, and rain pelted the glass.

"What's going on?" His dark eyes swam with concern, and Morag's breathing sped up again to have him so close. She remembered the first time she'd seen James, how she thought *other* girls might consider him hot. Turned out *she* was one of those other girls. It was his kindness, his humor, his love of his family, and music that endeared her to him, but he was, objectively, one hundred percent hot now she let herself admit it.

Which only made her heart beat faster. "I—I found out some information." She pointed up, hoping he couldn't see how flustered his proximity made her. "Are the others in the lounge?"

He nodded and motioned her in front of him. She slid past him, their bodies touching briefly, and felt the heat from the contact go from the top of her head to her toes. Keenly aware of James behind her, she led the way into the lounge to find the others sprawled on the couches and chairs.

Hamish lay on one couch and tossed his football over his head in a perfect spiral again and again. "I'm bored."

"Would you be bored if I told you our family is related to the Fin Folk?"

Hamish missed the ball, and it tumbled onto the floor as he sat up. "Uh, excuse me, can you repeat that?"

All of a sudden, the others surrounded her in a half-circle around Morag. Everyone peppered her with questions, except Paul, who kept his lips pressed tightly together. When Morag finished recapping everything Catherine had told her, he finally opened his mouth.

"This doesn't prove anything. It's more Tullimentay legends, not scientific evidence."

Juliette shot her brother a pitying look, but everyone else ignored him.

"Tomorrow is the solstice," Ivy said. "What do we do?"

"We should go see Ingrid."

"Uh, slight problem." Paul pointed to the leaded window where sheets of rain ran down as though a firehose sprayed it.

Ivy vibrated with excitement and pulled on Hamish's arm. "Text her. I don't know if she'll react well if you come straight out and ask her about the Fin Folk. Ask her about the solstice stuff first."

Hamish nodded a few times. A moment later, his thumbs flew over his phone.

"What if we just crash this solstice party?" James said.

"I don't think that's a good idea," Paul said.

"So, sit around and wait to get kidnapped?" Juliette said.

"Oh. My. God." Paul threw up his hands in disgust and returned to his chair by the fireplace.

"What did you ask Ingrid?" Morag asked Hamish.

"If I could come along to this solstice thing with her."

"And?"

Hamish grunted, his thumbs flying again. "She said it's not a good idea. I'm asking why." A second later, he frowned. "She says, 'It's a weird local thing.'" His thumbs blurred. "This is bullshit. I'm going to ask her to explain."

"Are there any other books or websites we could look at?" Juliette pulled out her phone.

Everyone spoke at once when a voice cut through it all. "That's enough." Startled, Morag turned around to see her dad standing in the doorway to the lounge. "I just came to check Morag got back safe in this rain. We don't want to worry your mother about anything else."

"Dad." Morag ducked her head, keenly aware James stood beside her. "I'm fine."

"I can see that. But I overheard you talking about this ridiculous Fin Folk stuff again. That's enough."

"Hear, hear," Paul muttered in the corner.

"In fact, you can all come downstairs and help me get dinner ready for when your mom gets home. We'll all have a nice family game night."

Hamish groaned.

"I'm doing some work for you tonight, Bill," Paul said.

"No. You'll be enjoying family game night, too."

Hamish snorted. "Ha!"

"That was the whole point of coming here," Dad said. "For our families to enjoy some quality time together. And we're going to have fun. Now come on."

Dad-mandated fun seemed like guaranteed misery, but by the end of the evening, Morag was surprised to find it *had* been fun playing Pictionary and charades. Françoise still wasn't feeling well, though, which was a shame since her Pictionary skills would've been top-notch.

Before bed, Morag gathered with the others in the upstairs hallway, and once again, their thoughts turned to the matter of the Fin Folk and the solstice tomorrow.

"Ingrid won't answer any of my questions," Hamish said. "I'm going over there tomorrow to demand she answer them."

"Demand?" Ivy said. "Not cool, bro. What if we all show up to, you know, hang out with her? Maybe we could get some info *and* have some fun, too."

"I like it." James fist-bumped his sister.

Hamish agreed.

"Should we try to do some more research?" Morag asked.

Paul heaved a long-suffering sigh. "Good night, everyone." He disappeared into his bedroom.

For a while, everyone hung out in Morag's room looking up stuff on their phones. But no amount of Boolean search terms gave them more information than what they already had. Midnight came and went.

It was officially the summer solstice, and they had no idea what that might bring. Like before, Juliette and Ivy stayed in Morag's room, and James let Hamish take his couch.

But Morag suspected sleep wouldn't come for any of them.

In the morning, it was still drizzling. When Mom overheard

Hamish talking about walking to Ingrid's, she immediately forbade Morag from going out.

"You can go without me." Morag hoped she didn't sound as pitiful as she felt.

"No way," James said. "Today we stick together."

Juliette looped her arm through Morag's. "The rain will stop. You'll see. Why don't we hang out in the *library?*" She emphasized the word and sent them a meaningful look.

Everyone, even Paul this time, hit the library to try to find more books about the Fin Folk, but they came up empty-handed. Out of sheer boredom, Ivy suggested a horror movie. The others agreed, but Morag stayed behind to continue her songwriting at the piano. The composition wasn't great yet, but that was okay. It was a work-in-progress, like her.

At last, the watery sun made an appearance, and Morag's mom deemed it safe for her to leave the castle.

"Take Pete with you," Gary said to James and Ivy. "He needs some fresh air."

As usual, Morag wore about fifty-eight layers of clothing in defense of the damp, chilly air, which made her curls go berserk. Juliette wore jeans paired with a flowing, yellow top embroidered with delicate orange flowers. Her blonde hair pulled half-up into two braids gave her a romantic air.

Morag patted her pocket for the reassuring crinkle of her traveling pharmacy. Hopefully, the rain would stay away. They strolled across the bridge, everyone laughing and shoving with pent-up nerves and excitement. The crescent of stitches around her kneecap pulled with each step, and she lagged behind to peek over the bridge. Morag fiddled with her necklace, running the pendant back and forth over the chain as she looked at the water.

The otter was back with a friend. The pair rolled and flipped around each other, and then froze as if sensing her on the bridge. Her heart thudded hard in her chest as they stared at her, and she stared back.

"Hey, there." Morag glanced at the others to make sure she wasn't noticed before she reached into her pocket, took out the folded piece of paper, and opened it. The otter in her drawing didn't do justice to the creature in the water, but it would have to do. "Here you go," she whispered and made an offering of her dream to the sea. She released her drawing over the bridge, along with any thoughts of continuing her art class or studying art in college. The paper fluttered down and floated on the water, bobbing on the waves.

It wasn't as sad as she thought it would be. She was Morag Davidson, not a Gaspar. No matter how much she might like to be part of that perfect family, she had to find her own way in the world. She had to stop trying to be someone she wasn't.

Everyone else had reached the end of the bridge, and when Morag looked back at the water, the two otters—and her drawing—had disappeared.

They made their way across the island and passed some sheep munching on a seaweed breakfast along the rocky shore. When they reached the school, a small group of parents approached the building with children in tow, weighed down with backpacks, duffels, and sleeping bags. Morag sensed a current of wildness in the children and nervousness in the parents. It wasn't a happy occasion.

"The solstice fête." Dread pooled in Morag's belly.

Parents huddled together outside the school talking while their children played in the middle, like herd animals circling to protect their young. "I think it's to keep all the children safe in one place," she said.

Pete perked at the sight of children. "Can we go play?"

"Sorry, little bro," James said. "You're stuck with us."

"Because Mrs. Heddle uninvited us," Juliette said under her breath.

Hamish called over his shoulder, "Hurry. There's Ingrid's house." The excitement was obvious in his voice.

Juliette sagged beside Morag. Her friend was hurting, and

it hurt Morag, too. She stuck out her bottom lip at Juliette. "I'm sorry."

"For what?"

"Hamish not noticing you," Morag said quietly. "He'd have driven you crazy, though."

Juliette sighed in admission and glanced at her brother Paul. "He likes you, you know. But I'm not sure the feeling's mutual anymore?"

Morag didn't reply. Instead, she found herself walking beside James, the tattooed boy with the face piercings. Morag, the girl with stage fright who played the piano in front of everyone, the girl who thought she was one kind of artist only to find out she was another, the girl who thought she'd loved Paul for years, who used to be able to ski with her family and fall in the snow to make angels without fear of dying, but now couldn't even handle the chill breeze playing across her cheeks without feeling a tingling warning.

Morag wasn't sure who she was anymore. But maybe that wasn't so bad.

A few raindrops splatted onto her head, and she did her best to ignore the incoming bank of clouds. Fortunately, they'd reached Ingrid's house. There was nothing but cold, gray sea behind it, dotted with the distant, hazy shapes of other Orkney islands. Smoke rose from the chimney, and the cacophony of barking dogs greeted them. Morag patted the dogs and stepped over the silver coins onto the front step, crowding behind her brother with the others to huddle under the small portico. Already, the rain picked up enough to patter on the roof.

Ingrid opened her front door, and her eyes widened in surprise. "Oh, hello. What are ye doin' here?"

Hamish lifted one shoulder to indicate the football under his arm. "We wanted to ask you to the park to play some touch football, but the weather isn't cooperating."

Ingrid gave him a wary look, and after a moment's consideration, she stepped back and opened the door wider.

"Mum?" she called. "We've got a few guests if that's okay?"

Seven guests to be precise. Feeling guilty, Morag followed Ingrid into the lounge.

"What are they doing here, Joyce?" asked a razor-sharp voice.

Morag cleared the lounge door to see Mrs. Heddle sitting in a chair. She slammed her cup of tea onto its saucer with a rattle.

Ingrid's mother jumped from the couch. "Susan, this is Hamish—"

"Davidson. Aye, I know." The woman's eyes stared back as cold as the sea outside the window. "Aye, I know *all about* yer family." She nodded slowly.

Behind them, the Gaspars and Bacons pushed into the overcrowded room.

The schoolteacher recoiled in her chair. "The entirety of America appears to have shown up in yer own home, Joyce."

Magnus lifted his hand in greeting and took a loud slurp of his tea.

Joyce did an admirable job of trying to ignore the other woman's rude behavior. "Everyone, this is Mrs. Heddle, our local schoolteacher."

"We've met." Morag matched Mrs. Heddle's stern look with her own. "I thought you'd be at the school for the solstice party."

Mrs. Heddle's eyes narrowed. "I'm here to pick up Bridget and Ingrid."

"They're no' going'," Magnus said.

Before this argument could continue, Pete burst into the room. "That dog licked me on the nose!" he said joyfully.

The transformation in Mrs. Heddle was astounding. She leaned forward in the armchair, a big smile on her face. "Who's this handsome lad?"

Pete held out his hand for her to shake. "I'm Peter Bacon. Do you guys have any cookies?"

Mrs. Heddle giggled. "Cookies. He means biscuits, aye? Joyce, give him some biscuits. Then I think these children need to be on their way, and I'll take Bridget and Ingrid with me." She pursed her lips at Ingrid's mom, daring her to disagree.

Ingrid's face turned so red, her freckles disappeared.

Magnus grunted. "The weather's no' so nice just now, Susan. No one's goin' anywhere."

The worsening rain beat against the windows in demonstration. How would Morag get home without dying? Why couldn't the weather cooperate for more than three hours at a time?

"Can I make ye tea?" Joyce made a desperate lunge toward the kitchen.

"Heavens, that's too much tea for anyone to make," Mrs. Heddle said. "Not that my sister ever listens to me."

Everyone rushed to reassure Ingrid's mother they didn't need tea.

Morag turned to Mrs. Heddle in surprise. "Joyce is your sister?"

"Aye." Mrs. Heddle nodded. "Everyone here is family one way or another. Sometimes, ye'd never believe the family relationships ye discover."

A willful streak overtook Morag. "I guess you heard we're distantly related to the Tullochs?" she said with false cheer.

Mrs. Heddle spluttered into her tea.

"*Do* you have cookies?" Pete asked, oblivious to the tension in the room.

"Here. I'll get the lad some biscuits." Mrs. Heddle glared at Morag and herded Pete into the kitchen. Everyone shuffled their feet and stole glances at one another.

"You have a lovely home," James said.

"Thanks." Joyce looked startled, perhaps not expecting such manners from a boy with an eyebrow ring. "I'm afraid it's no' quite big enough for the lot of ye, but there's always the barn. It's got a telly out there."

"I wanna see the barn." Pete came from the kitchen clutching two fistfuls of cookies. "Are there animals?"

Mrs. Heddle stood ramrod straight and laced her fingers at her waist. "I need to be on my way with my nieces. It's best ye all go home before the weather gets worse."

Morag wondered how it could.

"Speakin' of the weather," Ingrid said. "Morag'll need a ride, Mum. I can drive them back."

"To Screeverholme?" Mrs. Heddle's voice rose as high as her eyebrows. "I think no'. Didn't I make it clear about their family?" She lifted her chin in Morag's direction with a hateful glare. "The answer's no, Ingrid."

"Ingrid is *my* daughter. I believe I'm in my own home." Magnus pointed toward the front door. "It's my Land Rover sittin' in the drive out there last I checked. I'll make the decisions here."

"Ye can't possibly let the girl near there, Magnus. Not *today*. She and Bridget are comin' back with me to the school."

Ingrid's dad rolled his eyes. "I've tried to be understandin' of all of this, but I think I've reached my limit. I'm a doctor, a man of science." He scooted forward on the couch and dug into his jeans pocket to produce a set of keys. "Here ye go, Ingrid. Ye can drive yer friends home, all right? Just be careful, aye?"

Ingrid took the keys, her eyes darting between her dad and aunt as if she couldn't quite believe she was being allowed such freedom.

"Go." Magnus waved at them. "Take the whole bloody lot of ye out of my house." He dug into his pocket again, took out his wallet, and peeled off some orange ten-pound notes. The sight of them sounded a few aggravating B-flats in Morag's head. "Stop in at the pub. Play some games, have a laugh. Enjoy havin' some new people on this island for once." He scowled at his sister-in-law.

Mrs. Heddle's eyes blazed right back. "I think ye're a fool, Magnus."

"Nothin' new there, then, is it?"

Their group was too big to take in one trip. Hamish left with the first group, and Morag hoped he'd get some information out of Ingrid. Morag stayed behind with Paul, James, and Pete, while Bridget was ordered to show them the barn. Luckily, the barn was only a short distance from the house, and as Morag followed the girl outside, she wondered how she might question her.

James nudged Morag in a way that was probably only friendly but made her pulse take a sudden upswing. "You on for another music session tonight?"

"Assuming we survive the solstice, sure." She failed to stop a goofy grin, despite the flicker of fear. "I—I've got a song I've been working on," she blurted before she lost her nerve. It was even more terrifying to consider showing someone her music than her drawings. Was that because Morag believed her songwriting might actually be good? That, with work, it could be great?

"Let's give 'er a test spin." James waggled his pierced eyebrow. "I've written a few songs myself. Maybe we could collaborate on something."

"I wasn't aware you were a songwriter, Morag." Paul wedged between them and turned his back on James. "I'd love to hear one of your compositions."

"Okay." Was Paul jealous? Did he have a reason to be? Morag ducked her head to hide her bemusement and slipped into the dim interior of the barn.

It was a strange combination of a living room with a couch and television at one end and a proper barn with goats and ponies at the other. The warm barn smelled of animals and clean straw, and a few clucking chickens dashed here and there.

Paul and James became absorbed in the old farming equipment. An unspoken competition sprang up between them, and their comments grew ever more technical as they tried to impress or contradict each other with their knowledge of tractor engines. Morag left them to it to admire the animals.

Pete giggled as he fed bits of hay to an old nanny goat. That left Morag alone with Bridget, who stood on a stepstool feeding an apple to a pony. This was Morag's chance.

She leaned on the stall door and attempted to look casual. "Hey, Bridget. I always wear my silver necklace." Morag winked. *Okay, that was creepy.* She rushed on. "So, I'm safe from what we talked about."

Bridget stroked the pony's nose.

"But I'm still worried. You said there're scarier things in the sea. How do I stay safe from something I don't know about? Can you tell me more? I won't tell anyone." Now she sounded even creepier—like some stranger parents warned their children about. She'd been one step away from saying it would be their little secret.

Bridget gave Morag a cagey look and glanced in the direction of the others.

"What are they?" Morag whispered.

"Undead things. Ye can't kill them except to chop off their heads."

Morag's mind spun with possibilities. Vampires? Zombies? "What do they have to do with the Fin Folk?"

Bridget offered another apple slice to the pony who whuffled it from her palm. "I heard my auntie say the Fin Folk made 'em. An undead army to kill us."

Morag was too stunned to respond, and the Land Rover rumbled up outside, putting a stop to the conversation.

The drive to the pub turned tense as James and Paul competed to see who knew more of the Land Rover's specs. Ingrid rolled her eyes at Morag in the passenger seat.

Morag decided to put a stop to it. "Ingrid, what's the deal with the overnighter at the school?"

"I wish ye and Hamish would stop with the questions." Ingrid's hands tightened on the steering wheel. "It's a summer tradition for the children here. It's just an overnight camp to learn about the wildlife of Tullimentay." She sounded so pleased with this last sentence, Morag knew the sound of a well-rehearsed lie.

"Your aunt asked me to it the first day we met, but at the ceilidh, she uninvited me. Why would she do that?"

"Erm, who can say? She's always been a bit crackers. Maybe she worried ye'd be bored."

"Is that why your dad didn't want you going?"

"Look, here's the pub."

In other words, drop it already.

Morag climbed out, and her neck itched where the cold rain hit her skin. She hurried into the snug building and spotted Juliette sitting close to Hamish at a corner table, Ivy across from them. A popular British singer played over the speakers, and her powerful voice created hypnotic stars of red and navy blue. In no time, Morag sat by the fireplace of the old pub, an appropriate Scottie dog lying near the hearth at her feet.

Hamish lifted his head toward Ingrid at the bar. "She dodged all my questions and changed the subject."

Before Morag could respond with what Bridget had shared, Ingrid set pints of cider in the middle of the table. The owner of the mostly empty pub didn't bother himself with drinking ages. Ivy couldn't believe her luck. Mrs. Heddle's disturbing behavior and the tension between James and Paul and their frustration with Ingrid's reticence to speak about the Fin Folk evaporated in the festive atmosphere of the cheerful pub. Soon, everyone was laughing. Ivy, as usual, laughed the loudest. The afternoon wore on, cementing friendships between all present. By the second pint, Morag decided she was not only best friends with Juliette, but with Ivy, and Ingrid, too.

Ingrid, as designated driver, told them it was getting close to dinner, and she needed to go home. She took the first carload back to the castle, and Morag drank another pint waiting for her turn. The drive to Screeverholme passed in a blur. Morag staggered across the bridge, arms linked with Ivy and Juliette, and asked if she should get an eyebrow ring, too. She was vaguely aware Hamish was kissing Ingrid goodbye on the bridge, and it struck Morag as incredibly romantic.

She wished James would kiss her on the bridge. No, not James. Paul. She meant Paul. "No, I want to kiss James," she said out loud.

Juliette frowned. "What?"

But Ivy cackled. She looked around and spotted her brother walking behind with Paul and Pete. "Did you hear that, James? Morag wants to kiss you!"

"Okay. I'm never gonna say no when a pretty girl wants to kiss me." James strode forward, yanked Morag away from the other girls, spun her to him, and kissed her hard on the mouth. His lip ring, cold and smooth, added an element of interest to the kiss. Not that she had anything else to compare it to but a quick peck after last year's homecoming with Brandon Becker. This was a marked improvement.

James pulled away all too quickly and gave her a gentle push toward Juliette and Ivy before returning to hold Pete's hand.

Morag's hand drifted to her lips, warm from James's. He thought she was pretty? She felt a ridiculous smile spread across her face and looked over her shoulder.

Paul, stony-faced, stared back.

Ivy followed her gaze and pulled a face. "Uh-oh. Somebody doesn't look happy."

"He had his chance," Juliette said. "Anyway, it's probably better you don't date my brother. Might make it weird between us. And no worries about me dating yours." She tilted her head toward the bridge where Hamish was talking to Ingrid.

His voice carried along the bridge. "Ingrid, come inside. Just for a little while."

Morag and the others slowed to watch the exchange. Hamish pulled on Ingrid like someone trying to lead a stubborn horse. She dug her feet into the cobbled stones.

"No, I have to get back."

"I know there's a demon-man here, and the place is infested

with Fin Folk," Hamish said, "but I'll keep you safe."

Ingrid stopped digging in her feet, and Hamish accidentally pulled her into his chest. "What did ye say?"

"Fin Folk?" Hamish took advantage of catching her off guard and dragged her closer toward the castle.

"Stop sayin' that."

"Fin Folk!" Hamish's voice echoed off the castle walls. "Fin Folk, Fin Folk, Fin Folk. I'm not afraid," he said, with the bravado of the tipsy.

"Ye should be." Ingrid backed away from him. "I've got to go. Promise me ye'll be careful and stay inside tonight. Don't go around shoutin' things like that, aye?"

"Kiss me one more time, and I won't do it again."

Morag turned around to give them privacy. Her skin was tingling, and she needed to get inside. She passed the place on the bridge where she'd knocked her pencils into the water and thought again how she'd taken their return as a sign the Fin Folk might not be evil after all.

But Bridget told her the Fin Folk had created an army of undead. Not exactly a good-guy move. She considered all the things she'd seen with her own eyes—the slinking wolf, the horned man, the bear, and the dead sheep—and agreed with Ingrid. She'd rather not have her idiot of a brother shouting their name on the bridge, of all places.

Why tempt fate?

They might've gotten in trouble for drinking at the pub if they hadn't come back to the adults well into their cups. Beer bottles and wine glasses littered the kitchen table, but it wasn't a party atmosphere. Something felt off.

"Where's Mom?" Juliette asked.

Mike slouched at the long table, surveying them with bloodshot eyes. "Probably talking to her boyfriend." He pointed his beer at them. "You hungry for dinner? I hear it's gonna be good." He took a long swig.

"Mike." Morag heard the warning in her father's voice.

"Qu'est-ce qui ne va pas?" Paul asked.

Mike didn't take the hint to respond in French. "Your mother's having an affair. In better news, Gary is doing a stir-fry. Smells delicious."

Several long, stunned seconds of silence ticked by where no one seemed to move or even breathe.

As if stuck by a pin, Juliette gave a delayed gasp, breaking the silence. She looked stricken. "An affair? Seriously?" She pressed her hand to her milk-white cheek.

"It would appear so from the texts I found. You can ask her yourself when she shows her face again. Unfortunately, she can't leave until the next ferry in three days." Mike's mouth twisted as he turned in his seat to speak to Morag's dad. "Fantastic, isn't it? Stuck on an island with your adulterous spouse and no escape."

Dad put his hand on Mike's shoulder and squeezed. "Mike."

"Yeah." Mike pushed himself up to stand and staggered. "Should talk to my kids somewhere private."

"Or maybe wait until you're sober," Dad said.

Morag felt instantly sober herself.

Mom chopped carrots harder than necessary. "I wish we could get snow peas on the island," she said loudly. Funny it was now her trying to cover Mike's behavior.

Morag sank onto a bar stool at the counter. Rubbing her hand over her knee, she recalled the conversation in the bathroom. Mom had said everything wasn't as it seemed when Morag had pointed out Juliette's parents never fought. Had her mom known or merely suspected?

How much of reality did Morag misjudge—or miss altogether? Because she was only sixteen or simply unobservant? Either way, it left her unsettled to realize situations and people had hidden depths she hadn't suspected. Her earlier joy evaporated like the steam coming off the stir-fry pan. Françoise was cheating on

Mike. On her family. How could she?

Mom placed a coffee mug in Mike's hand and patted it with her own. Mike gave a weak smile and led Paul and Juliette out of the kitchen, all of them looking as sick as Mom had on the ferry. Morag wanted to comfort Juliette, but what could she say? As much as she loved the Gaspar family, it wasn't Morag's place to get involved. It wasn't her family.

But the Gaspars were *like* family, and it felt like someone died.

Dinner was a somber event. None of the Gaspars reappeared. Morag kept staring at the weapons on the wall, with all their promise of violence and wished they'd eaten in the kitchen instead. The banqueting hall was chilly without Mike feeding the fire.

The Bacons and Morag's family watched a movie in the lounge to distract themselves from the drama unfolding upstairs. Except for Pete, tucked up in his own tower above the kitchen, no one went to bed in case the Gaspars needed their space up there.

The weather refused to be upstaged and created its own drama. Rain lashed the windows with such intensity, Morag wondered if it could crack the glass. Wondered, too, what unknown risks Hamish had taken when shouting out the Fin Folk's name like that. If the Fin Folk could control the weather, was this personal? Gusts of wind drove the torrent against the castle. Lightning flashed in the sky, and thunder rumbled, growing closer, the storm a hungry beast ready to devour the castle whole.

Morag shivered. The carriage clock on the mantle chimed eleven right as a frantic knocking sounded on the castle's front door. Dad got off the couch, frowning at Gary. Together, the two dads headed down, everyone trailing behind. Morag's father pulled open the door onto the pounding rain. Ingrid's parents, soaked and wearing anxious faces, stepped inside the entry.

"Is Ingrid here?" Joyce shouted over the rain. "Have ye seen

Ingrid?"

Dad shut the door. A beat of deafening silence followed as Joyce's words sank in.

"We called Hamish," Magnus said, "but we didn't get an answer." His eyes went to Hamish.

Hamish pulled his phone from his pocket. "No signal."

Joyce clutched at his sleeve. "She's no' with ye?"

Hamish shook his head slowly, his brow furrowed. "She dropped us off around five."

Joyce gave an anguished cry and whirled around to bury her face in Magnus's chest.

"We found the Land Rover running in the road," Magnus said numbly. "She never came home."

Chapter 21

Joyce pounded her fist against her husband's chest. "My sister wanted Ingrid at the school. But ye weren't born here, and ye wouldn't listen. Ye've never been here when this happened. If Ingrid—" Racking sobs choked off her words and wrenched Morag's heart.

"I asked her to come inside." Hamish's features contorted in horror, and the Davidsons closed around him in support. Ivy, subdued for once, huddled between Gary and James in the chilly entry.

"The island's not that big," Dad said. "We'll form a search party and call the police."

Joyce issued a harsh laugh. "The police won't come. They never do."

Dad's frown deepened. "What do you mean, 'they never do'?"

Magnus held his wife tightly against him. "The weather. They can't come."

"The weather is always like this when they take one," Joyce

cried into his chest.

Dad looked helplessly at Gary who shrugged in bewilderment. "When who takes what?"

Magnus spoke over the top of his wife's head. "She means the Fin—"

"Don't, Magnus!" Joyce pulled from his embrace. "It's bad enough already. At least this way, they mightn't harm her."

Hamish's face crumpled in anguish, probably thinking how he shouted their name on the bridge. Morag certainly was.

"She must be nearby. She could've stopped to help an injured animal and—"

"Then why didn't we find her? What will it take for ye to believe? Ye know the curse is real. Look what happened to my niece. Or to any of us who try to leave the island." Joyce's voice shook. "The Land Rover's on the road, Magnus, and she didn't come home."

Magnus smoothed his hands over his wife's wet head. "What do we do, Joyce? Tell me, and I'll do it."

"She's gone. We'll never see her again." Her wails turned into a wretched howling.

Hamish buried his face in his hands. Juliette and Paul crept into the entry, attracted by the commotion. Juliette's face was blotchy from crying. She and Paul stared at the hysterical woman.

"Joyce, come sit down." Mom—always calm in a crisis—put her hand on Joyce's arm.

The woman flung it off with startling violence. "This is all yer fault. I know about the Tullochs in your family. Oh, aye, my sister told me." Joyce's face twisted fiendishly, and her voice dripped poison. "Why did ye come here? The Tullochs finally died, and ye took their place and kept the curse goin'. Leave!" Her voice rose to a shriek. "Go away!" She threw herself at Mom, hitting her face.

"Hey!" Dad's jaw dropped in outrage, and he moved to protect Mom.

Magnus grabbed his wife's arms and dragged her back. "I'm sorry," he choked out, wearing the same shocked expression as everyone else. "I'm so sorry." He turned abruptly and walked out, frog-marching the crying Joyce into the rainy night. The door slammed behind them.

No one said anything for several heartbeats.

"What the *hell* was that?" Gary asked.

"Are you all right, Lisa?" Dad bent to examine Mom's face with a tenderness that touched Morag.

Everyone burst out talking. About Ingrid, the curse, the Tullochs.

"I'm calling the police," Dad said to no one in particular.

"It's true?" Juliette stepped closer to Morag. "The Fin Folk took Ingrid?"

Paul scoffed. "Is it true shapeshifting, amphibious people came onto the island and dragged Ingrid away for a forced matrimony? Are you listening to yourself? More likely she snuck here to get some with Lover Boy, and the two of them are too afraid to tell her parents. I'd check Hamish's bed first."

"What did you say?" Hamish didn't wait for a response. He spun Paul around by his shoulder, cocked back his arm, and landed a solid punch on Paul's face.

"Hamish!" Dad, busy on the phone, gestured wildly at Gary, who moved toward the altercation.

Blood gushed from Paul's lip, and he retaliated by sweeping Hamish's legs out from under him. Hamish slammed onto the stone floor with a loud grunt, and everyone gasped. Morag covered her mouth in shock.

"Paul!" A red-faced Françoise appeared in the doorway, followed by her furious husband.

For several minutes, chaos reigned supreme. When the dust settled, they all moved upstairs to the lounge. Mom and Paul gave each other rueful looks before sinking onto the couch with bags of frozen vegetables on their faces. Hamish sat gingerly in a chair, his hand at the small of his back, and stroked Malcolm in his lap.

Dad cleared his throat and looked at their group, sitting or sprawled or perched tensely, depending on the person. "Magnus is right. The police boat won't come in this weather. Ingrid has to be around somewhere. We'll search the island."

Malcolm jumped off Hamish, who stood with a wince. "Great. Let's go."

James unfolded himself from the floor. "I'm in."

Ivy said, "Me too," echoed by Juliette.

"I *want* to help," Morag said. "But my stupid allergy means I can't go out in this storm."

Dad waved his hands around. "No. Only adults for the search."

Hamish stared his father down. "I'm eighteen. I *am* an adult."

Dad shook his head in exasperation but didn't argue. "Fine. Everybody else, go to bed. There's nothing you can do."

"Yo, I'm eighteen, too." James crossed his arms and stepped closer to Hamish.

Hamish clapped him on the back. "Thanks, man."

"No problem. Let's go find your girlfriend."

"Uh, I'm sixteen," Ivy said. "I can help."

"Not happening." Gary pulled on a pair of hiking boots. "You need to keep an eye on Pete for me."

A quick, heated argument, conducted solely through facial expressions, passed between father and daughter until Ivy threw up her arms. "Fine."

Morag waited for Paul to offer help, to remind everyone he was seventeen, which was close enough, but to her disappointment, he remained silent, the bag of frozen peas still cradled against his mouth.

As the adults put on jackets, Morag grabbed Hamish. Something Ingrid said kept rattling around her head. *It's where they take people.* "Hamish, do you think—" She hesitated. Morag didn't want to put him in danger, but what about Ingrid?

"Do you think she could be at the cave?"

He gave a grim nod. "Good idea." He rubbed his hand down his face. "She told me not to shout their name. This is my fault, right?"

"It's not." At least she hoped so. "If I bundle up, I could go with you."

"No way, Morrie. You wouldn't last a minute in this."

He turned away when Morag grabbed his arm. "Wait." She could help in this one, small way. Her fingers struggled with the clasp until the silver pendant slid free. "Wear this. It's silver. The Fin—" She wouldn't say their name. "The silver might buy you time." Morag helped him put it on, the delicate necklace absurd on her giant brother.

He tucked it under his shirt and zipped his coat. "Thanks." Hamish pulled her into a bear hug, and his stubble scratched her cheek. He was right. He was an adult now.

Kind of.

"Be careful," she said. "'Cause I don't really hate you."

He rolled his eyes in dismissal and punched her in the arm. "I know. No one could hate *me*, Morag."

Paul stepped forward. "It's not that I don't want to help—I just didn't want to leave the girls alone, okay?"

Sexist, yes, but Paul meant well, and he was who he was—somebody Morag finally realized wasn't for her—as anything more than a friend. A friend she had to admit she was glad would be staying here with her, given the circumstances.

"Sorry for what I said," Paul continued. "Hope you find Ingrid soon. Take this." He shoved a flashlight at Hamish.

"Thanks." Hamish took it, stunned. "Sorry about your mouth."

Paul shoved his hands in the pockets of his hoodie. "I deserved it. Sorry about knocking you on your ass."

Hamish's lip twitched. "You've got moves, I'll give you that."

Then all the adults were gone, leaving behind Morag, Paul, Juliette, and Ivy with Pete sleeping upstairs. Ivy collapsed onto a sofa and flipped through the television channels, Paul fed the fire, and Juliette sat on a chair under a lamp with her embroidery.

How could she embroider at a time like this? Morag paced and checked her phone every few seconds for updates but didn't have a signal half the time. "I hate being stuck here not knowing what's going on."

Malcolm meowed and rubbed himself against the bookcase in the corner. Morag walked over to where a book stuck out from the others. "What's this?"

"Nothing." Paul jackknifed up from crouching by the fireplace.

Morag ignored him and read the title of the protruding book with a smile at the cat. "Did you know Malcolm is a character in *MacBeth?*"

"Yes." Paul sounded impatient as he reached past her to shove the book back into place. Morag would swear she heard him sigh in relief, but it was instantly overlaid by a strange rumbling in the distance.

Thunder.

"Hey, what's this?" She pulled the book next to MacBeth off the shelf.

Paul tilted his head to read its title. "'*A Brief Summary of Tullimentay Folklore.*'"

Morag had focused her search for Fin Folk books in the library rather than the lounge since almost all of them here were tattered paperbacks. She carried the old green volume to an armchair and sank down. Malcolm jumped on her lap and began purring as if he approved of her reading selection.

Paul left her to argue with Ivy over whether they should watch a horror film or a space documentary, with Juliette acting as referee. Morag ignored them as she skimmed through the yellowed pages. It was written by a pompous-sounding English scholar who'd come to the island in 1897 to catalog local beliefs. Her eyes raced over the words when she saw chapter twenty-five, *Curse of the Orkney Sea.*

"Guys, shut the hell up." Morag cut off Ivy's screech as Paul dove over a chair to grab the remote from her. "Listen to this. 'The people of Tullimentay believe in a race of dangerous sea people called the Fin Folk who use the magic of the solstice to snatch a human for a mate. Mothers take special care to protect their children on the solstice as the Fin Folk will creep in at night to steal hairs from their heads to use in dark magic. Mary Tulloch, a local resident, is said to be part Fin Folk and was accused of casting a curse that prevents the locals from leaving the island on the solstice. The islander's hostility extends to any Tulloch, who are believed to draw the Fin Folk to the island in greater numbers'."

"It makes sense now why people wanted your family gone for the solstice," Juliette said, embroidery forgotten. "Mrs. Heddle wouldn't want you at the school if you might attract Fin Folk."

Lightning flashed outside and thunder rumbled. Morag stirred. "Maybe we shouldn't say their name."

"When it says they steal hair from kids, how much are we talking?" Ivy ran her fingers through her purple and red locks. "A couple of strands? Or are these kids left, like, totally bald here?" Her laughter was cut short by a piercing scream.

The cat jumped off the sofa with a hiss, and Ivy flew toward the doorway. "Pete."

Morag might not be able to go out in the storm, but she *could* go with Ivy. She rushed out of the lounge. The two of them, Malcolm on their heels, raced into the kitchen to the spiral staircase. Pete screamed again, and they pounded up the steps. What if the Fin Folk had come to steal Pete's hair?

Ivy flipped on the hall light and rushed into Pete's room. His bedside lamp threw out a faint circle of light over him cowering under a blanket, shaking like a small dog. Ivy launched herself onto the bed and drew the boy into her arms. "It's okay, Pete. I'm here now."

Morag hung in the doorway, unsure how to help.

"There was a man." Pete pointed at the leaded window. "There!"

The cat's golden eyes glowed green in the darkness as he let out a low growl that raised the hairs on Morag's neck.

"Shh." Ivy stroked her hand over Pete's hair to calm him. "You're okay."

"He knows I took it," Pete said. "He was pointing at it."

"At what?"

Pete scrambled out from under his blankets and ferreted under the bed until he lofted up the drinking horn. "This."

Morag's heart thudded heavily in her chest. One mystery was solved, at least.

"I stole it," he sobbed. "I knew it was wrong, but I wanted it." The gold bands gleamed in a flash of lightning as he set it on his nightstand.

"Is that from the Viking burial mound?" Ivy said. "Pete, that was naughty. We'll put it back tomorrow." She sent Morag a look of dismay. "You can sleep with me tonight, okay?"

Pete's lip wobbled. "Okay. I'm sorry." Then he shrank onto his bed and screamed. "He's back!"

Where the thin moonlight streamed into the room, a monstrous shadow fell on the wood floor, the outline of a man with two curving horns rising from his head.

Tears of terror sprang to Morag's eyes.

"Holy crap." Ivy jumped off the bed and scooped Pete against her.

Malcolm sprang toward the shadow with a yowl as Ivy pushed Morag through the bedroom doorway, plowing them into Juliette. "Go, go, go!" She shoved Juliette, who turned back down the hall.

"What's happening?" Juliette said.

"He's gone." Pete pointed over his sister's shoulder as she clutched him against her chest. "He disappeared, Ivy."

Morag didn't stop. For all she knew, it meant the monster was on the move. Malcolm slipped down the hallway ahead of them as if spurring them on.

"What's going on?" Juliette tried again as she hurried down the staircase.

Neither Ivy nor Morag answered, and they raced into the lounge.

Paul turned from his sadly smoking fire. "Everything all right?"

"There's a freaking monster in the castle," Ivy blurted. "So, I'd have to say no. Everything is *not* all right."

Paul made a brave show of poking around Pete's room while Morag huddled with the other girls and Pete in the hallway. No way in hell was she going back in there. Paul came back and declared Pete's bedroom was monster-free, but Morag and Ivy weren't reassured.

They decided hot chocolates in the kitchen might not be a bad idea. Malcolm accompanied them, and Morag felt oddly better for the cat's company. Juliette slammed cupboards louder than necessary, clanked spoons and cups, and generally did her best to stave off everyone's fear with noise.

Ivy lowered herself onto the bench next to Pete, and her hands trembled as she lifted her mug. "We need to get off this island."

Paul sat across from her calmly sipping his hot chocolate. "If there really are monsters here, Ivy, I'd have thought you'd want to stay. Enjoy all the excitement."

Her mouth fell open. "You're joking, right?" Morag supposed even Ivy's ability to relish a spooky thrill had worn thin. "This isn't a movie, Paul. It's real life."

He lifted an eyebrow. "You don't think all this talk of curses and Fin Folk is fun?"

"Don't say that," Morag muttered. "Don't say their name."

"You think I'd find it *fun* monsters are real and snatch kids away?" Ivy said. "Is it fun Ingrid is missing?"

Paul sighed. "Ingrid's going to be fine, you'll see. We saw some bioluminescence, some shadows, and you're this scared?"

"I want to leave, too," Juliette said. "As soon as possible."

"Gaspars are made of tougher stuff."

"The Gaspars are weak," Juliette snapped. "In case you didn't notice, our family fell apart tonight because of it."

That shut Paul up—for the moment at least. Ivy and Morag shared an awkward grimace.

Paul held his breath a moment. "I think everyone's getting carried away in group hysteria. There are rational explanations for all of this."

Ivy wrapped her arm around Pete's hunched shoulders. "I have no rational explanation for that shadow."

Another argument broke out, and Morag unsqueezed herself from the bench to put her empty mug in the sink. Malcolm scratched at the back door and stood on his back legs to reach his front paw toward the doorknob. Morag looked out the window where lightning forked across the gray sky, highlighting the headstones in the graveyard. The mounds looked swollen, the rain expanding the earth, and the graves brought to mind the disturbing image of ripening fruit ready to burst forth their crop of dead.

"You're not going out there, buddy," Morag said to him.

"Refusing to face reality is itself illogical," Ivy was saying.

Morag ignored the bickering at the table. Something was moving in the darkness of the barrow entrance. "What's that?"

No one heard her.

"It's not reality," Paul was saying to Ivy. "It's your imagination."

"I *saw* that shadow on the floor."

Another bolt of lightning tore open the sky, illuminating a formless shape emerging from the burial mound. Morag's eyes struggled with the dimness after the lightning.

"You saw a shadow, but your mind created a pattern from what your little brother told you."

As Morag's vision adjusted, she saw the shape was moving stiffly up the slope.

"It wasn't real," Paul continued.

A lead weight fell into Morag's chest. "Um, guys? I think *that's* real." She pointed out the window at the nightmare-come-to-life staggering through the graveyard toward the castle.

Chapter 22

Juliette and Ivy, with Pete trailing behind, got up to stand beside Morag. Juliette peered through the glass and jumped back with a strangled yelp. Morag didn't blame her. What they were seeing was terrifying.

"Don't look," Ivy said to Pete, who buried his face in her stomach.

Outside, the hulking shape drew closer, taking on the rough form of a man covered head to toe in black soil, like a golem come to life. Horns sprouted from the man's head. He carried something that looked like a staff, though it was hard to tell, as it too was covered in a thick layer of mud and dirt.

Ivy swore softly under her breath. "Tell me that's another wedding blackening."

"I don't think so." Morag's voice shook.

With each step he took, the grave dirt shook from his body, revealing more of the horror underneath.

A whimper escaped Ivy, and an impatient sigh issued from Paul as he scraped back the bench from the table. "What is it?" He marched toward the window. "Is it more scary glowing plankton or a grizzly or maybe—oh my god!"

Morag nodded in agreement, unable to tear her eyes away from the creature.

Paul put his hands on his head in astonished terror.

"What do we do?" Juliette asked quietly as if she might draw the creature's attention. She whirled around. "I'll make sure all the doors are locked." She checked the kitchen door before rushing from the room. Morag doubted locks would make a difference to the thing moving in their direction.

Morag switched off the overhead lights. Unfortunately, it made the gray twilight outside brighter so they could clearly see the full evil being unearthed in front of them. Dirt continued to fall away from the monstrous man approaching the castle.

He wore a rotting tunic with a tattered leather breastplate, leggings, and ragged leather boots crisscrossed with cords. It wasn't just his clothes that were decayed—*he* was. White bones gleamed under hanging strips of rotting flesh. Ribs here, a femur there, a glimpse of a humerus.

Dem bones, dem bones, dem dry bones, popped in Morag's head. Only these bones weren't exactly dry. Sinewy tendons and flaps of muscle stretched across them. Thick dirt caked his face from view.

Pete started crying while Ivy made meaningless soothing noises and pet his hair.

The scene was too ghoulish, too unreal to prompt any rational action, and Morag finally understood how someone could freeze up. She gave herself a mental slap. She couldn't stand here doing nothing and hope they'd be safe in the castle. A terrible thought struck her. Everyone else was outside. "We have to warn the others." Morag pulled out her phone, but her heart sank. "I don't have any signal."

Ivy swore. "Me neither."

Lightning flashed, and a moment later, a roll of thunder rattled the windows. The creature outside shook himself like a dog, and dirt flew from what remained of his body, at last revealing the terrible face, hardly more than a skull. No nose, no mouth, only decomposing skin clung to his cheekbones and jaw. He stared toward the castle with glowing blue eyes. Long blond hair blew across his face. Now Morag could see he wore a helmet sprouting two curving horns, and the item in his hand was a large battle axe.

Horror clenched her throat in a fist, and her legs trembled. She and Hamish had seen this creature—or one like it—in the castle before and another one down by the rocks.

"That's one of the Fin Folk?" Paul asked.

"I don't know." Morag bit her bottom lip. "Looks like a Viking from the burial mound."

"Definitely a Viking with that hat," Ivy said.

"It's a common misconception Vikings wore horns on their helmets." Paul's voice came out strangled and high. "They didn't."

"Well, don't tell this one. He might get mad." Morag fought an urge to giggle as hysteria set in.

"No, he's mad at me," Pete whispered. "I took his horn. It's all my fault."

If it was anyone's fault, it was Paul, Morag thought. He was the one who'd gone in the barrow first. If he hadn't gone nosing around in there, Pete never would've got the idea to do the same.

Paul, for the first time Morag could recall, had a stupid look on his face, like maybe he remembered he himself handled that drinking horn, and perhaps the Viking zombie wasn't too happy with him either. His hands seemed permanently stuck to the top of his head.

Juliette rushed back into the kitchen, slamming into Morag. "Look what I got in the banquet hall." She held up a dagger and pointed it at the window. "We've got to arm ourselves against— What *is* it exactly?"

"Oh, my god. Of course. It's a draugr." Ivy's voice rose in excitement, and Morag had a sneaking suspicion that part of the girl still enjoyed this. "Why didn't I think of it before?"

"What's a draugr?" Juliette pressed against Morag's side and stared at the creature turning in a circle.

"A draugr," Ivy said softly, "is a sort of ghost mixed with a zombie mixed with a wraith that guards its final resting place. A reanimated corpse from old Nordic cultures that can haunt people as an apparition or take on a corporeal form."

Paul stared.

"What? You're not the only one who reads. And this is kind of my arena. A pair of open scissors can keep them in their graves, but they'll come out if their treasure is disturbed." Paul swallowed when she said this and shared a guilty look with Pete.

"There were scissors," Pete wailed. "But I took them to dig in the dirt."

Ivy widened her eyes at Morag but patted Pete on the back. "It's okay, buddy. You didn't know. If I'd gone out to the barrow before, I could've figured the draugr thing out sooner. See what happens the one time I follow the rules?"

Nobody said anything for a minute. Morag hoped the creature would disappear, but it looked solid. Perhaps she and Hamish only ever saw one in ghostly form.

"Anything else useful you want to share?" Paul said.

"Uh, so yeah," Ivy said. "They can make birds fall dead out of the sky. Draugrs can control the weather. Shapeshift."

"A lot like the Fin Folk," Paul said through bloodless lips.

"I don't think that's one of the Fin Folk," Morag said. "Earlier today, Bridget told me the Fin Folk created an army of the undead. This must be what she meant."

Juliette's fingers dug painfully into Morag's arm. "How do we defeat a draugr?"

"This isn't a video game," Ivy said. "I don't know."

"Well, we have to do something," Paul said, and Morag detected a note of panic.

"You have to chop off their heads," Morag murmured, and their faces turned shocked. "Yeah. Bridget told me that, too."

"What's he doing?" Juliette asked.

The draugr swept his axe back and forth low to the ground and looked all around. His mouth fell open unnaturally wide, and a long mournful howl poured from his mouth.

"He wants his horn." Pete started crying again.

"Then we should give it back," Paul said.

Juliette gasped and pointed to the graveyard where the mounded graves trembled.

Morag's heart conceded temporary defeat and stopped beating for a moment or two. "Are you seeing this?"

"Of course, I'm seeing it." Paul clutched his hair. "I'm not blind."

Ivy pressed her phone screen some more, but the *Call Failed* popped up over and over, the screen bright in the dark kitchen.

Another bolt of lightning flashed followed by an ear-splitting crack of thunder. The draugr struck the staff of his battle axe on the ground. The trembling in the graves grew to a heavy shaking until one of the gravestones toppled over, and the mounds of earth started to crumble.

"Dead people are going to come out, aren't they?" Ivy spoke in a flat voice. "There's going to be actual zombies coming out of those graves."

"Guys!" Morag pointed. "What's that?"

"What the—" Paul slowly lowered his hands from his head.

Another creature slipped from the sea onto the shore of Screeverholme and crept behind the draugr.

Morag gasped. "*That's* a Fin Folk."

Wearing nothing but a dark fur loincloth, he was tall and pale with long limbs. Chains of silver coins hung around his neck. His elongated hands and feet were webbed like flippers, and the torrential downpour plastered dark hair to his skull. He wasn't ugly like the picture she'd seen—his slightly flattened features and overly round eyes looked human enough until his lips peeled back to reveal a mouth full of needle teeth, like those of a deep-sea angler fish.

Even more remarkable than his ghastly dentition was the Fin man's skin. Flashes of lightning revealed it was translucent and marbled, covered with pearlescent color and streaks of burning orange like a fire opal come to life. Morag watched in astonishment as colors pulsed over his skin.

"It's like a cuttlefish." Morag glanced at Paul, who nodded. This Fin Folk man's skin was similar to those squid-like cuttlefish that changed colors in bursts of patterns.

The Fin man carried a spear in his webbed hand. On another flash of lightning, the Fin man leaped at the draugr, crossing the distance of twenty feet in a single jump. He drove the spear through the draugr's back so hard it shot out the front of his chest.

The draugr screamed. Pete screamed as well. The dead Viking ripped the spear out the front of his chest, spraying putrid chunks of flesh and gore. He tossed the spear in the direction of the graveyard where the burial mounds stopped trembling.

Malcolm scrabbled harder than ever at the back door and let out an almighty string of yowls.

The Fin man threw himself onto the draugr's back with a battle cry that defied description. A low roar, like waves on rocks or whale song, a sound that should only be heard underwater. His skin rippled with bright swirls of green and yellow.

"Uh, Paul. I don't think we've been seeing copepods," Morag whispered. At the sight of those colors, her heart spasmed with overwhelming fear. The Fin man's skin throbbed from yellow to waves of crimson that fanned over his limbs. Rage filled Morag, sending molten heat through her core. Her fingers curled at her sides. The crimson swirled with a deep purple, and her fists clenched in determination.

"I won't die today!" Morag shouted. Everyone in the room jumped.

"Uh, okay?" Ivy said.

"Kill him!" Morag cried.

The draugr spun and clawed at the Fin man on his back.

The two creatures went down, fighting and rolling and making otherworldly noises. The Fin man's skin flashed yellow to red to purple and back again. Morag's emotions flipped through terror, anger, and a steely will to survive. In the dimness of the driving rain, the two men appeared as one single body gone mad— skeletal and flippered limbs flying—until the churning mass rolled into the sea with one last, soft rumble of thunder.

Morag's gaze switched from the water to the still graveyard and back again. Over and over. No movement. The rain eased to a soft drizzle.

No one spoke for a while, as if speaking might break the spell and make the roaring monsters return. Malcolm meowed and frantically scratched some more at the door. Paul reached over and opened it.

"No!" But Morag was too late. The cat streaked into the night, and to her amazed horror, galloped into the water and disappeared beneath its surface. She rounded on Paul. "Why did you do that?"

"I—I wasn't thinking. He seemed desperate to get out."

"Did he just drown himself?" Juliette sounded near tears.

"No," Morag said. "No way. He'll be back. You'll see." They watched and waited a few minutes, but the cat didn't reappear. "I'm not giving up hope." Morag turned to the others. "Did you feel it? Did you feel what the Fin Folk man was feeling?"

Juliette's brow wrinkled in confusion, a look mirrored on the others' faces.

"You didn't feel stuff when you saw all those colors on his skin?"

"I felt scared," Ivy offered.

"Me too." Pete braved turning from Ivy to add this helpful comment.

"Yeah," Morag said. "The yellow made me scared, the red made me angry, the purple made me, well—determined." Morag stared at her friends. "None of you felt that? Seriously?"

Paul shook his head.

"Synesthesia?" Juliette said.

Morag bolted upright with a searing epiphany. If Mary Tulloch, her ancestor, was related to the Fin Folk, then Morag was too. Maybe her synesthesia *wasn't* synesthesia. Maybe it was the result of being part Fin Folk.

"I don't get it," Ivy said. "If Fin Folk create draugrs to fight for them, why was that Fin Folk guy attacking one?"

"Maybe the draugr went rogue?" Paul turned to Pete. "Where's the drinking horn? I think now might be a good time to put it back in the barrow."

That was an exceptionally good—and brave—idea. "It's on Pete's night stand," Morag said. Maybe we should put the scissors back, too."

Ivy waved her phone in the air. "I've got a signal!"

Morag backed from the door, unable to take her eyes from the eerie, still landscape of sea and sky. Both she and Ivy called their parents, but no one answered. Paul returned to the kitchen with the drinking horn.

"I'll go with you," Morag said.

"No, Morag, it's too cold." He stopped in front of her and reached up to gently tug one of her curls. "I'm sorry I didn't listen to you before. Let me do this. I *need* to do this."

"Not alone." Ivy hiked her thumb toward the door. "Let's go."

Morag took watch with Juliette at the door. Her friend clutched her dagger with a menacing glare.

Watching Paul and Ivy's progress toward the barrow, Morag reached for her necklace, only to remember she'd given it to Hamish. She hoped her brother was okay and put her arm around Pete. The three of them stood in such utter silence that when Juliette's phone rang in her hand, she shrieked and dropped it along with the dagger onto the floor before snatching up both items.

"Mom," she said. "Come back here right away." Juliette started telling her mother everything they'd witnessed only to be cut off. Morag could make out the high pitch of Françoise's voice, but not the words. As Juliette listened, her face grew stony.

Morag hoped Pete couldn't feel how much she was shaking. The Fin Folk were real. *She* was part Fin Folk. Draugrs were real. There were Zombie Vikings that needed beheading.

Or maybe she'd never woken from her anaphylactic shock at the ferry terminal and was lying in a coma in a Scottish hospital having a vivid dream about mythological creatures.

"We all saw it, Mom!" Juliette sounded indignant. "It is so *not* some romantic fantasy I've imagined."

Françoise's voice squawked through the phone, and Juliette sighed. "Fine. We'll let you know if we see them." She shoved her phone in her pocket and threw open the door to let in Ivy and Paul, their gruesome errand complete and none the worse for it. Pete threw himself at his sister and clung to her like a starfish on a rock.

"Mom wouldn't listen," Juliette said. "She said to stay here. They're on their way back."

"Did they find Ingrid?" Morag asked.

"They split into groups. Our moms didn't find her. They haven't been able to get anyone else on their phones."

Paul frowned. "If they haven't found Ingrid, why are they headed back?"

"Because," boomed Gary from the kitchen doorway, "the effing islanders told us to go eff off. Something about you Davidsons being related to the Tullochs and a curse. Ordered us back to the castle. I swear, it's like a mob out of Frankenstein." He shrugged out of his dripping coat as he ranted. "All that was missing were the pitchforks."

Pete peeled himself off Ivy and flew across the kitchen to attach himself to his father. Gary hugged him tightly.

"It was like nothing you've ever seen," Gary said.

Ivy held up her finger. "Uh, Dad, speaking of like nothing you've ever seen. Wait till you hear what we saw."

Before she could tell him, Mom and Françoise appeared,

followed by Dad and Mike a moment later, both spluttering about the angry islanders.

"Bill, where's Hamish?" Mom said. "And James?"

Dad's mouth turned down. "I thought they were with you." He looked at Morag. "They aren't back?"

Morag's heart somersaulted as she and the others shook their heads. Ivy looked miserable. She wasn't having fun anymore.

"They'll be back soon, I'm sure." Mike patted Mom's arm.

No one else knew where Morag had sent Hamish and James.

"Wait, did you lock the door, Dad?" Juliette asked.

"No, why?"

Everyone started talking at once about the draugrs, the Fin Folk, where Ingrid could be, and what Hamish and James were doing.

Were her brother and James heading back to the castle at this very moment? Making their way over the bridge without any warning about skeletal Vikings and spear-laden Fin Folk? Or were they, as Morag suspected, at Hellyaskaill cave? If so, what were they encountering? She imagined Hamish and James twisting through the tunnels of Hellyaskaill, the place where people disappeared and were never seen again. She'd told them to waltz in there and offer themselves on a platter. And what, a silver necklace would keep Hamish safe? She'd been an idiot. If anything happened to them, it would be all her fault.

Of course, that had been before she'd seen a Fin man for herself and those needle teeth, before she'd seen a draugr in all its harrowing detail. She never would've sent them there if she'd known. Her gut twisted into burning knots. What if Hamish and James ran into the bear? What if a torrent of water washed them away? Hamish. Her big brother, always making her either laugh or cry, the brother who got into fights to protect her, and teased her out of being too serious.

Anguished heartbeats passed as she imagined her family, her life, without Hamish in it.

And James. The music they made together. Their quick kiss

on the bridge. She wanted to kiss him for real, kiss him longer. What if she never found out what that was like?

She wouldn't stand around waiting. Morag had known what that Fin man was feeling—she was the only one with synesthesia. If anyone could face the Fin Folk and maybe communicate with them, it was her. The Fin Folk already tried to send a message to her once before when they returned her pencils and gave her the drawing with the symbols. If Hamish and James were in danger of being taken by them, she might be their only shot at survival. That otter she'd saved had to be one of the Fin Folk. Perhaps they'd give her back Hamish and James as a debt they owed her.

A sinister voice in Morag's head wondered what she could do if a draugr had attacked them. It was too awful to contemplate. She shoved the thought away.

She needed guidance, and it wasn't going to come from the people in this room. Only one person on this island might be inclined to help another Tulloch with information. She needed to speak with Catherine.

No one would ever let Morag out into the cold, wet night. She'd have to sneak out. "I need to go to bed," she said to Mom.

"Are you okay?"

"My knee hurts. And my head." It wasn't a lie. "Will you wake me when Hamish gets back? I need to know he's okay. And bring me Malcolm if he comes back in? He ran out earlier. I'm worried about him."

At some point, Morag wanted Mom to realize she was gone in case she needed help herself.

"Sure, honey." Mom's eyes narrowed, and no wonder. It hardly seemed believable Morag was going to bed in all this excitement.

But the excitement was what saved her in the end. Dad announced another search party for Hamish and James this time—angry islanders be damned, and Mom, probably all too happy to have one child tucked away safely, told Morag good night, and joined in the discussion.

Chapter 23

Morag tugged up her scarf to cover everything but her eyes. The rain had stopped, the wind died down, and a hushed stillness lay thick over the landscape. The sea stretched out, gray as usual, but the sky had taken on the greenish, bruised shade people described before tornadoes. She missed darkness then. The utter, complete darkness. The reassurance of the cycle of day and night repeated *ad infinitum*. Here, the twilight gave her a feeling of something unfinished, an exhausting state of the perpetual.

Her footsteps crunched over the bridge, and the water lapped softly below. Heart pounding, she peeked over the side, afraid of what she'd see. Fin Folk? A draugr? Malcolm, washed up dead? Her shoulders tensed. She saw nothing. She set her sights on the rising hill of Tullimentay. Her layers of clothes, hat, and gloves, hastily donned in the hallway, managed to keep the cold at bay. Two flashlights and an epi-pen stretched her pocket.

She walked as fast as her painful knee allowed. Every small

noise, every sigh of wind scraped her nerves. Fear walked beside her like a palpable entity, Morag's only company. She felt like the last person on the planet, walking across this island on the edge of the world.

The entire way, she tortured herself with possible fates for Hamish and James, all ending in death or dismemberment. Dread settled in her chest. The pain in her knee became a welcome distraction. Her layers of clothing proved too warm, and perspiration broke out along her hairline. She hoped it wouldn't chill her.

The school came into sight, windows glowing, and people packed inside the classroom, Mrs. Heddle visible at the front. At each window, an adult stood as if on guard duty. After Gary's description of the islanders, Morag hurried past, keeping to the far side of the road. She let out a slow breath when she slipped past the school and approached Sinclair's.

Morag limped up the stairs to the apartment above the shop, and the door opened before she knocked.

"I saw ye in the road." Catherine cinched a purple robe around her waist. "It's no' safe for ye to be out and about with that mad crowd."

The woman's flat was as cluttered and stuffy as her shop. Magazines and books covered every surface, and candles, melting like Dali paintings, spilled across a coffee table. Morag yanked her hat off her sweaty head, and Catherine gestured to a sofa.

Duncan spotted her from his bed and seemed to think the late hour excused him from greeting duty. He only thumped his tail twice.

Morag sat and rubbed her throbbing knee, careful not to disturb the stitches. There was no time for niceties. "My brother and friend have gone missing. At Hellyaskaill. I need any information about the Fin Folk that could save them."

Catherine straightened like someone pulled a string in her spine.

"I know you believe in them, Catherine."

The woman nodded once. "Aye, as much as I've been trying to deny it, I can't anymore. Tell me what's happened."

Catherine massaged her hip as Morag caught her up. "You said Mary had weird skin that lit up. Do you know if it changed colors?"

Catherine stared. "Aye. My gran told me that's how the Fin Folk talk to each other."

"Does anyone in your family have synesthesia?"

"What's that?"

When Morag explained, Catherine smiled. "My dad saw people's names as a certain color. Mine was a peacock blue. Why do ye ask?"

Quickly, Morag told her about the Fin man's skin and how she felt his emotions. "But how could that help me communicate with them?" She balled her fists in frustration. "How do I ask the Fin Folk about Ingrid or my brother and friend? Hasn't anyone tried to contact them before? Or tried to get someone back from the sea?"

"Of course. Ingrid's dad was out there tonight, splashin' about and bellowin' at anyone who'd listen. He swam so far out, Mr. Murray had to fish him out with his boat. I heard a whole mob coming up the road from Hellyaskaill saying as they didn't find her there."

"They didn't mention my brother or James?"

"Not that I heard."

Morag's mind whizzed, the gears flying around ineffectually. "Is it really true people can't leave on the solstice?"

Catherine sighed. "Aye, so they say. Any islander who does so dies—drops dead, gets a terrible illness, or meets a grim accident. They can leave the island on other days, but if they fail to show up on the solstice, they'll die. Everyone thought the curse was lifted with Robbie Tulloch dead last year. Loads of people were planning to leave this solstice. Once they found out ye're a Tulloch too, they didn't want to chance it and decided to stick with Mrs. Heddle's plan."

"What's her deal?"

"Twenty years ago, her daughter went missin' on the solstice. The lass had leukemia—only fifteen. Some say—including the police—the girl drowned herself to end her suffering, and Mrs. Heddle, mad with grief, made up the Fin Folk story to believe she lived on underwater. Regardless, she was never seen again."

Morag suddenly pitied the teacher.

"Mrs. Heddle's made it her mission to guard the children of Tullimentay. Every solstice she organizes a lock-in at school with the parents standin' guard. No one's gone missing since. Until Ingrid."

A beat of silence followed as they no doubt both thought of Ingrid's fate. Morag cleared her throat. "Do you know anything about draugrs?"

"Draugrs? Ye must mean drogs." Catherine shuddered. "Ye'd do better to ask Ben about that."

Morag blinked. "Ben?" She recalled what Catherine had said before, that Ben and his family stood between the island and a sea of monsters. "Ben's some sort of draugr-slayer?"

"Aye. He once got into his cups at a ceilidh. Told me his entire family trained to kill drogs. No one on this island talks of them. It scares them even more than the Folk. People say the Fin Folk created the drogs from our dead as an unnatural army to fight for them. If you bury someone on this island, they come back as one. That's why they only cremate now." Morag pictured the church with no graveyard. "Ben's been mutterin' about drogs killing so many sheep this summer. He told me Screeverholme, with that old Viking barrow and graveyard, is covered with drogs ready to rise up if they or their treasure are disturbed—or if the Fin Folk commanded it."

Disturbed—like someone poking around in their barrow or stealing their special drinking horn?

"Ben might've stayed at Screeverholme, but last week, he said his girlfriend spotted one lurkin' outside her house. He wanted to protect her."

"But where did that one come from? Did his girlfriend bother a grave?"

"Doubtful. Land drogs only wake up if ye bother their graves or treasure. But Ben told me the ones who die in the sea are restless and can come out of the water at any time."

Morag had seen a draugr her first day boarding the ferry—that skeletal form in the water—and again as the shadowy shape lurking among the gravestones of Screeverholme, perhaps hauling its rotting body from the sea to investigate the newcomers.

Catherine glanced at Duncan, her face fearful. "I saw one once, with Duncan on the beach. It was almost dark, and he was havin' a grand time playin' near the shore when somethin' grabbed him and tried to drag him under. I rushed to help him and fell. Hurt my hip even worse. Duncan managed to get away, and I saw a bony arm disappear beneath the waves. I called Magnus for help, but I couldn't bear to tell him. I knew he wouldn't believe me. I tried to convince myself it was my imagination, but I've been afraid ever since. Duncan and I like to stick indoors now, don't we?"

Duncan groaned in response.

"What about the Fin Folk? Have you seen them?"

"No, and I intend to keep it that way." Catherine twisted her silver ring around her finger.

Morag touched the place where her necklace should be. Hamish. She glanced at her phone. Mom hadn't called, frantic to know where she was. That meant Hamish wasn't back. She'd lost half an hour getting to Catherine's and talking. "I should be going."

"I'm sorry about yer brother, but most likely he's lost in the cave. They'll find him. Don't worry, they do say they only ever take one. The drogs are another story," she added in a mutter. "Ye can't do naught but wait, Morag."

Like hell she'd wait while her brother was in danger. But she couldn't tell Catherine that. "You're right. I'm going home now." She held up her phone, hoping Catherine couldn't read the earlier texts from Juliette. "That's my dad texting. He's coming up the road now to take me home."

Catherine frowned. "It's cold out there. The rain will be back." As if to illustrate this point, thunder rolled in the distance.

"My dad sounded pretty mad. I better listen. I've got my jacket." Morag flipped her hood over her head and zipped her jacket to her nose, pulling her head in like a turtle. "I'll be fine."

The only sound was Duncan snoring as Catherine tapped her finger to her lips. There was probably no way she'd let Morag leave.

"I'd walk ye to meet him myself, but my hip is killin' me. Go on. I'll watch from the window."

Morag didn't hesitate, except to pat Duncan on the head on her way out the door, back into the night and its dangers.

Chapter 24

Morag looked over her shoulder at Catherine in the window, the woman's eyes drilling into her. She forced herself to move toward the castle, away from the direction of Hellyaskaill. She considered going home and asking for help. Did she think she could storm the cave alone and rescue Hamish and James? But if she returned to her family, they'd make her stay home, safe from the cold. They might not understand about the Fin Folk and how Morag could read their emotions.

So what if she could? Was reading their emotions somehow going to save Hamish and James? Save Morag?

She's rescued the otter and been thanked with the return of her colored pencils. That had to count for something. But she needed to let her family know where she was going. With her head start, they wouldn't be able to stop her, but she could make sure help was on its way.

How far could Catherine see down the road? It curved away and over the rise; Morag needed to get past that rise and double back.

People's voices carried around the curve in the road.

"—completely mad," a woman was saying. "They're tryin' to break down the door of Screeverholme. Those people have done no wrong."

Morag's fingers clutched the inside of her coat pockets.

"Aye, but neither did Ingrid." It was an older man's voice.

"They're Tullochs," said another woman. "It's *their* fault. If we offer one of the Davidsons to the Folk, they might give Ingrid back." Her voice sounded much closer. They'd be over the rise soon, and they'd spot Morag.

A delipidated stone barn stood nearby, its roof collapsing. Morag moved behind it and waited in the shadows for the group to pass. She risked a peek around the corner where two women and a man walked up the road.

"It's no' right," the first woman continued. "They're threatenin' them with guns."

Adrenaline zipped through Morag's veins as she ducked back around the corner of the barn.

"Och, it's just Arthur and his shotgun," said the man. "Practically an antique."

"Arthur or the gun?" asked the second woman.

"Both." He and the second woman laughed as thunder rumbled. "This storm is far from over, and it's no' safe out. Let's get ourselves home and dry and behind locked doors with a nice cup of tea."

The trio passed by Morag's hiding spot, their backs to her now.

The first woman tsked. "Listen to ye. Talkin' about tea when those people are in real trouble. It's no' right. I wish the police would get here."

"The police can't help in this matter, ye ken that well enough, Alice," said the man.

Their footsteps and voices were fading away. Morag caught snatches until one final disturbing sentence floated back, Alice's voice loud with indignation. "People could die tonight."

Morag's stomach somersaulted. She waited another minute or two to make sure the group was gone before snatching out her phone. "Mom?"

"Morag? You okay? Do you need something?"

Mom thought she was in her room, safe and sound at the top of the tower. She was about to shatter that illusion. "What's going on outside?"

"It's insane. A mob's on the bridge demanding we come outside and offer someone from our family to the Fin Folk. It's insanity. We can't get out to search for Hamish and James. And several of these lunatics have guns. Honestly, I wouldn't be surprised if some of them really did have pitchforks and—"

"No word from Hamish?"

"No. Eventually, Dad's gonna kill someone or get killed himself trying to get through these people." Fear and rage laced her words.

Morag hated to add to that mix, to her dad's determination to get through the armed group. "Mom? I know where Hamish and James went. The cave on the west end of the island. I'm going to find them."

"What? No. Anyway, no one can get through those people on the bridge."

"Mom, listen to me, okay? I'm not in the castle. I snuck out earlier to find Hamish and James." She held the phone from her ear as her mother squawked a stream of obscenities. She'd never heard her mom swear like that before.

"You will go straight to Catherine's right now and stay at her place."

"I'm not going to do that." She took a deep breath. "If you can get through, come to the cave, all right? Come help me. But don't let Dad get himself killed either."

"Morag—"

"Mom. I'm not leaving Hamish and James when I can help them. I promise I'll bring them back safe." Or die trying. Wasn't that the dramatic end to that promise? Another idea formed in her mind—a plan that could save everyone at the castle, Hamish and James, and save Ingrid, too.

"This isn't negotiable. You will—"

"I love you, Mom." Morag hung up on her mother. Her heart squeezed tight. In the heavy silence, she headed back toward Catherine's, staying off the road by sneaking behind the shops. She resisted scratching a welt on her cheek as she crept by a row of homes with dark windows. Ingrid's house loomed in the dimness, and she gave it a wide berth to avoid disturbing their dogs.

Once again, she felt truly alone and hoped she stayed that way until her destination.

Hellyaskaill.

The wind whipped up. The lighthouse swept a beam of light across the land. Morag walked toward the western edge of the island and soon heard the crashing waves. At the top of the cliff, she stopped to phone Hamish. No answer. Other than the waves, the headland was silent without even seals barking. Morag, like a miniature lighthouse herself, swept her flashlight over the area until she found the trailhead to the cave.

She made her tortuous way down the cliff face, and every switchback increased her heart rate. Her mouth was dry as it began to rain again. Several times she lost her footing on the loose rocks and almost fell. Her knee ached. The waves roared below like a hungry sea creature ready to devour her if she went over the side. She glanced down at the frothy sea and glimpsed a flash of shimmering green in the water.

The Fin Folk. All those nights, she'd seen them and not known.

She reached the bottom of the trail and put away her flashlight to free her hands for climbing over the boulders. The deep crack of the cave entrance looked like a sly, wicked smile, and she faltered. She drew a deep breath. Hamish and James were in there. They needed her. The rain fell harder. Fat, cold drops pattered her cheeks, raising several more hives. An ominous roll of thunder spurred her toward the cave and the shelter it offered.

Inside the cave, she pulled her flashlight back out and started down the narrow tunnel. After several turns, the sound of the sea disappeared, swallowed by the rock. The only noise was her ragged breathing. Could she really go through with her plan?

She tried to control her thoughts, but they spun out against her will. Morag thought of her family most of all. She loved them so much. She wasn't sure she could do what was needed. She thought of Juliette and her friends back home. She pictured trees and grass and the mountain snow of Colorado, her bedroom, and her family's battered piano. Trivial things, like pasta with garlic bread, fuzzy socks, and the feel of pages in a book.

She passed the carvings of the Fin Folk and what she now knew were draugr.

Thinking of facing a creature armed with needle teeth, however distantly related, was frightening enough. A Viking zombie? That was wet-your-pants, scream-like-a-little-kid, pass-out-on-the-floor scary.

She hummed the song she'd been composing. It echoed oddly off the walls, and she stopped. Growing terror took root in her chest, wrapping tendrils around her heart and lungs. Her imaginative, synesthetic brain did a bang-up job of conjuring a draugr waiting around every corner. Gradually, the smell of fish and wet dog grew stronger.

The bear.

The sound of rushing water signaled she'd almost reached the central cavern, and Morag guessed the geyser was erupting. A flickering light appeared at the end of the tunnel.

"Hamish? James?"

"Morag?" Hamish's voice sounded insubstantial, echoing in the large cavern ahead. "Run, Morag! Get out of here!"

Something growled, and the sound built into an angry roar. Morag's legs trembled, but she somehow moved forward, propelling herself toward a horrifying scene. In the cavern, about thirty feet away, Hamish and James stood with their backs pressed against the wall. In the flickering light of two burning torches mounted on the wall, a giant bear stood on two legs and loomed over Hamish and James. At her approach, the bear looked at Morag and let loose another roar.

"Run, Morag!" Hamish repeated. He clutched his bloody left arm to his chest.

A boiling rage filled her at the sight of her wounded brother. "I'm not leaving you." Her voice shook more in anger than fear.

The shaggy bear stood ten feet high. As he dropped onto four legs, his eyes glowed an unnatural blue. Like the draugr's. Morag gulped. This was no ordinary bear, but a supernatural creature.

"Morag. Go." James gasped in pain. He wasn't putting weight on his right foot.

"Hey, let them go!" Morag shouted.

Without warning, the beast charged Morag. Her bones turned to liquid mercury, heavy and useless in the sight of the oncoming bear.

The boys shouted, though she barely comprehended it through her terror. The bear skidded to a stop, pivoted, and charged Hamish and James. They all screamed. Snorting, the bear paced back and forth on paws the size of dinner plates, looking unsure of what to do with his captives. She couldn't believe he was real. Unlike the Fin man and draugr before, distant through a window, this bear was just feet away. Fear sharpened everything. She could smell his wet dog scent and see the bristly hairs along his back.

Morag spared a glance at Hamish. Blood saturated his sleeve, and a spasm of fear gripped her. Was the injury bad enough to cost his arm? He was conscious, though. That had to be a good sign. "Are you okay?"

"Sort of?" The whites of Hamish's eyes showed all around as he looked from Morag to the pacing bear. "You happen to bring any help?"

"I'm it. But I have a plan."

The bear, obviously disapproving of the conversation, let out a roar that hurt her ears.

"What do we do?" Hamish asked.

Morag knew exactly what to do, but if she thought too hard, she wouldn't be able to.

She smiled at her brother, trying to memorize what he looked like. His dark curly hair like hers, his heavy eyebrows, and wide mouth. With affection, she noticed the way his left ear folded over slightly. She looked at James as well, drinking in the slope of his shoulders, his graceful musician's hands, the sharpness of his jawline.

Her parents would understand, wouldn't they? She was doing it for all of them.

A geyser of water shot up, and the bear charged again, stopping in front of Morag. He pushed onto two legs and snarled, giving her a view of his enormous teeth. She'd never been so afraid. She might actually die, right here, right now.

The bear swiped at her chest, leaving behind burning lines of agony. Shocked, she staggered and fell onto the rocky ground, vaguely aware of Hamish and James shouting. She scuttled backward like a crab, but the bear crashed back onto four legs, trapping her between them. She curled in a ball as warm blood soaked her shirt. The bear roared, bathing her face in his awful breath. She slapped her hands over her ears and shut her eyes tightly. Tears leaked down her cheeks at the searing pain in her chest. The roaring stopped, and the bear huffed, rocking from side to side over her body.

She opened her eyes and locked on the bear's blazing blue gaze above her, but she spoke to her brother. "I love you, Hamish. Tell Mom and Dad I love them, too."

"Morag?"

Before she lost her courage, she yelled. "Let them go! Give back Ingrid. Take me instead."

"Morag, no!" Hamish cried.

Morag braced herself—to be killed, to be taken. But the bear turned to watch the center of the cavern. An otter with creamy spots on his chest slithered out of the hole—the otter Morag had saved.

The sleek animal squeaked, and the bear answered with a terrible bellow.

"That—that otter—he stole your necklace earlier," Hamish stammered.

The otter stood and began to spin, light and heat swirling around him. In turn, the bear stood, spinning faster and faster beside her. It was like being trapped in a tornado. She curled back into a ball, tucking her arms over her head. Heat rolled off the bear, and lights flashed through her closed eyelids. When it finally stopped, she opened her eyes.

"What the—" Hamish said.

Two Fin Folk men stood before them. The Otter-Man was gangly. Morag sensed he was young. Not a child, not quite adult either, like her. She averted her eyes from his nakedness and looked at his face. Wide green eyes gleamed from his flattened features. Blond fur-like hair covered his head. He wore her silver necklace.

The Bear-Man was tall and stout, with spiky dark hair. His eyes remained a ghostly blue.

The two Fin-Men faced each other with grimaces that revealed their needle teeth. Hamish took the opportunity to yank Morag toward him with his good arm. James leaned against the rock, favoring his right leg. His mouth hung slack with shock.

To her relief, the Fin Folk retrieved some bundles from the ground and covered themselves with loincloths made of seaweed. Otter-Man's skin rippled yellow and red, while Bear-Man's skin pulsed only a menacing crimson. Morag swiped her hand over her bloodied chest as an overwhelming fury took hold of her. When she focused only on Otter-Man, a healthy dose of fear mixed into her emotions. It was hard to separate her own feelings from those of the creatures.

"Do you feel what they're feeling, Hamish?" she asked. "Do you feel their emotions when their skin changes colors?"

Her brother gave her a bewildered look and shook his head.

Otter-Man opened his mouth, and again, the noises sounded like they should be uttered underwater. Like whale song. To her astonishment, the haunting music of the Fin Folk language flooded her with images. She saw herself, reaching for the otter, from his point of view. She clutched the sides of her head.

Otter-Man's memory played out in her mind as if it were her own. The scene of the otter rescue unfolded in her head, and she realized Bear-Man must be seeing it, too. His pulsating red skin faded to a sickly olive green. Shame rolled off Bear-Man.

"What's happening?" Hamish said.

"I—I can see what he's saying. The sounds make pictures in my mind, like a movie." It felt like tumblers sliding and clicking into place to unlock the mysteries of her unusual brain. "My synesthesia," she said in amazement, "is their language."

This is what it meant to be related to the Fin Folk.

Bear-Man turned to Morag and extended a flippered hand.

"What's he doing?" James asked.

"I think he's trying to apologize."

Screwing up her courage, she held out her shaking hand. Bear-Man's skin was firm and rubbery, like a dolphin's. As his webbed fingers closed over hers, he opened his mouth to pour out a deep song.

And he sang a story for Morag.

Chapter 25

Bear-Man's songs painted images—collective memories seen through his eyes and others before him. Morag shut her eyes, and slowly, a history of the Fin Folk took shape, playing like a disjointed film. Hamish and James sat next to her on the cave floor, her brother gripping her hand as she blocked out everything but Bear-Man's voice.

She saw an undersea world. Dozens of Fin Folk swam around her, their skin flashing the bright yellow greens of caution, the blues of contentment, and purples of determination. Fin Folk shape-shifted into seals and bulleted through the water to escape a pod of killer whales. Seeing through the eyes of another, sunbeams wavered through the water as she broke the surface.

Ships with sinister curving necks at bow and stern headed toward the island. Vikings who evolved from invaders to settlers. Time passed and the island changed, the humans building, farming, and fishing.

Another memory. The Fin Folk clambered onto the island, crept through human houses, and slipped onto ships. They offered fish to the frightened settlers, who traded bread in exchange. The Fin Folk gathered provisions from the land and explored the island's village. In time, some of the settlers chose to go with the Fin Folk into the sea.

The sun burned bright on the solstice, the one day the Fin Folk king could transform humans to live underwater. The king used a magical staff inlaid with mother-of-pearl—for transformations and to heal sick and injured Fin Folk and humans.

Morag gasped at the sight of a city, and Hamish's hand convulsed in hers. Glittering jewels of diamond, emerald, pearl, and sapphire covered the towering, reef-like structures floating underwater. Windows gleamed, lit by the life force of phosphorescent sea creatures.

The Fin Folk and humans had beautiful babies with pulsing skin. Ceremonies flashed by, and Morag sensed the reverence with which the Fin Folk handled giant shells or bone or metal objects taken from above. As the Fin Folk shared a meal of shimmering fish, happiness radiated off them in peach-colored flushes. A celebration. Joy. Love.

"Morag?" Hamish's voice intruded. "Tell me what's going on."

"He's showing me their history. Their lives."

James leaned against her as if he hoped she might transmit the images to him, too.

Bear-Man's voice grew harsher. One of the transformed humans came onto land and told of the glittering city below. The Viking settlers, with greed in their eyes, rowed out to sea and dove underwater to claim the riches of the city. A terrible battle broke out. Fin Folk poured over the sides of boats, pulled the warriors to watery deaths, or stabbed them with spears. The Vikings drove their weapons into the Fin Folk until blood spread in an oily red slick. The Fin Folk cried out songs of sorrow, and the humans screamed.

Morag shoved the heels of her hands into her eyes, but she

couldn't block the images as long as Bear-Man kept speaking. "Stop." Tears slid down her cheeks, as she wondered why he must show her this.

The images changed, though it was the same long day. The Viking men gathered on a small island, recognizable at once by its shape as Screeverholme without a castle. Fin Folk, as otters and seals and birds, watched the Vikings bury their dead in the burial mound and graves. One Viking stood apart, a giant of a man wearing a bear fur over his shoulders, clearly the leader. Gravely injured, blood seeped down his side as he ordered his men to roll a large boulder in place to mark the barrow.

The Fin Folk believed the battle was over, but the Viking giant snuck upon the Fin Folk king and wrestled his staff away. He used the staff to resurrect his men but died within moments. The magic worked. The Viking leader rose again as a fearsome, terrible draugr with gleaming red eyes, and his men rose with him. He and his draugr army fell upon the Fin Folk, killing most of them.

Thanks to the stolen Fin Folk magic, the draugrs could control the weather, gained power near the solstice, and could change form too, from animal to draugr and back again. They flowed into the city, ransacked it, and carried their plunder to the graveyard where the earl carried out one last task. The Fin Folk watched in puzzlement as he etched the runes into the rock of his burial mound. Then the draugrs slept away the years with their treasure.

Still, that was not the end. Bear-Man sang of the draugr's curse that brought back the dead on the island. Morag saw villagers buried on the island, sometimes with trinkets. An image played through her mind of a man disturbing one of the graves, a draugr rising to kill him. Other times one of the Fin Folk awoke a draugr, desperate to find a way to break the curse of this undead army, but always failing. She saw draugrs haunting people as ghosts, draugrs eating sheep in wolf form, and draugrs killing humans. A horrible litany of death by drowning passed by. Those lost souls went not into the earth, but watery graves, doomed to a restless existence as draugrs seeking revenge on the Fin Folk.

The Fin Folk and humans no longer had peace. The islanders wrongfully believed the Fin Folk created the draugrs plaguing their island. Fin Folk fought draugrs in the water, while humans killed any Fin Folk who came on land. Besieged on all sides, the Fin Folk population diminished. In order to bolster their numbers, they crept onto the shores of the island, into the settlers' homes, and chose a human to kidnap each solstice. Morag saw the Fin Folk take three people at once, only for their magic to fail to transform more than one each solstice.

Most of the settlers fled the island every summer. It became harder and harder for the Fin Folk to take the humans they so desperately needed to help them defeat the draugrs.

Bear-Man's song softened into melancholy. A personal memory, seen through his eyes. Bear-Man swam in the water with a Fin woman who looked like him. Morag sensed she was Bear-Man's sister. Together, they watched a handsome young man fishing near the shore.

Now Morag was underwater inside a reef structure where the Fin woman lay in a bed woven of seaweed and cradled a baby girl. The handsome young man was now a Fin man, but his features were still recognizable. He touched the baby, and great bubbles of laughter bloomed from him. Bear-Man stared in wonder at his niece.

Another memory and Bear-Man's voice turned darker. Bear-Man cried out to warn his sister and her mate of an approaching draugr. They tried to swim away, but Bear-Man's sister clutched her baby in her arms, slowing her down. The once-human Fin man turned to face the draugr and was ripped limb from limb. The draugr slashed open the Fin woman's throat, and as the baby drifted from her mother's limp arms, the creature wrenched the infant by her leg. Bear-Man's song of despair distracted the draugr into releasing her, but before Bear-Man could kill the monster, it fled into deeper waters.

Bear-Man tried to heal the baby's injured hip. He used a staff and used the magic in his own hands, but nothing worked. The draugr's dark touch couldn't be healed. Under Bear-Man's care, the baby grew into a toddler who struggled to swim. Bear-Man feared she wouldn't be able to escape a draugr in the future and would die.

Mary Tulloch was transformed into a human girl, her leg still injured, and returned to land. Bear-Man placed a life-saving curse on her. Cold would hurt the little girl, force her away from the sea and wind, to remain safely inside for always. Bear-Man transformed a fish into a pewter-colored cat to accompany the little girl on land and bring messages between land and sea.

Malcolm.

And Bear-Man cast one last curse. Anyone born on the island could no longer leave on the solstice. The Fin Folk needed the humans too much, needed to add to their number to fight the draugrs and keep the islanders—and Mary—safe. To keep the draugrs from spreading. An unforeseeable side effect of his curse caused any islander woman to die if she tried to have her baby elsewhere.

Morag opened her eyes as the images faded. She looked at Bear-Man in awe. The Fin Folk must live very long indeed if this was the uncle of her ancestor, Mary. Bear-Man's skin rippled a dull, flat gray of muted grief, which passed to Morag. He still missed his sister and the man. He missed his niece. And Morag was related to him. Sorrow flooded her at his pain, and also her own as she remembered her mission in coming here.

She touched his arm. "Let them go." She pointed at Hamish and James. "Give back Ingrid. I will go in her place."

"No!" James said.

"Morag, no! Not this again." Hamish grabbed for her, but she stepped away from him toward Bear-Man, who shared a look of confusion with Otter-Man.

"It will be easier for me, Hamish. I'm related to them. I can already understand their language."

"Well, they don't understand you," Hamish said, as the two Fin-Men continued to stare at Morag in incomprehension. "Stop being so noble."

Then it dawned on her. Of course! The last piece of the puzzle. She could never sing words without her synesthesia overwhelming her. Morag opened her mouth and let her song pour out, picturing Ingrid going back to her parents while envisioning herself going into the sea.

She couldn't stop other images from making it into her song. Her parents, Hamish, her friends, grandparents, aunts and uncles and cousins, her home, her school, and more. Tears streamed down her face at the thought of losing them all, at the thought of her family's grief at losing her.

Bear-Man stepped in front of her and traced his webbed fingers down her cheek to wipe away her tears. He shook his head and sang back, startling her with his image not of a memory, but his imagination. Morag standing with Hamish and her parents, her entire family smiling. He'd seen her family before, come into Screeverholme Castle that first day to spy on them. She felt what he said, saw it in the pearly iridescence of his skin. Love. Her family loved her, and she loved them. Morag was his family, too, and he would not take her when she didn't wish to leave them.

"They—they won't take me," she said to Hamish and James and turned back to Bear-Man. "Then, please. Give us back Ingrid." She filled her lungs to sing her request, but the continuing pain in her torn chest made her gasp.

Bear-Man noticed and placed his flippered hands on her shoulders, pinning her to the wall. A pulsating golden hue started at his head and swept down his arm. Warmth radiated into her chest, a searing pain took hold, and she cried out.

"Hey!" Hamish grabbed Bear-Man's arm but couldn't budge him.

After a few seconds, the pain receded. Only tingling warmth

remained. She pulled her sticky shirt away where the bloody slashes had healed into four pink lines. Otter-Man uttered a few noises, and in her mind, she saw herself slam onto the rock that day under the bridge. Bear-Man moved his hand to her knee. Again, a searing pain came followed by a tugging sensation. She ripped up her pant leg. The stitches had pulled through the healing skin. The dark threads fluttered to the cave floor.

"He healed it!" She turned to an astonished Hamish. "He healed me."

She pointed to Hamish's arm. Bear-Man hesitated. He ducked his head and forced Hamish to look at him as he sang. "You're his kin. He wants you to know he's sorry."

"If he's really sorry, tell him to give back Ingrid."

Before she could, Bear-Man turned to James and spoke.

"He's sorry for you, too," Morag said. "He wants to heal you both."

Golden light pulsed along Bear-Man's arms and hands as he healed first Hamish and then James.

Hamish flexed his fingers, bent his elbow, and rotated his shoulder.

James hopped to his feet. "Good as new. Maybe better."

"Now get back Ingrid," Hamish said.

Morag concentrated hard on picturing Ingrid and sang out a plea for her return.

Bear-Man stared at her with a sad expression and motioned for them to follow him down one of the tunnels. Morag had a bad feeling, and her fear increased with every step. About twenty feet in, Bear-Man lifted his pulsing hand and waved it in front of the rock face. The rock shimmered and the mirage disappeared to reveal a small niche. Several burning torches illuminated Ingrid unmoving on a pile of furs. Morag's breath caught in her throat.

"Ingrid!" Hamish rushed to where she lay and knelt beside her. "She's alive, but she's hurt!" He pulled back Ingrid's rain slicker to reveal blood on her right shoulder. Gently, he eased the sleeve down to a deep puncture wound surrounded by black skin. He flashed Morag a furious face. "Look what they've done to her."

Dismayed, Morag turned to the Fin-Men, and this time, Otter-Man sang. Images of Ingrid stopping in the road where it ran nearest the shore. A wounded sheep struggled in the headlights, and Ingrid climbed out of the Land Rover to help it, much like Magnus's explanation for her disappearance. A draugr, hiding behind a stone wall, shot her with an arrow. Bear-Man slipped from the water and rushed up the shore to the road, and the draugr disappeared over the island. Otter-Man helped Bear-Man carry Ingrid to Hellyaskaill, away from the prying eyes of islanders.

They tried to heal her without success, and a series of pictures rolled by in her head. Many Fin Folk over time bore wounds from draugrs that could only heal when the draugr who'd injured them was killed. Bear-Man hadn't been able to kill the draugr who hurt Mary, and she hadn't healed either.

"What's he saying?" Hamish's words shook with rage.

"It wasn't them. It was a draugr."

"A what?"

As quickly as she could, Morag summarized everything Bear-Man had told her about the Fin Folk and the draugrs. Hamish and James paled.

Hamish stroked Ingrid's hand. "What do we do?"

Otter-Man crouched beside Hamish and held out a bloodied arrow, the flight feathers black and red. He opened his mouth, and Morag spoke for him. "Fin Folk magic can't heal a draugr wound. Ingrid is free to go, but she'll never heal until we kill the draugr that hurt her. The one who uses arrows with those flights. When he dies, she'll heal." At those words, something nagged at the back of Morag's mind, but she couldn't think what. Something about killing the draugrs.

Hamish took the arrow from Otter-Man with a fierce expression. "I'll find this draugr and kill him myself."

"Ye'll do no such thing," growled a voice behind them, and with a guttural shout, Ben lifted a sword and charged Bear-Man. Malcolm ran to Ben's side.

As Ben swung his sword, Morag and Malcolm both sprang in front of the Fin man. "Stop!" Morag cried. "Don't hurt him."

The sword stopped inches from her head. Bear-Man's arms circled Morag protectively, warm and clammy.

"Don't worry, Morag," Ben said. "I won't let him harm ye."

"No. They're not bad, Ben. There's so much you don't understand." It was difficult for *her* to understand, but she needed to explain it to Ben. "Since I'm part Tulloch, I'm related to them through Mary." Her heart swelled with unexpected pride. "I'm part Fin Folk. When they speak, I see in my mind what they're saying, and I can speak to them."

Ben shook his head in disbelief and confusion. Bear-Man gently pushed Morag aside and stepped toward him, and Ben's hand tightened on his sword. Bear-Man opened his mouth and whale song spilled out. Slowly, he held out his hand to Ben.

"He says he wants peace with humans," Morag said. "He knows what you are—a draugr-slayer. I mean, drogs. You have a common enemy. He appreciates what your family has done all these years to keep the islanders safe from drogs. It helped keep his people safe, too."

Ben scratched his head, which might have been amusing in other circumstances, as he clearly struggled to make sense of her words. "But they made the drogs to—"

"No. The Viking settlers did that. The Fin Folk aren't bad," she repeated. "Obviously kidnapping people wasn't great, but it's a long story."

Ben stared at Bear-Man and back to Morag, his brow furrowed in deep thought as no one spoke or moved.

At last, Bear-Man addressed the cat, and Ben took a staggering step back.

"Malcolm is with the Fin Folk," Morag said. "He came with Mary Tulloch onto land all those years ago to guard against draugrs and keep the Fin Folk safe from humans. He changes into a fish and carries messages to them."

Ben stared at the cat in amazement. "I grew up with Malcolm at Screeverholme. As did my father who was caretaker of the castle before me, and his father before him. I—I thought he was just a magic cat who warned me of danger."

Oh, is that all?

"It makes sense now," Ben said slowly. "I've killed many draugrs over the years, but never once managed to catch a Fin Folk. Malcolm must have always warned them."

Ben looked at Bear-Man's outstretched hand for a long moment and finally shook it with a dumb-founded face. The Fin man's skin glowed purple with determination.

"He means it," Morag said. "He wants peace."

"He might want peace, but he won't find it tonight." Ben gave them a somber look. "Malcolm found me at my girlfriend's. I came outside and met Crusher. He said most of the islanders went to Screeverholme to demand some sort of sacrifice. Malcolm led me here. I should've stayed at Screeverholme the past few days, but I wanted to protect my girlfriend. I thought yer families would be safe, what with ye Davidsons being related to the Folk, but that's the very thing that put ye all in danger from the islanders." He gripped Morag's shoulder. "I'm sorry. I wasn't a good caretaker after all."

It was natural for him to want to be with his girlfriend. Morag saw how young Ben actually was, how heavy a burden he'd been carrying. "Uh, that's okay. Anyway, we have bigger problems than the islanders." She told him about the draugr, about the trembling graves.

Ben's face went white. "I wouldna thought ye goin' near the burial mound would be enough to rouse them. I fight drogs that come onto land now and again, but nothin' like ye're describing— like one tryin' to summon more from the graves."

"I know why." Morag told him about Pete and the scissors and the stolen drinking horn. "But Paul and Ivy put the horn back."

"It's too late for any of that." His lips pressed tight. "The process of awakenin' them has begun, and on the solstice to boot." Ben was as grim as she'd ever seen him. "We've got to get yer families away. If the drogs are wakin' up properly—Screeverholme's like a wasp's nest of them. When it bursts open, it's the last place any livin' creature should be."

And it was where their family and friends were stuck.

Chapter 26

Bear-Man and Otter-Man carried on a conversation, and Morag translated. They would gather what was left of the Fin Folk, gather their strength for what Bear-Man saw as their final stand. He and Otter-Man glowed a deep purple.

The two Fin-Men disappeared without a splash into the hole in the cavern.

"Let's go," Ben said.

Hamish picked up Ingrid's limp body, and James grabbed Morag's hand. "You did great," he whispered. "With your beautiful voice."

Morag warmed at his words, and they hurried to follow Ben up the tunnel, Hamish trailing behind as he carried Ingrid. Morag climbed the cliff in the freezing rain and tried to ignore her hives and the wheezing rattle in her throat. At the top of the cliff, they piled into Ben's tiny car. Poor Ingrid was squashed between her and Hamish, her head lolling when they buckled her in. Morag swallowed two antihistamines. She hated taking something that might make her sleepy, but anaphylactic shock would be a tad inconvenient, too. Danger would keep her alert.

Ben floored it, and the little car raced across the island. The dashboard clock showed two in the morning. The closest thing to full night this far north in summer. A minute later, they pulled in front of Ingrid's dark house. Hamish got out and pounded on the door until he gave up and returned to the car.

"Three guesses where her family is," Ben said.

Driving sixty miles an hour got them across the tiny island in mere minutes. Several cars were parked near the Screeverholme bridge. Even though Morag expected them, it was still a shock to see people waiting on the bridge. A flash of lightning illuminated the group, about forty strong. Less than half the islanders. At the sight of the car's headlights, they turned.

"Welcome committee's here," James yelled over the pounding of the rain on the car roof.

"Wait here, Morag," Ben shouted. "Lads, ye come with me. Hamish, bring Ingrid." Morag opened her mouth to protest, but he lifted his hand. "No. I want ye out of the rain and cold until I can talk some sense into them."

Morag reluctantly agreed. Hamish hooked his arms under Ingrid and gently lifted her out of the car. He slammed the door shut with his hip. Ben opened the trunk and hefted out his sword.

Morag crawled into the front seat to peer through the windshield. Rain sheeted down the foggy glass. Ben, James, and Hamish, with Ingrid in his arms, were no more than blurs approaching the bridge.

Ben stepped toward the small crowd. He talked, raising an arm from time to time and gesturing with his sword. Joyce rushed from the crowd at Hamish and Ingrid, and the people closed around them. A few minutes later, Hamish carried Ingrid back across the bridge with Joyce to deposit her in the Land Rover. Joyce got in the driver's seat, and Hamish attempted to get in with her, but the vehicle took off without him. Morag watched the red taillights disappear up the road before returning her attention to Ben and the crowd.

Despite Hamish bringing Ingrid back alive, it didn't appear to be going particularly well with the islanders. Admittedly, Ingrid hadn't been returned in great shape. Morag wiped the windshield with her sleeve. Her view cleared enough for her to see the group engulf Ben, Hamish, and James. Without thinking, she jumped out of the car and ran to the end of the bridge where the group was shoving and shouting and pushing them.

A burly man grabbed Hamish by the arm. "Let the Folk have this one. Maybe then they'll heal Ingrid."

"Get yer hands off him!" Ben shouted. He lunged with his sword, and the man released Hamish. Ben immediately shoved Hamish behind him. "Get to the castle." He swung his sword in an arc, creating a circle around the three of them. Slowly, Ben, Hamish, and James shuffled back toward the castle.

Someone fired a gun, and Morag screamed. A man held a pistol over his head and pointed it toward the sky. "Not a step further."

Someone was going to get hurt or worse, and she only knew one way to stop this.

Morag put her fingers in her mouth and gave a piercing whistle. Some of the group turned toward her. She cupped her hands over her mouth. "Hey! It's Morag Davidson. You want a sacrifice for the Fin Folk? Take me. I can communicate with them."

"What did she say?" One of the islanders started toward her.

"I can talk to the Fin Folk," she shouted as loud as she could. "They can have me. Let my brother go."

Now she had the attention of the entire group. She circled her arm. "Come on. Let's go to Hellyaskaill. I'll offer myself there." No need for them to know her offer had been refused.

She might not be in danger from the Fin Folk, but she had her doubts about the mob. Her heart lurched as the group pushed and heaved in her direction along the bridge like a single beast.

Ben shoved Hamish and James in the opposite direction

toward the castle. The boys ran the remaining distance. The castle door opened, and they disappeared inside. At least they were safe for now.

The crowd had almost reached Morag. She hadn't thought too hard about this plan, only that she needed to get the islanders off the bridge so her family could leave Screeverholme. Her face itched badly. She wasn't going to last long in this cold. She turned and started toward Ben's car, and the group picked up speed.

Morag's skin tingled, and pressure bloomed in her ears. A sizzling noise came right before the world exploded in bright light and ear-splitting sound. She collapsed to the muddy ground, clutching her ears. A lightning bolt was burned into her retinas, still bright against her tightly closed eyelids. People shouted and screamed. Ozone hung heavy in the air. She scanned her body for injuries and found none. She stood up on shaky legs, scared of what she'd see.

People huddled in small groups and checked each other over. Morag stepped closer to Screeverholme and gaped at the sight. Lightning had struck the bridge, and the center half of it had crumbled away to leave an impassable gap. There was no way to reach the castle. No way to get to her family. And no way for them to flee Screeverholme.

A woman shrieked and pointed at the castle wall where a pair of draugrs skittered like spiders straight up toward a window. Morag's stomach dropped like an anchor to her feet, weighing her down with horror.

Everyone else had the same reaction, frozen in fraught silence. Then group hysteria took hold. Suddenly, everyone was yelling and running from the castle at the same time Morag roused herself to run toward it. The group passed her by, forgetting Morag in their terror. Within moments, they'd disappeared up the road and abandoned Screeverholme to its fate.

Morag stood at the edge of what was left of the bridge. A few stones tumbled from the ragged gap in the middle. Across the broken bridge, someone opened the castle door. Her father. The draugrs froze on the castle wall and began a rapid descent.

"Dad! Shut the door!" She pointed, jumping up and down. "Shut the door!"

She was sure he couldn't hear her, but he looked up. The draugrs were only about twenty feet above his head. Her dad shouted something she couldn't catch and slammed the door. One of the draugrs shrieked, and the pair started back up the wall toward the window.

Her family was trapped in that castle. They needed to get off the island, but how? Despairing, she stared at the black water. Her despair evaporated when she spotted it—Ben's rowboat tied to the small mooring.

Morag rushed down the muddy slope, slipping and sliding. Hives covered her body, and the swelling made her clumsy as her allergic reaction ramped up. There was no time to hesitate or think. That boat was everyone's only ticket off the island, away from the draugrs. She threw herself into the dubious watercraft. Her fingers fumbled at the rope to untie it.

Waves thrust the little rowboat up and down, and the wind tore her hood from her head. She squinted through the pouring rain to find a place where she could land on Screeverholme. There! The boathouse at the eastern edge.

The rope came free, and she grabbed hold of the oars. It took some time, but she managed to turn the boat around and point it toward Screeverholme. She pulled the oars through the water while keeping an eye out for the treacherous rocks. Already, her arms felt like wet paper, and she'd only rowed twenty feet toward the castle. Gusts of wind clawed at her face and whipped hair into her eyes.

Pull, pull, pull. The muscles in her arms trembled. Each breath came wheezier than the last. Thunder growled, and the waves tossed the boat this way and that. She fought to stay pointed toward the boathouse, but the water and wind had different ideas. Wave after wave carried her to the western edge of Screeverholme, closer to the graveyard.

So stop fighting it. Getting to the castle was all that mattered. She'd drag the boat up on that side. Her spirits rose as the land grew nearer, then sank when she saw she might overshoot Screeverholme entirely. If so, she'd end up adrift in the open North Sea where she'd most certainly die.

Using her last reserves of strength, she rowed toward the western edge, toward the graveyard and the safety of the kitchen entrance. Once more, electricity crackled in the air and tingled along her body. An instant later, the sky ripped open with a cannon shot of thunder, and lightning hit the island of Screeverholme. A deafening crack like a gunshot followed. The graveyard stood in stark relief as if lit by stadium floodlights. The lightning had split open the boulder marking the barrow, and the ground trembled.

Morag blinked as the bright spots from the lightning faded. When her vision cleared she saw the true horror. Draugrs poured from the barrow. Draugrs pulled themselves from the sea onto the island. Draugrs clawed up the sides of the castle. The smell of putrid decay carried across the gale as they burst from their graves.

She rowed hard for shore, though monsters waited there. She rowed for her family. She rowed for her friends. A roar came from her right. A wave, growing bigger by the second, rolled her way. She pulled the oars as hard as she could, but it was instantly upon her. Ten feet high, the wave crashed down beside her. The boat soared into the air. Her raw hands gripped the sides, but the boat flipped over, and she lost her grip. She plunged into the sea. The breath squeezed from her lungs as frigid water closed over her head.

Morag slipped into icy darkness.

Chapter 27

Morag woke with a gasp. Her heart galloped like a racehorse on stimulants, and her limbs shook. It was warm. Deliciously warm. Was she dead? She opened her eyes and found herself on the couch in the castle lounge. Her family, James, Ivy, Paul, Juliette, and Otter-Man stared at her.

Otter-Man.

His Fin Folk face pressed in among those of her family and friends. It was the weirdest thing she'd ever seen. Behind him stood Bear-Man.

"She's alive!" Mom pulled her into a bone-crushing embrace. "Thank god the epi-pen worked."

"I see you've met the Fin Folk," she said calmly. "Otter-Man. And that's Bear-Man." Something snagged around her neck, and she touched the silver pendant on her necklace. "Thanks," she said to Otter-Man.

Dad gawped at the Fin-Men and back to Morag. "He showed up at the kitchen door with the big one about five minutes ago with you in his arms."

"Dad wanted to kill them," Hamish said, "but I explained they were cool."

"Thank you." Mom grabbed Otter-Man and hugged him. His skin pulsed a bright orange, and Bear-Man's was the light turquoise of amusement.

"Mom, you're embarrassing him."

"Oh yeah," Hamish said. "Forgot to mention Morag can communicate with them."

"Mom, can you feel what they're feeling when you look at the colors of their skin?"

Her mother shook her head with a stunned expression.

Juliette's and Paul's mouths hung open. Everyone goggled at the Fin Folk in shock except Hamish and James, who'd had a little more time to adjust to their existence.

"That's, uh, some set of teeth they've got," Dad said.

Malcolm weaved between Hamish's legs, and Morag noticed the sword in her brother's hand. She pushed herself up to sitting. Everyone but Mom was armed. "Where did you get all those swords?"

"The banquet hall," Ivy said. "It was my idea."

"They look sort of—rusty."

"Yeah, Ben said they have to have iron in them to kill the draugrs," Ivy said. "The more the better."

Malcolm jumped on Morag's lap and meowed. "Guys, I think he's trying to tell—"

Glass shattered downstairs, and Mike's voice carried up from below. "A little help here!"

Malcolm streaked out.

"What's going on with the draugrs?" Morag said.

"Yeah, about that," Hamish said. "We're overrun. We're probably all gonna die."

"Hamish!" Mom said.

"But you're still alive for now, so that's good." Hamish grinned at her.

"What's the plan?" Morag asked.

"Hold them off enough to row more people across in that tiny rowboat Otter-Man brought with you," Dad said. "Gary got Pete to Catherine on the other side, but he can't get back to us. Hamish is right. Outside it's teeming with those monsters."

James pushed in closer. "Once the solstice is over, Ben can leave the island again. If we can get everyone off Screeverholme, he'll start flying people off Tullimentay before it's overrun by draugrs. There's only one plane, but there are boats, too. Everyone can try to get to Sanday."

"Where *is* Ben?" Morag asked.

As if in answer, he shouted from downstairs. "Could use yer help here."

"Okay, where's my sword?" Morag stood, but her shaking legs gave out, and she collapsed to sitting.

Mom put her hand on top of Morag's head. "You're not going anywhere, young lady."

Everyone else went downstairs, leaving Mom, Morag, and Otter-Man alone.

Otter-Man opened his mouth, and Mom stared slack-jawed at his singing. "You can understand that?"

"Yes." She avoided her mom's eyes. "Where's my sword?" she asked again.

"What did he say?"

"He's going to protect me." She sighed. "So you can go help the others."

Morag wanted to argue. She should fight for her friends and family, but she was too weak to walk, let alone lift a sword. She allowed Otter-Man to carry her upstairs to her bedroom, the highest point in the castle. He deposited her gently on her bed, took the sword strapped to his back with seaweed, and stood guard at the door.

It felt like years since she'd been in this bed. Though it was tempting to burrow under the covers, she wanted to charge downstairs to help, not be shut up like a princess in a tower. Knowing those wraith-like creatures swarmed over the castle while she lay here was killing her.

She focused and sang a picture to Otter-Man of her getting up from the bed and going downstairs to fight.

Otter-Man shook his head and flashed an image of her resting.

She balled her fists and sang him a hypothetical story of Otter-Man healing her from her ordeal.

Otter-Man came to her bed wearing a sorrowful expression. He showed her the other Fin Folk using staffs to heal badly injured people. Then he showed her Bear-Man and older Fin Folk healing others with less serious injuries, their hands glowing. He showed her the small hands of young Fin Folk, none of them glowing.

He held up his hand where a small spark of yellow flashed down from his shoulder to one finger.

"Okay, I get it, you're not old enough to heal well yet, but can't you try?" She sang an image of her family, surrounded by draugrs. "Please. I have to help them."

He moved closer to the bed and bent down, their eyes locking. He stared at her for a few seconds and held his hand up again, his eyes squeezed shut. After a moment, golden light pulsed down his arm, and he touched her head. It felt like warm water running down her body, along with an intense sense of well-being. She got off the bed feeling mostly restored.

A shadow darkened the window. "Look out!"

A draugr crashed through the window where she'd stood so many nights. The skeletal man wore a leather breastplate and carried a bow. He notched an arrow and aimed. Otter-Man raised his sword, but before he could turn, an arrow sprouted from his chest. Blood spread across the Fin man with alarming speed, and he collapsed. Otter-Man cried out, and the image, a command showing Morag fleeing the room, was so strong, it took everything she had not to obey. She wouldn't leave him to die.

The draugr stepped toward Otter-Man, notching another arrow. A rancid miasma rolled off the creature. Morag snatched up Otter-Man's sword from the floor. It was heavier than she expected. With a yell to summon all her strength, she swung the blade at the draugr's head, but only managed to slash his shoulder, knocking him off balance. The draugr screamed a metallic screech that tore at her eardrums. The ragged flesh over his jaw ripped apart to reveal bone and teeth. He looked at her with pale eyes filled with rage and slithered back out the window, heedless of the broken glass.

Trying to catch her breath, she sank beside Otter-Man, who'd gone the color of cream.

"No. No, no, no." She took his flippered hand in hers. "I'm going to get help."

Otter-Man lifted his other hand and touched her cheek. Her tears fell into his webbed fingers. He let out a feeble, breathless song of sound. Though the images came blurry and colorless, she recognized them at once. It was her again, on the rocks, reaching down to free the otter that day. To free Otter-Man.

Another image, one he'd hoped would come to pass. Morag swimming with Otter-Man underwater, meeting his family. His hand flopped down, and the image evaporated.

"No." Pain lanced through her. She was losing him.

Otter-Man's skin flickered once, twice, then faded to clear. She could see into his body; bones, veins, internal organs, the carnage that was his chest, the blood seeping everywhere. His heart and lungs moved feebly.

Morag gritted her teeth and stood, gripping the sword so hard, her fingers ached. She took note of the yellow fletching on the arrow. She'd find that draugr and kill him herself. Otter-Man's gaze stared at nothing, but his heart still beat. "I'm going to save you."

She rushed from the room and started toward the staircase.

A draugr crested the top, a spear in his bony hand. With an outraged cry, she charged him with the heavy sword, lifting it to strike. In a flash of movement, the draugr used his spear to knock the blade from her hand. She darted forward to retrieve the sword, but he stepped on the hilt, his blue eyes gleaming, and lunged toward her with the spear.

Morag spun and headed for the opposite end of the hall. A draugr with a poleaxe burst from that staircase and blocked her way.

She was trapped and unarmed. With no time to think, she threw herself through Paul's doorway, slammed the door, and turned the lock. There were only two hiding places. Under the bed or in the wardrobe. Footsteps sounded outside the door. She slipped into the wardrobe and pulled it shut. A line of light came through the gap where the doors met.

She waited, her heart beating like a rabbit's. The bedroom door rattled. Maybe draugrs were easily dissuaded. An explosion of splintering wood destroyed that hope as the two creatures broke down the door and entered the room.

Chapter 28

Morag was going to die among Paul's neatly hung clothing. The draugr carrying a poleaxe used it as a walking staff, the haft thudding on the wooden floor, and his breaths came as rattling rasps. She could see them both through the crack, sniffing the air through the holes in their skulls where noses should be. Their rotten stink made her gag. She suppressed it, but the tiny noise she made was enough.

The draugr, a thin line of him visible between the doors, raised his poleaxe. A wedge of blade smashed through the wood, stopping an inch from her face. Morag screamed and pushed herself deeper into the wardrobe. Her scream spurred them into a frenzy. The poleaxe wrenched free, giving her a bigger view of the draugr through the hole left behind.

What's the plan, Morag? She had no plan, no plan, no plan.

Cornered, she squeezed tighter against the back of the wardrobe. Something dug into her back, and her fingers scrabbled for it. A doorknob! Like Narnia, she thought hysterically and turned it. The back of the wardrobe opened.

She slipped into the darkness, and her foot caught on a step. She slid on her backside down a tightly spiraling staircase. After a few bruising steps, she braced her hand on the wall and stopped herself. Banging and metallic screams came from above. She wasted no time and continued down the stairs as fast as she dared, clinging to the wall for balance. She smacked into a solid surface at the bottom. A quick feel around in the dark revealed another doorknob. What waited on the other side?

She held her breath and cracked open the heavy door onto the lounge. Paul *did* say he had a secret in his room—a secret passage. That explained how he kept disappearing, like during hide and seek or after that argument with Hamish when he vanished from the lounge.

Noises came from far away, but the lounge itself was quiet. She rushed into the empty room and saw she'd come through the bookcase. The copy of *MacBeth* stuck out. Morag closed the bookcase and pushed the book in. Something rumbled upstairs, which must have been the door closing in the wardrobe. No wonder Paul got nervous when she'd messed with that book. She'd almost learned his secret.

She only hoped she'd trapped the draugrs in the passage. Now she needed to find the draugr who'd hurt Otter-Man.

Shouting carried up from the first floor. Paul's voice. Dad, Françoise, Mike. She stepped into the hall and peered around the corner. Assured no draugrs waited there, she jogged down the stairs to the entryway to find everyone blocking off the castle entrance. Mom was nailing boards over a window while the others moved furniture into the entry. A pile of swords lay in the center of the stone floor.

"Morag!" Dad said. "What are you doing here?" He stopped helping Mike and Hamish, who were shoving a table across the door.

"Otter-Man is dying." Saying it out loud made it real, and she fought back tears. "There are two draugrs upstairs, and my bedroom window is broken so more can get in."

At her words, everyone froze in their work.

"They were in your room," she said to Paul. "I might've trapped them in the secret passage."

"I know the passage." Ben lifted his sword toward Dad. "We'll check the bedroom." He turned toward Mom and Françoise. "You two check the lounge." He pointed at Mike. "You board up Morag's window."

"Stay here," Dad said. The adults disappeared up the flight of stairs.

"Stay here? No way." Morag selected a sword from the pile. "I have to find the draugr that hurt Otter-Man."

Hamish gave her a grim nod. "I need to find the one that hurt Ingrid."

"But how do we do that? Go out there and hunt them?" Morag asked.

"We're kind of trapped," Juliette said. "Have you seen outside?"

Morag stood on tiptoe to look out the remaining unboarded window. A mass of moving bodies seethed in the lashing rain, interspersed with bursts of yellow and red light from Fin Folk locked in an epic maritime battle.

There were too many draugrs everywhere to possibly kill them all. There had to be another way. What was their weakness? Iron, yes. For a moment, she considered making some sort of nail bomb and just as quickly dismissed it as impractical. Even if they had the supplies to create such a thing, iron nails weren't enough to take down a draugr. That was the difficultly of killing an undead army—they were already dead. Only beheading them one by one could stop them.

Unless . . .

The nagging fuzzy thought from earlier came into focus.

She stepped back from the window. "Remember the runes, Paul?"

Paul straightened "Yeah. I memorized them."

"What was the part about as long as the earl was alive—"

"Not alive. It said, 'Until he falls the final time, he and his men shall live forevermore.'" He stared at her for a few beats, and then his face lit up. "You're thinking—"

"We have to kill the Viking earl." If her skin could change color, it would be purple. "He's their leader. If those runes are right, if he dies, all the draugrs from the graveyard die. All of us will be saved—Ingrid and Otter-Man too."

Ivy frowned. "How are we supposed to find this earl guy?"

Morag closed her eyes to remember what Bear-Man had shown her. "He's way bigger than the others with bear fur over his shoulders and red hair. And I think he's the only one with red eyes."

"Great," Hamish said. "That's a tremendous help. I'll be sure to look deeply into each draugr's eyes."

"It's something," she snapped. "We can't just stand around helpless. Hole ourselves up while the Fin Folk die out there. Die protecting us."

Juliette put her hand on her shoulder, and the smile of her best friend gave Morag a shot of courage. "What do you propose we do, Mor?"

Her brother and friends all stared at her, looking for guidance. What exactly *did* she propose? Charge out into the rain to find the earl?

What had Pete said? *I stole his horn and now he's mad.* "I have an idea." Everyone waited expectantly. She loved these people so much. The thought of any of them dying was much worse than the fear she felt for her own life. "We should—"

A loud crash came from the lounge above. There was no time for plans or speeches. Hamish ran for the stairs, but Paul grabbed his arm. "Wait. Spiral stairs are good for battle only when you have the upper ground. Let them come down, and we'll take them together."

Hamish gave a quick nod. They positioned themselves on either side of the staircase. An axe blade crunched through the castle door and from the hallway behind them, another draugr marched toward the group. All hell broke loose. Ivy swung her sword at the pair in the hall, Hamish and Paul took out one of the draugrs which fell in a heap at the bottom of the steps, and Juliette braced herself for a fight at the front door, James at her side.

Morag grabbed him. "Come with me."

James frowned. "We need to help them."

"We need to do this more."

"Go," Juliette said. "We got this."

James followed Morag out of the entry. "Where we going?"

"The graveyard."

"I was kind of hoping you'd say Forty Whacks." He followed her down the hall and into the kitchen. "It's this fun axe-throwing venue Ivy loves. Great for stress relief and—whoa, okay!"

Morag had whipped open the kitchen door onto two growling draugrs who barreled inside. One sported fresh battle wounds in the form of dangling ribs. With a comic high scream, James lifted his leg and kicked the one in front, knocking it into the second, and they both sprawled on the kitchen floor. Morag seized the opportunity and lifted the heavy sword to chop off the first one's head with a satisfying thwack. James beheaded the second to send its leering skull spinning toward the table.

"Way more fun than Forty Whacks." James grinned.

She grinned back.

Wind whistled through the broken door. In the eerie northern twilight of the *simmer dim,* dark shapes moved from the shore toward the castle.

"You sure about this?" James asked. "The graveyard?"

"I'm sure."

"What's your plan?"

"It's pretty simple. Piss off the draugr earl." She pointed at the stone pillars in the graveyard. "He won't appreciate me desecrating his burial site."

They stepped closer to the mangled frame of the back door.

James sucked in a breath. "There must be dozens."

Five or six draugrs were within yards of the kitchen. Several battled with Fin Folk near the shore, and an occasional loud Fin cry filled her head with tormented images. A black cat dashed from the graveyard and transformed into a draugr. It must have been the cat Malcolm chased away the day she and Paul went into the barrow. To their left, more draugrs pulled themselves out of the water. In the graveyard to the right, the mounds had split open like burst blisters. The mouth of the barrow yawned dark and empty.

Hopefully empty.

"I'll hold off these guys." James lifted his head toward the water and the half-dozen headed their way. "You run for the barrow. And after this, we go home, and I take you axe-throwing." He grabbed her and swung her toward him to press his lips to hers. "Now go!" He shoved her forward.

Morag hurled toward the burial mound, risking a glance back. James took a casual step out the kitchen door. The guy was actually *sauntering* toward the draugrs. She took a split second to marvel at that before zeroing in on the barrow entrance. She threw herself down the slope into its darkness where the pair of scissors lay in pieces. Stones held up the crumbling dirt. Inside, it smelled damp and moldering. She took out her phone and turned on the flashlight.

A hole gaped open in the dirt wall ahead of her, where the draugrs must have spilled out. She drew a shaky breath and shined her light inside.

She stepped into the space, empty of draugrs, but not empty. In the far corner lay piles of silver coins and jewels in every hue. Even under layers of dirt, they shimmered in the light of her phone. Behind the stacks of coins, the bow of a large boat peeked through the soil. The entire place reeked of old death. Against every instinct, she fought through the stench, propped her sword against the dirt wall, and rushed over to paw through the treasure. If she could find the drinking horn, maybe the earl would come for her. "Hey!" she shouted, the silver coins clinking as she sifted them through her hands. "I'm desecrating your grave, idiot!"

She couldn't find the horn though, and nothing happened. No sudden appearance of a vengeful Viking. "Your boat sucks. *You* suck!" She was starting to enjoy herself. "My grandma could pillage better than you!" Still nothing. She spat on the ground. "That's what I think of your precious grave." She stuck some silver coins in the pockets of her jeans. Where was he? If they didn't kill the earl soon, Otter-Man would die. If he hadn't already. Ingrid would never wake again.

Something gleamed in a loose pile of dirt. Morag dug, and her fingers closed around the smooth drinking horn. James shouted her name outside.

Grabbing up her sword, she ran out of the barrow to find James facing three gigantic wolves, one white, one brown, and one black like the one she'd seen near the castle. The white one crouched down and slunk toward James. Morag clutched her sword and charged with a banshee shriek. The wolf leaped at James. There was no way to reach him in time. Things might unfold in slow motion in a movie, but in real life, everything occurred too fast to tell what was happening, and then James lay under the snarling wolf. The brown beast closed in on him, and the black wolf turned its attention toward her.

She strained to bring up the heavy sword as the wolf sailed at her head. The beast's teeth sank through her right forearm to scrape bone. She screamed at the crushing pain before adrenaline and shock blocked most of it. The wolf moved in for another bite. Fury coursed through her as she managed to slice it, making it yelp and back away only to circle her again. She crouched low and tried to lift the sword with her non-mangled left arm.

The wolf leaped again.

Chapter 29

Morag braced for impact, for the crush of the wolf's slathering jaws. A darker shape loomed above her. Bear-Man! He swooped in to bite the wolf through the skull and sent it flying with a mighty shake of his head.

"Thank you," she breathed.

Her arm tingled as she smiled up at the massive bear on his back legs before her. He gave a single nod, dropped to the ground, and landed on top of the drinking horn she'd cast aside in the heat of battle. The horn shattered under his massive paw, and the ground trembled. Before Morag could think what it meant, Bear-Man stampeded into the wolves attacking James and scattered them like stuffed toys. James pushed himself to his feet, his clothes torn and bloody.

The tingling intensified in her arm, and she ripped back her sleeve to watch her shredded arm knit back together. The cry from James told her the same thing was happening to him, proof the draugrs who'd attacked them as wolves were dead.

Before she could enjoy the moment of triumph, Bear-Man

bellowed. Draugrs swarmed him in such great numbers, he crashed to the ground under their force.

"No!" Morag stumbled as the earth trembled. She thought it was from Bear-Man's terrible fall, but the rumbling didn't stop, it grew. In every direction, draugrs rushed toward her and James, the mass of them broken only by small circles where flashing Fin Folk fought them. The ground shook harder, and Morag threw out her arms to keep her balance. The draugrs parted, and an enormous shape like nothing she'd seen yet began to stride along the shore. If monsters had their own nightmares, *this* was what they'd dream of.

Demonic horns sprouted from his skull. Blood-red eyes blazed in a face that was a wretched mess of bone and torn flesh. A bear fur complete with an attached head draped his shoulders. He wore leather armor, and high leather boots wrapped his feet. He carried an enormous battle axe, phosphorescent blue light dancing along the blade's edge. His bottom jaw opened wide with a battle cry that made every human and Fin Folk on Screeverholme clutch their ears.

The sound rattled Morag's ribcage, and she wondered if her heart would stop. The draugr earl was finally here.

And he looked very, very angry.

His every step shook the ground. Morag's insides liquified in terror. She tightened her fingers, numb with fear, on her sword. As he marched, the draugrs closed rank behind him. The battles between the draugrs and Fin Folk ceased as all stood in awe of this ancient chieftain.

James moved to her side, and his resolute look put some steel in her spine. He squeezed her hand. "If I have to die with someone by my side, you're not such a bad choice."

"No one's going to die," she said fiercely. She glanced at Bear-Man, unmoving, and hoped it was true.

The Viking earl stopped five feet in front of her and looked at the shattered horn. When his gaze lifted to Morag, his red eyes shone like twin lakes of fire. She relaxed her grip on the sword and regained feeling in her fingers. Things might not have been moving in slow motion, but she was noticing every detail of her last moments.

The rise and fall of her chest, the faintest hint of salt water under the stench of death. The way the wind died down, and the air felt heavy. The warmth from James's hand as she slipped hers away. The lack of pupils in the earl's red irises, the smooth white arch of his exposed collarbone, the leather thong wrapped around the haft of his battle axe.

This detail, of all of them, gave her courage. Evil magic had taken over this man, but a man he'd once been, one who sat and perhaps wrapped that axe himself. A living, breathing man who'd had a mother and father, eaten meals, run in the sunshine, and laughed with friends.

And sure, he'd done his fair share of plundering. But to live this hellish existence? She should end his misery.

The brief flash of compassion disappeared as the earl raised his battle axe. She swung her sword, but the axe came down, down, down, and broke her blade in half. James lifted his sword, and a nearby draugr sent it flying with a flip of an axe haft.

The earl raised his axe a second time, and she braced herself for the final blow. Her life didn't flash before her eyes; she felt only overwhelming grief at her impending death.

Shotgun fire blasted from the water, and the chief turned.

Morag didn't take time to understand. She stumbled away, heaved up James's sword in both hands, and whirled around, swinging it high with the momentum of her turn to bring it to the earl's neck. The impact jarred her to her shoulder joint. The sword was too heavy, and he was too tall. She'd missed her mark. The earl roared, the blade wedged in his waist. She braced her foot on the draugr's thigh and tugged at the blade with a sickening squelch until it came free, and she fell onto her back.

For one horrifying beat in time, the world condensed to Morag and this mighty draugr. He stepped toward her—red eyes fixed on her face—as he lifted his axe for the third time.

She flinched, not ready to die.

Suddenly, Bear-Man slammed into the back of him. Morag scrambled to her feet as the earl folded over and stumbled in Morag's direction. Bent at the waist, the draugr was finally within her reach. Using every bit of strength left in her body, Morag lifted the sword and brought it down as hard as she could on the ancient Viking's neck. His severed head tumbled to her feet, and his body collapsed and shook the ground one last time.

She held her breath, her heart suspended in her chest. Did the runes tell the truth? Several long seconds of silence spun out as everything and everyone came to a stop and waited.

Then, as if invisible marionette strings had been cut, the draugrs collapsed as one where they stood with a crashing clatter of bones and old armor.

The Fin Folk erupted in cheers, and their songs painted beautiful colors in Morag's mind. She sank to her knees in the mud, weak with profound relief. After a few, deep breaths, she pushed to her feet, and James pulled her tightly against him. Her family spilled out the broken back door to join her and James. Morag hugged her parents, hugged Hamish, and Juliette.

When she eased away, she spotted Mr. Murray's fishing boat on the water with him at the helm. Crusher stood on the portside with a shotgun in his hands. His entire band, along with other islanders, had packed into the boat with their guns, shovels, and cricket bats. Not everyone on Tullimentay had chosen to abandon them.

The boat landed on the shore, and people spilled onto the rocky beach. The islanders and Fin Folk squared off in two opposing lines. They cast wary looks at one another, the Fin Folk flashing sickly green with suspicion.

"Come on," Morag said to her family and friends, and they hurried to join the stand-off. Morag took position next to Bear-Man, fully healed again.

Suddenly, the Fin Folk dropped to their knees and softly sang—their skin deep indigo. The Fin Folk king was approaching.

Shocked, Morag turned to see in person what she'd seen in her mind.

Otter-Man strode forward, fully recovered, carrying the mother-of-pearl staff.

"*You're* the king?" Otter-Man seemed so young, so deferential of Bear-Man who now kneeled beside her, but perhaps the older Fin man was his trusted advisor or bodyguard.

She started to kneel, too, but Otter-Man stopped her and pulled her into an embrace, his skin glowing with gratitude.

He lifted the staff and opened his mouth. A rich melody spilled out, and all around, the Fin Folk murmured.

"What's happening?" Dad asked Morag.

She smiled at the islanders and raised her voice. "He's lifting the curse. From now on, you're free to leave the island on the solstice. Now the draugrs are dead, there won't be any more kidnappings. He wants Fin Folk and humans to live in peace again and help one another. There will be more dangers." The image of a sea monster flitted through her mind, making her pause. "But together you will be stronger. From now on, humans and Fin Folk will choose if they will be together. A special pact will be forged between you." She pointed at Magnus. "He's calling you forward."

Magnus looked at the other islanders, who shuffled nervously. Catherine gave an encouraging nod, and the doctor stepped forward. Bear-Man stood and took a small blade from the seaweed hilt at his side. Magnus flinched, but Bear-Man handed the knife to Otter-Man, who drew it across his palm.

"He wants you to know they only took Ingrid because she was injured by a draugr," she explained, reliving in her mind the moment when Bear-Man snatched Ingrid after she was struck by the arrow. "They wanted to keep her safe until she could be healed, as she is now, but they would've brought her underwater to live with them. He wants to repay his debt for his actions and shake your hand."

"I gathered that." Magnus pointed at the blade, and the

islanders gasped when he cut his own hand. "Now we shake. A blood oath for peace."

They shook hands. Then Otter-Man sang again.

"He's calling you, Catherine," Morag said. "You may have been adopted, but you're no less of a Tulloch, a descendant of Mary."

The group parted so a bewildered Catherine could step forward. Bear-Man's arms thrummed with golden light as he placed his hands on her head. She cried out, and the islanders pushed forward.

Morag threw her arm in the air. "No, wait."

A few minutes later, Catherine gasped. "My hip. It's right. It's finally right." She lifted her leg and gave a few kicks. "He's healed it somehow. I don't know how, but he's done it, sure enough." She skipped through the people, and Crusher let out a booming laugh.

Then it was Morag's turn. Otter-Man held her hands and sang to Morag, the one who carried the most Fin Folk inside her. He sang, and as he did, he lifted the curse of the cold that had separated Morag from the sea.

Chapter 30

"Come back inside, you two." Mom stood at the repaired kitchen door. Malcolm sat at her feet, and his golden eyes fixed Morag with a disapproving look. "It's freezing."

"I know! Isn't it great?" Morag spun in a circle with James beside her while the cold rain plastered her hair to her face.

Mom muttered, "Crazy kids!" and slammed the door.

Morag had noticed Catherine briskly walking across the island earlier in the chilly weather. Morag had only suffered her cold affliction for a few weeks, and she was so relieved to be cured. She could only imagine how Catherine felt with her lifelong limp gone at last.

Now Morag could stand in the cold rain with James as long as she liked. "I still can't believe we survived." She couldn't stop grinning.

James grabbed her and hugged her again. He did that a lot lately. "Should we go inside and work on our music?"

Our music. She smiled at him. "In a minute." Crusher had sent her a copy of their recordings to use for her college applications to music programs. She'd dropped her AP art class and enrolled in a music course from a community college back home that she could do online.

Which was good, since she was in no rush to leave the island—or the islanders.

The day after the big battle, Catherine told Morag about her efforts at the school to recruit help for Screeverholme, her desperate drive across the island door-to-door to gather aid for the Americans. In the end, what finally convinced almost half the islanders to load into Mr. Murray's boat were Crusher's pleas when he and his band reminded everyone of the ceilidh. How Morag and James connected with them through their music and showed themselves to be a part of Tullimentay. He and Catherine told the islanders that Morag and the others were children of the island too, even if Mrs. Heddle couldn't see it.

Mrs. Heddle's daughter had appeared a few days ago on her shocked mother's doorstep. Years before, the Fin Folk had cured her cancer and taken her away to live with them. She'd placed a wriggling baby girl into Mrs. Heddle's arms—a baby with pulsing skin and frighteningly sharp teeth, but adorable, nonetheless. At least according to both the Fin baby's grandmother and her great-aunt Joyce. Mrs. Heddle begged Morag for forgiveness for everything, including leaving the note on the castle door.

Together, Mrs. Heddle's daughter and Morag translated for the Fin Folk and began repairing the mistrust between both peoples. Most important had been explaining that Fin Folk hadn't created the draugrs. Metaphorical and literal bridges were being built as the islanders and Fin Folk started construction on a new bridge to Screeverholme and lent the castle occupants boats to use.

The Fin Folk took to shifting into humans from time to time and sharing pints in the pub with real humans, though their whale song still made everyone jump in alarm when they spoke. One particularly handsome one had already caught the eye of Ingrid's friend. As for Ingrid, she was fully recovered and finally allowed to visit the castle, which she did daily to see Hamish.

Many of the islanders had also taken to visiting the Fin Folk in the water—dressed in wetsuits to stay warm. Crusher turned out to have more than musical talent. He was a certified scuba instructor. He taught Morag how to dive so Otter-Man could personally give her a tour of their Fin Folk city, slowly being restored to its former glory with the treasure retrieved from the barrow. As further proof of their peace pact, Otter-Man shared some of the treasure with the islanders, who were using the funds to repair the bridge and update the school.

Everyone agreed no one from the outside world could ever know about any of what had happened. They needed to keep the Fin Folk and the island safe from the curious—or those greedy for jewels or the limited amount of healing the Fin Folk could provide people. The islanders were good at keeping secrets, and the Fin Folk were good at disappearing if need be. At least one Fin Folk had been known to go freshwater and live in a certain loch, and no one had proof yet.

Juliette and Paul were staying on the island for the rest of the summer while Mike and Françoise had returned home to negotiate their divorce and new living arrangements. Not everything turned out perfectly in life.

But sometimes things turned out okay. Morag's parents hadn't stopped holding hands since the night of the solstice and seemed eager to work things out. Hopefully, they would.

Things weren't always what you thought. Like Juliette's parents, and Mom and Dad. Like the Fin Folk. Like Morag—the part Fin Folk girl with synesthesia and a gift for music who brought down monsters.

Or James, the tattooed boy who'd stolen her heart. Her heart swelled now, looking at his crooked smile.

"Come on, let's go play that music." James bent and kissed her, and his mouth was warm in the cold rain.

Acknowledgments

This story will always hold a special place in my heart because I was able to share it with my children when they were younger. There was something indescribably fun about reading aloud my own novel to my kids. So first and foremost, I have to thank Isabelle, Zoe, and Luke for listening to your mom's book with such enthusiasm.

Because I wrote this book earlier in my writing career, it took a lot of hard work to transform it into something publishable. I especially appreciate the suggestions and developmental ideas put forth by editor Ejay Dawson and the support and advice of Susan Brooks at Literary Wanderlust. Thank you also to JV Arts for their cover.

I lived in Glasgow many years ago, and I've visited family living in Scotland over the years. I've been lucky enough to stay in not one, not two, but three different Scottish castles. None of those experiences, however, prepared me for writing about the wholly unique setting of Orkney. Its culture, folklore, and dialect are its own, and I'm incredibly indebted to the website https://www.orkneyjar.com and its site owner, Sigurd Towrie. All mistakes are mine alone, and I hope the people of Orkney forgive me some poetic license in creating the imaginary Tullimentay island and running away with the idea of the Fin Folk.

As a grammatical side note, I also took some liberties in making the plural of draugr be draugrs in this story for simplicity's sake.

I love to use music to get into the mood of a story. I have to thank the band The Magnetic North and its atmospheric album Orkney: Symphony of the Magnetic North for providing the most fitting soundtrack to this book. Of Monsters and Men filled in much of the other scenes. If you're curious what songs Morag's "synesthesia" sparked for her throughout this story, you can find her playlist on Spotify as Morag's Playlist Curse of the Orkney Sea.

As always, I couldn't be a writer without critique partners like Amy Wilson and Amanda Nay or so many members of Rocky Mountain Fiction Writers.

I wouldn't be the person I am without my wonderful family. Thanks to my mom, my in-laws, and my as-good-as-family friend, Danielle Greenleaf. Most of all, thank you to my husband and best friend, Jon. You're the one I write for, if you didn't already know it.

I'd be remiss if I didn't thank my moral support crew of my pug, George, and my cats, Delilah and Wanda, who are always willing to keep me company when I'm writing.

And thank you, the reader, for taking time out of your busy life to read my book. I hope I entertained you!

About the Author

Joy grew up in California and obtained a Zoology degree from UC Davis. Animals always feature in her stories. She enjoys imagining something creepy in every situation, starting with a fourth-grade theater production when she became convinced a monster lived under the stage. So it's no surprise that she loves including scary elements in her writing. She's the author of the horror romance, Old Cravings. When she's not writing, she's lucky enough to work in a library surrounded by books. She currently lives in Colorado with her family and a passel of pets who hog the couch.

Printed in the USA
CPSIA information can be obtained
at www.ICGtesting.com
LVHW040802060923
757193LV00006B/86